About the Auth

Tracy Corbett lives with her partner Simon in Surrey and works part-time for a local charity. Tracy has been writing for a number of years and has had a few short stories published in *My Weekly* magazine. As well as belonging to a local writing group, she enjoys amateur dramatics and can regularly be found dressing up in strange costumes and prancing about the stage pretending to be all manner of odd characters. *Starlight on the Palace Pier* is Tracy's third novel.

Also by Tracy Corbett:

The Forget-Me-Not Flower Shop
The Summer Theatre by the Sea

Tracy Corbett

STARLIGHT ON
THE PALACE PIER

avon.

A division of HarperCollins*Publishers*

www.harpercollins.co.uk

Published by AVON
A division of HarperCollins*Publishers* Ltd
1 London Bridge Street
London SE1 9GF

www.harpercollins.co.uk

A Paperback Original 2018

Copyright © Tracy Corbett 2018

Tracy Corbett asserts the moral right to be identified as the author of
this work.

A catalogue copy of this book is available from the British Library.

ISBN: 978-0-00-829948-4

This novel is entirely a work of fiction. The names, characters and
incidents portrayed in it are the work of the author's imagination. Any
resemblance to actual persons, living or dead, events or localities is
entirely coincidental.

Typeset in Birka by Palimpsest Book Production Limited, Falkirk,
Stirlingshire
Printed and bound in UK by CPI Group (UK) Ltd, Croydon CR0 4YY

All rights reserved. No part of this text may be reproduced, transmitted,
down-loaded, decompiled, reverse engineered, or stored in or introduced
into any information storage and retrieval system, in any form or by any
means, whether electronic or mechanical, without the express written
permission of the publishers.

MIX
Paper from
responsible sources
FSC™ C007454

This book is produced from independently certified FSC™ paper
to ensure responsible forest management.

For more information visit: www.harpercollins.co.uk/green

Acknowledgements

I always enjoy carrying out research, and I'd like to thank a few people for helping me with this book. Firstly, my lovely friend Beccy Wire, whose regular jaunts to Brighton proved extremely helpful. Also, Nick Bates and Anneli Sandstrom for sharing their in-depth knowledge about the city and how it's changed over the years. They gave me some great insights and information, so a huge thank you. I'm just sorry I wasn't able to include all the stories – I'll have to set another book there, I think!

I'd also like to thank my wonderful brother, Kevin, who thanks to his continuing ability to regularly injure himself, was able to enlighten me about torn knee tendons and ruptured Achilles. Who knew his clumsiness would prove so useful? Thanks, Kevin. And try and stay off the crutches for a bit longer, yeah?

This is my third book, and I've come to realise the value of the wonderful book blogging community and my fellow writers who take the time to review new releases and share their reviews and quotes via social media. It's such an amazing thing you all do, so thank you! Your support means so much.

The Avon team continue to be amazing, championing me as an author and helping me to develop new ideas and produce the best version of my stories. The whole team are fab, but particular thanks to Victoria Oundjian and Molly Walker-Sharp for guiding me through the process, as well as being jolly nice people. I'd also like to thank my agent, Tina Betts, who continues to support and encourage me. It's very much appreciated.

And finally, a huge thank you to all you lovely readers for enabling me to continue with my dream and write stories. If you'd ever like to get in touch, please feel free to drop me a line – especially if you have a funny story – I'm always on the lookout for new book ideas! Contact details can be found on my website: www.tracycorbettauthor.co.uk.

For my Mum & Dad,
who have just celebrated their 60th Wedding Anniversary!

Chapter One

Becca Roberts got off the bus outside the grand Queens Hotel and made her way along the promenade towards Ruby's Guest House, the place she called home. The sea breeze increased as the English Channel came into view, choppy and grey, chucking waves of foam over the harbour wall. Wispy clouds obscured the sun, but that didn't detract from the spectacular view. No matter where she'd lived, or travelled to since moving away to attend dance college, Brighton always appealed, whatever the weather.

She stopped to rub her knee. Waking up with a raging hangover had killed any desire to do her strengthening exercises today. Her physio wouldn't be happy. He also wouldn't approve of her hobbling down the road weighed down by a lumpy rucksack and dragging a heavy suitcase, but needs must.

And anyway, she was used to pain. Injury was an occupational hazard for a dancer. At some point, everything in your body would hurt. But this latest injury wasn't a niggle that

1

could be cured by massage, painkillers and ice. And that was something she was still struggling to get her head around.

The sight of her mum's bright yellow front door cheered her a little. Ruby's Guest House was a three-storey Georgian townhouse situated in the Artists' Quarter, bang smack between the old burnt-out West Pier and the replacement Palace Pier. The 'Vacancies' sign creaked in the breeze as she approached. God, she'd missed this place.

Despite ringing the bell twice and knocking, no one answered. She tried the door, unsurprised to find it open. Her mum had been known to leave a key in it overnight.

'Anyone home?' she called out, carrying her suitcase over the threshold. 'Mum?'

Still no answer. She spotted a Post-it Note stuck to the mirror hanging in the hallway.

In the kitchen prepping lunch. You're in the Seventies Suite! Come and find me when you're settled. Mum. x

Becca smiled. The Seventies Suite was her favourite. She dragged her suitcase upstairs and down the landing. As she opened the bedroom door, she was hit by bright swirls of orange patterning on the wall and a lime-green duvet cover with a multitude of cushions strewn about the bed. A lava lamp sat on top of a chunky bedside cabinet, next to a yellow plastic clock. The room glowed, helped by the orange curtains and huge sash window.

She couldn't help laughing as she kicked off her shoes and jumped onto the queen-sized divan. She'd spent many a night

2

lying on this bed during her teenage years, gossiping with her cousin about boys... Well, one boy.

Themed rooms had been her dad's idea. He'd spent six years designing and constructing the different spaces, researching and sourcing suitable décor and putting his carpentry skills to use before dropping dead of a heart attack aged forty-six. It had seemed so cruel that after all his hard work, he hadn't lived long enough to complete the project and enjoy it.

Shaking away the sadness, she rolled off the bed and headed for the bathroom, enjoying the feel of the deep-pile rug beneath her feet. Like the bedroom, the en suite was styled to reflect the Seventies, including a pampas bath suite and psychedelic tiling. She noticed a large crack in the shower screen and made a mental note to tell her mum. Ruby's Guest House was normally in tip-top condition, something her dad had always insisted on.

After a quick shower, in the hope it might ease her hangover, she slung on a pair of jeans and a loose-fitting crop top and headed for the stairs.

All the bedroom doors were closed, except for the one leading to the sewing room. She stuck her head around the door, eager to admire her mum's latest work-in-progress. But instead of the usual collection of haberdashery neatly displayed on the shelving, she was greeted with mayhem and clutter. Rolls of material lay on the floor, two partially dressed mannequins were shoved against the wall and various boxes of ribbons and accessories obscured the floor. The place was a mess.

Strange. Her mum was usually such a stickler for a tidy workspace.

Her pondering was cut short by a sharp pain shooting up the back of her leg. She spun around, knowing full well what... or rather *whom*...she was about to encounter. True enough, Mad Maude was on the attack. The devil incarnate. Satan with fur.

She swiped at the cat, but her reflexes were too slow to outwit her nemesis. Maude's orange fur expanded as she clawed at her enemy's leg. Why her mum put up with such a psychotic animal, she didn't know. Surely it couldn't be good for business? But then, Maude didn't pick on anyone else. It was only Becca she had a vendetta against.

Grabbing Maude by the collar, she prised the cat away, knowing she only had seconds to make her escape. Chucking Maude onto the beanbag, she hobbled for the door, slamming it behind her and holding on to the handle. For all she knew, the damn cat could open doors.

Various screeching noises could be heard from the other side. Becca waited until it had gone quiet before she let go and limped downstairs. Bloody cat.

She was so distracted, she nearly knocked into an elderly woman heading into the dining room. 'Goodness, where's the fire?' the old woman said, looking alarmed.

'I'm so sorry. I didn't see you,' which was hardly surprising;

4

the woman was barely four feet tall. Okay, bit of an exaggeration. But she was tiny. 'Are you okay?'

'Of course I am.' The woman sounded indignant. 'How frail do you think I am?'

Becca figured this was a trick question, so refrained from answering. 'It was my fault entirely. I was escaping Mad Maude. I'm not a fan of cats,' she added, feeling an explanation was required. 'Particularly not ones with a personality disorder.'

The woman laughed. 'In that case, you're forgiven. I'm familiar with Maude's antics. You must be Ruby's daughter? She mentioned you were arriving. Delighted to meet you.'

The woman's eyes travelled the length of Becca's body, taking in her ripped jeans, leopard-print nails, big hoop earrings and blue-tipped peroxide hair. Her expression indicated disapproval.

Becca fought back a smile. As outfits went, this was conservative. She held out her hand. 'Lovely to meet you. I'm Becca.'

'Mrs Busby.' The woman tutted at the sight of Becca's black bra visible beneath her white top. Her mum had often mentioned the old woman during their phone calls. She sounded like quite a character.

The woman held out her arm and nodded towards the dining room. 'Shall we?'

Becca had never escorted anyone into lunch before.

Oh, well. Always a first time for everything.

She led the old woman through the doorway, expecting to find the room bustling with guests and chatter, but instead found the sparse conservatory empty apart from one elderly gentleman seated at a table. He was wearing a smart blazer.

When they entered, he rose from his chair and pretended to tip his non-existent hat. 'Good afternoon, Milady. And how are we this fine lunchtime?'

Mrs Busby responded with a dainty curtsey. 'I'm very well, thank you, Dr Mortimer.'

He held out a chair for her. 'Allow me.'

Becca felt like she'd been transported to a bygone era.

'And who do we have here?' The elderly gentleman subjected Becca to the same once-over Mrs Busby had given her. His reaction seemed far more approving.

'Ruby's daughter,' Mrs Busby answered. 'She's moved into the guest house and doesn't like cats.' Her voice lowered to a whisper as though Becca wasn't standing there. 'I think she might be one of those hipster types, but she has nice manners, so I think we can overlook her other foibles.' The woman pointed to Becca's bellybutton ring, poking out from beneath her top.

Foibles? Becca was too amused to be offended. She'd never been called a 'hipster' before.

Before she could respond, the double doors leading to the kitchen opened and her mum appeared looking hot and flustered, carrying a tray of freshly baked rolls. Her dark hair had streaks of grey in it and she'd lost weight over the summer, but her face brightened on seeing her daughter. 'Becca, love. You're here.' She looked around for somewhere to dump the tray, balancing it on one of the empty tables. 'Good journey?'

'Not bad, thanks.'

Becca was enveloped in a big hug. Ruby Roberts smelt of warm yeast mixed in with fabric conditioner.

God, she'd missed her mum. 'Where's Jodi? Is she home?'

'She's gone for an interview. She'll be back soon.'

'An interview? God, I hope she gets it.' Part of the appeal of moving back home was the chance to reconnect with her cousin, who also lived at the guest house.

Her mum tugged on Becca's hand when it became clear Mrs Busby was eavesdropping. 'Come through to the kitchen,' she said, ignoring her guest's disgruntled expression. 'Be with you in a moment, Mrs Busby. Coffee coming up, Dr M.'

The doctor saluted. 'Excellent. Got quite a thirst on me today.'

Her mum mumbled, 'Nothing new there then,' and led Becca away from prying eyes.

The kitchen at Ruby's Guest House was an impressive open-plan room styled with large pieces of vintage French furniture. The ceiling was high and beamed, with fitted skylights to let in light, even on a dreary day. So it was something of a shock to discover pots and pans piled in the sink and baking produce strewn across the table.

Becca assessed the marked paintwork and grease-stained oven. 'Is everything okay, Mum?' The place was a far cry from its usual immaculate state. But then, she hadn't been home for three years. Her mum had always insisted on visiting her in London, claiming she didn't want her daughter incurring any unnecessary expenditure. But now she wondered if there'd been an ulterior motive.

Her mum turned and smiled. 'Absolutely peachy.' There was something a little forced about her jovial tone. 'Lunchtime is always a tad crazy.' Which was odd, as there only appeared to be two guests. 'But enough about me. How did it go with the consultant? What did he say?'

Becca sighed. She'd been dreading this conversation. 'He said the surgery was successful. The patellar tendon has been reattached and he's pleased with the mobility I've been able to regain through physio.'

'Well, that's great...isn't it?' Her mum was astute enough to sense a *but* coming.

'On top of an already weakened Achilles, I won't be able to dance again...not professionally, anyway.' Somehow saying the words aloud made them feel more real and she was hit by a wave of grief.

Even before Becca had visited the consultant, she'd known this would be the likely outcome. There was no way her body could endure the daily slog of classes and performances required to continue dancing, but despite this reasoning, her reaction to hearing the verdict had reduced her to a blubbering wreck.

Her mum pulled her into a hug. 'Oh, sweetheart. I'm so sorry.'

Becca savoured the moment. It'd been a long time since

anyone had held her. She hadn't realised how much she'd needed it. 'It's not like he didn't warn me. I guess I was hoping for a miracle. Stupid, huh?'

'Not stupid at all.' Her mum rubbed her back. 'Dancing is your life, your dream – of course you don't want it to end.'

'Let's face it, it's not like I had much of a career to lose. Working in clubs and on cruise ships is hardly performing at the Folies-Bergère.' Tears threatened again, so she stepped away from her mum's embrace and perched on a kitchen stool.

Maybe that's why it hurt so much – it was the end of what might have been. All those years of auditions, rejections and doing her utmost to make it as a dancer had counted for nothing. She'd never got to experience the thrill of performing to sell-out arenas like her flatmates had done, touring with Take That or Kylie. Her one highlight had been starring in a pop video for a rap artist she couldn't remember the name of.

She didn't have the right body shape for ballet and her singing voice wasn't good enough for musical theatre, so regular work was hard to come by. But she'd never given up, and despite being told 'no' ninety per cent of the time, she'd developed a thick skin and given it her all while hoping for that big break.

Her mum's frown didn't let up. 'You're a beautiful dancer and don't ever think otherwise. It's a tough business, but you did your best and that's all that matters.'

She loved her mum's positivity, but she felt too raw to be rational. 'Doesn't matter now. It's over.'

Her mum looked pained. 'So what are you going to do?'

That was the million-dollar question. What the hell *was* she going to do? 'I have no idea.'

Life after dance was always going to be hard, but in hindsight, she should have come up with a contingency plan. Both her flatmates had combined dancing with studying for degrees, but Becca had barely scraped through GCSEs. Maybe she would have done better at school if her life hadn't been turned upside down so cruelly. But the combination of her dad dying and getting her heart broken at sixteen had made focusing on school impossible.

Her mum rubbed her forehead, leaving a smudge of flour. 'What about pursuing a career away from dance? You've tried a few things over the years.'

'I'm not sure cleaning up after goats at London Zoo, or selling newspapers at Waterloo station count as viable career options.'

Most dancers took other jobs at some point during their careers, but she'd had more than her fair share of 'filler jobs', reluctant to commit to anything long-term in case her big break was just around the corner.

Her mum smiled. 'Whatever you decide, you have my support – you know that. Take your time, lick your wounds and when you're ready, get back out there. You've got a lot to offer; you just need to find a new dream.'

A new dream? Her mum made it sound so simple. What could possibly replace the buzz of performing? Dancing was a drug. It was all she'd ever been good at.

They were interrupted by Dr Mortimer yelling from the dining room. 'I'm ready for my coffee, Mrs Roberts!'

'Be with you in a tick!' Her mum rolled her eyes. 'Bloody man.'

Becca hopped off the stool. 'Talking of dreams, what's with the sewing room? I thought you had plans to open it up for guests?'

Her mum filled the cafetière. 'I did, but there's not much point when I only have two people staying. And besides, I enjoy sewing. I decided it was better to keep the space for myself.'

Becca loaded up the tea tray. 'Fair enough, but there's still quite a lot of refurb to be done on the guest house and you're not—'

'If you dare say "getting any younger" I'll throttle you.' Her mum's gaze narrowed.

Becca held up her hands in mock surrender. 'I was going to say…you won't be able to finish the other rooms if you don't bring in enough income.'

Her mum went over to the hob, rubbing the small of her back. 'Yes, well, my plans have been put on hold for a while. Like I said, with only two guests it seems pointless to furnish extra rooms when there's no demand.'

Becca wondered what was going on. The guest house

boasted nine rooms, all with en suite facilities and separate living areas. It was situated in a prime location on the seafront. And although there were still two rooms unfurnished, the place was normally full, even during the winter months. 'But without extra rooms, you won't be able to expand if demand picks up.'

'The Carpenter's Room and the Floral Suite are available.'

'Which are both single rooms. You need at least another double.' Becca filled the kettle, trying to be useful. 'What's going on? Is there something wrong?'

'There's nothing wrong.' Her mum was a terrible liar.

She tried again. 'Are you having money problems? Is that it?'

Her mum turned to face her. 'I'm fine, sweetheart. Really. There's nothing for you to worry about.'

Becca recognised the expression on her mum's face; it was the one she wore herself when trying to convince the world she was okay about her dance career being over. A brave façade concealing the pain lying beneath. Well, she wasn't fine. And neither, it seemed, was her mother.

But further delving would have to wait, as her cousin appeared in the kitchen. Becca rushed over and threw her arms around her. 'It's so good to see you!'

Jodi hugged her back, and then pulled away. 'What the boggin' hell have you done to your hair?'

Becca grinned. 'Like it?'

Her cousin studied Becca's blue-tipped hair tied into high

12

bunches. 'On anyone else it would look bonkers. On you it looks ridiculously cool...even if you do resemble a Smurf.'

Becca laughed. 'Talking of hair.' She fluffed up Jodi's mass of black curls. 'What happened to the cornrows?'

'Too high-maintenance. I decided it was time to embrace the 'fro.'

'I like it. It's bang on trend.'

Jodi laughed. 'Listen to you, Gok Wan.'

'When you're stuck working in a newsagent's booth at Waterloo station all day there's not much else to do other than flick through magazines. The natural look is in, you'll be pleased to know.'

Jodi laughed. 'Yippee, fashionable, at last.'

Becca slipped her arm through Jodi's. 'I hope you don't have plans tonight, because we have some serious catching up to do. You up for a night on the town?'

Jodi raised an eyebrow. 'Does the Pope wear a silly hat?'

Becca laughed. 'Excellent. I was thinking the Gin Tub. They have a tasting event.'

'Sounds suitably inebriating. I could do with getting obliterated.'

Becca gave her a questioning look. 'Didn't the interview go well?' She knew her cousin's efforts to find a job were proving hard work.

'Actually, it went okay. But it's only a temporary position. I should hear tomorrow.'

They were interrupted by a screech. Maude had appeared

and leapt into the air when the steam from the oven startled her.

Jodi intercepted and grabbed the cat, dangling her in front of Becca. 'Fancy a cuddle?' she said, enjoying an opportunity to tease her cousin.

Becca backed away. 'No, thanks.'

'She's just being friendly.' Jodi stroked the cat's orange fur.

'I'm serious, Jodi. Don't you dare let her go. She's out to get me.'

Jodi looked down at Maude. 'Is Becca being a tinsy-winsy bit paranoid?'

When Jodi pretended to throw the cat, Becca ran over and hid behind her mum. 'Mum, tell her!'

'I'm not getting involved,' her mum said, laughing. 'Honestly, it's like having a pair of teenagers in the house again. Give Maude to me,' she said, taking the cat. 'Now, will you troublemakers be wanting dinner later?'

'No thanks. We'll grab something when we're out.' And then Becca had a thought. 'You're welcome to join us, if you want?'

Her cousin did a double-take.

'That's sweet of you, but Maude and I are happy staying in and watching *Corrie*. Aren't we, Maude?' The cat hissed. 'Manners, young lady. Come on, let's put you outside so I can finish lunch... And don't forget your key,' her mum called back from the doorway. 'I won't be happy if I have to get up in the early hours to let you girls in like last time... And don't drink too much.'

14

Becca winked at Jodi. 'Don't worry, we'll be good.'

'Well, that'll be a first,' her mum shouted from outside.

Jodi raised an eyebrow and followed Becca upstairs. 'What was that all about?'

'How do you mean?'

'Inviting your mum to join us? You've never done that before.'

Becca shrugged. 'I thought maybe she needed cheering up.'

Jodi stopped walking. 'Why? Has something happened?'

'I was hoping you'd tell me. She seems a little...off. You know, sad. She looks tired and she's lost weight. She says she's fine, but I think she's hiding something.'

'I hadn't noticed.' Jodi looked stricken. 'I'm a terrible niece.'

'No, you're not. And it's always easier to spot something when you're not around all the time.' Becca followed her cousin into The Beach Room. The turquoise room was huge and sea-facing, with white shutters and a large ceiling fan to keep it cool during the height of summer.

Becca kicked off her boots and opened the double-slated doors leading to the built-in wardrobe. 'What do you fancy for tonight, bohemian chic, or racy reggae?'

Jodi sat on the bed and unlaced her Converse trainers. 'Don't care. Nothing too revealing. Last time I spent half the night with my boob hanging out and not realising until the barman handed me a bulldog clip.'

Becca laughed. 'I'd forgotten about that.' She flicked through Jodi's meagre collection of clothes. Mostly jeans, a few summer dresses, some nice items from the local boutiques in Brighton that her mum had bought her for various Christmases and birthdays. And then something caught her attention. She pulled out an orange tunic emblazoned with the words *Pho-King Good* on the front and laughed. 'Why on earth have you still got this?'

Jodi didn't reply, but her cheeks flushed.

Becca immediately stopped laughing. 'Oh, God, you're still working there, aren't you? I'm sorry, I didn't realise. Why didn't you tell me?'

'Because it's embarrassing?' Her cousin looked mortified. 'It's not great as jobs go, but Mr Pho trusts me and I'm earning money, even if it's minimum wage. It's better than being unemployed.'

Becca went over and squeezed her hand. 'It's so unfair that no one will give you a job. You have so much to offer.'

Jodi shrugged. 'That's the way it is. You know the worst part?'

Becca shook her head.

'When the judge sentenced me to six weeks in prison, I didn't think it was such a big deal. I'll do my time and make amends, I thought.' Tears appeared in her eyes. 'When I was released, my probation officer told me I'd been given a second chance. I'd paid my debt to society and it was up to me whether I continued with a life of crime, or resisted reoffending and turned things around.'

'And you have, Jodi.'

16

'As far as everyone else is concerned, I can't be trusted. I'm a risk that isn't worth taking.'

Becca slid her arm around her cousin. 'I wish there was something I could do.'

Jodi rested her head on Becca's shoulder. 'There is. Take me out and get me drunk.'

Becca hugged her. 'That, I can do.'

Chapter Two

Friday 8th September

Jodi washed her hands in the dingy restaurant bathroom, trying to remove the smell of burnt oil, lemongrass and fermented fish that had saturated her clothes and skin. It didn't matter how many times she washed her tunic, there always seemed to be a hint of Thai curry invading her wardrobe. She didn't mind working at the restaurant, she was grateful for the income, but waiting tables wasn't her dream job.

She dried her hands and removed her tunic, rolling it into a tight ball and stuffing it into her bag, trying to contain the potent smells. Maybe she didn't deserve a dream. Perhaps she'd given up her right to lead a better life when she'd gone off the rails and ended up in prison. Maybe karma was wreaking its revenge.

But if that was the case, then she wouldn't have been offered a job at the Starlight Playhouse, would she? It might not be permanent, but it was the type of job she'd always wanted.

When she'd attended the interview, she'd assumed it would

go the same way as all the others. The interviewer would switch from being impressed by her first-class business degree and glowing references from her tutors, to discovering her criminal record, and the vibe would instantly change. Awkward glances would be exchanged, followed by concerns about her 'lack of work experience' or 'suitability for the position'.

No matter how hard she'd studied, how many nights she'd volunteered at the homeless shelter, or how much commitment she'd shown over the years waiting tables for Mr Pho at the local Thai restaurant, she couldn't seem to escape her past.

But Carolyn Elliot-Wentworth hadn't been put off by Jodi's stint in prison. And if she'd remembered Jodi from her days spent attending the youth club at the Starlight Playhouse a decade earlier, she hadn't acknowledged it. Instead, she'd offered Jodi the position of business manager for a fixed three-month period. The salary wasn't great, and it was only twenty hours a week, but it would give her some much-needed office experience.

Plus, if Becca could be persuaded to apply for the dance teacher position being advertised, she might even get to work alongside her cousin. It was almost perfect.

Jodi had one reservation. It meant working at the scene of her teenage misdemeanours. Was that a good or bad thing? She didn't like being reminded of her past. But maybe that was the point. It was karma again, ensuring she could never escape her mistakes. A daily reminder that she needed to stay on the straight and narrow.

She said goodnight to Mr Pho and headed into the street, unsurprised to find it full of revellers. It was Saturday night. The party had only just started.

Like most of the locals, she usually avoided using the main road that led away from the railway station down to the seafront. The area was frequented by pale-skinned out-of-towners who'd travelled down for the weekend, eager to get pissed, hook up and start fights. The *Pho-King Good* restaurant was situated in the heart of the tourist area. As such, it attracted large groups of twenty-somethings, eager to line their stomachs with cheap curry before consuming barrel-loads of booze.

One such group were hanging around outside the restaurant. They'd been in earlier, already drunk, making her job torturous. She was used to dealing with unruly behaviour, attempts to chat her up and ask whether she had a boyfriend. It was all part of the job. But she'd be lying if she said it didn't upset her when reference was made to her ethnicity. They say alcohol makes a person tell the truth, that inebriated people become brutally honest and offer unfiltered opinions. Whereas a sober person would keep their prejudices under wraps, a pissed person might not.

One of the guys whistled as she walked by. 'Hey, sexy.'

He stunk of smoke. Yet another pungent smell to add to the stench infiltrating her clothes.

'Anyone ever told you, you look like Thandie Newton? I wouldn't kick her out of bed,' he said, showing off to his mates.

Jodi ignored him.

Her relationships with men had been influenced by several things, most of which revolved around her upbringing. Apart from witnessing her mum shacking up with numerous blokes, her own destructive behaviour had attracted a certain 'type' – one she was no longer interested in. As with job hunting, man hunting had proved disappointing. She'd had one semi-serious relationship in her early twenties, but the moment she'd plucked up the courage to tell Ned about her criminal past, he'd suddenly developed a desire to go travelling. Despite promising to contact her on his return, he never did.

And that was the problem: if they were decent blokes, they didn't want a girlfriend with a criminal record. And who could blame them?

The guy stepped in front of her, blocking her route. 'Want to join the party?' He offered her the joint he was smoking.

The smell acted as a trigger, a time capsule that transported her back to her teens. Of waking up with no recollection of where she'd been, or what she'd done the previous evening. Of nights spent in police stations waiting for her mum to pick her up. Aunty Ruby showing up instead and taking her back to the guest house to sober up. Crying her eyes out, as she dealt with the comedown of a drug-fuelled night.

She'd grown up in Hove, the posh end of town – although there'd been nothing privileged about her upbringing. Her mother had lacked direction, until she'd met Ratty. To this day, his real name remained unknown. All Jodi knew was that he was a musician from Jamaica, who played steel drums in a reggae band and spent one summer in 1988 touring the UK with her mother in tow.

By the time he left England and headed home to the Caribbean, Adele Simmons was in love, addicted to the 'groupie' lifestyle and six weeks pregnant. Unfortunately for Adele, it was all downhill after that. She flitted from one man to another, trying to find another Ratty, and increasingly annoyed that her youth, fun and night time partying had been curtailed by a screaming baby.

Consequently, Jodi grew up without a father and with a mother who resented her. She'd accepted being passed from one relative to another, while her mother entertained numerous male 'friends'. She did what the other kids did, watched films at the Duke of York cinema, hung out at the skate park and ice-skated at the now closed Ice Cube. When she reached her teens she realised her mum's lifestyle wasn't normal. Her reaction to discovering that her mum was the talk of the school gates, was to rebel. When Adele failed to respond to her daughter's pleading for her to change her ways, Jodi switched to behaviour that ensured her mum *had* to pay attention to her. But even that hadn't worked.

She preferred to avoid thinking about her mother, who was currently shacked up with her latest man in Glasgow and no longer part of her life.

Side-stepping the guy with the joint, Jodi walked off,

ignoring his drunken suggestion that she 'go back to where she came from'.

Ignorant arse. She came from bloody Brighton.

Her teenage years hadn't all been rotten. Her best memory was from the summer of 2005 when one of her favourite bands, The Kooks, had moved into a property in Adelaide Crescent and used to sit outside on the lawn practising their latest songs. She and Becca had felt so cool, so grown-up hanging out with them. The memory made her smile.

But her smile faded when she turned into East Street and saw a homeless man lying on the ground. He was wrapped in a blanket, his worldly goods stored in carrier bags next to him. She dug out her tips from the night and placed the coins into the hat lying next to him.

'Would you like details of the homeless shelter?' she asked, crouching down, but he was asleep. She tucked his hat under the blanket, out of sight, and left him alone.

Her life could so easily have ended up the same way. Aunty Ruby was the reason it hadn't. Her aunty had taken her in after she'd left prison, helped her study for her GCSEs, A levels, and had been thrilled when Jodi finally obtained her degree last year.

When Jodi reached the guest house, she found the place in virtual darkness. Pushing open the front door, she spotted Mrs Busby carrying a tea tray across the foyer. It was a nightly ritual. Two glasses of hot milk, one for her and the other for Dr Mortimer, accompanied by a packet of Milky Ways.

23

Jodi ducked behind the front desk, unwilling to be collared and grilled. Neither of her aunty's long-standing guests knew about her past and she wanted to keep it that way. But it was getting increasingly tricky to keep the truth hidden, especially when the pair couldn't understand why 'a nice girl like her' seemed so inept at finding a job.

While she was hiding, she heard a noise coming from the study. When she was sure Mrs Busby had disappeared, she crept over and peered around the study door.

She loved her uncle's old study. There was something about the smell: a mixture of worn leather and old books. It was also the room where her aunty spent a good deal of time. It seemed to give her comfort.

Over the years, books on gardening, horticulture and organic produce had been added to the tall bookcases, already crammed with publications about science, religion, cricket and war history. The dark green carpet was covered with a thick woven cream rug and a vase of fresh flowers adorned the window ledge, next to the nautical weather predictor. But other than that, it remained as her uncle had left it – more of a safe haven than a shrine. A place her aunty could retreat to when life got too much.

Her aunty was sitting in the wingchair, her legs tucked up, spinning the chair around, faster and faster, with a glazed look.

Jodi leant against the doorframe. 'Bad day?'

Her aunty nearly fell off the chair. 'Goodness, you made me jump.'

'Sorry.' Jodi went into the room. 'Everything okay?'

'Fine, love. I was lost in thought. I've been trying to balance the books.'

Jodi noticed a pile of invoices on the desk. 'Is there a problem?'

'Other than my lack of enthusiasm? Not really.'

Guilt kicked Jodi in the ribs. Why hadn't she realised her aunty was struggling? Her cousin had spotted it straight away. 'Do you have to do this tonight? Can't it wait until morning?'

'Possibly, but I've been putting it off for over a week.' She sighed. 'It's not my favourite pastime, but the books won't balance themselves.' Flicking on the desk lamp, her aunty reached across for her reading glasses. 'Of course, it might help if the books actually tallied for once. Dealing with the accounts was always Derek's area of expertise.' Her expression turned melancholy. 'Still, it wasn't like the poor man expected to die so young. It took us both by surprise.'

Jodi dumped her bag on the floor and went over to the desk. 'You seem dejected, Aunty.'

'Oh, ignore me, love. My back's playing up. It always makes me crabby. Anyway, how are you? Busy night at the restaurant?'

'Hectic.' She perched on the desk, noticing a discarded travel brochure in the waste paper bin. 'Have you been to see your GP?'

Her aunty pushed her hands into her lower back, stretching out the muscles. 'It's nothing a hot bath and a decent rest won't solve.' She stopped. 'And losing a few pounds.' She visibly sucked in her tummy.

Jodi smiled. 'You look fine, but you could do with a holiday.'

'If only.' Her aunty rolled her eyes. 'I think the five-a.m. starts are taking their toll. If I'm not in bed by nine p.m. these days, my body objects.' She let out a sigh. 'Mind you, my body seems to object whatever I do, so I'm not sure why I bother.'

Jodi rescued the brochure from the bin and flattened out the pages. The front cover depicted a white boat cutting through deep blue water, advertising a cruise around the Mediterranean. 'What you need is a change of routine. A wise person once told me, if you carry on doing what you've always done, you'll only ever be what you've always been.'

Aunty Ruby laughed. 'Very profound... Ghandi?'

'You, actually.'

'I said that? Goodness.'

'It was good advice.' Jodi gestured to the brochure. 'Yours?'

Aunty Ruby looked away. 'When would I get the chance for a holiday?' Her cheeks had coloured, so Jodi knew the brochure was hers.

Her aunty resumed spinning on the chair. 'But perhaps I do need a change. When I opened up this morning I caught the reflection of a middle-aged woman staring back at me in the glass. It took me a moment to realise the woman was me. I'm sure the last time I looked my hair was still brown. Now look at it?' She pointed to her wavy bob. 'I look like Miss Marple.'

Jodi laughed. 'You do not. But if you don't like it, why don't you colour it?'

'I'd look like mutton dressed as lamb.'

'No, you wouldn't. The colours you can buy these days look really natural. And besides, only the other day you were telling me how much you admired Helen Mirren. And I'm sure she dyes her hair.' Jodi placed the travel brochure on the desk, hoping the enticement of a holiday might prove tempting.

Her aunty looked thoughtful. 'Helen Mirren, eh?' And then the chair stopped spinning. It had unwound in height. She peered over the top of the desk, making Jodi laugh with her miffed expression.

Maude interrupted them, sauntering into the room carrying something mangled between her teeth. She dropped the carcass by Jodi's feet and looked up, radiating an air of arrogance as she turned tail and sauntered out again.

'That's right, leave me to clear it up,' her aunty called after her, struggling to get out of the unwound chair.

Jodi went over to help, steering her aunty towards the door. 'I'll deal with this. Pour yourself a glass of wine, have a warm bath and then go to bed. In the morning, I'll sort out the accounts.'

'Oh, you don't have to do that.'

Jodi looked at her. 'Actually, I do. In fact, I don't know why I haven't offered before. What's the point of studying for a business degree, if you don't use it to help your family? You've helped me enough over the years; it's time I repaid the favour.'

27

Jodi might be struggling to persuade an employer she was trustworthy and loyal, or convince a guy she wasn't trouble waiting to happen, but she could prove to her family that their belief in her was justified. Because without them, she'd be lying in a gutter under a blanket somewhere...like that homeless guy, wondering what the hell had gone wrong with her life.

Chapter Three

Saturday 9th September

Becca was suffering with her second hangover in the space of forty-eight hours. She'd met up with a couple of old school friends last night and had ended up at Patterns. Why had she drunk so much? Her head hurt, her eyes hurt, even her hair hurt. But most of all her knee hurt. Too many gin cocktails coupled with dancing in high heels until the early hours had aggravated her injury...again. If she carried on like this she might never make a full recovery. But it was hard to remain focused on her rehabilitation when she knew her dancing career was over.

Still, she didn't want to walk with a permanent limp, so she needed to dial down the abuse and let her knee heal, which was why she was sitting in the kitchen with an ice pack balancing on her knee. Two paracetamols and two ibuprofens had dulled the pounding in her head, but she still felt battered.

It wasn't the best preparation for an interview. But then, she wasn't even sure she wanted the job. Teaching was certainly an avenue lots of dancers chose after retiring, but they were usually the ones who'd had successful careers and had taken teacher training courses. She hadn't done any of that. She'd never considered herself the teaching type. On the other hand, she needed a job. And Jodi was desperate for an ally, so Becca had contacted Carolyn Elliot-Wentworth and applied for the position.

She drank another glass of water and forced down a slice of toast, but she knew fresh air would be the only real antidote. A walk up to Preston Park would do her good, plus it would help strengthen her thigh muscles, something the consultant said was necessary to protect her knee from future injury.

Yesterday's clouds had blown away leaving a lovely September day. It was warm enough that she didn't need a coat, so she headed away from the marina up towards Victoria Fountain, reacquainting herself with her home town. Once a place filled with cheap housing, hippies and squatters struggling to make a living, Brighton had been transformed into a thriving town full of artists and celebrities.

She upped her pace, fighting the urge to limp. It took a while for the stiffness in her knee to ease, but gradually the pain subsided enough that she could almost ignore it.

Late-night partying wasn't a new phenomenon. As a dancer, most of her gigs had been in the evening and it would be gone eleven by the time she left the venue. With the buzz of adrenaline flowing, sleep was impossible. So she'd often joined the other dancers and headed off to a club, staggering home in the early hours before collapsing into bed. There wouldn't even be the luxury of a lie-in the next morning. She'd be up early for class, putting her body through its paces, running through the necessary drills, jumps and turns, always trying to perfect her technique.

She'd learnt early on that you had to love dancing to stick to it. It gave you nothing back in return, no painting to display on a wall, no poem to be printed or sold, nothing other than that single fleeting moment when you felt alive. Dancers endured constant pain, rejection and injury. Not to mention years of intense training, poor salaries and cruelly short careers. And yet she'd never met a dancer who didn't think they had the best job in the world. That rush of exhilaration, moving your body to express yourself, creating a moment of magic that transported people out of their everyday lives.

And now it was over. She stopped and took a breath, hit by another wave of grief.

Okay, so she might never dance professionally again, but that didn't mean she had to give up completely, did it? People danced in wheelchairs, for Christ's sake. She wasn't about to let a couple of dodgy tendons stop her.

It wasn't long before she reached Preston Park, the site of many a music festival in days gone by, and the place where she'd spent so much of her youth.

She walked through the ornate iron gates, glancing up to see whether the pillars still had lion heads perched on top. They did. She made her way up the long driveway to where the once grand stately home was situated. From the outside, the Starlight Playhouse hadn't changed. The red brickwork still looked impressive, the array of tall sash windows dominated the view, and the green countryside framing the estate was stunning.

As she neared the building, her mind tumbled back to the summer of 2005 when Jodi had dragged her along to the Friday night youth club. It was a strange venue to host a horde of boisterous teenagers who had little regard for an impressive structure built nearly four hundred years earlier. It was only now that the idea of using a listed building to house a games room and a disco seemed bizarre.

The memories evoked a mixture of emotions. Her teenage years had been mostly happy, filled with love, dance classes, and an idyllic lifestyle by the seaside. She'd never been interested in boys or dating, unlike her cousin, but she could still remember every moment of that first night at the youth club. Most of the kids were hanging around outside, smoking and drinking. Not Becca. She'd wanted to dance, imagining herself starring in The Pussycat Dolls video for 'Don't Cha' rather than hooking up with boys...until she'd met Tom Elliot.

Tom was two years older, drove a scooter and was the most gorgeous creature she'd ever seen. He went to a private boys' school and was posh, clever, and above all, mysterious. When he'd initially approached her and asked her out, she'd panicked and turned him down, intimidated by his confidence and ease. He'd shrugged and said, 'That's a shame,' and walked off. She'd spent a miserable week regretting saying no and wishing she could turn back time. The following Friday night, he'd approached her again and repeated his offer. This time, she'd said yes.

Of course, he was also the boy who broke her heart nine months later. But she didn't want to think about that, especially as shortly after her dad had died.

Shaking away the sad memories, she climbed the steps and approached the impressive front door. There was a sign detailing opening hours for the café. She doubted it was still being used as a youth club, but she was curious to see inside.

The open-plan foyer looked the same. The parquet flooring was badly scratched. The dark wooden panelling covering the walls had faded from the sunlight burning through the windows, and the huge chandelier hanging from the ceiling lacked a few bulbs.

Ahead was the main reception, a large desk housing a computer rather than the ancient till that used to sit on top a decade earlier. There was no one manning the desk and no one in sight. Her footsteps echoed up to the high ceiling as she walked across the foyer.

She glanced through the archway leading to where the grand staircase was roped off with a 'No Entry' sign. Her mind travelled back to a time when she'd been allowed upstairs to the family's living quarters. The upstairs had been frozen in time, a representation of centuries past with its ornate furniture, tapestries and family heirlooms. But the downstairs had been dragged kicking and screaming into the twenty-first century – even if it had never quite finished its transition.

She checked her watch. Ten minutes before her interview. She went in search of the café, eager to rest her knee.

Painful memories aside, the Starlight Playhouse was a fantastic place to explore. She remembered Tom telling her the manor house had been used as a collection centre during the First World War. People from the surrounding areas would drop off woollen garments to be sent to France. During the Second World War, the Royal Navy Hospital had evacuated from Southsea and set up medical facilities at the manor. At the end of the war, residency had reverted to the Wentworth family.

She reached the café and became aware of laughter. A woman was seated at one of the wooden tables, seemingly talking to herself, amused by something. Becca looked around, but there was no one else about. The décor hadn't changed. The red velvet chairs were past their best and the cream walls still had scuff marks depicting the outline of non-existent paintings. But the view from the glass doors leading to the landscaped gardens was as impressive as she'd remembered.

She startled when the swing doors leading to the kitchen burst open. A surly man appeared wearing chef whites. He went over to the woman seated at the table and pointed to a cup. 'You want refill?' His voice was deep and thick with an eastern European accent.

The woman looked up, initially baffled, but then smiled. 'Thank you, Petrit. That would be lovely.' She pushed her glasses up her nose, but they immediately slid down again.

Becca instantly recognised Carolyn Elliot-Wentworth. The owner of the Starlight Playhouse. More significantly, Tom Elliot's mother.

Becca had been surprised when Jodi had told her Carolyn was still running the place. Even as a naive sixteen-year-old, she'd realised the woman had issues. Judging by her fumbled attempts to align teacup with saucer, Becca suspected alcohol was still a factor.

Not that she was in a fit state to pass judgement; she'd knocked back enough gin cocktails in the last few months to sink a ship. But her reliance on alcohol was temporary, an aid to easing both the physical and mental anguish caused by surgery and the demise of her career.

But maybe that's what every alcoholic said in the beginning. No one set out to become addicted. She made a mental note to quit using booze as a crutch.

Once the surly man had disappeared into the kitchen, Becca tentatively approached the woman. 'Sorry to disturb you, but it's Carolyn, isn't it? You probably don't remember me, I used to come here as a teenager with my cousin.'

The woman looked up. There seemed to be a time delay before she registered Becca's words. Her head tilted to one side, followed by a frown when her glasses slid off her nose and landed in her lap. Eventually the penny dropped. 'I know you,' she said, squinting. 'You used to come here as a teenager.'

Becca managed a smile. 'I did, yes. Becca Roberts. How are you, Mrs Elliot-Wentworth?'

The woman waved her hand. 'Oh, please, call me Carolyn.' She stood up, leaning against the table for support. Her glasses slid off her lap and fell to the floor. 'Come closer.' She peered at Becca, her face morphing into recognition. 'That's right. You're...?'

'Becca.'

'That's right. Becca. Tom's Becca.'

Becca flinched. She hadn't been *Tom's* Becca for over twelve years.

'You went off to be a dancer. I remember. Beautiful girl.' Carolyn cupped Becca's cheek, her hand somewhat unsteady. 'Look at your hair!' she said, flicking one of Becca's blue-tipped bunches. 'What brings you here?'

Becca smiled. 'I'm here about the dance teacher position? Jodi said the current lady's retiring and you're looking for a replacement.'

Carolyn looked confused. 'Who's Jodi?'

Oh, hell. Please don't say the woman had forgotten she'd hired her. 'My cousin, Jodi Simmons? She's starting work this week as business manager.'

'Oh, of course! Silly me. Yes, that's right.'

Relief flooded Becca. 'She's really looking forward to working here.'

'I'm so pleased. And you're quite right, we do need a replacement for Mrs Morris.' Carolyn gestured for Becca to sit down. 'Do take a seat. Are you still dancing?'

Becca's knee complained as she sat down. 'Not at the moment. I've moved back to Brighton to recover from a knee injury.'

'Oh, that's a shame. I remember Tom telling me how beautifully you danced.'

Becca flinched.

Needing a distraction, she retrieved Carolyn's glasses from the floor and handed them to her.

Carolyn looked confused. 'What are these? Oh, my glasses. I was wondering where they'd got to.' She put them on. The woman must be late fifties, but she was effortlessly stunning. Slim, high cheekbones, a regal quality to her stance. But there was also a reddening around her cheeks, and her blue eyes were cloudy and bloodshot. 'Have you taught dance before?'

Becca shook her head. 'No, I haven't.'

Carolyn pushed her strawberry-blonde hair away from her face. 'Qualifications?'

Becca decided honesty was the best policy. 'Unfortunately not. I've only recently discovered that my dancing career is over. This is the first job I've applied for.'

Carolyn frowned. 'Oh, so no references?'

'Afraid not.' This wasn't going well. Becca decided to be proactive. 'What kind of dancing do you teach here?'

'Kids' ballet and adult beginners' tap.'

Okay, nothing too challenging then. That was a relief. 'I studied both ballet and tap extensively, so I have the relevant skills, just not in teaching. But I'd be willing to learn.'

Carolyn sighed. 'It's not ideal...but the truth is, I've been advertising for months and only had two applicants. Neither of them wanted the job.' She looked around the café, her expression wistful. 'I know I've let the place go, but one day I hope the Starlight Playhouse will become the thriving arts centre I dreamt it might be.' She sighed. 'But I can't do that if there's no income and the classes provide that. At least, they used to. Numbers have dropped off since Mrs Morris announced she was retiring. Today's her last day.'

Becca could see the woman was in a fix. And she knew all about trying to hold on to a dream that was rapidly fading. She might not have the relevant teaching experience, but she was positive she could rise to the challenge. After all, they were kids. Adults starting out. How hard could it be? 'I appreciate taking me on is a risk, but I'm keen to develop my skills and make the transition into teaching.'

Carolyn grabbed her hand. 'You know what? Let's give it a go. Why don't you take this afternoon's class and we'll see how you get on?'

Becca started to panic. 'You mean, like a trial run?'

'Exactly. If you do okay, the job's yours.'

Oh, hell. That left her no time to prepare. Still, she'd be a fool to turn it down. 'Thank you so much for this opportunity, Carolyn. I won't let you down.'

38

'I know you won't.' She squeezed Becca's hand. 'My son always said you had a good heart.'

Then why did he break it? Becca immediately squashed the thought. It was no longer relevant.

Carolyn moved away from the table. 'Come into the office. I have paperwork.'

The surly man appeared from the kitchen with a fresh cup of coffee. When he saw Carolyn leaving, he grunted. 'You no longer want?'

'Leave it there, Petrit. I'll be back.'

He dumped it on the table, sloshing liquid into the saucer.

'Don't mind him,' Carolyn said. 'He's from Romania.'

Becca wasn't sure what to make of that. She followed Carolyn into the office, which was situated behind reception.

'There's normally someone manning the desk, but Vivienne's off today.' Carolyn fumbled over a set of keys, dropping them twice before finding the one required to unlock the door.

The office wasn't big, and it felt smaller due to the piles of files stacked on the floor. A couch was shoved against one wall and the filing cabinets were crammed full of documents, preventing the drawers from closing. The desk was cluttered with mugs, boxes and papers scattered across the leather top.

'Where are the timetables?' Carolyn picked up a stack of papers. 'I can never find anything.' She sifted through the documents, discarding them, adding to the mess on the floor.

She pointed towards the ancient computer on the desk. 'Can you use one of those?'

Becca nodded. 'Yes, but I'm no expert.'

'Me neither. It's such a stress. Tom's tried to teach me, but I still can't work the ruddy thing. I much prefer pen and paper.'

A chill ran over Becca's skin. 'Does Tom visit often?' No way was she about to take a job if there was a chance she'd see Tom Elliot again. She wasn't that desperate for work.

'Not as much as he'd like, or me for that matter. His job keeps him busy.'

Okay, so minimal risk of a chance meeting. She could work with that.

'He lives in London. He's a criminal defence barrister.'

He'd achieved his dream then.

Becca watched Carolyn rummage through a desk drawer. 'Looks like you'll be glad of the help in the office.'

'Hmm...what?' Carolyn looked up. 'Help in the office? Sadly, no. Vivienne, my front-of-house manager, tries to keep the petty cash up to date, but she doesn't have enough time to do everything.'

Becca froze. 'I meant my cousin Jodi.'

Carolyn resumed rummaging. 'Nothing would please me more than getting some help, but we can't afford another salary. I can barely cover the cost of the staff we have. Maybe one day, when things pick up.'

Oh, hell. This didn't bode well. 'But Jodi's starting work here this week, remember?'

'Ah, here it is!' Carolyn wiped crumbs away from a sheet of paper. 'The timetable.' She handed it to Becca. 'I knew it was here somewhere.'

But Becca was more concerned Carolyn kept forgetting she'd offered her cousin a job. 'Thanks for this. I'll take a look. So, about my cousin...?'

But Carolyn had slumped onto the couch, her feet tucked under her, her glasses skew-whiff. She looked exhausted, as though searching for the timetable had siphoned all her energy. Becca was about to repeat her question, when Carolyn yawned and said, 'The ballet class starts at two,' before drifting off to sleep.

Becca felt uncomfortable about leaving her unattended. But what was she supposed to do? She removed Carolyn's glasses and placed them next to her. It was like old times, when she used to help Tom put her to bed.

Closing the door behind her, she went into the café and knocked on the kitchen door.

She had to step back when the doors swung open. 'What?' the man said, looking her up and down.

'Carolyn's asleep in the office.'

He folded his arms across his chest. 'What you want me to do?'

Helpful. 'Err...nothing. I just thought I should tell you. Will she be okay?'

He grunted. 'She always sleep.' And with that, he let the doors swing shut in her face.

Charming.

Still, she had bigger things to worry about. Like trying her hand at teaching. And whether Carolyn would wake up before the class started.

More importantly, whether Carolyn would remember she'd offered her cousin a job.

Chapter Four

When the buzzer of doom sounded, Tom Elliot uncrossed his legs and stood up. The jury had reached a verdict and were ready to come back into the courthouse to deliver their conclusion. Guilty, or not guilty? That was the question.

He glanced behind him to where his client sat in the dock, looking surprisingly cheerful for someone inevitably facing jail time.

Tom gave his client a questioning look, checking he was prepared for what was about to happen. Bobby Franco grinned and gave him a thumbs-up, which in the circumstances, was both highly inappropriate and stupidly optimistic.

The trial hadn't exactly gone well. Bobby Franco was a fifty-year-old dishonest rogue who liked to bet on the horses and spent most weekends fighting at his local pub. On this particular occasion, he'd been charged with shoplifting. It was Tom's job to defend him. Something that didn't fill him with joy, but was a necessary evil of his trade.

It was a far cry from the high-profile cases he'd read about in the newspapers when he'd decided on a career in law aged just seventeen. But representing the likes of Bobby Franco was the reality of being a barrister. It paid the bills. Even if it didn't prove very fulfilling. He firmly believed in everyone's right to be represented in court, and some of his clients were even innocent. But the pressure to win cases, coupled with his stress levels exacerbating his asthma, meant being a barrister wasn't all it was cracked up to be.

The sound of footsteps approached. The jury. The door opened and in they walked, a mixture of modern society, some willing to serve justice, others forced to participate in their civic duty. Beads of sweat broke out under his wig. He could always predict the outcome of a case by whether the jury looked at him as they returned to their seats. On this occasion, they avoided eye contact. It was curtains for Bobby Franco.

The foreman, a man with tattoos and a ponytail, stood up. The court clerk approached him. 'Have the jury reached a verdict upon which you are all agreed?'

Tattoo man nodded. 'Yes.'

No hesitation. No hint of 'reasonable doubt'.

'Do you find the defendant guilty or not guilty of the theft of two marital aids from Ann Summers retail store in Reading?'

'Guilty.'

What a surprise.

'And is that the verdict of you all?'

'It is.'

Tom glanced at Bobby. That was what you got for nicking a vibrator and a blow-up doll and trying to abscond with the items stuffed down your trousers.

But Bobby didn't look remorseful. Far from it. He looked... smug.

'Mr Thomas Elliot.' The sound of the judge's voice snapped Tom back to attention. 'Your client has been found guilty on the most overwhelming of evidence.'

You don't say. 'Yes, your honour.'

'In fact, this case shouldn't have been in my court. This type of case should have been heard by the magistrates. Did you advise this man to elect to come to the Crown Court and waste thousands of pounds of taxpayers' money?'

Tom had predicted a bollocking. He tried to look contrite. 'No, your honour. It was my client's decision.' And a stupid one. But as his barrister, the judge clearly felt Tom should have dissuaded his client from the theatrics of trial by jury. What was he supposed to do? Bobby Franco wanted his day in court and every defendant was entitled to be tried by their peers.

The judge turned his wrath on the client. 'Robert Lewis Franco, you will go to prison for thirteen weeks.' And with that, the judge flounced out of the court in true dramatic style. Job done.

The client's response was to laugh. Thirteen weeks was nothing. He'd served longer for ramming a shopping trolley into a security guard at Tesco.

The jury started whispering.

Bobby Franco was led from the dock.

Tom picked up his briefcase and left court seventeen, heading for the grand Robing Room upstairs. His chest was tight. He stopped in the corridor and patted his pockets, searching for his inhaler. His phone vibrated.

He checked the display, knowing it would be either his mother or his ex-girlfriend, both of whom had already called several times that day, despite him telling them he was in court and uncontactable.

It was Izzy. Should he answer it, or smash the phone against the nearest bench seat? Tempting. But she'd only keep calling. He raised the phone to his ear, his brain telling him it was a bad idea.

'Hi.' She sounded hesitant.

There was a time when the sound of her voice would have brought a smile to his face. Now it was just an unwelcome intrusion. A reminder of the life he no longer had, or wanted.

'Tom...are you there?'

He needed to stay strong and not soften at the break in her voice. 'I'm here.'

She sighed. 'I'm sorry about last night... Are you okay?'

He swallowed. Was he okay? When she'd walked through the front door of the place they'd shared for two years and were currently selling, her arms around another man, he'd stood there waiting for pain to hit him full in the chest. But it hadn't come. He'd felt...nothing. Well, not entirely nothing,

46

a slight twinge, a stirring sense of familiarity, but nothing crippling. Strange then that the sound of her voice could threaten to weaken his resolve, when seeing her hadn't.

'What do you want, Izzy?'

'We didn't get a chance to speak yesterday.'

'There isn't anything left to say.'

She paused. 'Isn't there?'

He opened his briefcase, praying he'd find his inhaler inside. He could feel the sweat trickling down the back of his neck, an indicator that an asthma attack was looming. 'Not as far as I'm concerned.'

'I don't think you mean that.'

He closed his eyes. Life with Izzy had been a constant yoyo. She'd loved city life, parties, notoriety, and most of all, money. But her desire for endless excitement had proved incompatible with his demanding job and unwillingness to 'party' with her. Her boredom and frustration with his supposed conservatism had her seeking thrills elsewhere. The arguments would increase, accusations would be thrown and eventually she'd storm out. But the remorse would soon kick in and she'd come back, promising to change her ways. Of course, she never did. And he'd been a mug for thinking otherwise.

'It feels so final, putting the apartment on the market and everything.' Her voice broke. 'Are you sure this is what you want?'

His eyes flicked open. What *he* wanted? *Jesus!*

It would be so easy to remind her of all the reasons why

it'd ended. Reasons caused mostly by her, not him. But he was past the point of caring. He was done arguing. He took a deep breath. 'We've been here before. It's time for us both to move on.'

'I just wanted to make sure, before...before it's too late.'

The tightness in his chest squeezed, increasing the need to administer a shot of Ventolin. 'I have to go... I hope everything works out for you. Bye, Izzy.' He ended the call before he heard her voice again and found himself caving...again. And that would make him the biggest idiot on the planet.

It was no good, he needed his inhaler. He must have left it in the Robing Room.

He'd just reached the end of the corridor, when his phone buzzed again. Christ, she was trying his patience today. He snatched at his phone, only realising at the last minute that it wasn't Izzy. It was his mother.

He pressed the button for the lift, deciding his lungs weren't up to climbing the stairs. 'Hi, Mum.'

No response. This wasn't unusual.

He tried again. 'Mum...? Everything okay?'

A few seconds passed before she spoke. 'Tom, love?'

There was a slur to her voice. He checked his watch. Twenty past three. Great. She'd either hit the bottle early, or she was still hungover from last night.

The lift doors pinged open and he stepped inside. 'Is there a problem? Only I'm at court today. Can I call you back later?'

Another delay before she responded. 'I have a problem.'

Several. But now wasn't the time to be pedantic. 'What's wrong?'

'I don't know how it happened.'

Oh, Christ. 'How what happened, Mum?' He pressed the lift button for the third floor.

'It just arrived. With no warning.'

Trying to get to the crux of his mother's many issues was a bit like pulling teeth. There were days when she got her shit together and was the funny bright person she truly was. But those moments were obliterated by the days when she succumbed to the booze. He should be used to it. Dealing with her drinking had been a constant throughout his thirty years, but it never got any easier. 'You need to be a bit more specific, Mum. What has arrived?' Post? Aliens? Dinner?

'A unicorn.'

A...*what?* He hadn't seen that one coming. 'A unicorn?'

'Yes. An inflatable one, to be precise.'

Was there any other type? Jesus, how pissed was she? 'And how did this unicorn arrive?'

'FedEx.'

At least she hadn't said, 'It flew in through the window.'

The lift doors opened and a couple of barristers got in, dressed in their full regalia. Oh, great. An audience.

'And what do you want me to do about it?' he said, trying to keep his voice low. Tame it? Ride it? Or merely inflate it?

'I want to know how it got here. I wondered whether you'd ordered it?'

49

'And why would I do that?'

'You often order things for me.'

'Yeah, food or clothing, not inflatable unicorns.'

One of the barristers turned and looked at him.

Tom shrugged. Don't ask, he wanted to say.

'Well, if you didn't order it, then who did?'

Tom rubbed his chest. He was starting to wheeze. 'What does the paperwork say? Does it say where it was ordered from?'

There was a delay while she no doubt searched for the paperwork.

The lift reached the third floor, enabling him to escape.

Trying to manage his mother's affairs back in Brighton was getting harder. It was one thing to pay bills, send her food, or check she got up every day, but trying to ensure she was managing her business adequately was another level of responsibility entirely.

His mother was the daughter of a titled family who'd accumulated several properties built in the 1700s. When his grandfather had died in 1979, the estate had been divided up between his two offspring. Uncle Henry had inherited the castle in Scotland and Windsor townhouse, while his mother had been lumbered with the crumbling manor house in Brighton. Uninspired by the thought of managing the upkeep of a Grade Two listed building with its multitude of antiquities and issues, his mum had applied to the local authority for planning permission to turn the entire lower ground floor into an arts centre. She'd had grand ideas to build a theatre, a cinema, several art studios and a café for local artists. Although permission was granted for the renovations, the project became too expensive to complete.

Over the years, the Starlight Playhouse had been used as a youth centre, a camera club and housed the occasional art display. But only the café attracted any regular custom, along with the solitary hirer of the dance studio.

Eventually, his mother came back on the line. 'I found it,' she said, accompanied by a rustle of paper. 'It came from eBay.'

Tom checked her eBay account. Unsurprisingly, he discovered an order for 'one inflatable unicorn'.

Shaking his head, he lifted the phone to his ear. 'The order was placed on the fourth of September. What were you doing last Monday?'

'Monday, you say?' A pause followed. 'No, I definitely didn't order anything last Monday. Are you sure it wasn't you?'

'It definitely wasn't me.'

'Maybe the account was hacked?'

There were times when he wanted to laugh – if he didn't find the situation so tragic. 'I doubt a hacker would have the items delivered to you, Mum. That would rather defeat the object of a scam.'

'Oh, yes, I suppose you're right.'

'You also ordered a set of acrylic paints. Does that ring a bell?'

Pause. The sound of breathing. More rustling of paper. He waited for the penny to drop. 'Now I come to think of it...'

And here it came.

'...I do remember ordering paints. I was going to design a mural for the foyer. A magical woodland scene with an enchanted leprechaun and a...'

'Unicorn?'

Pause. 'A unicorn...yes.'

Tom opened the door to the Robing Room. 'Anything else I can help with?'

'Err...no, love. I'm good, thanks.'

'I'll call you later, okay? Love you.'

'Love you too.'

Tom ended the call. He needed his inhaler...now!

Chapter Five

Jodi's resolve was being tested to the limit. Her boots were still damp from yesterday's downpour and now the wind had decided to join forces in annoying her, flipping her hood back as she headed up the long driveway towards the Starlight Playhouse. She gave up the battle and let go of the hood; it served no purpose this morning other than to risk strangling her.

Despite the challenges of a bumpy bus ride and the arrival of more rain, she reached the playhouse with a few minutes to spare. It was her first morning working in an office. Her big chance. An opportunity to put theory into practice and test out the skills she'd learnt on her degree course. She was determined to put her insecurities behind her and not think about her past misdemeanours, her lack of workplace experience, or the imposing surroundings. Instead, she'd focus on the task in hand and prove to the world that she wasn't a liability, but a useful person to have around. Excellent plan.

But as she climbed the stone steps leading to the front

door, her foot slipped on the wet and she lost her balance. She tried to grab the railing, but her hand slid off the slimy surface and she found herself tumbling backwards. She landed with a thud at the bottom, knocking the wind from her lungs. Pain hit her in several places. Hard concrete dug into her back. Her right hand was twisted beneath her.

For a moment, she didn't move. She couldn't – it hurt too much. Rain dripped onto her face, her hand stung like crazy and her throat constricted with self-pity. Her aunty and cousin had a habit of falling over, or tripping up, but she'd always considered herself fortunate not to have inherited the family's 'clumsy' gene. But maybe she had? It had just taken longer to surface.

A more likely explanation was that she was suffering with new-job jitters.

Rolling onto her front, she dragged herself upright. She was soaking wet, covered in dirt and bleeding. She glanced down at the damage. The top layer of skin was missing from the palm of her right hand. Just what she needed.

She limped up the steps, her hand shaking as she opened the ornate wooden door. Thoughts of strong tea, disinfectant, and a set of waterproof plasters kept her going. But logic should have warned her luck wasn't with her this morning. As she unbuttoned her mud-splattered coat trying not to dirty the floor, a cold chill tickled the back of her neck.

Sensing movement, she turned sharply and came face-to-face with... *Boggin' hell!* The Woman-in-Black. She'd seen the stage play; she knew her fate. Death awaited anyone who saw the apparition. Except, on closer study the woman didn't appear to be a ghost. For a start, there was a strong waft of perfume radiating off her and her attire wasn't eighteenth-century widow, more twenty-first-century couture.

'May I help you?' The woman's gaze homed in.

'I'm Jodi Simmons. I start work here today.'

The woman's expression was as sharp as the edges of her black asymmetric bob. 'I doubt that very much. I'm the front-of-house manager. If a new member of staff had been taken on, I think I would know.'

Okay. How was she supposed to respond to that?

And then a horrible thought occurred. Maybe Carolyn had changed her mind? Or worse, she'd forgotten she'd made Jodi the offer? Oh, hell.

Thankfully, her new boss appeared at that moment. 'Darling, girl. Welcome to the Starlight Playhouse.'

Carolyn Elliot-Wentworth was still a force of nature – tall, blonde and beautiful. She was dressed in a floaty summer dress with a long woollen cardigan shoved over the top. The belt of the cardigan had come loose and was dragging on the floor behind her, but she didn't seem to notice. Her hair was knotted at one side, but she was smiling and looked genuinely happy to see Jodi – even if there was a slight falseness to her exuberance, as though her flamboyance was driven by an external force.

She ushered Jodi into the reception area. 'Come inside, you're drenched.'

Jodi experienced a rush of relief. It hadn't been a horrible misunderstanding. She was expected. 'Thank you so much for this opportunity, Mrs Elliot-Wentworth. It's a real privilege to be working at the playhouse.' Which was entirely true. Quite apart from gaining some much-needed work experience, it was the most amazing building she'd ever seen...damp patches and musty smell aside.

'Please, call me Carolyn.'

The Woman-in-Black didn't look happy. 'May I have a word, madam?'

Madam? Jodi wondered whether she should call Carolyn that too?

'Can it wait, Vivienne? I need to show Jodi around and introduce her to the team, and then I have a meeting.' She paused. 'At least, I think I have a meeting. Do I have a meeting?'

When Carolyn looked directly at her, Jodi blinked, wondering if it was a trick question. 'Err...I don't know.'

Carolyn's frown indicated this was the wrong answer.

Jodi swallowed. 'Maybe it's noted in your diary? Would you like me to check?'

'Oh, I don't keep a diary. It's all in here.' Carolyn tapped the side of her head.

Clearly it wasn't, but Jodi wasn't about to point that out.

Thankfully, Vivienne diverted Carolyn's attention. 'The accountant has phoned again, madam. He's yet to receive the last five months' accounts. This is the seventh time he's called in the last week.'

Carolyn waved her hand about. 'He's so pushy. I've told him I'm dealing with it. Tell him I'll call him back later today… or maybe tomorrow. Thursday at the latest.' She went to walk off and then abruptly turned back. 'Oh, silly me. I haven't made the necessary introductions. Jodi, darling. This is Vivienne King, our front-of-house manager. And Vivienne, this is Jodi. She's our new business manager.'

Jodi smiled.

The Woman-in-Black didn't.

Carolyn lowered her voice in a conspiratorial fashion. 'Vivienne helps me with the paperwork sometimes. Do let her know if you need anything. I'm sure she'd be happy to assist.'

Jodi seriously doubted that.

A feeling compounded when the woman's beady eyes took in her state of disarray. 'You seem to have met with an accident.'

Jodi followed the woman's gaze down to her muddied coat. 'I'm sorry, yes. I fell.' When she glanced back up, the woman was staring at her hair, which had probably started to frizz thanks to the rain.

'So it would appear.' In a movement so smooth it was almost feline, the woman turned her back on her. 'You'll find a sink in the toilets adjacent to the café, Ms Simmons. Please ensure you clean up after you.' A waft of perfume filled the air as she glided away, disappearing into the shadows in a manner that would make Mrs Danvers seem positively warm.

Carolyn took hold of Jodi's hand. 'Don't mind her. She's a sweetie really.'

Jodi felt this was highly unlikely, but she was happy to be proved wrong.

'Now, where were we?' Carolyn gave her another expectant look.

'You were about to show me around and introduce me to the team?'

'Oh, that's right. I was. This way.' She hooked her arm through Jodi's and manoeuvred her down the corridor.

Jodi had hoped she might be able to stop off at the loos and tidy herself up, but Carolyn seemed to have forgotten her battered state. The stinging in her hand was getting worse, not helped by her new boss gripping it. There was a slight tremor to Carolyn, accompanied by a sweet cloying smell that radiated off her as they walked together. Jodi was no expert, but along with the slightly slurred speech and inconsistent walking pace, she suspected Carolyn still had issues with alcohol.

They arrived at the café, which was empty. Unsurprising really, considering it was only nine a.m. The noise of a hedge trimmer drew their attention outside. A burly middle-aged man was up a ladder tending to the bushes lining the large courtyard.

Jodi's eyes fell on the ornate statue of a lion, minus an ear. Shame dragged her mind back to the summer of 2005 when she'd climbed up the thing, showing off to her mates by pretending to ride it, before toppling off, taking its ear with her and landing with a thud on the solid concrete. She couldn't blame clumsiness for that one; it had been pure drunken anarchy.

Surprisingly, when faced with an inebriated teenager wreaking havoc at her playhouse, Carolyn hadn't called the police. Instead, she'd arranged for a taxi to take her home. Jodi hadn't appreciated Carolyn's kindness at the time, but she certainly did now.

Carolyn opened the French doors and waved at the man up the ladder. 'Eddie, darling? Can I introduce you to someone?'

The man cupped his ear, indicating he couldn't hear. He climbed down, and walked over. Actually, walked was the wrong word. It was more of a meander, slow and controlled, like a cowboy in an old film. He was wearing an Indiana Jones hat, which he tipped upon reaching them. His overcoat was dripping wet.

'This is Jodi...' Carolyn's face scrunched up in concentration as she clicked her fingers, trying to remember her new worker's surname.

Jodi helped her out. 'Simmons.'

'Simmons, that's it. Jodi Simmons.' Carolyn put her hand on the man's arm. 'This is the wonderful Eddie Moriantez. He's been here for years and looks after the grounds and does a bit of maintenance.' She turned to Jodi. 'He used to be in the navy,' she added, her pretence of a whisper failing.

'Oh...right. Great to meet you.' Jodi held out her injured hand and braced herself.

Thankfully, the man declined. 'I won't, if that's okay. I'm filthy.' He held up his hands, which looked clean enough. She suspected he'd noticed her injury and was letting her off the hook. 'Muddy work.' He smiled, his expression both relaxed and amused. She decided Eddie was going to be a lot easier to get along with than Vivienne.

Carolyn immediately turned back to Eddie. 'We won't keep you,' she said, already shutting the doors. 'I'm sure you're eager to get back to trimming the bushes. There really isn't anything worse than an untidy bush.'

Jodi and Eddie exchanged an amused look. 'I best get back to it then,' he said, tipping his hat. 'Can't have an untidy bush.' He ambled off, chuckling.

Yep, she was going to like Eddie.

'Kitchen next.' Carolyn steered her towards a set of swing doors to their right.

The kitchen was cold and uninviting with a severe lack of modern appliances. A huge iron range with various copper pots hanging down from the surround dominated the far wall. An island filled the middle of the room with a rack above. She half expected to see a selection of game hanging from it, like in an episode of *Downton Abbey*, but there wasn't any. She couldn't see a dishwasher, but there was a microwave and a coffee machine next to the deep ceramic sink. Cooking in there wouldn't be particularly easy, she imagined.

A man was standing at the island chopping. He didn't look up when they approached.

'Petrit, I'd like you to meet my new assistant, Jodi...' More clicking of the fingers.

'Simmons.'

'Simmons!' Carolyn laughed. 'Why do I keep forgetting?'

Jodi felt it wouldn't be prudent to answer.

'Petrit Manaj is our resident chef. He looks after the café.' Her voice lowered. 'He's from Romania.'

Jodi was starting to realise that everyone who worked at the playhouse had a tagline. She wondered what hers would be? *This is Jodi...she has a criminal record.* God, she hoped not. She'd just have to hope Carolyn's poor memory extended to Jodi's antics as a teenager.

The man carried on chopping, the large knife slicing down on the board as if he was trying to obliterate the coriander.

'Petrit, stop a moment, will you. My head's banging.' Carolyn covered her ears.

The chef dropped the knife, making it clatter. He turned and gave Jodi what could only be described as a death stare. He had deep-set eyes that burned beneath a thick unibrow. His face was angular and covered in unkempt stubble. But it was the disdain in his expression that gave most cause for alarm. Jodi recognised the look. It was the same look the lad from the restaurant had given her the other night, the one who'd shouted abuse in the street.

Refusing to be intimidated, she held out her hand. 'Pleased

to meet you.' She held eye contact, daring him to refuse her offer of introduction.

Her resolve weakened slightly when he gripped her hand, making her flinch. 'You contaminate my kitchen,' he said, marching over to the sink and washing his hands.

She wondered if he'd still have washed his hands if there'd been no blood? Sadly, she suspected he probably would have.

Carolyn frowned. 'Are you bleeding? How on earth did you do that? We need to get that sorted.'

Jodi was sensing a pattern.

Carolyn gave Petrit a friendly wave and then ushered Jodi out of the kitchen. 'He makes the most delicious goulash,' she said, hooking her arm through Jodi's. 'Now, I think that's everyone.' And then she stopped. 'No...I've forgotten someone. Who have I forgotten?' She looked at Jodi, waiting for an answer.

Jodi wondered if this was some kind of initiation test. If it was, then she suspected she was failing.

'Leon!' Carolyn's exuberance almost knocked Jodi off her feet. 'Of course, silly me. Our gorgeous bar manager.'

Supporting a swaying Carolyn, Jodi was led through to the adjacent bar area, which was basically a narrow counter with a few tables overlooking the gardens. Jodi's hand was stinging and she wished she could tidy herself up, but her boss wasn't done with the introductions. She'd just have to hope that the bar manager was politer than Petrit...

And then she saw him.

The impact was hard and fast. She hoped her sudden intake of breath hadn't been audible.

'And that's Leon.' Carolyn sighed. 'I told you he was gorgeous.'

Gorgeous didn't come close.

The guy behind the bar looked to be of similar age to Jodi and with similar colouring. His hair was shaved short, with neatly trimmed facial hair that made his eyes stand out. And boy, did they stand out. They looked almost green...no, light brown...or maybe hazel? It was difficult to tell in the dismal light with the rain pounding against the windows. Whatever the colour, they bored right into her, pinning her to the spot, igniting such heat she half-expected steam to start rising from her damp coat.

And then he smiled.

Boggin' hell. It was the kind of smile that could stop traffic.

'Hi,' he said, leaning on the bar, the outline of his toned arms visible beneath his casual shirt. 'Leon Malone.'

'Jodi Simmons.' Her voice sounded calm. She wasn't sure how – her heart was hammering away.

His gaze travelled down to her hand. 'Do you need something for that?'

Observant too.

'It's only a scrape. Nothing major.'

He handed her a paper napkin. 'Looks painful.' His hand brushed hers and she could almost feel the electricity firing up her arm. Bloody hell.

63

Get a grip, she told herself. She was here to gain work experience, not flirt with the staff. Swooning after a fit bloke would be a distraction she didn't need. She hadn't spent the last seven years turning her life around to be derailed on her first day.

'There's a first-aid box in the office. You'll find plasters and antiseptic cream inside. Let me know if there isn't. The contents don't always get replaced,' he said, glancing at Carolyn, who didn't seem to notice.

Jodi wondered which was going to be the bigger challenge: dealing with a rude chef, the icy front-of-house manager, or trying not to swoon over the hot barman.

'Jodi used to come here when it was a youth club.' Carolyn leant against one of the bar stools. 'She made quite an impact.'

Oh, God. Jodi wanted the ground to swallow her up.

'Is that right?' Leon raised an eyebrow. 'How so?'

Jodi couldn't believe Carolyn was about to shaft her and tell the gorgeous bar manager about her wayward youth. How did she even remember?

Carolyn laughed. 'Blowed if I know. I can't remember what I had for breakfast. Whatever it was, it made quite an impression on my son.'

Phew. Of sorts, anyway. Did Tom know she was working here? Somehow, Jodi doubted it.

Leon looked right at her. 'I can imagine.'

Carolyn clapped her hands. 'Introductions over. Time to get to work.' She slid her arm through Jodi's. 'Now, tell me what you know about QuickBooks. I haven't a clue and I have a stack of invoices that need entering.'

Five months' worth, by the sounds of it.

And then Carolyn stared down at her bloodstained hand. 'Goodness me, how did I do that? I'm bleeding. Leon, where's the first-aid box?'

Jodi held up her hand. 'I think it's my blood, Carolyn.'

Carolyn's gaze switched from her own hand to Jodi's. 'When did you do that?'

It was official. Jodi was starring in her own version of *Groundhog Day*. 'I fell down the steps outside.'

'Well, why didn't you say something? We need to get that sorted.' She took Jodi's arm and headed in the direction of the office.

Jodi glanced back at Leon. 'Thanks for the napkin.'

A wry smile played on his lips. 'No worries. Good to have you on board.' He resumed drying glasses, leaving Jodi to wonder whether working at the Starlight Playhouse was going to be even more challenging than she'd imagined.

Chapter Six

Wednesday 13th September

Becca had learnt early on in her career that being a dancer wasn't a glamorous existence. From dusty, dirty rehearsal rooms, to dressing rooms that needed more than a lick of paint. Not to mention the touring, getting home late at night, the money that you weren't paid and the endless physical hard work. You had to sacrifice a social life. You had to get used to being told no a lot, taking criticism, being told you weren't good enough. The love you had for dancing had to be bigger than all the negatives. And she'd dealt with that. She'd been stoic, dedicated and resilient...but nothing could have prepared her for the horror of teaching a class of seven-year-olds.

The trial lesson last Saturday hadn't started well. Mrs Morris had been so relieved a potential replacement had finally been found, that she'd packed up and gone home. Talk about landing her in it. But she hadn't let this dent her confidence, and had set about trying to win over a group of tiny tots. Her plan was to begin with the basics, assess their abilities and then build on their technique, as her teachers had

66

done with her. Which was fine in principle. It was just in practice that it failed.

Half the kids hadn't turned up for the class. The ones who did were unruly, wouldn't listen to instructions and spent the entire hour running around the studio making an absolute din. Far from reining in their unruly offspring, the parents had stood around the room glaring at Becca, clearly holding her responsible for their children's lack of discipline. One boy nicked a girl's hairnet and refused to give it back, making her cry. Two other girls started bickering and ended up crying, and one kid ran across the studio so fast he smacked into the mirrors, resulting in more crying.

Becca had been close to tears herself.

But this was nothing compared to the parents. One outraged mother removed her child mid-class, stating in a loud voice that Becca was an 'utter disgrace'. Three parents announced at the end of the class they wouldn't be returning, and one woman questioned whether Becca's 'unconventional' appearance was entirely 'appropriate' for the role of a dance teacher.

Part of her had wanted to question why they allowed their children to behave in such a rowdy manner, but she'd held her tongue. She suspected teaching was like the world of show business, where everyone knew everyone. If word got out that she had a bad attitude, then it would be game over.

But it'd been tough. She'd never struggled to be civil before. But then she'd never been faced with a horde of competitive parents, who did nothing but criticise her appearance, her lack of control, or her ability to teach.

The distressing thing was, they were right. She was a useless teacher.

The only chink of light had come at the end of the class when one of the mothers had thanked her for helping her kids understand the meaning of 'turnout', something they'd struggled with under Mrs Morris. She'd introduced herself as Rosie and promised to return next week. She'd even left smiling, seemingly oblivious to just how disastrous the class had been.

Despite all this, Carolyn had still offered Becca the job. She wasn't naive enough to believe this was because she'd impressed Carolyn. Far from it. Carolyn hadn't even witnessed the debacle – she'd still been asleep in the office – which meant the offer was based purely on Carolyn's desperation to find a replacement teacher, and not on Becca's ability. It wasn't exactly a glowing endorsement. And now Becca had to do it all again. This time with the adult tappers.

While she waited for the class to arrive, she took the opportunity to stretch out her hamstrings. Flexibility was the key to any style of dance. Stiff joints and tight tendons didn't allow for freedom of movement.

She went over to the barre and began her routine, using the time to have a proper look around. She'd been so busy on Saturday trying to control the kids that she hadn't paid much attention to the state of the dance studio. On first glance, it looked fine. It was a decent-sized space, with a wooden sprung floor, a mirrored wall, and a ballet barre running the length of the room. But on closer inspection, she could see damp patches on the walls, cracks in the plasterboard and chunks missing from the floorboards. It looked tired and scruffy, like the rest of the building.

She was mid-stretch when the doors behind opened. A couple entered, both very tall and model-thin skinny. They wore matching woollen coats and hats, despite the mild weather. They ignored Becca and shuffled over to the furthest seats, as if trying to hide.

She went over. 'Hi, I'm Becca. I've taken over from Mrs Morris.'

They acknowledged her with shy nods, but didn't hold eye contact.

Becca tried for a welcoming smile. 'And you are?'

They looked at each other, as if silently questioning who was going to answer.

Eventually, the guy spoke. 'I'm Nick. This is my wife, Cassie.'

'Lovely to meet you both. Have you been coming to the class long?'

They shook their heads. 'First time,' the man replied.

Thank God for that. She figured it would be easier if people had nothing to compare her with. 'Welcome to the class. Do you have tap shoes?'

More head shaking. The couple were synchronised, if nothing else.

'Not to worry. But if you enjoy the class and want to keep

coming you'll need the correct shoes. I can give you a list of stockists if you need them.'

The doors opened again and two women came in. Unlike Nick and Cassie, these two didn't appear to suffer from shyness. One was short and round with a mass of curly grey hair, and the other was medium height with fabulous red hair and an equally fabulous cleavage. They immediately came over. 'You must be our new teacher,' curly-haired woman said. 'I'm Miriam, lovely to meet you.' She held out her hand.

The woman had a firm grip. 'Good to meet you. I'm Becca.'

'Cute hair,' the woman with the big boobs said. 'I'm Wanda. Wanda from the US.'

'Nice to meet you, Wanda from the US.'

Wanda laughed, a big throaty sound. 'Well, aren't you a breath of fresh air. Quite the opposite to Nearly-Dead-Morris.'

Miriam smacked Wanda's arm. 'She was the same age as me, thank you very much.'

Wanda shrugged. 'I say it as I see it.'

'Well, I wish you wouldn't.' Miriam walked off and sat down.

Wanda followed. 'Someone's got their knickers in a twist.' She let out another throaty laugh. 'Don't you just love that word? Knickers? We don't have that in the US.'

Becca suspected she was in for an interesting evening. Clearing her throat, she faked a confidence she didn't feel and addressed the group. 'Shall we get started? For those of you who have tap shoes please put them on, and then find a space on the floor.'

Five minutes of faffing followed as Wanda and Miriam struggled to locate their shoes, put them on and tie the laces. Miriam was dressed in a brightly patterned smock dress, whereas Wanda wore the full dance regalia: Lycra catsuit, leg-warmers and top-of-the-range tap shoes. Nick and Cassie, who looked like they'd just come from work, were dressed in head-to-toe grey. Collectively, it was a sight to behold.

Becca was just thinking it couldn't get any more bizarre, when the doors opened and another woman joined them. 'Sorry, I'm late,' she said, hurrying in. She dropped her bag, tripped over it and then dropped it again when she tried to pick it up.

'That's Mi-Sun,' Wanda said, in a loud whisper. 'She's from Korea.'

And Becca thought dealing with the kids was hard.

Still, at least this lot weren't running around the room screaming. Not yet, anyway. 'As we have two new people in the class and I'm new myself, let's start with a few basic steps to get us warmed up. Okay?'

Four expectant faces stared at her.

Mi-Sun ran to join them, tripping up as she did so.

As a fellow klutz, Becca could empathise. 'Okay, could you all spread out so you're not on top of each other?' They shuffled about. Wanda and Miriam both wanted to be at the front. Nick and Cassie hid at the back. Mi-Sun was left in the middle

71

on her own. 'Right. The first step we're going to learn is called the shuffle.'

'Oh, I know this.' Miriam launched into a demonstration, followed by Wanda, who wasn't about to be outdone. What with Miriam's curves and Wanda's cleavage, there was quite a lot of bouncing going on. The floorboards got a good workout.

'That's great, ladies. But let's break it down for the rest of the class.' She waited until the floor stopped vibrating. 'The shuffle is a combination of two basic moves, the brush and the strike. Let's start with the brush.' She was met with three concerned expressions and two bored ones. Miriam and Wanda failed to hide their frustration at being made to start from the beginning.

Oh, well. Nothing she could do about that. Even with no teacher training she knew she could only go as fast as the slowest person in the group.

Becca turned to face the mirrors. 'Stand on one leg and lift your other foot. Now swing the foot forward, brushing the ball of your foot against the floor.'

Nick lost his balance.

Cassie lifted the wrong leg.

And Mi-Sun fell over.

Becca rushed over to pick her up. 'Are you okay?'

The woman nodded.

'Let's try again, shall we?' Becca stood next to Mi-Sun, one eye on Nick and Cassie behind her. 'Lift your foot, swing it forwards, brush it on the floor.'

Nick accidently kicked Cassie.

Cassie lifted the wrong leg.

And Mi-Sun *almost* fell over.

Did that count as progress? Becca wasn't sure.

'Try again,' she said, as they attempted to copy her. 'That's it. Don't let your heel touch the floor, Nick. And again.'

After ten minutes of practice, and aware that Miriam and Wanda were bored, Becca resumed her position at the front. 'Now you've all mastered the brush,' she managed to say, without any hint of irony, 'let's move on to the strike. This is simply the same movement in reverse. You swing your foot backwards, instead of forwards. Then we build up speed so that it looks like this.' She did a quick demonstration, pleased to note that her knee didn't object too much. 'Can you see what I'm doing? Brush, strike, brush, strike.'

Several attempts were being made to replicate the move, but none of them looked anything like a shuffle.

Nick lost his balance.

Cassie got her feet entangled.

And Mi-Sun fell over.

Becca sighed.

It was going to be a long evening.

*

By the time she got home, she was mentally exhausted. Her plan to cover how to do a step-ball change and a buffalo step had gone completely out of the window. They'd spent the entire hour trying to master the shuffle...and failing. Despite her constant coaxing and reassurances that they were making progress, her pupils remained unconvinced. And with good cause. She'd never realised teaching involved so much lying.

What had become evident during the hour-long session was that whereas Miriam and Wanda didn't suffer from a lack of confidence – or opinions, for that matter – their enthusiasm far outweighed their skill levels. Nick and Cassie were acutely self-conscious, body-conscious and painfully shy, and poor Mi-Sun had absolutely no coordination. She was like a drunk Bambi...on ice.

Collectively, the group had the core strength of gravy and the flexibility of iron piping. Becca had been completely out of her depth. She was just grateful that once again Carolyn hadn't been there to witness the car crash; she'd gone to bed early with a mysterious 'virus'.

Becca let herself into the guest house, surprised when it looked like no one else was home. She found her mother and cousin upstairs in Jodi's bedroom trying to fix a leak in the en suite.

Her mum was gripping a pair of pliers, trying to turn off the tap, which didn't appear to be budging. Her cheeks were flushed and her hair was sticking up all over the place.

Becca leant against the doorframe. 'Problem?'

'What gave you that impression?' The pliers slipped off the

tap and banged against the splashback. Her mum whacked the sink in annoyance.

Jodi's expression indicated all was not well.

Becca reached over and patted her mum's back. Hardly the most useful of responses, but she felt something was needed. 'Can I help?'

Her mum moved out of the way. 'Be my guest.' She stretched out her back, grimacing as she did so. Becca supposed it was times like this that her mum missed her dad. He'd been such a competent handyman.

She picked up the pliers. Having lived in a shared house with a landlord who'd never carried out any repairs, she was used to getting her hands dirty.

Jodi edged away, not trusting her cousin to be any less lethal than her aunt. 'How did the tap class go?'

Becca pulled a face. 'About as well as the ballet class.'

'That good?'

'Like herding cats.'

There was a knock on the door. 'There's quite a bit of noise coming from up here,' Mrs Busby called from the hallway. 'The doctor and I are trying to watch *Frost*.'

Her mum slumped onto the toilet seat.

'David Jason is such a good actor, don't you think?' The old woman shuffled into the bedroom. 'Pardon my intrusion, but it would be a shame to miss it.'

Her mum forced a smile. 'Apologies, Mrs Busby, but we have a leak. I'll get it fixed as soon as possible.'

'Oh, dear. That won't do.' Mrs Busby looked down at the wet floor. 'The doctor was very disappointed there was no suet pudding for supper tonight. It is Wednesday, after all.'

Becca jumped in before her mother said something she'd regret. 'Sorry about that, Mrs B. As you can see, we're a little busy. Why don't you go back and finish watching the telly, and we'll try not to make so much noise?' She shut the en suite door, hoping the old lady would take the hint.

She did, not before commenting, 'Why you don't telephone a plumber, I don't know.'

Becca watched her mother grip hold of the edge of the loo seat. 'Does she have any idea how much a plumber would charge to come out at this time of night?'

Not for the first time, Becca wondered if her mum was having money problems. She didn't like to keep asking, but she couldn't help if her mum refused to tell her what was up.

'So what went wrong at the tap class?' Jodi asked, tactfully changing topic.

Becca twisted the tap, but it wouldn't budge. 'It would be easier to tell you what went right. I couldn't even get them to pick up the basic steps. And there were only five of them. How on earth am I going to cope with a class full? It seems wrong to take Carolyn's money. It's like I'm defrauding her.' She gripped the pliers around the tap and twisted.

'So what are you going to do?'

'Quit.' The pliers slipped off the tap. 'Shit.'

'Oh, that's mature. Is that how you dealt with adversity when you were a dancer?'

Becca twisted the tap again. This time it shifted a fraction. 'It's different.'

'How so? You wouldn't expect to perform in a show without rehearsing, so why would you expect to teach a class without training?'

The tap slowly began to move. 'Exactly. I have no training.'

'So you've got a bit of catching up to do. Suck it up.'

The tap shifted. The dripping stopped.

'Oh, well done, love.' Her mum patted her on the shoulder.

'Yeah, well done,' Jodi said in a sarcastic tone. 'Just as well you didn't *quit*.'

Becca poked her tongue out at her cousin. 'So what do you suggest? It's not like I can fast-track through years of teacher training ahead of next week's class, is it?'

'No, but you can do other things.' Jodi followed her into the bedroom, leaving her mum wringing out her wet sleeve. 'There's heaps off stuff on the internet. You're bound to find videos on teaching and people-management. You just need to dig deep and persevere.'

Becca flopped onto the bed. 'You make it sound so easy.'

Jodi glared at her. 'Did you seriously just say that to me?'

Becca propped herself up on her elbows. 'Sorry, you're right. I'm a crap cousin.'

'You are, but you're forgiven.' Jodi sat down next to her. 'Nothing will be as bad as the first lesson.'

She raised an eyebrow. 'You think?'

Jodi's expression turned ponderous. 'It's a bit like sex. You can read about it, watch other people doing it, study the mechanics of it, but nothing prepares you for the real thing. The first time is always a bit of a disaster.'

Becca laughed. 'I can't believe you're comparing teaching to fu—'

'*Oi*! I can hear you,' her mum called from the en suite.

'Sorry!' Becca pulled a face at her cousin.

Jodi grinned. 'As I was saying, you need to muddle through as best you can. Next time will be better. You just need to practise, like you do with—'

'I'm still here!'

'—learning to play the piano,' Jodi said, making Becca laugh. 'Keep at it. And then once you're feeling more confident, we can look at ways to increase attendance. Maybe design an advertising strategy.'

'Very corporate.'

Jodi swiped her with a pillow. 'Don't take the piss.'

Becca squealed when Jodi poked her in the ribs. 'I'm not.'

'You are. I worked bloody hard for my degree.'

Becca grabbed a second pillow. 'I know you did. You were a model student. I bow down to your superiority... *Ow*, stop it!'

'Then stop being sarcastic. As the new business manager at the playhouse, I want none of this quitting nonsense, okay?' Another blow dislodged one of Becca's bunches. 'You need to listen to someone with the necessary skillset in business management.'

Becca retaliated, swiping at her cousin with the pillow. 'Know-it-all-knickers.'

Jodi threw the pillow, but Becca ducked and it connected with her mum as she walked out of the en suite. 'Oops! Sorry, Aunty Ruby.'

They were subjected to 'the stare'. It was a look they'd experienced many times during their teens. It was usually followed by a grounding.

Becca hid behind her cousin. 'You've done it now. Mummykins isn't happy.'

Jodi nicked Becca's pillow and resumed hitting her. 'Arse-lick.'

Becca fell back onto the bed laughing, relieved when she saw her mum laughing too.

Chapter Seven

Tuesday 19th September

Tom buttoned up his three-piece suit and straightened his wig and gown ready for the first hearing of the day. Wearing a double-breasted jacket was a requirement of all barristers when appearing in the Crown Court. If you turned up wearing a single-breasted, or heaven forbid, you weren't wearing a waistcoat, then you'd be strung up by the judge and sent packing from the courtroom. He'd learnt that the hard way.

His client today was a twenty-five-year-old man charged with affray. Together with seven of his mates, his client had got completely pissed whilst out on a stag do and managed to get into a massive fight with another group of lads also celebrating their forthcoming nuptials. Their fiancées must be so proud. Unfortunately the fight was caught on CCTV, so there was little Tom could do in terms of mounting a defence.

Cases involving alcohol never sat well with him. It was too close to home. He'd lost count of the number of times he'd been contacted by the police to inform him that his mother had been found wandering down the road inebriated and was currently sleeping it off in a cell. He'd jump in his car, race down to Brighton and assure the desk sergeant that it wouldn't happen again. But of course, it would. His mother's reaction to waking up in a police cell varied from mortification and tearful apologies, to angry insults and accusations. '*I have it under control*,' or '*You never want me to enjoy myself*,' were common. '*It's your fault I'm this way*,' stung the most.

He knew that shifting the blame, manipulating loved ones and becoming abusive were all part of the illness, but it didn't make it any less painful. The idea that one day her behaviour might result in her appearing in front of a judge made him sick to his stomach.

But the upside of today's case was that it was being heard at Snaresbrook, one of his favourite courts. It was situated in the borough of Redbridge and was a beautifully ornate building with wonderful gardens and even a lake. Inside it was like Hogwarts, with its magnificent staircases, impressive turrets and mysterious locked doors. It was a showcase for how a Grade Two listed building could look if money wasn't an issue. Next to Snaresbrook, the Starlight Playhouse looked like a rundown brothel.

He'd just left the Robing Room when he heard his name being called.

At first, he didn't recognise the voice. Why would he? He

hadn't spoken to his father for several years. It was only when he turned and saw Harvey Elliot walking towards him that his brain made the connection. His initial instinct was to run, but that wouldn't be overly mature, and besides, his feet wouldn't cooperate.

'When I saw your name listed today, I hoped we'd bump into each other,' his father said on reaching him. 'Good to see you, son.' He held out his hand.

Tom stared down at his father's outstretched hand, wondering if someone had transported him to a parallel universe – one where they weren't estranged and his father hadn't walked out on his mother eight years earlier. Tom's gaze lifted to his father's face, visibly older than when he'd last seen him, his hair and moustache silver-grey, his eyes surrounded by wrinkles and framed by thick-rimmed glasses with bizarre purple-tint lenses.

His father was a Silk. Queen's Counsel to use its proper title. Their gowns were made of silk – hence the name, and they were considered the heavyweight boxers of the criminal justice system. They strutted and postured in court like sprinters before a hundred-metre final, acting as though they were intellectually superior to everyone else in the room.

His father's attitude to parenthood had been just as intimidating.

Tom instantly felt his chest tighten.

But he was no longer a spineless teenager, too afraid to stand up to his father, or disobey his ultimatums. He might not be equal in terms of barrister status, but there was no way he was about to pretend the past hadn't happened.

His father appeared unperturbed by his son's refusal to shake his hand. 'How are you, Thomas?'

It was such a simple question and yet one that was fricking hard to answer. How was he? What? For the past seven years? He opted for brevity. 'I'm fine.'

'And work?'

'That's fine too.' Tom wasn't about to share his growing sense of dissatisfaction about his career. Not least because his father wouldn't understand. He'd never been 'soft' like his son.

'What time are you due in court?'

There was no point lying – the trials were listed on the wall. 'Soon.' He kept his response vague.

'Tricky case?'

'Not really. Was there something specific you wanted?' Tom rubbed his chest, wishing he'd taken a shot of Fostair this morning as a preventative.

His father glanced behind, waiting until the corridor cleared before speaking. 'I wanted to let you know that I haven't been... well.'

Time slowed. It took a moment before he realised the thumping he could hear was coming from his chest. But he wasn't going to soften, not after all this time. 'I'm sorry to hear that. Nothing serious, I hope.'

Harvey Elliot cleared his throat, as though debating whether to continue. 'I was having chest pains. I was admitted to London Bridge Hospital for an angiogram. The test results showed the onset of atherosclerosis. It causes angina.'

'Right.' It felt like a pathetic response to such a big announcement, but what was he supposed to say? Despite everything that'd happened, he'd act like the dutiful son and bury the hatchet? That wasn't going to happen. There'd been too many arguments over the years, too many hurtful accusations.

His father waited, but it was obvious Tom had nothing more to add. 'I thought you should know.'

'What's the prognosis?' Tom felt he needed to know what he was dealing with, even if they had burnt their bridges.

'Medication. Eating better, taking more exercise. Less stress.' His father tried for a good-natured smile. 'Torture, right?'

Tom didn't feel like engaging in friendly banter. 'Surgery?'

'Not at this stage. Hopefully it can be managed without the need for surgical intervention.'

'Well, thanks for letting me know. I hope things improve.' He went to leave, but his father caught his arm.

'The thing is, it's made me re-evaluate my life. Lying in a hospital bed waiting for results tends to focus the mind. Makes a man think about his life, his...decisions.'

Tom turned to look at the man who'd made his teenage life hell and walked out on his mother when she'd needed him the most. 'And what conclusions did you come to?'

'I decided that I didn't want to miss out on any more of my son's life.' His father took a step closer. 'It's time to bury the hatchet. I'm willing to move forwards, if you are. I was hoping we could call a truce and forgive each other. What do you say?'

Tom rubbed his chest. 'You think I need *your* forgiveness?' He studied his dad's face. There wasn't a hint of insecurity. 'I'm curious. What terrible crime have I committed that requires your forgiveness?'

'You've barely spoken to me in seven years—'

'And why is that?'

His father sighed. 'Because you felt the need to punish me for leaving your mother.'

The man wasn't stupid; he'd give him that. 'She has an illness. She needs constant help and yet you decided to put your own needs ahead of hers.'

His father frowned. 'Do you have any idea how hard it was for me?'

The blood drained from Tom's face. 'Hard for you?'

There were so many things Tom could have said, but at that moment he was genuinely lost for words. His father thought it would be that simple? That he could just decide it was time for them to 'move forwards' and forget everything that had gone before. Jesus. He really was a piece of work.

Tom was saved from saying something he'd regret by his phone pinging with a message. He glanced down, expecting to see Izzy's name. They'd accepted an offer on the flat and were close to exchanging contracts. But it was a missed call from his mother.

85

Ignoring his father, he pressed play. *Did you know you could get green apples…? From now on I'm only going to buy green apples. No other colour… Can you get other colours? Pink? I'd like pink apples. Add green and pink apples to my grocery shopping this week. Thank you, darling. Love you.*

Tom didn't know whether to laugh or cry. The world was conspiring against him. An unwinnable case, his father having a mid-life crisis, and his mother losing the plot. And it was only bloody nine-thirty.

He turned to leave. 'I need to deal with this.'

'Will you think about it?' his father called after him.

There was nothing to think about. Some things were beyond repair.

The relationship with his father was one of them.

Chapter Eight

Saturday 23rd September

'You cannot exclude my child,' the woman said, squaring up to Becca. 'You have no right. I'm paying you to teach my kid to dance, not inflict this rubbish on them. It's not even dancing.' She gestured to where the kids were balancing beanbags on their feet, trying to flick them up and catch them standing on one foot.

'You're right. It's not, but—'

'If I wanted my kid to mess around playing games, I'd do it at home. I wouldn't pay some jumped-up freak to do it for me.'

Freak? That was a new one.

The woman jabbed a finger. 'Get on with teaching them to dance and don't tell my kid he can't join in, you hear me?'

Becca was conflicted. Part of her wanted to give in, especially as the other parents were nodding in agreement, supporting the woman's grievance. But she knew she had to make a stand. If she didn't, things would never improve. She couldn't spend every Saturday morning shouting until she was hoarse. 'I'm sorry, but I can't agree to that.'

The woman looked incredulous. 'Excuse me?' She turned to the other parents. 'We're paying for you to teach our kids ballet, right? Nothing else.'

A few mothers nodded in agreement.

'So get teaching, or we're gone.' The woman folded her arms, ultimatum delivered.

Becca could feel the burn of numerous eyes on her. She was a pathetic excuse for a teacher. But she was trying her best to remedy that. She was at a crossroads where she needed to make a decision. Give in, or stand her ground.

There was no real dilemma. She'd rather risk losing half the kids than give in to their bullying parents. Having said that, she'd be a fool if she didn't try to win them over. Without any pupils, she wouldn't have a class. Or income. And Carolyn was relying on her to help improve the fortunes of the playhouse. She had to try and turn the situation around.

She gestured to the kids, who were oblivious to the heated discussion taking place by the piano. 'If these kids are serious about making it as a dancer, then they need to learn the art of listening.' *And discipline*, she added silently, something that was also currently lacking. 'Until we reach a point where I'm convinced every child understands that if they don't listen they can't join in with the class, then I can't move forward with more complex activities.'

Becca had spent the last two weeks trawling through numerous videos and articles, and quizzing her mum about teaching. Her mum's message had been clear. There was absolutely no point in teaching her students about adagio, fouette, jeté or pirouettes, if they didn't listen. If you didn't listen, you couldn't learn. So, much to the horror of the parents, she'd begun today's class by announcing that from now on there would be rules, and if those rules were broken, there would be consequences.

'Mrs Morris never had a problem with our kids,' the woman said, urged on by the other mothers. 'Maybe you're not cut out to be a teacher.'

This was entirely possible. But it was Becca's class, and she needed to develop her own way of teaching. And that didn't include spending the entire hour shouting and being ignored. If the parents didn't like it, tough.

'I'm sorry you don't agree with my approach.' Becca feigned a confidence she didn't feel, trying to hide her shaking hands. 'It goes without saying that I'd love for your children to remain in my class.' She looked at the parents, some of whom avoided eye contact. 'But I honestly feel this is the best approach. However, the decision is entirely yours. If you'd prefer to try a different class elsewhere, then that's your prerogative. I'll refund you this term's money.'

They hadn't expected that. There was a murmur as the mothers huddled together, discussing what to do next.

Becca had no idea how Carolyn would feel about refunding the fees. She was taking a big risk, but it was the only way she could wrestle control of the situation.

She spotted Ben and Phoebe's mother standing to one side.

When Rosie smiled and discreetly gave her a thumbs-up, her panic levels lowered. The woman would probably never realise how much that single show of support meant.

The ringleader approached with the verdict. 'I'm taking my kids to someone who knows what they're doing. They're good kids. I don't appreciate you treating them like they're not. I'll expect a cheque in the post. I want a full refund, you hear me?' The woman yelled at her three kids, and then dragged them from the room.

Becca waited to see who else would follow. Two other mothers scuttled out, heads down, their kids in tow. That left five kids from the original class and two new starters. It had been three, but one mother left before the class started, unimpressed by the state of the dance studio. Oh, well, you couldn't win them all.

As the door banged shut behind them, Rosie came over. 'That must have been hard. But you did the right thing.'

Becca sighed. 'I hope you're right.'

Rosie smiled. 'Take it from me – children need boundaries. And they need to learn the consequences of pushing those boundaries. I'm more than happy for you to discipline my kids. Anything that makes my life at home easier.' There was a sadness to her expression, which lifted as quickly as it had arrived. 'Just out of interest, why are you getting them to juggle beanbags?'

'It helps improve balance,' Becca said, watching the kids flipping up the beanbags trying to stay upright. 'If you watch

Lionel Messi playing football, or Roger Federer on the tennis court, they could literally be falling over and yet somehow still make the shot. It's what sets them apart. And it's the same with dance. Balance is the most fundamental attribute a dancer needs.'

'I never realised. Maybe I should take it up myself.' Rosie gestured to her walking stick, which until that moment Becca hadn't noticed. 'I always wanted to dance, but never learnt as a child. It's too late now, I'm forever falling over.'

Becca didn't want to pry, but her reaction must have given her away.

'Multiple sclerosis.'

Becca flinched. 'I'm sorry to hear that.'

Rosie didn't look more than early thirties. She was slim, with a lovely open smile and wavy brown hair that fell around her shoulders. Life could be so unfair.

'It flares up every now and then. Doesn't make dealing with two energetic kids any easier. Luckily, I have Dan to help me, my other half. He's a saint.'

And Becca had thought dealing with a ruptured Achilles and severed patellar tendon was hard? She vowed never to moan about her injuries again.

Rosie nodded to the kids. 'Can I give you a word of advice?'

'Please do. You might've noticed I'm new to this.'

'Kids need discipline, you're right. They also need a lot of encouragement. Good behaviour should always be praised.'

She touched Rosie's hand. 'Thank you, I'll remember that.'

Becca turned to the class. 'Excellent work, kids. You've done really well today.' She was rewarded with a few beaming smiles.

Rosie smiled. 'See? You'll have them eating out of your hands in no time.'

Becca could only hope.

Despite the first forty-five minutes of the class being torture, the last section flew by. The kids seemed to enjoy the balance games and there was definitely less crying than the previous two weeks. It was too soon to believe progress was being made, but she'd be lying if she didn't feel relieved that the more 'vocal' mothers had quit the class.

A few of the kids said goodbye as they left the dance studio. Rosie's kids even gave her a wave. Maybe she was starting to win them over? She hoped so. For Carolyn's sake, if nothing else.

Becca decided she needed to address the state of the dance studio with Carolyn. All the advertising in the world wouldn't improve numbers if the décor put people off.

She pulled on a pair of joggers over her dance tights and zipped up her hoodie, ensuring she kept her muscles warm. Her knee felt pretty good today, but her Achilles was tight. The scar was itching, something that happened on occasion.

She caught sight of her reflection in the mirror. *Freak*, one of the women had said. It seemed a little harsh. She'd toned down her clothing for the classes, opting for traditional ballet attire instead of her modern dance gear, removing all jewellery and keeping her nails neutral.

That just left her hair, which although still blonde with blue ends, was neatly twisted into a knot at the base of her neck. For her, it was positively conservative. What else could she do? It wasn't like her tattoo or bellybutton ring were on show.

She flicked off the light and locked the door.

It shouldn't matter what she looked like. She should be judged on her performance, not her appearance. Not that she was glowing in that department either. But at least she could do something about that. Changing how she looked was not an option. It was who she was.

She passed through reception and knocked on the office door.

No answer.

She tried the handle in case Jodi was wearing her headphones. Her cousin wasn't expected to work on a Saturday, but she'd offered to do a few hours ahead of her shift at the restaurant later. Carolyn had a habit of talking to herself, so Jodi had started wearing headphones to block out the noise.

The door was unlocked, but Jodi wasn't at her desk. Becca was about to leave, when she realised Carolyn was asleep on the sofa. She was curled up, one arm flung off the side, her head at a strange angle.

Becca went over and removed Carolyn's shoes. She lifted her head and placed a cushion underneath, trying to make her more comfortable. The sofa was too small for her tall frame, but there was nothing Becca could do about that. The woman smelt of booze. The office keys were clutched in her hand.

She slid the keys from Carolyn's hand, intending to give them to Jodi when she saw her.

When she stood up, she noticed the wall safe was open. She couldn't imagine that had been intentional. Carolyn had probably got distracted halfway through a task, as so often happened.

She went over and shut the door. The office looked much tidier now. Jodi had spent her first week filing, shredding and finding homes for various things. She'd always known her cousin would impress. She'd just needed someone to take a chance on her. And now Carolyn had.

Shutting the office door, she headed down the corridor towards the café. A couple of creative types wearing tie-dye overalls were enjoying a brew; other than that, the place was deserted. The Starlight Playhouse boasted an art studio, a small cinema, a theatre and a grand ballroom, and yet all the rooms lay empty, unused, failing to generate any income. It was a travesty. And a waste too. This place could be a thriving arts centre if it was in better shape.

As Carolyn wasn't in a fit state to discuss the repairs, she decided to ask Eddie Moriantez instead. She'd seen him fixing a door hinge and sanding down a splintered bench seat this week.

Before she could track down the handy groundsman, she heard heated voices. As she rounded the bend, she saw her cousin locked in battle with the front-of-house manager.

'You're being unreasonable,' Jodi said. 'Why won't you give it to me?'

'Madam may trust you, but I don't.' The woman lifted her chin, looking down on Jodi like she was something attached to the bottom of her heeled court.

Becca wanted to thump her.

'Until I receive express authority from madam, I will not comply with your request.'

'What is it you think I'm going to do?' Jodi looked perplexed. 'Open an offshore account? I'm just asking for the password to QuickBooks.'

'If madam wanted you to have access, she'd have given you the password.'

'Carolyn isn't feeling well,' Jodi replied. 'She's lying down. I don't want to disturb her.'

Becca caught sight of Eddie coming through the French doors. He was carrying a toolbox.

As much as she wanted to stay and defend her cousin, she'd learnt over the years that Jodi didn't appreciate people wading in to help her. Confident her cousin was more than a match for Vivienne, she left Jodi to continue her battle and went after the groundsman.

She caught up with him as he reached the ballroom. She hadn't been inside since returning to Brighton – the door had always been locked – but the sight that greeted her was no less impressive than it had been twelve years earlier when Tom had shown her around.

She squashed the image of Tom that popped into her head. Nothing good would come from reminiscing.

The grand ballroom was huge with wooden parquet flooring and a high ceiling painted in the style of the renaissance artists. Angels were depicted in full flight, armed with crossbows, flying between the clouds, the moon and the stars.

The walls were painted white, decorated with intricate carvings adorned with gold leaf. At the far end, a grand fireplace sat beneath a gigantic mirror. Three chandeliers hung from the ceiling, ornate and fragile. A grand piano sat in the corner, hidden underneath a dustsheet.

It was breathtaking. A stunning space, waiting to be filled with royalty and nobility. It was only as she walked further into the room that its beauty became overshadowed by disrepair. Paint peeled away from the artwork on the ceiling. Cracked plaster hung from the walls. Several panes of glass were cracked. The chairs, once plush and ornamental, looked tired and worn.

Eddie was up a ladder inspecting the water-stained ceiling.

Careful not to make him jump, she approached. 'Eddie? Do you have a moment?'

He glanced down. 'Hey there, Becca. How was ballet class today? It sounded lively from outside.'

She'd warmed to the groundsman the instant she'd met him. He had kind eyes and was always cheerful. Next to the sombre front-of-house manager and grumpy chef, he was a breath of fresh air. 'Less disastrous than last week. It's a work in progress.'

'You'll get there. Nothing worth achieving is ever easy.'

'That's just the sort of thing my mum would say.'

He laughed. 'Sounds like a woman worth listening to.' He aimed his torch at the ceiling. The shake of his head indicated all was not well. 'Did you want me for something?'

'It's about the dance studio. What are the chances of you fixing it up a bit?'

He sighed. 'It's on the list, but so are lots of other jobs.' He shrugged. 'There's not enough budget to get all the work done.'

'But income will only increase if we get more people using the facilities. The state of the dance studio is putting people off. Is there really no way you can bump it up the pecking order?'

He shone his light on the ceiling. 'See that? There's a leak in the roof, which is affecting this room and the art studio next door. If we don't get it seen to there's a risk the whole lot will fall down.'

'Oh.'

He climbed down the ladder and fetched a drill from his toolbox. 'In terms of priority, this takes precedence. Sorry.'

'Fair enough. I thought it was worth asking.'

'What are you doing in here?' The sound of Vivienne's voice made Becca jump. She turned to see the woman marching towards her, her heels clicking on the flooring like rapid gunfire. Against the white walls, her black flapper dress seemed even more sinister than normal.

'I was talking to Eddie.' Although why Becca had to justify herself, she wasn't sure.

'This room is off limits. You're not authorised to be in here. Kindly leave.'

Eddie climbed up the ladder. 'Steady on, Vivienne. She was only asking about repairing the dance studio.'

Vivienne ignored him and glared at Becca. 'The running and upkeep of this establishment is no concern of yours. You're engaged to deliver two dance classes per week. Nothing more. Kindly know your place.'

Know your place? Well, that told her.

Becca glanced up at Eddie, who shrugged as if to say, 'What can you do?'

Not a lot, it would appear. 'Apologies, Vivienne. I was trying to help.'

'Madam doesn't need your interference...' And then she froze, her eyes widening as though she'd seen an alien. 'What are you doing with the office keys?'

Becca glanced down. She'd almost forgotten about them.

Before she could answer, Vivienne snatched them from her. 'I'll take those.' There was a definite accusation in her tone. Although quite what Becca had done, she didn't know. 'That will be all, Miss Roberts.' The woman gestured to the door.

Becca was being dismissed like a naughty chambermaid caught stealing from the minibar.

No wonder Jodi referred to her as the Woman-in-Black.

Vivienne King was positively evil.

Chapter Nine

Monday 25th September

Jodi read the details again just to be certain she wasn't imagining it. Nope. She wasn't going mad. The invoice was for the purchase of one inflatable unicorn. How on earth was she supposed to categorise that? She certainly couldn't list it under utilities or maintenance. Perhaps it counted as publicity? She'd enter it under miscellaneous and check with Carolyn later.

Not that she'd seen her boss so far today and Jodi had been in since eight, despite a late finish at the restaurant last night. But she didn't mind. She was eager to get to grips with the accounts. Except, she wasn't. Her uni course had covered many things, but not how to deal with lost receipts, unknown expenditure and a boss whose behaviour swung from boisterous, to morose, to sleepy, on a daily basis.

A knock at the door preceded Eddie's jovial face appearing. 'Am I interrupting?'

'Not at all. Come in.'

'You asked me to look for a couple of receipts.' He entered the office, smelling of freshly cut grass. 'I managed to find one for paint, but not Polyfilla.' He pulled out a crumpled receipt. 'Sorry about the Sellotape – I had to stick it back together. I'm moving house so I've been having a clear-out. I must've shredded the other one.' He was like a big kid apologising to his teacher because the dog ate his homework. 'I've never been asked to keep receipts before.'

Jodi's heart sank. 'I wonder how Carolyn keeps her accounts in order?'

'I'm not sure she does.' He wiped his grass-stained hands on his combat trousers. 'In future, receipts will be kept, ma'am.' He gave her a military salute.

She laughed. 'Navy, right?'

'Twenty-five years.' There was a note of pride in his voice.

'How did you end up here?'

'I took early retirement after my wife died. I needed a change of lifestyle. A slower pace.' Judging by his relaxed demeanour the change had worked. 'I miss being at sea, but I get to be outdoors working here, which is the next best thing.'

'The grounds are amazing.' The house might be in a shocking state, but the gardens were immaculate.

'The grounds were landscaped a couple of centuries ago. It's mainly maintenance now, which fortunately doesn't cost a lot.'

He made a good point. It was the house that drained all the funds. Although it was difficult to assess the financial state of the playhouse due to poor bookkeeping. It was bad, but as to how bad, was anybody's guess.

He smiled. 'You need anything else?'

'If you're moving house I'll need to update your personnel records. Can I have your new address?'

He grimaced. 'The place I was due to move into has fallen through. I'm looking for another room. I'll let you know when I find somewhere.'

'When do you need to move out?'

'Three weeks.'

'Boggin' hell, that's tight.'

He laughed. 'Tell me about it.'

'Good luck finding somewhere.' She turned back to her PC. 'Oh, Eddie, have you seen Carolyn this morning?'

He stopped by the door. 'She mentioned something about meeting with the local council to discuss a grant. No idea whether the meeting was here or at the council offices.'

'Oh, okay, thanks.' She returned to updating QuickBooks, now that she had the password, and entered the paint purchase. She had no problem categorising that one. Unlike the unicorn. 'Right. One down, thirty-seven to go.'

She printed off the list and headed into the foyer. The Woman-in-Black was sitting behind reception, her bony shoulders visible through the thin fabric of her blouse. She looked like a Chanel waxwork dummy. Stylish, yet rigid.

'Morning, Vivienne. Everything okay?'

The woman assessed Jodi's very non-designer Primark skirt and top. 'Can I help you?'

In two weeks of working at the playhouse Jodi had yet to

see the woman smile. 'I'm trying to track down a few receipts.'

Vivienne turned away. 'Madam never requires receipts.'

'So I gather, but I've spoken to the accountant and he needs them to certify the accounts. Without them, he can't evidence the expenditure.'

Vivienne bristled. 'Are you accusing me of subterfuge?'

'Not at all.' Particularly as Jodi wasn't sure that was the correct word. 'I'm simply asking if you have receipts for any of these purchases.' She showed Vivienne the printout, but the woman refused to look at it.

Jodi sighed. None of her lecturers had warned her it would be like this. She tried a different question. 'Do you have a record of the room hirers, or class attendances for the last five months?'

Vivienne looked dismissive. 'I do not.'

Count to ten, Jodi told herself. 'Well, from now on can you log any income received and keep receipts so that I can reconcile the books?'

'Until madam informs me of the change herself, I will continue as before.'

Jodi sighed. 'You're obviously very loyal to Carolyn. I would've thought you'd want to support me in trying to help her sort out the accounts.'

Vivienne turned her head. 'That is not my concern. You have no authority to change the terms and conditions of my position.'

Jodi blinked. 'I'm simply asking for a few receipts. Is that really so hard?'

'If madam wishes to change the procedure then naturally I will comply.'

'Fine. I'll speak to Carolyn and ask her to talk to you.' If she could find her.

Jodi left reception, her confidence dented. She'd never let Vivienne see it affected her, but she'd be lying if she didn't admit it hurt. It wasn't just the bookkeeping. Whatever she asked for it was met with resistance and rudeness. Why was she resented so much?

She headed towards the café, expecting to have an equally challenging time with the churlish chef. He hated her too. She tried not to take it personally, but it was hard. But then, she reasoned they were rude to Becca too, so maybe they had a problem with all interlopers.

The sound of loud laughter hit her the moment she turned the corner.

She'd found Carolyn.

Jodi passed through the bar, glancing across to see if Leon was there. When he smiled her mood lifted a little. And then she reminded herself that she was an independent woman who didn't need a man to validate her worth. Yeah, good luck with that.

Leon nodded to where Carolyn was entertaining a group of men. His wary expression told her trouble was looming. Oh, good. Like she didn't have enough to deal with.

Four men were seated in the café, mesmerised by the exuberance of the woman regaling them with the history of the playhouse. Either that, or they were stunned into submission. Both, probably.

Carolyn was wearing a suit, which should have given the impression of a professional businesswoman. Unfortunately, it was a raspberry colour and full of creases, and her cream blouse was a little too sheer. With the sunlight hitting her from behind, the men were getting a good view of what lay beneath, which wasn't much.

'In 1891, noted architect Temple Moore remodelled the manor house designing the hard landscaping at the rear.' Carolyn gestured to the gardens, her arm nearly smacking one of the men. 'The east wing remains untouched along with the four-storey tower.'

Jodi crept past, not wanting to distract her boss in full flow. Her arrival in the kitchen elicited a grunt from Petrit, who was beating the life out of a lump of dough. 'What you want?'

'I need to ask you about receipts, Petrit.'

'Too busy.' He slammed the dough down on the worktop. She ignored the speckles of flour landing on her grey skirt. 'You said that yesterday and the day before.'

'I cook. No time for receipts.'

She was tempted to point out that if he arrived for work when he was supposed to he'd have the time. But Petrit's poor time-keeping was a battle for another day.

She was about to leave, when she spotted a stack of empty wine bottles by the bins. Were they Carolyn's? She'd never seen her boss drinking, but she must be consuming a lot of alcohol to act the way she did. 'Are those yours?' They were the same brand used in the bar.

'For use in kitchen. For cooking.' He thumped the dough.

'All of them?' What was he cooking, coq au vin for the entire population of Brighton?

He glared at her. 'You accuse me of stealing?'

'No, I'm asking if they came from the bar?' When he shrugged, she tried again. 'Petrit, I need to know if bar stock is being used in the kitchens.'

'You speak with boss. Not me.'

'It's a simple question.'

'You ask too many questions!'

She held her ground. 'And you don't answer any of them.'

'Speak with boss.' This was followed by a tirade of Romanian. 'Leave kitchen! Too busy to answer questions from peoples like *you*.'

She flinched. 'I'll leave the printout here for you to look at. I'll be back tomorrow to see how you've got on.' Unwilling to turn her back on him, she shuffled sideways and hurried out of the kitchen.

Unnerved as she felt, it was quickly overshadowed by the sight of Carolyn holding her skirt above her knees and doing what appeared to be the cancan.

Jodi hurried over to the bar so she could observe from a safe distance. Should she intervene? Or stay out of it? As she mulled over her options, she realised she was thirsty. She'd kill for a coffee.

Leon placed a cappuccino in front of her. 'You look like you need caffeine.'

What was he, a mind-reader? 'That obvious, huh?'

He leant on the bar. 'Are Petrit and Vivienne giving you a hard time?'

'No more than normal. They don't seem to like me.'

Leon shrugged. 'Don't sweat it. Vivienne's annoyed because Carolyn didn't give her the business manager job.'

'You mean, she applied for my job?'

Leon slid a bowl of chocolates towards her. 'Yep. She's been here for years, so it didn't occur to her Carolyn wouldn't give it to her.'

Things were starting to make sense. 'No wonder she hates me.'

Leon frowned. 'It's not your fault. Vivienne wasn't the right person for the job. You are.'

She glanced down at her coffee. 'You don't know that.'

'Sure, I do.' When he grinned, her belly flipped. 'And Petrit's problem is that he's a lazy arse. He figured with Vivienne in charge he'd continue to get away with stuff, but you're no pushover. He's met his match and he doesn't like it.'

'Well, at least now I know.'

Leon glanced over at Carolyn. 'I'll have a word with them.'

'Please don't. It's my problem, not yours. I'll talk to Carolyn...' who was at that moment laughing flirtatiously at something one of the men had said. 'Talking of Petrit, what's the deal with him taking wine from the bar? Is that usual?'

Leon dragged his eyes away from the floorshow. 'He's supposed to log what he takes, but I'm not here all the time, so I don't always know he's taken stuff until I do a stock check.'

That surprised her. 'How often do you check the stock?'

'Weekly.'

'And do you keep receipts for everything you buy?'

A smile played on his lips. 'They're in a folder under the till.'

'You're the only person who seems to understand the need for accountability. Everyone else reacted as though I was asking for their spleen... Well, apart from Eddie.' She sipped her coffee. It was heavenly.

'Must be my upbringing. I've always been a good boy.' He winked at her.

She laughed. 'Why do I find that difficult to believe?'

He leant on the bar. 'How's your coffee?'

'Lovely.' She took another sip. 'So, how long have you worked here? If you don't mind me asking.'

He unwrapped a chocolate. 'Two years.'

'And do you enjoy it?'

'Mostly.' He offered her the chocolate. 'Certain people I could do without. It's a shame the place isn't busier. Carolyn has her issues, but maybe that's why I stay. Loyalty.'

She took the chocolate. Strawberry cream. How did he

107

know that was her favourite? Must be a lucky coincidence. 'It's a good attribute to have.'

He shrugged. 'Working here gives me plenty of free time to write.'

Jodi glanced over when Carolyn began singing Vera Lynn's *We'll Meet Again*. 'What is she doing?'

'I think she's demonstrating.' Leon tilted his head. 'She received a grant from the council to entice people from hard-to-reach communities to engage with the arts. I heard her talking earlier about the link between singing and improving mental health.'

When Jodi turned back she almost bumped noses with him. Embarrassed, she covered it by taking a sip of coffee. 'So, what do you write?'

His expression turned sheepish. 'Songs.'

'You're a songwriter?'

His cheeks coloured. It was barely visible beneath his dark skin, but she noticed just the same. It was adorable... Not that she was interested. 'Kind of. It's a work in progress.'

She took another sip of coffee. 'I'd love to hear you play. Where do you perform?'

He rubbed his shaved head, an awkward gesture that made him seem younger than his twenty-something years. 'My bedroom mostly. I've uploaded a few tracks to YouTube, but haven't plucked up the nerve to play a live set yet.'

A loud crash interrupted them.

Jodi turned to see Carolyn falling into her visitors' table, sending cups and saucers flying. What followed next was embarrassed laughter from Carolyn, Leon jumping over the counter, and the disgruntled men from the council wiping spilt liquid from their suits.

It was carnage. And yet another scenario not covered on Jodi's course. 'I'm so sorry, gentlemen,' she said, racing over. 'Let me fetch a cloth.'

The men didn't look happy. Who could blame them?

Carolyn wriggled free from Leon's grasp. 'I'm fine,' she said, pushing him away. 'Let go of me.'

Leon's expression told her they had a problem. Like Jodi didn't already know that.

'Perhaps it would be better if we rescheduled the meeting for another time?' Jodi said to the men from the council, gesturing towards the exit. 'Let me show you out.' And with that they left, eager to distance themselves from the exuberant owner of the playhouse.

When Jodi returned, she discovered Carolyn shouting at Leon. 'You've stolen my shoe? Give me back my shoe!'

'Your shoe is on the floor, Carolyn. Let's get you upstairs.'

She dug him in the ribs. 'I don't want to go upstairs.'

He held on to her, careful not to hurt her. 'How about a coffee and a lie-down?'

'I'm not tired.' And then she threw up, right down the front of his *Superdry* T-shirt.

Leon bit his lip, as if holding back an expletive.

Carolyn burst out crying. 'I'm so sorry, Leon.'

He held her as she cried. 'It's okay, Carolyn. It'll wash out.'

Petrit appeared from the kitchen, the doors banging shut behind him. He didn't look happy.

Leon eased Carolyn over to Jodi. 'Take her into the office. I'll help Petrit clean up.'

Petrit started grumbling, but Leon ignored him. Jodi admired his restraint. She mentally added 'equality and diversity' to the growing list of items she needed to discuss with her boss...when Carolyn sobered up.

By the time they arrived in reception, Carolyn's crying had reduced to a whimper.

Vivienne stood when they neared. 'What have you done to her?'

'I haven't done anything, Vivienne. If you want to help, get her a strong coffee, please.'

The woman harrumphed and strode off.

Jodi led Carolyn into the office and sat her on the couch. 'Let's get you out of that jacket.'

Carolyn looked down at the mess. 'Oh, God. What have I done?' She began hitting her thighs, pummelling her fists harder and harder. 'Why do I do this?'

Jodi grabbed her hands. 'Stop that.' When she was certain Carolyn had calmed down, she removed her jacket and handed her a water bottle. 'Drink this.' Jodi used the remaining water to rinse Carolyn's hands and wipe them clean.

Carolyn didn't say a word. Her mood had switched from gregarious to gloomy.

The door opened and the Woman-in-Black appeared. 'Madam's coffee.'

'Thank you, Vivienne.' When it became clear she wasn't about to leave, Jodi said, 'That will be all.'

A disgruntled Vivienne exited, banging the door behind her. At least Jodi knew the source of Vivienne's resentment now. Jodi had nicked her job.

Jodi turned to Carolyn, feeling like she was at a crossroads. She'd only worked at the playhouse for two weeks, but every day there'd been an incident of some kind. It was clear that the staff had become accustomed to Carolyn's antics and didn't bat an eyelid when she caused mayhem. Maybe Jodi should follow their example and ignore Carolyn's catastrophic behaviour? Soothe her, patch her up and let her sleep it off, pretending like it had never happened... Or maybe she should face it head-on. Ignoring the situation hadn't worked, so maybe it was time for a few home truths.

She handed Carolyn the mug of coffee. 'I gather the meeting was about a grant you've received from the council?'

Carolyn sipped her coffee.

When nothing was forthcoming, Jodi continued. 'And how do you feel it went?'

Carolyn ignored her.

Jodi felt like she'd been transported back to her teens when Aunty Ruby used to question her after a night spent misbehaving. Her aunty had never shouted or yelled hurtful comments like her mother had done, she'd just calmly pointed

111

out the error of her niece's ways, shaming Jodi to her core. She'd learnt a lot from her aunty.

It was time to put that learning into practice. 'Do you think they were impressed? Do you think they left here believing their money to be in safe hands?'

Still no response.

Jodi had been the same. Sullen and silent. 'Or do you think they left thinking the owner is a mess, a woman who despite being clever, kind, and more than capable of managing the playhouse is an unreliable...alcoholic?' There, she'd said it.

Carolyn threw the mug of coffee against the wall. 'You don't know me!'

The mug didn't smash, but the contents splashed across the desk, soaking the few receipts Jodi had managed to collect. Helpful. 'So, you're not an alcoholic?'

There was a tremor in Carolyn's hands. 'I can stop anytime I want.'

Jodi nodded. 'Good to know... Then, why don't you?'

Tears ran down Carolyn's face. 'You don't understand.'

'I understand more than you realise.' She knelt down and took Carolyn's hands. 'You may not remember what I was like as a teenager, but I was a mess. I used to rely on drugs and alcohol to get me through the day. It was a way of masking my problems and escaping reality. I could justify it to anyone who challenged me. I didn't care about the consequences of my actions, or the people I hurt.'

112

Carolyn stared at her skirt, her body twitching like an exposed nerve.

'Watching you just now, I remembered being fifteen and setting fire to a bin at school. It caused mayhem. The fire service and police were called and the school had to shut. I thought I was so funny, so clever, so popular with the other kids. But I wasn't. I was a pain in the arse. A disruption that everyone just wanted to go away.'

Carolyn shook her head. 'It's not the same. You don't know how hard it is. It's not my fault—'

'Yes, it is.' Jodi cut her off. 'And do you know how I know that? Because I said the same thing. It wasn't my fault. It was the school. The police. My mum. If it weren't for her, I wouldn't have felt the need to escape. But it wasn't her fault. She was an excuse. It was *my* problem. Do you know when I realised that? When I was sitting in a prison cell.'

Carolyn looked abashed.

'You need to face up to your problems, Carolyn. You need to accept help and take ownership of the situation…before it's too late.'

Carolyn started sniffling.

Jodi squeezed her hands. 'All you need to do is accept that you need help. It'll be hard, but it's better than the road of self-destruction.'

Carolyn burst out crying and slumped onto Jodi.

Eventually, the tears subsided and drowsiness took over. Jodi removed Carolyn's one remaining shoe and covered her

113

with a blanket. Then she went over to her desk and logged onto QuickBooks, even though challenging Carolyn about her drinking was bound to result in her dismissal.

She just hoped it was a price worth paying.

Chapter Ten

Tuesday 3rd October

It had been an odd week at the Starlight Playhouse. It had started at last week's tap class when Becca had tried to teach her adult tappers a basic eight-count routine. Mi-Sun had moved left instead of right, tripped over Wanda's foot and crashed into Miriam, who subsequently fell over Nick and hit the wall with an almighty thud. A series of yelps had followed as Miriam tried to remain upright, culminating in the ballet barre being yanked from the wall and Miriam sliding to the floor.

Mi-Sun had been close to tears. Wanda had a bruised foot where Mi-Sun had stepped on it, and Miriam was left with a large splinter in her hand. Anyone would think Becca had been running a boxing class rather than a dance class.

Consequently, she'd been forced to cancel the rest of the classes until the damaged studio could be repaired. But it wasn't all negative. She'd used the excuse of a broken ballet barre as a bargaining tool to obtain permission to tart-up the rest of the dance studio.

Carolyn had initially been reluctant, but Becca had worn her down, offering to carry out the work herself and assuring her boss that costs would be kept to a minimum. So, with Eddie's help, she'd set about sanding and varnishing the wooden floor, filling and painting the walls, and making good the ballet barre.

Without the classes running the playhouse had felt deserted. There was no music or children's laughter to fill the space. The building had felt cold and soulless. It was a place that needed life. It needed people. And maybe Becca needed that too. As infuriating as her pupils were, she'd missed them this week.

She got up from the floor and stretched out her knee. Sitting crouched on the floor painting radiators wasn't a good position. Her knee complained when she stood up.

Eddie appeared through the doors carrying one of the industrial lights she'd acquired from a recently closed abattoir. 'One down, four to go,' he said, placing the light on the floor.

She rubbed her paint-covered hands on her overalls. 'Do you need a hand?'

'I'm good, thanks.' With a smile, he disappeared through the doors.

Visiting the abattoir had been a surreal experience. Thankfully, there'd been no trace of animal slaughter on the premises, just a load of equipment in need of a new home.

Eddie appeared carrying another light. 'I can't believe you

managed to get hold of these. They really didn't want any money for them?'

Becca stretched out her Achilles. 'I think the liquidator wanted some cash, but Jodi bamboozled him with talk of BS wiring regulations and the need for them to supply a valid installation certificate. In the end, he gave in and told her to take them.'

Eddie laughed. 'I didn't realise Jodi was familiar with electrical regulations?'

'Oh, she's not. She googled it and called his bluff. He knew less than her, so her master plan worked.'

He shook his head. 'Perhaps I should take her with me house hunting.'

'Any luck finding somewhere?'

'Not yet, but I'm seeing a couple of places this afternoon. Fingers crossed.' He went to collect another light.

Yesterday's trip hadn't started out brilliantly as both her mum and Jodi had been in low spirits. Her cousin's melancholy stemmed from an incident last Monday involving Carolyn getting hammered and throwing up over bar manager Leon. Jodi had returned to the guest house despondent and fully expecting to be fired.

Becca hadn't been there to witness the episode, and Jodi wouldn't divulge much. All her cousin would say was that she'd confronted Carolyn about her drinking and the playhouse owner hadn't taken the criticism well.

Her cousin had been on tenterhooks all week, expecting

an *Apprentice*-style 'you're fired' meeting. But it never came. Whether Carolyn had forgotten, or whether she was choosing to ignore it, remained a mystery. Jodi arrived for work each day full of trepidation, but other than being a little subdued, Carolyn had acted normally... Well, normally for her. So for the time being, Jodi remained in her position.

As for her mum, Becca had been unsuccessful in determining the root cause of her unhappiness, so she'd focused on cheering her up instead. The three of them had spent yesterday morning shopping. The day had begun with a wicked breakfast at Buddies Café on the seafront, followed by a visit to Snoopers Paradise, the most amazing junk shop in Brighton. The trip had finished with the visit to the abattoir. They'd arrived home with a set of second-hand fold-up chairs for the ballet mums to sit on, several large framed prints of ballerinas to give the newly painted walls some colour, and the pendant lights. And all for under a hundred quid. Bargain.

Becca wasn't naive enough to believe one shopping trip would cure her cousin and mum's blues, but it had temporarily given them a lift. It'd been like old times.

Eddie arrived with another light. 'I've just seen Carolyn. She's called a staff meeting.'

'Is that unusual?'

'I'd say.' He put the light down. 'I've worked here nearly ten years and we've never had a staff meeting.' He shrugged. 'I guess there's a first time for everything.'

'When is it?'

'Now. Everyone's required to attend. I hope it's not bad news.'

Becca hoped so too.

She checked her overalls for wet paint. Happy she was semi-decent she went into the loos to wash her hands. Her reflection revealed a smudge of paint on her cheek and lopsided blue bunches. Maybe she'd go for purple next? Now the judgemental mothers were out of the picture she didn't have to contain her appearance so much. Hence her psychedelic nails and semiquaver earrings.

Becca was the last one to arrive for the meeting. The office wasn't big and felt cramped with seven people inside. Eddie and Leon were sitting on the sofa looking chilled. Vivienne was seated in one of the office chairs, her back rigid, her hands folded neatly in her lap. Carolyn was standing behind the ornate leather-topped desk looking unusually restrained in a navy tunic and leggings, her hair tied back, not a trace of make-up. Jodi was tucked into the corner as if hiding.

It was only when the door slammed, Becca realised Petrit was standing next to her, his arms folded, his scowl already at 'warning' level, which didn't bode well. She wanted to move away, but there wasn't enough room.

Carolyn cleared her throat. 'Thank you all for coming. I appreciate this is an unusual request, but I have an important announcement.'

Jodi sunk further into her chair. Surely Carolyn wouldn't

fire her publicly? If she did, she'd have Becca to answer to, boss or no boss.

Carolyn's thighs rested against the desk, as if it was the only thing holding her up. 'I'm an alcoholic,' she said, her voice shaky. This was followed by a weighted pause, as if she expected an outcry and a barrage of questions.

Everyone remained silent.

Carolyn glanced at all six faces, looking for a reaction. 'This doesn't come as a shock?'

Eddie, Leon and Becca exchanged an awkward look.

Jodi stared down at her lap.

No reaction from Vivienne or Petrit.

'Right... Well, that probably tells me all I need to know.' Carolyn tried for a self-deprecating laugh, but it fell a little short. 'And I thought I'd kept it so well hidden.' When no one contradicted her, she swallowed uneasily and continued. 'It's been brought to my attention that I might not be as in control as I'd thought. And that my recent actions have impacted on others.' She clutched her hands, as if trying to stem the shake. 'As such, it's been suggested that I seek...help. Professional help.' She glanced at Jodi.

The silence was excruciating.

Poor Carolyn. Here she was, sharing her shameful secret and everyone already knew. Only Jodi had the courage to look her in the eye.

Becca had no idea what the appropriate response was to such an announcement, but keeping quiet felt equally uncomfortable. 'That's very brave of you, Carolyn. I'm sure I speak for everyone in wishing you the best and hoping you get the help you need.'

Carolyn let out a breath. 'Thank you.'

Another awkward pause.

'Is there anything we can do to support you?' Leon asked, evoking a nod from Eddie, who added, 'Yes, anything we can do, just name it.'

Becca could have kissed them both.

'Thank you, I appreciate that...and yes, there is something.' Carolyn pushed her glasses up her nose. 'I've booked myself onto an eight-week residential course at a local rehabilitation centre. I'll be absent from the playhouse for the duration of the course. In my absence, I feel it necessary to appoint a deputy.'

Vivienne sat up straighter.

Petrit grunted.

'Someone I trust implicitly,' Carolyn said.

Vivienne gave a small nod.

'Someone who I know will keep the playhouse running, ensure you are all looked after, and who will have the courage to make tough decisions when needed.'

A smug-looking Vivienne glanced at Jodi. It didn't take a mind-reader to work out what her first 'not-so tough' decision would be.

In just a few weeks, her cousin had proved herself to be reliable, loyal and trustworthy. She'd sorted out the office, arranged a payment plan with the playhouse's creditors and drafted a marketing plan for improving business. Letting her go would be a backward step. It would be wrong of Vivienne to sack her just because she didn't like her. But then, she didn't like Becca, either. So maybe she'd get rid of her too.

The idea of stopping teaching filled Becca with sorrow. How crazy was that? She hadn't even wanted the job in the first place. And now she didn't want to stop. She was making progress, albeit slowly. She was learning too, mostly by her mistakes, but at least she was taking ownership of her failings and trying to improve. And now it was under threat, all because Vivienne wanted to be top dog.

Carolyn continued. 'I know this appointment might not be to everyone's satisfaction, but I have to follow my heart and go with who I feel has the best credentials.' Carolyn smiled at Vivienne, whose returning smile was more of a self-satisfied sneer. 'Which is why I've decided to leave the running of the Starlight Playhouse to Jodi and Becca.'

What? Becca's shock was overridden by Vivienne's strangled cry and Petrit's grunt, which was so loud it made her jump.

'This is outrageous.' Vivienne stood up, sending the office chair rolling backwards.

'My mind is made up, Vivienne.'

'But they've barely been here a month. You don't know them. You can't trust them.'

'They've more than proved their trustworthiness.' Carolyn gestured to Jodi, who looked as shocked as Becca felt. 'Which is why I've entrusted Jodi with the combination for the safe and added her as a bank signatory.'

Vivienne looked like she was about to combust. It was the most animated Becca had ever seen her. 'Madam, I urge you to reconsider. You're placing the future of the playhouse in the hands of two people who have no vested interest in its continuation. I've served this place for years, I've served *you* for years, always doing my utmost to protect the interests of the Elliot-Wentworth family.'

'And I'm very grateful, Vivienne. Really, I am.' Carolyn placed her hand over her heart. 'Your loyalty means the world to me.'

'Then why are you favouring them...' Vivienne pointed at Becca and Jodi '...over a long-standing member of staff?'

Carolyn looked momentarily lost for words.

Eddie came to her rescue. 'I think it's a great appointment, Carolyn. Becca and Jodi will do a fine job. They have my full support.' He raised his hand as if voting them in.

'Mine too.' Leon glanced at Jodi.

'And we all know why that is, don't we?' Vivienne snapped at Leon, sounding like a spiteful schoolgirl. 'We've all seen the way you look at her. No prizes for guessing your agenda.'

Becca's mind was being dragged from one shocking announcement to another. Leon had the hots for her cousin? How did she not know this? Had Jodi noticed? Or was she keeping quiet? Too many questions. Now wasn't the time to dwell.

'My mind is made up,' Carolyn said, seeming to summon her last drop of strength. 'It's a decision I've not come to lightly, but I feel it's the right one. As a favour to me, and as a show of loyalty to the playhouse, I would be grateful if everyone could support this appointment and do their best to make Becca's and Jodi's task as easy as possible. Will you do that for me?'

Eddie and Leon nodded.

Petrit barged past Becca and exited the office, mumbling in Romanian.

'Vivienne?' Carolyn looked at the Woman-in-Black, whose angry face matched her dark red lipstick.

'I'm not happy about the situation, but as you're refusing to see sense, I have no alternative but to accept.' Vivienne walked over to the door, her chin lifted. 'I just hope madam doesn't regret the decision.' And with that, she was gone.

Carolyn smiled at Becca. 'I hope it wasn't too impertinent of me to appoint you both without discussing it with you first?'

Becca glanced at Jodi, who still looked a little poleaxed. 'I'm honoured you think we're up to the job.' Bloody hell, was she up to the job? She had no idea. 'I mean, I know Jodi is; she has a business degree. But as for me, well...what I mean is, I'll do my best.'

'I know you will. Your creativity combined with Jodi's business acumen is the perfect combination. You'll make a great team.'

Jodi stood up. 'Thank you, Carolyn. You have no idea what this means to me. I won't let you down.'

'I know you won't, darling girl.' She took hold of Jodi's hand. 'I have every faith in you.'

'Me too,' Leon added, his eyes fixated on her cousin. Definitely smitten.

'And me.' Eddie gave Jodi a thumbs-up.

Carolyn smiled. 'Thank you, I'm lucky to have you all. Vivienne will calm down eventually.'

Becca wasn't so sure.

'Now, if you'll excuse me, I'd like a private word with Jodi.'

Becca exchanged glances with her cousin. Boy, did they have a lot to chat about later. They'd be running the playhouse together? It was too much for her head to compute.

Becca followed Eddie and Leon out of the office, still dazed, responding on autopilot as they congratulated her and patted her on the back. And to think she'd thought Carolyn had called the meeting to sack Jodi.

Unsure what to do with herself, she went into the dance studio and finished painting the radiator. There was no effort required in painting. The upward strokes of the brush helped to occupy her hands, whilst her brain continued to spin. How did she feel? Excited? Scared? She wasn't sure. This was another challenge. A test of her mettle. But unlike dancing this had more to do with her mind than her body. A dodgy knee wasn't going to stop her. A couple of disgruntled staff members, on the other hand, might.

Wiping excess paint from the brush, she wrapped it in a cloth. She rolled up the dustsheet and stood back to admire her handiwork. The studio looked much better. It was a masking job, rather than a full refurb, but with white walls and brighter flooring, it already looked more inviting.

Picking up the remaining paint, water bucket and roller tray, she carried them outside onto the fire escape.

The thought of line-managing Vivienne and Petrit didn't fill her with joy. She was confident Eddie and Leon would cooperate, but the other two? Not so much. Despite this, she couldn't deny the frisson of excitement she felt. It was another possibility. Another path to walk down and see where it led. And to think, only a month ago she was jobless, homeless, and with no idea what her future held. Now, she was teaching and about to co-manage an arts centre.

It was heady stuff. But then she remembered it was a failing arts centre. The Starlight Playhouse wasn't a thriving hub of creativity; it was a neglected manor house in dire need of refurbishment. Still, they could turn things around and build on its reputation. Reverse its fortunes and repay Carolyn's faith in them...except there was no budget for investment. However she looked at it, the tablecloth wasn't big enough to cover the table.

She leant over the railing and shook out the cloth, emptying dried Polyfilla into the skip below.

The main thing was she wasn't doing it alone. She'd have Jodi. Together they would overcome adversity. They were a team. Wonder Women united. And if this opportunity led to a permanent position for her cousin then it was worth the hassle.

She stepped back, not realising the roller tray was behind her. Her foot slipped on the paint almost sending her over the railing onto the concrete below. In her effort to stay upright, she knocked over the water bucket and paint tin, sending the contents flying.

As if in slow motion, the airborne paint descended like a snowstorm, landing on a black BMW that had just screeched into the service yard below. As the white paint hit the front window obscuring the view, the driver hit the brakes, sending the car into a spin. It clipped the corner of the recycling bin before coming to a halt.

There was a moment's silence before the driver's door flew open and a man appeared. 'You've got to be frickin' kidding me!'

Time slowed.

Becca's heart rate sped up.

A buzzing noise filled her head.

She clutched the railing, trying not to fall.

His hair was still blond – but gone was the indie-grunge mess of his teens. Now it was styled in that designer 'just got out of bed' look that only the naturally blessed could get away with. Gone was the long parker coat, DM boots and jeans with zips sewn into them. He was dressed in a light grey suit with a darker grey waistcoat and no tie. The top button of his white shirt was undone. He looked slightly dishevelled and sexy as hell. But this was nothing compared to the startling blue eyes framed by long spidery lashes that were currently darting about like laser weaponry looking for the person who'd covered his car in white paint.

And then he looked up.

Oh, shit.

She did the only thing she could think of.

She ran.

Chapter Eleven

...continued

One moment the woman was standing there; the next she was gone. Tom blinked. Had she been an apparition? He turned back to his car, wondering if he was hallucinating. It was almost as if...? No, it wasn't possible. It couldn't be her. He looked back up at the fire exit. No one was there.

His mind was playing tricks on him. He was tired and stressed. He hadn't slept much over the past week, thanks to Izzy refusing to sign the flat sale contracts, claiming she was 'having second thoughts' about selling. An emotional exchange of words had followed with him trying to convince her that selling was the right thing, and her pleading to 'give them another go'. By the time they'd finally exchanged contracts he was exhausted.

What with the added pressure of trying to juggle court cases and manage his mother's affairs, sleep had become an impossibility. His asthma was bad too, to the point where he'd been prescribed Clenil Modulite to reduce the inflammation in his lungs and prevent a full-blown attack. He'd been advised to reduce his stress levels, which was laughable.

He looked at his car. The windscreen and bonnet were covered in white paint and there was a dent in his front wing. He kicked the rear tyre. 'Shit.'

He wasn't about to start cleaning up the mess wearing his suit. He had a change of clothes in the boot along with a few personal belongings. The rest of his stuff was in storage. The decision regarding where to live following the flat sale had been decided when he'd received a voice message from his mother telling him she was off to rehab. The Starlight Playhouse would be his home for the next eight weeks.

He glanced up at the fire door one last time, just to check the paint-thrower hadn't reappeared. She hadn't. Whoever it was, she wouldn't get far. And when he found her, he'd give her a piece of his mind – whether she was a dead ringer for his childhood sweetheart, or not.

He walked around to the front of the building. The grounds stretched ahead of him looking impressive. Eddie had kept on top of things, which was one less problem to worry about. He didn't visit the playhouse often. For the most part he could manage his mother's affairs remotely. But the news that she was off to rehab meant staying in London was no longer an option. Not at the moment, anyway.

The reception area hadn't changed. Neither had the woman behind the front desk. She was a scary apparition, her black apparel a reflection of her sombre personality. Vivienne was old-school. Her father had served the family at a time when the Starlight Playhouse was still a manor house and she'd been brought up to revere the aristocracy. She believed in the hierarchy of position within a household and didn't take kindly to those of lower rank 'acting above their station'. But she was fiercely loyal to his mother, so he could forgive her occasional snobbery. 'Hi, Vivienne. Is my mother around?'

'Master Thomas, what an unexpected surprise.' She smoothed down the front of her black dress. 'Madam will be so thrilled to see you. As am I. You couldn't have called at a more opportune moment.' She lowered her voice. 'There have been some developments concerning the playhouse. I don't want to alarm you, but I fear madam is not thinking rationally.'

His mother's actions were rarely rational, so this wasn't ground-breaking news. However, he wasn't about to start gossiping about his mother's mental state. 'Is she in the office?'

'Madam is upstairs packing. Has she mentioned her...trip?'

She made it sound like his mother was heading off to Venice for the weekend. 'She has. Thank you, Vivienne. I'll head up and see her.'

'I hope this means you'll be taking over management of the playhouse in her absence, Master Thomas?'

He glanced back. 'That's the plan.'

Vivienne smiled. The kind of smile a snake would inflict upon a defenceless mouse before devouring it.

He climbed over the rope cordoning off the private quarters

and headed up the grand staircase, patting the bust of Uncle Henry as he passed by. Large oil paintings hung from the walls, depicting his ancestors in stately attire, from full battle regalia, to women wearing elaborate gowns and bored expressions. His mother had descended from a titled family, but his paternal family came from Billericay, diluting his blue blood somewhat. And he was fine with that.

The manor house was spread over three floors. The basement wasn't used anymore. It mainly stored heirlooms, paintings and furniture, moved down there when the ground floor had been converted into an arts centre. The east tower wasn't used either, other than by him. He was the only person who'd preferred the solitude of the tower to the drama below, spending his teenage years trying to escape his father's temper and his mother's drunkenness.

The galley corridor was unchanged, as were three of the original bed chambers. Dark wooden panelling covered the walls, adorned with shields and spears and rich fabric tapestries. The furniture was chunky, ornate and uncomfortable. During the renovations, four of the bed chambers had been converted into a living area, and his mother's private study was also up here. Now the place looked tired, dusty and smelt of damp.

He found his mother in her study, flicking through old photos. He leant against the doorframe and watched her. He was glad she'd booked herself into rehab. But he wondered what had changed her mind. She'd always resisted when he'd suggested it before. 'Hi, Mum.'

Her face broke into a smile. 'Tom, darling!' She moved around the desk to greet him.

He met her halfway, pulling her into an embrace. She smelt of coconut, which was a massive improvement on day-old gin. She'd lost weight and he could feel her ribs. But she was sober and didn't appear hungover, so they might be able to have a sensible conversation. 'So, big news, I hear?'

She drew back and looked at him, her eyes scanning his face. 'I'm sorry I left a message. I should've spoken to you in person, but I didn't want an interrogation. I needed time to adjust to my decision.'

He frowned. 'When have I ever interrogated you?'

'Oh, darling, you do it all the time. And it's okay, I deserve it. I know it's because you care.' She turned back to the desk and picked up a brochure. 'The programme lasts eight weeks. Here are the details.'

He took the brochure, still smarting over her accusation. 'How did you find this place? Have they been recommended? Do they have a good reputation?'

She gave him one of her looks.

'What? This isn't an interrogation, this is a concerned son asking his mother what research she's done to ensure this is the best place to get help.'

She tilted her head to one side, flecks of grey visible in her blonde hair. 'The place was recommended by my GP. It has an excellent reputation.'

'Good.' He read the blurb on the front. 'The Sunrise

Rehabilitation Centre boasts a safe and nurturing environment, offering personalised treatment plans and twenty-four-hour care.'

'I visited the place on Friday. I'll have my own room, daily one-to-one counselling and group therapy sessions.' She sounded like she was describing a fancy spa retreat.

He tried to mask his hurt. 'Why didn't you ask me to come with you?'

She raised an eyebrow. 'Because you would've taken over, and this was something I needed to do on my own.'

Wow. A sober Carolyn Elliot-Wentworth was a lot more assertive than her pissed counterpart.

'They also have music and art therapy, and offer yoga and meditation, which helps with the detox process. That's the worst bit, apparently.' She turned away, busying herself with papers on the desk. 'Detox can take between seven to ten days, but I'll be supported throughout.'

He wasn't about to let her struggle alone. 'You'll have me too, so you won't be on your own.'

She turned to look at him. 'No visitors, I'm afraid.'

He frowned. 'For how long?'

'The duration of the programme.'

'They can't ban your son from visiting.'

'I've signed a contract. I've agreed to the terms.'

He flicked through the brochure. 'Where's the number? I'll call them.'

She removed her glasses. 'I know you mean well, but you need to let go. Just as I have to.'

'What does that mean?'

She paused, as if trying to assimilate her thoughts. 'I'm trapped in a vicious cycle of shame and guilt. The only way of maintaining long-term abstinence is to face the root cause of my addiction, which will be painful and no doubt humiliating. Until I've faced my demons, I won't be able to move forwards. And that will be impossible to do if I know my son will be there to witness my collapse.' She cupped his cheek. 'Family will be invited to a meeting once the programme is complete to discuss supporting me on the road to recovery. I would love for you to come to that.'

He swallowed back the lump in his throat. 'I'll be there.'

'Thank you, darling.' She kissed his cheek. 'Now, let me finish packing and then we can grab a coffee before you head back to London.'

'I'm not going back to London. I'm staying here.'

She seemed confused. 'Why?'

'To manage the playhouse, of course. If you're going to be away for eight weeks, then someone needs to run the place.'

'Which is why I've appointed a deputy.'

'I know Vivienne's loyal, but she's not up to taking on the playhouse.'

She sighed. 'It's not Vivienne.'

'Who, then?'

'Look, all you need to know is that the playhouse is in safe hands. So, thank you for the offer, but it's not necessary.' She walked out of the study.

What the hell was going on? He followed her. 'Why are you being so cagey?'

'I'm not.'

'Yes, you are. Who is this safe pair of hands?'

'There's two of them actually.'

'Okay, so what are their names?' He caught up with her by the bust of Uncle Henry. 'Mum, please. If you're not here, then I need to know who I'm dealing with. Supposing something happens? An emergency?'

She stopped walking. 'Fine. I'm leaving the running of the playhouse to Becca Roberts and Jodi Simmons.' Having dropped her little bombshell, she hurried down the staircase, leaving him too shocked to move.

So, it had been her.

And then his brain caught up with his ears. 'You're leaving them to run the playhouse?'

He followed his mother to reception. 'I'll be in my office, if anyone needs me, Vivienne.'

'Of course, madam.' Vivienne looked a little stunned when her boss slammed the office door.

'Mother, wait up. We're not done.' He ran across reception.

'Is everything okay, Master Thomas?' Vivienne gave him a quizzical look.

'No, it isn't.'

'I take it you've heard the news.' She lowered her voice, checking no one could overhear. 'I think madam is under some sort of voodoo spell. She's been brainwashed by that

136

dark girl into handing over the playhouse. You have to make her see reason, Master Thomas.'

As much as the idea of Becca and Jodi running the playhouse filled him with horror, his objections were based on historical fact, not the colour of Jodi's skin. Voodoo spell? Christ, the woman was ignorant. 'Thank you, Vivienne. I'll handle this.'

He entered the office to find his mother rummaging through the desk drawer. 'Where are my spare keys?'

'Mum, will you please talk to me.' He closed the door, preventing Vivienne from eavesdropping. 'How the hell are Becca and Jodi involved with the playhouse?'

'Becca teaches dance here.' She unearthed the contents of the drawer. 'She moved back to Brighton to recuperate from an injury. I offered her a job.'

He tried not to conjure up an image of Becca dancing. He didn't need the distraction. 'Right. And Jodi?'

'She's my new business manager.' She sifted through the wastepaper bin, emptying the contents onto the desk. 'Where are those keys?'

'You gave the job to Jodi Simmons? Did you know she has a criminal record?'

She didn't look up. 'Yes, she told me.'

'And you think that makes her a suitable candidate to take charge of the playhouse, do you? To look after the finances and handle money?'

His mother stopped searching and pinned him with a

disappointed look. 'Since when did you become so judge-mental? I thought I'd raised you better than that.'

'This isn't a judgement. It's a fact. She was jailed for theft.'

'Yes, and since then she's turned her life around. She's obtained a business degree and proved herself to be trust-worthy.'

He seriously doubted that.

'I don't know how I managed without her,' she said. 'I fully intend to offer her a permanent position when our finances improve.'

'They won't improve with those two in charge.'

'You're being childish.'

He stepped closer. 'And you're being taken for a fool. Please reconsider, I'm begging you. This is a huge mistake.'

She gave him a steely glare. 'I've offered Becca and Jodi joint running of the place for the next eight weeks and I'm not about to retract my offer. No matter what you say.'

'Fine. Have it your way, but at least give me an equal say. I've come here intending to stay for the duration of your treatment. I have a vested interest in the playhouse too. This is my family home. And besides, the Starlight Playhouse is your dream. Please let me co-manage it with them, for my sake, if not for your own.'

She sighed, no doubt worn down by arguing. 'Fine.'

'Thank you.' He needed to save her from herself. She wasn't thinking clearly.

'But don't take over and make all the decisions. You may

138

not trust them, but I do. They've brought more positive change in the last month than I've managed in twenty years, so listen to their ideas and respect their opinions. Okay?' She held out her hand, forcing him to cement their agreement with a hand-shake. 'Thank you... Ah, here they are!' She found the keys under the desk. 'Now, I need to finish packing. Jodi has gone to the bank to withdraw funds—'

'Is that wise?'

She folded her arms across her chest.

He held up his hands in surrender. 'Fine, whatever.'

'If you're staying, you'll need to make up one of the guest suites.'

'I'll stay in my old room.'

She looked incredulous. 'It's freezing up there.'

'The fresh air will do me good.'

Wasn't that an understatement.

He marched outside, his chest tightening with every breath. So much for reducing his stress levels. He felt like he was about to explode. The world was conspiring against him. His father, Izzy, and now his mother, forcing him to relive a time in his life he'd rather forget.

He rested his hands on his knees, trying to draw in deep breaths. His bloody inhaler was in the car. A car that was currently covered in white paint. White paint that had been thrown by Becca Roberts. 'Damn it.'

He closed his eyes. His mother had no idea what she'd done.

He could still remember with clarity the night his life had started to unravel. They'd been at one of those house parties where adults were absent and trouble escalated as word spread that a good time was to be had. Booze, drugs. Never his scene, but a factor whenever Jodi Simmons was present. The party had got out of hand. The neighbours had called the police, complaining of noise and the smell of cannabis. The sound of sirens had sent the kids running before the police arrived. But a drunken and drug-fuelled Jodi had tied the back of his scooter to the garage door in an attempt to be 'funny'. When he'd driven off with Becca riding pillion, the scooter had flipped and they'd ended up in an ambulance being treated for cuts and bruises. When his dad had arrived at A&E to collect him, he'd had a fit. Tom had been grounded for weeks, despite not having actually done anything wrong.

And that was the thing about Becca and Jodi: they'd dragged him into their antics. Maybe not Becca so much, but in the end, even she'd had a brush with the law. It was trouble he could do without.

Rubbing his chest, he continued walking, aiming for the back of the playhouse where his paint-splattered car was parked. He heard running water before he turned the corner. The sight stopped him in his tracks. Becca Roberts was washing his car.

For a moment, he just stared. It was like he'd been transported back in time. She was wearing white overalls and pink Converse trainers, her blonde hair had blue ends, tied into bunches that swung about as she rubbed paint away from his windscreen. She was holding a hose in one hand, a sponge in the other, making more mess than she'd created. A surge of something filled his gut – he had no idea what. Dread, probably.

When she dropped the sponge, picked it up and resumed rubbing, his temper flared. 'For crying out loud!'

His yell startled her. She turned, still holding the hose… and sprayed him with water.

Cold hit him like a hammer blow, sucking the air from his lungs.

He couldn't move; his body had gone into shock.

Becca tried to redirect the hose, tripped over the bucket and soaked him again.

Self-preservation kicked in. He ran over to the wall and turned off the outside tap. He was drenched. His suit, his shoes, his hair. Wet clothes clung to his skin, uncomfortable and cold. He turned to glare at her. 'You did that on purpose.'

Becca was on the ground where she'd fallen, water dripping from the end of the hose. 'Of course I didn't. You startled me. What were you thinking, shouting at me?'

'Because you dropped the sponge and didn't rinse it out.'

'So?' She clambered to her feet, favouring one leg.

'The ground is covered in grit. You've probably scratched my paintwork.'

She threw her hands in the air. 'Oh, pardon me for trying to do you a favour.'

He marched over, his blood boiling. 'A favour? You were the one who threw paint over it in the first place.'

She looked up at him. Her wide blue eyes, pink lips and cute nose forever imprinted on his brain. 'It was an accident, you arsehole. You seriously think I'd stoop so low as to chuck paint over your car?'

'Where you're concerned, anything's possible.'

She jabbed his chest with a finger. 'Don't you dare presume to know me. You haven't seen me for twelve years.'

'No, but you're still capable of causing mayhem, by the looks of it.'

'You arrogant arse.' She smacked him in the face with the sponge.

It didn't hurt, but he was shocked nonetheless. Too stunned to speak, he stood there, watery paint trickling down his face and onto his suit jacket. When he found his voice, he said, 'Expect a dry-cleaning bill.'

'Do what you like. As long you piss off back to London, I don't care.' She turned, kicking the gravel, dirtying her pink trainers.

'Believe me, I'd love to, but I'm stuck here babysitting you and your bloody cousin for the next eight weeks.'

She stilled. It was like someone had electrocuted her. Even her blue bunches stopped swaying. She turned slowly to face him. 'What did you say?'

'That's right. I've come back to manage the playhouse while Mum's in rehab. Imagine my surprise when she told me she'd put you and your cousin in charge. I don't know what your game is, but if you're planning anything dodgy think again. Because I'll also be here co-managing with you, and I won't be as easy to impress.'

The colour drained from her face.

He knew the feeling.

Chapter Twelve

Wednesday 11th October

Becca tried to hold her hand steady, which was hard when she was laughing. Even more so, as she didn't want her pupils to know she was laughing. 'Okay, cut!' She lowered her phone, wiping a tear from her eye.

'Are you laughing?' Miriam leant against the ballet barre, trying to catch her breath. The barre held firm, a testament to Eddie's workmanship.

Becca realised they could see her. Damned mirrors. 'Sorry, but I'm laughing with you not at you, I promise.' She hoped that was a suitably diplomatic response. 'It's looking really good, honestly.'

Wanda pulled a face. 'Honey, you're a terrible liar.'

'I'm not lying. We just need to give the routine more energy.'

'More energy? I'm dying here.' Miriam was bright red in the face, the same colour as her tights.

Everyone had been asked to wear red for the evening's class. Their outfits ranged from Wanda's blood-red wrap-dress to Cassie's muted burgundy cardigan. Nick had on a red

144

sports hoodie, and Mi-Sun wore a beautiful traditional Korean Hanbok made of pure silk. The idea of matching outfits had been to promote 'The Playhouse Tappers' in a showreel. With such contrasting shades and styles, her master plan had fallen a little short, but they certainly looked colourful.

'Shall we try again?' Becca looked at her tappers, none of whom looked particularly enthusiastic about being filmed.

'Are you sure this is a good idea?' Nick had his arm around Cassie. 'Will people be impressed by us lot prancing about?'

'Are you kidding me?' Becca smiled encouragingly. 'They're going to be blown away by you guys.'

'But we keep making mistakes,' Cassie said.

'It doesn't matter, I can edit the clips later. I'm not planning on showing the whole routine, just a few seconds of dancing with captions to advertise the classes. It's purely for promotion. I won't use anything that doesn't show you at your best. I promise.'

'And where will this video be shown?' Miriam's breathing had returned to normal.

'Various social media sites. We're trying to build a following and encourage more people to join the classes.'

'Who's we?' Wanda looked suspicious.

'My cousin Jodi's helping me. She's great with marketing ideas.' Becca went over to her amp. 'Shall we try another take?'

The group nodded reluctantly and took up their starting positions.

'Now, remember. The camera flattens everything so you need to give it ten times more effort to make it look good on film. Don't worry if it's not perfect. The key is to smile and look like you're having fun.'

She was about to press play, when the doors to the dance studio opened and in walked Tom Elliot. He stopped abruptly when he realised a class was in progress.

All eyes turned to look at him. Wanda let out a low whistle.

Becca couldn't blame her. He made quite an impact standing there dressed in dark suit trousers, no jacket, just a waistcoat over a baby-blue shirt that magnified the colour of his eyes. Eyes that had once transfixed her.

Wanda beckoned him in. 'Well, don't just stand there, honey. Come in and join the class.'

Becca didn't believe for a second he was there to tap-dance. More likely he was checking up on her. She'd managed to avoid him since her altercation with him last week when she'd dropped paint on his car and soaked him with the hosepipe, but she knew her luck was running out.

Co-managing the playhouse was a daunting enough prospect without the added pressure of dealing with Tom Elliot. The man who'd betrayed her. Who'd succumbed to pressure from his dad and ended their relationship when she'd needed him the most. She'd switched from being hopelessly in love, happy and adored – to feeling broken-hearted and utterly miserable. But she was older now and a lot wiser. And no longer under his spell.

She matched his frown. 'Did you want something? Only we're in the middle of class.'

He shook his head. 'Nothing that can't wait. Apologies for interrupting.'

'You can interrupt me anytime, honey.' Wanda's big laugh filled the room.

'Wanda, really.' Miriam shoved her friend. 'The man's half your age.'

Wanda grinned. 'That's how I like 'em.'

Tom didn't leave. Why, Becca had no idea. He was a distraction she could do without.

Turning back to the class, she pressed play on her phone. One Republic's *Counting Stars* burst from the speakers. 'Wait for my count...and five, six, seven, eight...step, step, shimmy, shimmy...'

Reflected in the mirrors she could see Tom watching the routine, his frown unrelenting. Seeing him again had caused a host of memories to surface. Her brain had been flooded with images, good and bad. Dragging her from ecstasy to torment, filling her with both resentment and deep-rooted longing. It'd taken her years to get over him. Maybe if she'd met someone else who'd made her feel the way he had, the wound would have healed. But no one had ever come close. And that didn't make seeing him again any easier.

After a minute of watching her pupils step on each other's feet and crash into each other, he left the dance studio. Good. She didn't need him interfering.

147

'That's great, everyone...heel tap...kick ball change...to the left, Mi-Sun...to the left!' Only Cassie seemed to be coping with the step combination. Becca zoomed in on her feet, hoping for some decent footage. 'Brilliant! Now, big finish... and cut!'

Five exhausted dancers slumped onto their seats.

Miriam fanned her face. 'That's me done.'

Becca went over. 'That was so much better. I've got enough material to make a showreel. Thanks, everyone. See you all next week.'

A good deal of puffing and grunting followed as they packed up and left. She'd have to work on their stamina if they were going to manage a routine that lasted longer than thirty seconds, but she was pleased with their progress.

She changed out of her tap shoes and laced up her rainbow boots, tying her dance hoodie around her middle. After flicking off the lights, she locked the doors behind her.

Despite being eight p.m. on a Wednesday evening, she was unsurprised to find Jodi still working – or to discover her locked in battle with the front-of-house manager.

'I'm not being unreasonable,' her cousin said, looking flustered. 'Leaving personal information on view in reception breaches data protection regulations.'

'Madam never mentioned any regulations to me.' Vivienne was being her usual helpful self. 'You probably made them up.'

'I assure you, I haven't made anything up. You're welcome

to read through the regulations yourself. I'll email you a link to the government website.'

Vivienne looked appalled. 'I don't use email.'

'Then I'll print off a copy. But from now on, please don't leave staff contact details lying around in reception. Okay?'

The Woman-in-Black didn't look happy. She picked up her bag. 'Goodnight, Ms Simmons. I'll leave you to lock up. No doubt you'll do a better job than me.'

Jodi sighed. 'Not at all, Vivienne. I'm very grateful for your help—'

But the woman had marched out the door, her black coat flapping behind her like bat wings.

Jodi looked dejected. She slumped against the reception desk, her mass of hair twisted into a tight bun. Her gorgeous hair looked better loose, but she was trying to appear more businesslike.

Deciding her cousin needed cheering up, Becca dropped her bag and started singing '*Ding-dong the witch is dead*' in a high-pitched voice. She danced around the foyer, hopping and twirling, wiggling her bottom.

Jodi's face broke into a smile. 'Nutter.'

Becca pirouetted up to her and tapped her on the nose, making her laugh as she sang, '*Sing it high...sing it low,*' switching to a deep voice.

Jodi's laughter only stopped when Tom appeared from the office.

The sight of Tom's confused expression undermined Becca's

composure and she bumped into the leaflet rack nearly toppling it over.

There was a time when her daft antics would have made him laugh. Not anymore.

Oh, well, it was no skin off her nose. Hooking her arm through Jodi's, she led her cousin away from reception. 'Some people have no sense of humour,' she shouted over her shoulder, loud enough for him to hear.

Jodi looked forlorn. 'He's been watching me like a hawk all day. Questioning everything I do, like he's waiting for me to trip up. It's exhausting.'

Becca wanted to thump him. How dare he treat her cousin like that! 'Don't let him get to you. You're doing a great job. Carolyn wouldn't have left you in charge otherwise.'

'Both of us, remember?'

How could she forget? 'And now it's three. We're like the Three Musketeers.'

Jodi looked at her. 'More like The Good, The Bad and The Ugly.'

'Charming; which one am I? On second thoughts, don't answer that.' Becca squeezed her cousin's arm. 'Come on, it's not that terrible.'

Jodi raised an eyebrow. 'Who're you trying to convince, me or you?'

'Both. Now come and have a drink. I need to revive my courage levels before my battle with Tom-the-Tyrant.'

Jodi managed a smile. 'Nice name.'

'I thought so.'

Leon was serving behind the bar. He smiled when he saw Jodi. The smile of a besotted man. Becca thought Jodi might need a gentle nudge in the right direction. Reassurance that she was worthy of a decent guy's attention.

Becca climbed onto a stool. 'So, apart from dealing with the tyrant, is everything else okay?'

Jodi sat next to her. 'Not really. We received a letter today from the council about the community engagement grant. They weren't impressed following their visit here a couple of weeks ago. They don't feel enough is being done to meet the terms of the award.'

Becca frowned. 'That doesn't sound good.'

'It's not. They're asking for a report evidencing progress. They plan to revisit the playhouse in a few weeks' time to reassess. If they're not satisfied enough steps have been taken to rectify the situation the grant will have to be repaid.'

'Oh, crap. Has Tom seen the letter?'

Jodi nodded. 'He's written back asking for more time, explaining the owner's receiving medical treatment and is indisposed.'

'Do you think that'll be enough to stall them?'

Jodi shrugged. 'Who knows? It's not great as plans go. It feels like we're letting Carolyn down by not taking action in her absence.'

Becca nodded. 'I agree. We can't sit back and do nothing. Any ideas?'

'Not yet, but I'm working on it.'

'Good. I'll put my thinking cap on too.'

Leon finished serving and came over. 'What can I get you both?'

'Orange juice for me.' Becca turned to her cousin. 'Jodi?'

'Glass of water, please. And a packet of crisps. I'm starving.'

'Coming right up.' Leon ambled off.

Becca helped herself to a few bar nuts. 'That reminds me, did you know Mum served readymade pizza for dinner last night? When I got home I thought Mrs Busby was going to pass out, she was so shocked. She said she'd never had pizza before.'

Jodi stifled a yawn. 'I wasn't there, I had a shift at the restaurant last night.'

'Oh, right. Do you think that's odd? I mean, Mum usually cooks a homemade meal.'

Leon placed their drinks down.

'Thanks, Leon.' Jodi gave him a shy nod. 'Maybe Aunty Ruby was tired, or didn't feel like cooking.'

Becca sipped her orange juice. 'Maybe. But I was thinking, if I can get Tom-the-Tyrant to agree to my tea dance idea, then I might persuade Mum to come along. Dancing is a proven way of lifting a person's mood. It might cheer her up a bit. What do you think?'

'It's worth a shot. When are you going to speak to Tom?'

'I suppose there's no time like the present.'

Leon appeared with a cheese toastie. 'You need more than

crisps,' he said, handing Jodi the plate. 'Cappuccino on its way.'

Becca smiled. She was glad someone was looking out for her cousin. 'Enjoy your toastie,' she said, nudging Jodi in the ribs. 'And don't work too late. You do too many hours.'

Jodi took a bite of toastie. Her expression indicated it was heavenly.

Becca looked at Leon. 'Tell her, will you?'

He handed Jodi her cappuccino. 'You know what they say, all work and no play.'

Becca left her cousin in Leon's capable hands, and went in search of the tyrant.

He was in the office working on his computer. He didn't look up when she entered.

Taking a deep breath, she sat in the wingback chair, aiming for an air of nonchalance.

He carried on typing. 'Ever heard of knocking?'

'Why would I knock? This is my office too, remember?'

'How could I forget?'

She swivelled in the chair, making it squeak.

It had the desired effect. He stopped typing. 'Did you want something? I'm busy.'

'That's okay, I'm happy to wait.' She leant back in the chair, making it squeak louder.

He turned to face her. 'What?'

She gave him her best fake smile. 'I have an idea for increasing income.'

He raised an eyebrow. 'Which is...?'

'Weekly tea dances.'

If she was expecting rapturous applause it didn't happen. Why, she wasn't sure. It was a great idea. It had come to her when she'd stopped to watch a brass quartet playing at the bandstand on the beach at the weekend. An elderly couple had got up to dance and she'd been struck by how charming it was.

Tom remained unimpressed. 'What's it got to do with me? Dance classes are your department.'

'I want to hold them in the grand ballroom.'

He turned back to his laptop. 'The ballroom's out of action. The roof needs repairing.' Negativity radiated off him like an electrical current.

She began to fidget, crossing and uncrossing her legs. 'I know, so we repair it.'

'We can't afford to.'

'Maybe if we bodge it temporarily we could make it good enough to use.' Her foot caught on a cable hanging down from the desk, making the desk lamp wobble. She reached out to catch it just as Tom-the-Tyrant turned to look at her.

His eyes darted from the lamp to her. 'Bodge it?'

She pushed the lamp back onto the desk, annoyed that he made her flustered.

'This is a stately home we're talking about, not a garden shed. The repairs need to be carried out by a specialist roofer.'

'We can't afford a specialist roofer.'

'I'm aware of that, which is why we can't get the work done.'

'But we wouldn't need a specialist roofer if we bodge...err... temporarily fix it.'

He looked agitated. 'The Starlight Playhouse is over four hundred years old. Do you have any idea the damage a rogue builder could cause? Cost aside, this family have been patronising Walker Gibbs for fifty years. My mother would see it as disrespectful to terminate a long-standing relationship, simply because you've obtained a cheaper quote.' He patted his pockets, searching for something. 'It's a matter of loyalty.'

'It's a matter of affordability.' She adjusted the lopsided lampshade, hoping he wouldn't notice.

'Either way, we don't have the money.'

The lampshade dropped again. 'But unless we invest we'll never be able to generate more income.'

He sighed. 'So use the dance studio for these...whatever they are.'

'Tea dances.' She lifted the lampshade again. 'And it's not big enough, or the right space. Ballroom dancing needs a suitable backdrop, and the right atmosphere. We could get a pianist in. It would be a real social event, something to bring people into the playhouse. It might even count towards the grant requirements.'

He shot her a look.

'Jodi told me about the letter.' She sat back in the chair. 'So what do you say?'

He opened his briefcase. 'No.'

'Think of the publicity.'

'No.'

She looked at the man before her. Where was the playful, romantic, sweet seventeen-year-old boy who used to play love songs down the phone to her? He'd been replaced by a grumpy, arrogant, combative man. Tom Elliot might be gorgeous on the outside, but underneath he was a changed person, and not for the better. 'Jodi thinks it's a good idea, so that's two votes against one.'

'And yet my answer is still no.' He removed an inhaler from his briefcase.

'That's not democratic.'

'Tough.' He administered his inhaler.

She stood up, ignoring the fact that he was holding his breath while the drugs kicked in...or maybe relishing the fact that he couldn't answer back for a few seconds.

She leant on the desk, faking a confidence she didn't feel. 'You're not the only one running the place, you know. And if you think being a bastard towards Jodi and trying to bully us into walking away will work, then think again. We made a promise to Carolyn to keep things going and that's exactly what we intend to do. And that includes coming up with a plan to ensure we don't have to repay the council grant.'

It was a bold statement. One that might have had more impact if the lamp hadn't chosen that moment to topple over. Unwilling to allow her clumsiness to ruin a dramatic exit, she marched over to the door – her anger tapered slightly by the realisation that he still suffered with asthma.

'Becca...?'

She turned back. 'What?'

'The answer's still no.'

And to think, for a second she'd almost started to feel sorry for him.

Chapter Thirteen

Thursday 12th October

Tom was struggling to concentrate. The Starlight Playhouse was eerily quiet. Only a couple of visitors in the café kept the place from being completely deserted. There were no dance classes or art lessons taking place, nothing that required his attention, and yet his mind refused to stay focused on his pre-sentence report.

He leant back in the office chair, stretching out his back. Jodi was sitting at the other desk, her face tense as her eyes darted from the receipts laid out in front of her to the spread-sheet on the computer. Unlike him, she didn't seem to be struggling to concentrate.

Which was a puzzle. The Jodi he'd known had been skittish and wired. The joker, who'd held court with her outrageous pranks, never knowing when to rein it in, or when to apply the brakes before plunging off a cliff at a hundred miles per hour.

Looking at her now you'd never guess she was the same person. Even her appearance was contained. Her mass of hair was tamed into submission. Her clothes were grey and under-stated. She was no longer the court jester. Now it was like she craved invisibility.

A rap on the door interrupted his thoughts.

Vivienne marched in looking annoyed.

Jodi didn't notice. Or if she did, she chose to ignore her.

Vivienne coughed loudly. 'I received your note,' she said, screwing up the Post-it-Note and throwing it in the waste paper bin. 'You wanted to see me?'

Jodi looked up. 'I did, yes. I'm trying to make sense of the petty cash system.'

Vivienne frowned. 'Why? I look after the petty cash.'

Jodi nodded. 'I know, but it's my job to reconcile the accounts. Carolyn said you run a float system?'

Vivienne lifted her chin. 'Do you have a problem with that?'

Jodi opened her notebook. 'Where do you log the expenditure?'

Vivienne rolled her eyes. 'Petty cash is for incidentals. Stamps, stationery, consumables and such.'

'All items that should be recorded in the accounts.'

'Madam never—'

'...required receipts. Yes, so you keep saying.' Jodi handed Vivienne a receipt book. 'From now on I'd like all expenditure recorded in this book and receipts kept.'

Vivienne frowned. '*I* look after the petty cash system.'

'And this is how I'd like you to manage the system going forwards.'

Vivienne looked at Tom, hoping for an ally. 'Master Thomas? Will you please explain to Ms Simmons that the current system is perfectly adequate.'

He wasn't sure it was. Keeping receipts didn't sound like an unreasonable ask. The finances weren't in great shape, which was why he'd recently engaged the services of an accountant. But maybe he needed to check with the professionals first before wading into the argument.

'Carry on as you were, Vivienne. I'll speak to the accountant and get back to you.'

Vivienne relaxed. 'Thank you, Master Thomas.' She gave Jodi a smug look and left the office.

He could feel Jodi's stare boring into the side of his head. 'I'm not about to piss off a long-standing member of staff just because you have a different way of doing things.'

'So even though I've studied finance and I'm in regular contact with the accountant discussing these matters you still don't trust my judgement?'

He looked at her. 'You want me to trust you?'

The look on her face told him he'd struck a nerve.

Tough. His mother might believe she'd changed, but as far as he was concerned the jury was still out.

Talking of juries, he needed to get back to his pre-sentence report. He turned back to his laptop, but the door opened again.

Petrit appeared holding a piece of paper. 'What is this?'

Jodi glanced up. 'It's a timesheet, Petrit.'

160

'I already give you timesheet.'

'There were errors on the previous one.'

'What errors?' His face darkened, contrasting with his chef whites.

Jodi flipped through her notepad. 'Monday 2nd October you arrived for work at eight-forty-five not eight a.m. as stated on your timesheet. Tuesday 3rd October you arrived at eight-fifty. Thursday 5th October it was nine-ten. I have them all listed. Shall I go on?'

'You spy on me?'

'I'm simply pointing out that the times listed on your previous timesheet weren't correct.' Jodi turned back to her computer. 'When I receive a completed timesheet with the correct start times I'll ensure your wages are paid into your account.'

Tom wasn't sure what Petrit would have done if he hadn't been sitting there. As it was, he stormed out, slamming the door behind him.

Jodi flinched.

Tom could see she was unnerved. He wasn't her biggest fan, but she didn't deserve to be treated like that.

He got up and left the office, closing the door behind him. He could do with a break.

Part of him wanted to go after Petrit and have words. The other part of him wanted to stay well out of it. He had enough on his plate. He didn't need the hassle of dealing with disgruntled staff too. But maybe that's what he'd signed up for by taking over the place.

Needing to clear his head, he went through the French doors into the sunshine. It was a gorgeous autumn day. The view down to the lake was stunning. The sun bounced off the reds and golds in the trees, creating a warm glow that reflected off the water.

He continued down the pathway and under the stone arch. The gardens looked lush and green, the foliage turning in colour, not yet ready to tumble. The house might be in desperate need of repair, but the gardens weren't. The pathway snaked through the trees and down to the bridge. He stood on the brow and looked over the edge, hoping the sight of running water might ease the tightness in his chest.

Why had he thought returning to the playhouse would make his life less stressful? If anything, it was making things worse.

His first week had been riddled with problems. It had started when he'd dropped his mother off at the rehab centre and she'd told him it was time for him to make amends with his father. He hadn't even known they were still in contact. It was a miracle he hadn't crashed the car. Consequently, it hadn't been the touching send-off he'd planned. He'd driven off angry, only regretting not saying a proper goodbye when he'd arrived back at the playhouse, grumpy and wheezing.

And then Izzy had called. A tearful phone call telling him she hadn't moved out of the flat and her parents had frozen her allowance again – something they regularly did when her partying got out of hand. He didn't like the idea of making

162

her homeless, but completion on the sale was due next week. When he'd pointed this out, he'd been accused of being unreasonable, selfish and uncaring. How the situation was his fault, he wasn't sure. So, she was still in the flat, ignoring his calls, and refusing to move out.

On top of this, his asthma was getting worse. Aggravated by trying to manage the damp playhouse and deal with two nemeses from his past. So much for reducing his stress levels. He was at breaking point.

Seeing Becca again had caused a reaction like a flame being ignited. His temper, usually in check, had exploded, hurtling him into full-blown rage. His behaviour hadn't been exactly gentlemanly and he was ashamed. But all the grief and guilt he'd repressed over the years had surfaced like a tidal wave, threatening to drown him. Seeing her again physically hurt, like someone had cracked open his chest with a tyre iron. And it wasn't like he could walk away. He was forced to interact with her on a daily basis and pretend he was okay. Well, he wasn't okay.

He crossed the bridge and walked around the lake, searching for a sense of calm. He used to spend a lot of time out here as a kid. With no siblings, he was used to his own company, entertaining himself, except when his cousins had visited. He'd enjoyed riding his bike around the grounds, camping out under the stars, or staying in the treehouse.

His dad had built the treehouse during a brief period when his mother's drinking had been under control. Calling it a treehouse was an understatement. It was a two-storey construction with a wood burner and electric generator, the precursor to glamping. They'd enjoyed one summer filled with barbecues and family parties before his mother had fallen off the wagon again.

After that the treehouse remained unused... Well, until his teens, when he'd discovered an entirely different use for it. But his breathing wasn't up to thinking about nights spent rolling around the lumpy airbed with Becca Roberts.

Most of his teenage years had revolved around caring for his mother. And he'd been fine with that, despite its hardship. He'd had a few mates, but it wasn't until he'd met Becca and Jodi that life suddenly became a lot more interesting. They'd balanced out the pain of seeing his mother pissed or hungover all the time, bringing laughter and fun into his life. He remembered their first summer together, hanging out on the beach, at the open-air cinema, ice-skating at the Cube and going to raves at Black Rock. They'd introduced him to a side of Brighton he hadn't known existed.

He stopped to admire Eddie's handiwork. The shrubs were trimmed back, and the trees cut to equal height. He crossed the expanse of grass towards the house, looking up at the ornate structure with its impressive architecture and multitude of windows. It was a surreal feeling, knowing this was his home. He loved the place, but it wasn't without its challenges. He supposed it was like being in a long-term marriage, you had to take the good with the bad, for better and for worse.

Sunlight glinted off the art studio windows. The doors were open. Eddie was up a ladder. Becca appeared, shielding her eyes from the sun. A third person joined her, a man carrying a clipboard. The man was sketching something, showing Becca his drawings.

Tom headed over. 'What's going on?' he said, his tone terser than intended.

Becca's smile was tight. 'This is Tom Elliot, the man I was telling you about. His mother owns the playhouse.' She was wearing chunky ankle boots over lime-green leggings and a short black dress. Her blue-blonde hair was tucked behind her ears, revealing asymmetric earrings the same colour as her tights.

The guy held out his hand. 'Marcus Forbes, Forbes and Daughter Roofing. Good to meet you.'

Tom shook the guy's hand, before turning to Becca. 'Can I have a word?'

'Certainly.' She smiled at the roofing guy. 'Excuse us, Marcus. I won't be a moment.' She sashayed down the steps, mesmerising poor Marcus, who had no idea he'd unwittingly stepped into a minefield.

She waited at the bottom, her arms folded, her stance switching to fight mode.

Tom followed. 'Care to explain what's going on?'

'I'm getting a quote to fix the roof.'

Just as he suspected. 'We discussed this and agreed a specialist roofer was needed.'

She leant against the wall. 'No, we argued and you tried to overrule me.'

'Either way, you should've consulted me before arranging a site visit.'

She inspected her orange nails. 'You would've only said no. I wanted to find out for myself what the options were.'

He rubbed his chest. 'There are no options. We need a specialist roofer.'

She shook her head, making her earrings swing. 'Forbes and Daughter are a reputable firm who specialise in period buildings. They might not be Walker Gibbs, but they come highly recommended.'

'By whom?'

She avoided eye contact. 'Toptrades.'

He couldn't believe what he was hearing. 'Are you serious?'

She pushed away from the wall. 'Look, before you blow a gasket, just listen to reason. Despite what you think, I did take on board what you said, and Marcus agrees that using a company like Walker Gibbs to replace the damaged roof would be sensible.'

He lifted his hands to the sky. 'Thank you.'

'However, Marcus is quoting for a temporary fix, not replacing the whole roof. A decent repair should last a few years, which will allow enough time for fundraising. More significantly, it means we can use the art studio and the ball-room for functions, and try to appease the council. Something that currently isn't possible.'

'How much?'

'Approximately two grand.'

He stepped away. 'For a temporary fix?'

Her hands went to her hips. 'Look, it's a great space, but it's not getting used. If we can fix the leak, then we'll get more people hiring it.'

'We can't afford two grand.'

'I know, but Marcus is offering a repayment schedule.'

He was distracted by a floral scent emanating from her. 'It's too risky. The answer's no.'

Her gaze narrowed. 'Because we can't afford it, or because you don't think a temporary fix is a good idea?'

'Does it matter?'

'Yes, it matters.' She advanced on him. 'Jodi and I are working our arses off trying to improve bookings and advertise this place, and if you're going to block every idea we have just to be bloody-minded, then things are never going to improve, are they?'

He tried not to look at her glossy lips. 'I'm not being bloody-minded.'

She looked incredulous. 'Are you for real?'

'Fine. I'm not against the temporary fix idea...providing the company checks out, and not just on...whatever that site is called—'

'Toptrades.'

'Right.' He backed away. She was a distraction he could do without. 'Even then we still can't afford it.'

167

She paced, dragging his eyes from her lips down to her shapely legs. 'If Jodi and I can raise the money needed, will you agree to get the work done?'

'I'll think about it.'

'Not good enough.' In one swift movement, she was in his face, her blue eyes pinning him with a glare. 'Yes, or no?'

For crying out loud. 'Yes.' Anything to get her off his case. And besides, the likelihood of her being able to fundraise in eight weeks was highly unlikely.

'Good, because we have our first tea dance arranged for tomorrow afternoon.' She hopped up the steps and sashayed away.

'Not in the ballroom?' he called after her.

She didn't answer and kept walking, swinging her hips in hypnotic fashion.

He tried again. 'The ballroom is out of use, Becca. The roof leaks.'

'Only when it rains!' She spun around, dazzling him with a smile. 'The forecast says no rain, so we're fine.' And with that, she ran over to Marcus.

He stood there, wheezing, unable to chase her down.

Eddie appeared next to him. 'She's a breath of fresh air, isn't she?'

Tom turned to look at him. That wasn't the description he'd use.

Chapter Fourteen

Friday 13th October

A bang from the landing jolted Becca awake. She stirred slowly, dragging her mind from deep slumber. As she blinked away sleep, bright swirls of orange patterning on the wall came into semi-focus. The yellow plastic clock on the bedside table told her it was gone eight, so she rolled out of bed and padded into the bathroom. She had errands to run, but she didn't need to be at the playhouse until later, so she was relishing the opportunity of a slow start.

In truth, she needed a break from dealing with Tom-the-Tyrant. In addition to being grumpy and stubborn, he was a lot more assertive than he used to be. Arguing made her feel out of her depth. Not to mention clumsy. He made her doubt herself – not that she'd ever let him see that. Standing her ground was a challenge. But gone were the days when she'd follow him around like an obedient puppy, hanging on his every word. She was an adult now. She needed to rid herself of those silly romantic ideals of her teens and get over Tom Elliot once and for all.

Showered and dressed, she headed onto the landing, only to find Mad Maude blocking her path. The cat was sitting on the top stair, her fur expanded, eyeing Becca like she was her next victim.

Determined not to be outwitted, Becca viewed it as a golden opportunity to practise being assertive. If she couldn't win a battle with a cat, what chance did she have with Tom-the-Tyrant? 'Move, Maude.'

The cat ignored her.

'I've just been giving myself a talking-to about standing up to bullies. So you'd better budge, because I'm going downstairs whether you like it or not.'

Maude's response was to bare her teeth.

'Don't say I didn't warn you.' Taking a deep breath, she edged past, keeping her back to the wall.

Maude waited until the opportune moment before lashing out, leaving a bloody claw mark on Becca's forearm.

'Bloody cat!' Becca ran downstairs, rubbing her arm.

Her mum was in the breakfast room. 'Morning, sweetheart. Help yourself to cereal and fruit.' And then she saw her arm. 'What happened to you? Don't tell me...Maude?'

'The one and only.' Her arm stung like crazy.

'I'm sorry, love. There's a packet of antiseptic wipes in the cupboard. Do you need plasters?'

'No, it's fine. It's only a scratch.' She tried not to feel disgruntled.

'Would you like some breakfast?' Her mum balanced the jug

170

she was carrying on the table. 'I could make scrambled eggs.'

'I'll sort myself out, Mum. You have enough to do.' Becca found the wipes under a pile of napkins. The cupboard was stuffed full of junk, no longer neat and tidy. Another indication that all was not well in the Roberts household. 'You're still coming to the tea dance this afternoon, aren't you?'

'Of course, love.' Her mum's smile was half-hearted. 'Looking forward to it.'

It didn't take a mind-reader to work out Ruby Roberts wasn't overly enamoured by the idea. But how was her mum going to meet new people if she didn't try new things? And she might enjoy it once she got there.

Cleaning her arm with the wipes, Becca watched her mum tend to Mrs Busby and Dr Mortimer, serving them two helpings of Shredded Wheat. Her mum said if she'd known about their colossal appetites before they'd moved in she'd have doubled the rent.

'Omelette, Mrs Busby?'

'Two lightly boiled eggs today, please. White soldiers, not too thick.' Mrs Busby was wearing a tweed pinafore dress. Very Miss Marple-esque.

Her mum's jovial tone didn't waver. 'What about you, Dr Mortimer?'

'Full English for me. Need to keep my strength up.' He patted his bulging stomach.

Her mum returned to the kitchen, her rigid smile the only giveaway she was fraught.

Becca went over to the elderly couple. 'Do you have any plans this afternoon?'

Mrs Busby peered over the top of her specs. 'When you get to our age, you rarely make plans.'

Becca smiled. 'Well, would you both like to come to a tea dance at the Starlight Playhouse?'

Dr Mortimer cupped his ear. 'What did she say?' His hearing aid was lying on the table next to his pill bottle.

Mrs Busby leant forwards. 'Do we want to go to a tea dance this afternoon?'

He looked mystified. 'What's one of those?'

'It's a social event,' Becca said, speaking loudly. 'Ballroom dancing, with afternoon tea served. Nothing formal, just a chance to meet people and socialise. Would you like to come?'

His silver moustache twitched. 'I had planned to watch a film.' A cloud of confusion descended on him. 'Although for the life of me, I can't remember which one. I can't seem to stay awake these days. I barely make it through *Death in Paradise* before nodding off.' His laughter was tinged with sadness.

'Maybe some exercise will do you good, William.' Mrs Busby lowered her voice. 'His memory isn't so good. It makes it very hard to go anywhere.'

'You wouldn't have to stay long.' Becca addressed them both, feeling uncomfortable excluding the doctor.

'What do you think, William?' Mrs Busby almost shouted. 'Shall we?'

The doctor tipped his non-existent cap. 'Only if you can keep up with the old fella?'

Mrs Busby scoffed. 'Men lined up to dance with me back in the day.'

Becca wasn't surprised. The old woman was still nimble on her feet well into her eighties. 'Do you have a favourite dance, Mrs Busby?'

'The foxtrot. My late husband and I used to whiz around the dance floor.'

Becca laughed. 'I'll bet you did. It would be lovely if you would both come this afternoon. Mum's coming, and I'll be there too.'

'Not dressed like that, I hope?' Mrs Busby's opinion of Becca's skinny jeans and off-the-shoulder top with a red bra strap showing wasn't favourable.

'I'm heading into Brighton to buy something more suitable,' Becca said, getting used to the old woman's disapproval. 'So will you come?'

Mrs Busby nodded. 'It'll do us both good. Don't you agree, William?'

'All being well,' Dr Mortimer added. 'Nothing's a certainty when you get to our age.'

She left them to their Shredded Wheat and went to check on her mum.

With the promise of three people guaranteed she was hoping the first tea dance wouldn't be a complete washout. Fingers crossed a few more people would show up. They'd been advertising on social media, but there hadn't been much time for word to spread. But if she could take some photos this afternoon, then she could create a few more posts and hopefully build momentum.

Back in the sanctuary of the kitchen, her mum was busy frying sausages and bacon, keeping one eye on the tomatoes sizzling on the grill. Smoke rose from the toaster. The coffee percolator made strange noises. Her mum mumbled incoherently, jabbing the sausages with a fork, as though they'd committed a crime. And then the smoke detector went off.

Her mum looked close to tears. 'Could this morning get any worse?'

'It's okay, I've got this.' Becca ran into the hallway to silence the excruciating squeal of the alarm, before returning to the kitchen to help finish breakfast.

By the time she'd rescued the sausages and bacon, boiled Mrs Busby's eggs and served it all up, she had some appreciation of what her mum dealt with every day.

When she came back into the kitchen and found her mum slumped against the back door, she handed her a steaming mug of coffee. 'Go and sit in the sunshine. I'll clean up in here.' She cut her mum off before she could protest. 'Just let me help, okay?'

Her mum obeyed and went into her patio garden.

Becca cleared away the breakfast things, loaded the dishwasher, put on a pile of washing, and dusted and hoovered the entire guest house.

It was therefore a little later than planned before she headed into Brighton. She didn't mind. She wouldn't be much of a daughter if she didn't help around the guest house. She made a mental note to help a bit more.

It was another glorious October day. Windy on the seafront, but trailing off as she headed deeper into the narrow lanes in search of an outfit for her first tea dance. Brighton had endless fascinating shops. She wandered around the North Laine area, buying a pretty mauve scarf for her mum and a silver belt for Jodi, which she hoped might go with the cute black dress her mum had got her cousin last Christmas. For herself she chose a midnight-blue Fifties dress from Tuff Tarts, combining it with a pale pink petticoat and matching neck scarf. Very retro. Perfect for the tea dance.

She ambled through Kensington Gardens, stopping to watch a guy in period dress riding a penny-farthing. As she watched him perform to the gathering crowd, she spotted numerous posters advertising Brighton's Annual Arts Festival.

Intrigued, she went over and read the details.

There were several events taking place, including a new play at the Rialto and two music recitals, one at the Brighton Centre and a classical offering at the Pavilion. There was also an open-house arts exhibition. She remembered visiting one a few years back with her mum. It had seemed surreal walking into a stranger's home and looking at their work, but the event had been hugely successful and generated an influx of visitors to the town.

An idea popped into her head.

She looked at the date. Twenty-fifth of November. That was six weeks away. Would that be enough time to pull something together? It was too good an opportunity to pass up on. They'd be fools not to take part.

With her mind already buzzing with ideas, she headed for the playhouse, pleased to note that her knee didn't twinge once during the forty-minute walk. She was making progress. She might even venture onto the dance floor this afternoon.

Her enthusiasm took a minor dent when she raced up the steps leading to the playhouse and almost ran smack into Eddie.

'I've been looking for you,' he said, reaching out to catch her. 'We have a problem.'

And her morning had been going so well. 'What kind of problem?'

'Vivienne's refusing to hand over the key to the ballroom. She says it's not safe to use and won't relent until Master Thomas instructs her otherwise.'

Becca sighed. Flaming woman. 'And where is *Master* Thomas?' she said, resisting the urge to call him a few other names.

'Last I saw he was in the office.'

Well, she'd be having words with *Master* Thomas. 'Thanks for the heads-up, Eddie.'

'Good luck,' he called after her as she ran off.

Tom-the-Tyrant was in the office frowning at his laptop.

He seemed to do a lot of frowning. His blond hair was tousled and the sleeves of his lilac shirt were rolled up. Why he insisted on wearing a waistcoat, she didn't know. Anyone would think he was working at the Old Bailey, not a rundown arts centre.

Jodi was also there, studiously working away. It wasn't exactly a companionable silence. The atmosphere at the abattoir had been warmer.

She marched over and stood by the desk, her good mood morphing into annoyance. No way was he going to ignore her. 'We can do this the hard way or the easy way,' she said. 'But either way, we're using the ballroom this afternoon for the tea dance.'

He swivelled in his chair to look at her. 'Good morning to you too.'

She held out her hand. 'I'd like the key to the ballroom, please.'

His baby-blues dipped to her hand and then up to her face. 'I don't have it.'

'But you can get it. So ask Vivienne to hand it over.' She leant on the desk, feigning an assertiveness she didn't feel. 'This is the easy way, in case you hadn't realised.'

He sighed. 'Be reasonable.'

'I'm being perfectly reasonable.' She straightened. 'If there was a valid reason why we couldn't use the ballroom then I wouldn't be pushing this. But the surveyor reported that structurally the room is safe. If the weather was bad and the roof was leaking, I'd be the first to agree we couldn't use it, but it hasn't rained for days. So can you please ask Vivienne to unlock the room.'

'And what happens next week if it rains?'

'Then we relocate to the dance studio. But for today I'd like to use the ballroom. That way I can take photos and promote the event, which will hopefully increase attendance and enable us to raise the money necessary to fix the roof. As you agreed.'

Jodi made an odd noise, like a stifled laugh.

If Tom noticed, he chose to ignore it. 'Technically, I didn't agree. You stormed off before we'd finished arguing.'

'But you did agree to the idea of fundraising?' She gave him a questioning look. 'And we can't increase income unless we bring in—'

'—more users, yeah, I get it.' He made her wait a good few seconds. 'Fine.'

Fine? He was agreeing? 'Right. Well, good. That wasn't so hard, was it?'

Jodi mumbled, 'Quit while you're ahead.'

She had a point...but Becca wasn't done.

She perched on the edge of the desk, causing him to raise an eyebrow. 'Was there something else?'

'I have an idea about how we can improve community engagement.'

He closed his eyes. 'Oh, joy.'

She ignored his sarcasm. 'Are you aware there's an arts festival taking place in Brighton at the end of next month?'

He shook his head. 'No, should I?'

'There are posters all over town. It looks like a massive event. I think we should take part.' Her declaration wasn't met with the immediate enthusiasm she'd hoped for.

He leant back in his chair. 'Take part how exactly?'

She hopped off the desk, needing to express herself. 'Think about it. The Starlight Playhouse would be the perfect backdrop for displaying local artists' work. Not to mention a great way to promote the venue. We could host a few exhibitions and use the theatre to put on a dance showcase. It would give my pupils a goal to work towards, and show the council we're committed to meeting the terms of the grant. What do you say?'

He gave her a loaded look. 'How much will it cost?'

Killjoy. 'Well...I don't know. I've only just had the idea.'

He rested his arms on the desk. 'So you want us to commit to putting on a huge event, incorporating all areas of the playhouse, with no idea of the costs involved?'

Smartarse. She turned to her cousin. 'I'm sure Jodi will help me draw up a proposal.'

'Well, until she does, the answer's no. Anything else?'

Her face felt hot. 'No.'

'Good. I'll ask Vivienne to unlock the ballroom.' He got up and walked over to the door. 'Coming?'

She wasn't sure who'd won the battle.

When he tapped his watch, and said, 'I haven't got all day,' she followed him out.

So much for not behaving like an obedient puppy.

179

Chapter Fifteen

Saturday 14th October

There were some days when Jodi wished she'd stayed in bed. Today was one of them. It had started this morning when a mother and toddler group had descended on the café. One of the baby's nappies had failed to contain its load and another child spilled sticky orange juice everywhere. Petrit had refused to help, stating he was 'on a break', and disappeared outside for a smoke, leaving Jodi to clean up the mess herself. When she'd returned the mop and bucket to the kitchen, he'd emptied the contents into the sink before she'd had a chance to move away, and bleach had splashed all over her black suede shoes.

Lunchtime had provided the next challenge. The sandwich she'd made had mysteriously disappeared from the fridge. She'd later found it dumped in the bin. No doubt it was retribution for asking Petrit to refrain from smoking outside the front of the building. It could equally have been Vivienne – who was still sulking because Jodi had pointed out that using a fire extinguisher to prop open an emergency exit breached health and safety regulations.

Life did test her at times.

She'd retreated to the relative sanctuary of the office, where she could work on a budget for Becca's showcase without further confrontation. Her cousin's brief was clear. The event needed to be an extravaganza...but without costing a shedload of money. Not a tall order at all.

Even discounting publicity costs, they'd need additional staff and security to man the event, not to mention catering, bar stock, tickets and programmes. She hadn't even started costing staging requirements, props and costumes. Keeping expenditure at a minimum was proving a challenge.

But she wasn't about to let her cousin down. It was a great idea and one she felt Carolyn would approve of. It would also go some way to meeting the grant conditions. Realisation that her salary was funded by the grant had only fuelled her determination to come up with a workable plan. Petrit and Vivienne could humiliate her all they liked, she was not about to quit.

She'd been working for several hours when Tom entered the office wearing his usual formal suit, complete with permanent frown. He was followed by Vivienne, who was playing the role of his shadow, her black attire adding to the eerie effect. But Vivienne King was no Peter Pan. She was more Captain Hook.

Tom cleared his throat. 'It's been brought to my attention that the balance in the playhouse bank account is considerably lower than it was a week ago.'

'Twenty thousand pounds lower,' Vivienne chipped in. 'And *I* haven't made any withdrawals.'

Tom shot the Woman-in-Black a look. 'Thank you, Vivienne. I'll deal with this.'

Vivienne bowed her head. 'Apologies, Master Thomas. You know what this place means to me. I'd hate for madam's dream to be destroyed by skulduggery.'

Skulduggery? Jesus.

'Like I said, I'll handle this.' The firmness in Tom's voice shut Vivienne up. 'I'm assuming there's an explanation?' Unlike Vivienne, he wasn't starting off with an accusation – even if the tone of his question reeked of suspicion.

Jodi stood up. Their 'superior' act was intimidating enough. 'I opened two new accounts earlier this week with higher interest rates,' she said, reaching for the paperwork. 'Twenty grand was transferred to the new accounts.' She pointed to the relevant transfers. 'As you can see, there's been no...skulduggery.'

Tom studied the paperwork. 'You didn't think to run this by anyone first?'

'Too big for her own boots,' Vivienne said, eager to back up the 'master'.

'I'm acting on the accountant's recommendations,' Jodi said, sick of being forced to justify her actions. 'He said failure to implement a suitable reserves policy wasn't good business practice. I was going to circulate the draft procedure this afternoon for your approval.' She handed Tom the document. 'Restricted reserves have been set aside to cover business closure costs and staff redundancies should the playhouse fall into receivership. The balance of the council grant has been transferred to non-restricted reserves, which can be used to cover ongoing repairs and maintenance, plus one-off expenditure like the showcase event.'

That got Vivienne's attention. 'What showcase event?'

Tom ignored her. 'I haven't approved the showcase.'

'But you did agree to consider a proposal.' He couldn't deny it; Jodi had been in the room.

'What showcase event?' repeated Vivienne.

'Consider a proposal, yes. But judging by the lack of available funds it's unlikely I'll be signing off on any significant non-essential expenditure.' He was using his 'I'm in charge' voice. The one she imagined he used in court.

But Jodi hadn't spent years studying for a business degree to be dismissed as though she knew nothing. 'The reserves have been slowly reducing over the years, without enough adequate income to replenish them. You don't need me to tell you this can't continue. The playhouse will fall into receivership within a year unless further funding can be sourced. Sooner, if we have to return the grant.'

Vivienne looked alarmed.

Tom's frown deepened.

Jodi continued, 'Reducing our expenditure isn't viable. We're already running at baseline, so that only leaves income

183

generation as a means of saving the playhouse.' She waited for the gravity of her words to hit home. 'Which is why Becca and I are actively trying to formulate a plan.'

Tom handed back the paperwork. 'I'm not making any decisions until I read the reserves policy and proposal for the showcase.'

'You'll have them by Monday.' She sat down at her desk, aiming for an 'I'm busy and need to get on with my work' vibe.

Tom took the hint and left.

Vivienne followed him out. 'What showcase event?' she said, unhappy at being kept out of the loop. 'Why wasn't I consulted, Master Thomas?'

Jodi sighed. There'd been no apology for wrongly accusing her of 'skulduggery'. No thanks for the work she was doing to secure the playhouse's finances. Just continued distrust.

Boggin' hell, she hoped all this would be worth it.

Her stomach rumbled. She needed a drink. She also needed to chase Petrit for his timesheet. The café stopped serving food at four – not that she wanted to eat anything made by Petrit, he'd probably sprinkle arsenic over it. But a bag of crisps from the bar would keep her going. Plus, the thought of seeing Leon cheered her a little.

Not that she was interested. Yeah, right.

Leon was behind the bar cleaning glasses in preparation for a busy Saturday night, which for the playhouse meant more than five people at any one time. It was a shame. The setting was great, the beer was good, and the barman was cute as hell...

Stop it, she told her traitorous brain.

Leon came over. 'Hey, there. Having a good day?'

'I've had better.'

His smile faded. 'Petrit or Vivienne?'

Both. 'Nothing I can't handle,' she lied. 'Any chance of a packet of crisps? I'm famished.'

'Sure.' He fetched the basket. 'No lunch today?'

'I ran out of time.' It sounded less pathetic than saying 'some nasty bully binned my sandwich'. 'I'm heading home soon. I'll eat later.'

He didn't look convinced. 'Sea salt and balsamic vinegar?'

'Perfect. Can you add it to my tab?'

'It's on the house.' His smile was back.

God, he had a lovely smile. She mentally kicked herself. *Stop ogling!* 'Thanks, but I'd rather pay. I don't want to give anyone a reason to question my integrity.'

He leant on the bar. 'They wouldn't succeed. You're one of the most hardworking and honest people I know.'

Oh, if only he knew... Thank God he didn't know. She shuddered at the thought.

Thanking him for the crisps, she headed into the kitchen, ready for what she hoped would be her last battle of the day.

Petrit was scraping the dregs of what looked like a tomato sauce from the bottom of a large pan. 'Work finished. I go home,' he said, without looking up.

'I need your replacement timesheet.'

'On side,' he barked, turning so sharply he sprayed her with tomato sauce.

Wet sauce trickled down Jodi's cheek. Her Primark shirt and skirt were splattered with red splodges. Had he done that on purpose? She wasn't sure. Either way, he didn't look particularly apologetic.

She picked up the timesheet. Swallowing back tears, she grabbed a handful of kitchen towels and left.

Leon was serving a customer. He did a double-take when he saw her, looking alarmed until he realised she wasn't covered in blood. His expression darkened. His eyes shifted to the kitchen door and then back to her. 'Are you okay?' he mouthed.

No, she wasn't. But she nodded, faked a smile and headed outside. She couldn't deal with Leon's kindness. It was too much. She felt too exposed.

The gardens provided a refuge. She ducked behind the hedgerow away from prying eyes. The earlier sun had lost its intensity. The breeze had picked up. She wiped tomato sauce from her clothes and face.

She didn't hear Eddie approach, and jumped when he said, 'What happened to you?' His smile faded when he saw she was crying.

The next thing she knew, she was in his arms. 'It was an accident. I'm fine.'

'I don't believe that for a second.' He rubbed her back. 'Another run-in with Petrit?'

186

She pulled away, embarrassed. 'It's nothing, really.'

'Say the word and I'll speak to him, okay? He shouldn't get away with this.' He looked at her with such concern it made her heart pinch.

She suddenly understood why the bullied kids from school hadn't wanted their parents 'telling teacher'. She'd been a tough-nut at school; nobody messed with her. Now look at her. She was a quivering wreck.

Pulling herself together, she accepted Eddie's offer of his handkerchief and dried her eyes. 'Thanks. I'm just tired. It's been a long week.'

'You work too many hours. Go home and have a restful weekend.'

If only. She had a shift at the restaurant tomorrow. But Eddie was right: she'd more than done her hours. Heading home was the sensible course of action. 'Thanks, Eddie. I'll do that... Any luck finding a place to live?'

He scratched his stubbly chin. 'I thought I'd found somewhere, but the landlord didn't seem eager to address the condensation problem. I decided to give it a miss.'

'Where will you stay?'

He shrugged. 'I'll find a B&B somewhere.'

She was struck by an idea. 'There's a spare room at my aunty's guest house. You could always stay with us until you find somewhere permanent. I'm sure it would be okay.'

He seemed to mull it over. 'I wouldn't want to impose.'

'You wouldn't be, and I can vouch for you. You're trustworthy and clean up after yourself.'

He laughed. 'I know who to come to for a reference. Let me have a think about it. Now, why don't you head off.'

'I'll do that.' She gave him an awkward hug. 'Thanks, Eddie.' After the day she'd had, his kindness meant a lot.

She headed inside, leaving Eddie to continue pruning. She'd work on the showcase budget at home. She needed a break from the Starlight Playhouse.

She sensed Leon watching her as she hurried through the bar. She didn't want him to know she'd been crying, so she kept her head down. Thankfully Vivienne was nowhere to be seen and Tom wasn't in the office. She scribbled a note saying she was leaving and picked up her bag. Crikey, it was heavy.

By the time she was on the bus, her feet hurt and her back was aching. A young girl sitting opposite gave her a strange look. She couldn't think why. And then she remembered her bleach-spotted shoes and tomato-splattered clothes. The strange look was justified.

She lifted her bag onto her lap, puzzled by its bulkiness. She unearthed a carrier bag she didn't recognise, and briefly wondered if she should drop the contents into a bucket of water. But there were no explosives inside, only a freshly made egg mayonnaise roll, a mango smoothie and a single wrapped chocolate. Strawberry cream. Her favourite.

She smiled, despite herself.

There was also a book. She read the cover. *The Art of War* by Sun Tzu. Curious, she read the synopsis: *The Art of War is an ancient Chinese work detailing every aspect of warfare, military strategy and tactics.*

And then she spotted the Post-it Note: *Thought this might help.J Don't let the bastards get you down. Leon. x*

Throughout the pages were further Post-it Notes. She turned to the first one. *Success requires winning decisive engagements quickly.* She smiled and flicked to the next one. *How to win confrontations.* Her smile grew wider as she read the next one. *Appear weak when you are strong, and strong when you are weak.* The final one made her laugh. *Know your enemies as well as you know yourself.*

Her chuckling made the girl opposite look over. Her face said 'nutter', but Jodi didn't care, and settled down to read the book.

She was still smiling by the time she arrived at the guest house.

As she came through the front door, she found her aunty on the floor with a scrubbing brush in hand. 'That darn cat,' she said, rubbing at the bloody stain. 'A pigeon, would you believe.'

Jodi dumped her bag on the floor. 'The art of war is to subdue the enemy without fighting, Aunty.'

Aunty Ruby sat back on her haunches. 'And how do you suppose I do that?'

'No idea. I'll let you know when I've finished the chapter.'

189

Jodi nodded to the book in her hand. 'Why are you wearing a hat?'

Her aunty got to her feet and whipped off the hat revealing... *Oh, boggin' hell*...a shock of bright yellow hair. The kind of yellow that clashed with her aunty's pink top.

'Not exactly Helen Mirren, is it?'

'Err...not really.' Jodi had never seen her aunty with anything other than brown hair... And then the penny dropped. 'Is that why you didn't come to the tea dance yesterday?' She hadn't seen her aunty since Thursday night.

Aunty Ruby nodded. 'I couldn't face everyone.' She transferred the mangled pigeon into a rubbish bag. 'Audrey from next door's mother died and they found a hair colour in the old woman's bathroom cabinet and gave it to me.'

Jodi was tempted to ask how the old lady died? Peroxide poisoning?

'Like a fool, I thought I'd try it out.' Her aunty pointed to her mop of yellow waves. 'It's a disaster.'

Jodi searched for a suitable platitude. 'It's not *that* bad.'

'You're a sweet girl, but you can't fib to save your life.' Her aunty removed her rubber gloves. 'My own stupid fault. Why I thought dyeing my hair would make me feel more vibrant, I don't know. I've just succeeded in making myself into a laughing stock.'

Jodi went over. 'No one's laughing at you. I agree the colour is...' she glanced up at her aunty's hair '...not quite the right shade for your skin tone, but—'

Her aunty burst out laughing. 'You can save the tact. I'm aware how dire it looks.'

'Perhaps try a softer blonde. Maybe a honey colour rather than...' Jodi searched for the appropriate description.

'Egg-yolk yellow?'

Jodi laughed.

'I think I'll revert to brown. It's safer that way.' And then she spotted Jodi's stained clothes. 'What happened to you?'

'I was engaged in warfare without a suitable battle plan.'

'Goodness.' Aunty Ruby looked perplexed. 'We'd better put the kettle on then. Hungry? I've been baking.'

Jodi followed her aunty into the kitchen, spotting a tray of teacakes cooling on the countertop. 'Do you want one?'

'Goodness, no.' Her aunty pulled in her tummy. 'Not that anyone would notice my wobbly waistline at the moment. I'm sure I could grow two noses and everyone would still be fixated on my hair. Mrs Busby thought it was a wig and Dr Mortimer thought I'd spilled a tin of paint on my head.'

Jodi sliced a teacake in two. 'They'll get used to it.'

'I certainly won't. Tell me about your day? What happened?'

Jodi sighed. 'Apart from being splattered in tomato sauce, it was like every other day. Tom and Vivienne hovered over me every time I opened the petty cash tin as though they expected me to abscond with the money, and I spent the entire time trying to justify everything I did. It was exhausting.'

'And unfair.' Her aunt debagged the tea. 'Can't they see how hard you're working?'

'Doesn't look that way. Anyway, enough about me. What's happening with you?' She smeared the teacake in butter. 'Becca was disappointed you weren't at the tea dance.'

'I feel bad about that.' Her aunty removed milk from the fridge. 'How did it go?'

'Only Mrs Busby and Dr Mortimer showed up.'

'Oh, no.' Her aunty looked mortified. 'Now I feel terrible. But how could I go looking like this?'

She had a point. 'On the plus side, it was lovely to see Becca dancing again. She and Dr Mortimer did a waltz.'

Her aunty teared up. 'Well, I'm sorry I missed that.' She carried the mugs through to the lounge. 'How did her knee hold up?'

Jodi followed. 'Fine, even when Dr M trod on her foot.'

'Poor Becca. I wish I'd made the effort to go now, yellow hair be damned.' She sank into the floral couch, tiredness enveloping her.

'You don't seem very happy, Aunty. Becca's noticed it too. You say you're okay, but something's wrong. What is it? We might be able to help.'

Her aunty sipped her tea, as if formulating her thoughts. 'Running this place was mine and Derek's dream,' she said, looking around the chintzy lounge, with its open fireplace and mismatched fabrics. 'And I enjoy it...most of the time. But it's hard work, especially doing it by myself. I'm getting older. I tire easily.' She lowered the mug. 'Lately, I've found myself resenting running around after everyone. Some days it feels like I've had enough.'

'Are you thinking of selling?'

Her aunty shrugged. 'I did contemplate it a couple of years ago, but when I broached the subject with Becca she became very emotional, reminding me it was "Daddy's dream". I haven't had the heart to tell her I'm single-handedly running "Daddy's dream" into the ground. Besides, there's Mrs Busby and Dr Mortimer to consider. It seems heartless to make them homeless at their time of life.'

'If selling's not an option, what *do* you want?'

'I don't know.' Her aunty slumped against the floral cushions. 'But I want to do more with my life. Does that sound selfish?'

'Not at all. Does this have something to do with the travel brochure I found in the bin?'

'In a way, yes. I've always wanted to travel.' She sounded wistful.

'Then book a holiday.' Jodi wiped her hands on a tissue, determined to help her aunty. 'Becca and I can look after this place. There's no excuse for you not to go.'

'That's sweet of you, but I can't afford it. Until the guest house repairs are sorted, I don't feel I can justify forking out for a holiday.' She sipped her tea, clearly fighting back disappointment.

And then Jodi remembered her conversation with Eddie. 'I might have a solution to that. A way of bringing in more money, getting the repairs done and going on holiday. How does that sound?'

Her aunty raised a dark eyebrow...a contrast to her mop of yellow hair. 'Like it's too good to be true.' She put her mug down. 'I'm listening.'

Jodi smiled. 'His name is Eddie Moriantez.'

Chapter Sixteen

Wednesday 18th October

Becca moved across the floor testing out the stability of her knee. She was pleased to note it felt solid beneath her. Her right leg was always going to feel different to the left, tighter and less flexible, but there were no outward signs of weakness. She no longer limped, or favoured one side. To anyone watching, she looked balanced. But she wasn't exactly pushing the boundaries. She was choreographing a simple routine, using basic steps that didn't require much exertion. Still, she had to start somewhere.

The lights in the dance studio flickered. She stopped dancing, waiting to see if the power would shut off. They'd had two power cuts already today. The beautiful autumnal weather had finally broken, replaced by the tail end of storm Ophelia sweeping across the country. Rain pelted against the roof. The wind made eerie noises.

The lights flickered again, accompanied by a buzzing sound.

She didn't want to deal with a power cut. Not on her own.

She'd stayed behind after tap class to work on the routine for the showcase. Announcing to her tappers that she wanted them to perform in front of a paying audience had been met with a mixture of responses. Wanda and Miriam had loved the idea of showing off their talents. Cassie and Mi-Sun, not so much.

Nick had been the surprise package, encouraging his wife and assuring her she 'was good enough'. And he was right. Cassie had made the most improvement. Her only issue was a lack of confidence. Nick's pep talk had persuaded the whole group to learn the routine with the option of pulling out if they weren't happy. It was a risky strategy, but Becca hoped to win them over with a fun routine they'd enjoy performing.

Getting the routine to work was the challenge. She had two tall dancers, two short ones and Mi-Sun bridging the gap. Her instinct was to place Cassie and Nick centre-stage. But when she'd lined them up during class, poor Miriam and Wanda had looked like a couple of bookends shoved at either end of the line.

The studio lights dipped again. Loud whirring and buzzing followed.

Becca checked her phone was still in her pocket. She might need it later.

Leon and Eddie had finished for the night. Tom was in court today, and Jodi had a shift at the restaurant. Vivienne and Petrit refused to work extra hours these days, so it was left to her to lock up.

A deep rumble rattled above drowning out One Republic's *Counting Stars*. She'd decided to build on the short routine her tappers had already learnt for the promo video. With less than six weeks to the festival, she figured she needed to keep things simple.

Another clap of thunder boomed above. The noise of drumming rain increased.

And then the lights went out.

Damn it! She crossed her fingers, hoping the electricity would spring back to life. When it didn't, she dug out her phone and switched on the torch function. She opened Eddie's text and read his instructions for dealing with a power cut. The prospect of heading down to the deserted basement of an old stately home in complete darkness, with a storm raging outside, didn't fill her with joy. It terrified her. She felt like one of those victims in a teen horror movie who entered the monster-filled cellar armed only with a torch and dressed in a see-through nightie. It didn't take a genius to work out they were about to be bumped off. Especially when the spooky music built to a crescendo, announcing the arrival of an axe-wielding maniac.

A bang made her jump.

She needed to stop thinking about monsters in the cellar and find the fuse board.

She untied her loose-knit tunic from around her waist and pulled it over her head. The torchlight made her cream top look yellow, which reminded her of her mum's hair. What had her mum been thinking? Becca almost hadn't recognised her. It was yet another indicator that all was not well in Ruby Roberts' world, and that was something that could no longer be ignored.

But that was a problem for another day.

She changed out of her tap shoes, slipped on her gold trainers and left the dance studio. Gingerly, she made her way through reception and under the archway leading to the grand staircase. The playhouse was eerie enough fully lit. In darkness, it was positively daunting. Her phone didn't provide much light. Numerous pairs of disapproving eyes lining the walls watched her as she felt around for the concealed panel in the wall.

The temperature dropped as she stepped into the stairwell. The stone wall was cold to the touch. Narrow steps spiralled downwards. The chill increased the lower she descended. When she reached the bottom, she was distracted by a light moving around. Had Eddie left a torch for her? How was it moving? Oh, God, someone was down here...

And then something touched her leg.

She screamed, recoiling from whatever had touched her.

Torchlight spun around and landed on her. 'Why did you scream?'

It was Tom-the-Tyrant. She might have guessed. What had she said about monsters in the cellar? Although this one was unlikely to attack her with an axe...at least she hoped not.

'Something brushed my leg,' she said, glancing down at the culprit, a roll of hessian matting.

Tom moved towards her. Even in the dim lighting she could see he was wearing a suit. Didn't the man ever relax?

'I assumed you'd met Harold,' he said, ducking under a beam.

'Who's Harold?'

He aimed his torchlight over her shoulder.

If she'd screamed when the matting touched her leg, it was nothing compared to the noise she made when she turned and saw part of a skeleton embedded in the wall.

She jumped backwards. 'Buggering hell! Who...who is that?'

'Don't know, only know him as Harold.' The scarily nonchalant way in which he responded to the question was unnerving, as though he were merely introducing her to a living relative.

'Have you reported it?'

A beat passed before he looked at her. 'Who to?'

'I don't know, the police... *Crimewatch*, or something.'

And then he did something that scared her a lot more than finding a monster in the cellar. He smiled. The tension he normally carried in his face disappeared. His expression morphed from mildly amused to releasing a pair of killer dimples. It had been a while since she'd seen that smile. Twelve years, to be precise.

His grin didn't relent. 'Harold's at least three hundred years old. I don't think they'd be interested.'

'How...how did he get there? In the wall... Do you know?'

Tom reached out and ran his hand over the exposed skull. His long elegant fingers were something else she'd forgotten

199

about. 'We don't know for certain. Burying people in walls was a common enough punishment, even for the Wentworths. But it was most likely one of the workmen involved in the renovation of the place. Although how he managed to cement himself into the partition, we have no idea.'

A clap of thunder made her jump.

Tom seemed to find her nervous state amusing. 'Why are you here so late?'

She edged away from the skeleton. Whatever the reason, it wasn't normal to have a corpse residing in the wall of your home. 'I've been working on the tap routine for the showcase.'

'Which hasn't been agreed yet.'

'The good news is that my tappers have agreed to take part.'

'Nothing has been agreed—'

'That just leaves my ballet class. But I'm confident they'll want to perform.'

'Are you listening to me?' He shone the torch at her. 'I said, nothing has been agreed. You shouldn't be talking to your students about this.' His smile had vanished. He was back to being grumpy. Good. It was safer that way.

'The festival's in six weeks' time,' she said, shielding her eyes from the light. 'We can't afford to wait.'

'We can't *afford* the expenditure.'

God, he was infuriating. She shone her phone into his eyes. See how he liked it. 'Have you looked at Jodi's proposal?'

'Yes.'

'And do you agree it's modest, it's thorough, and strikes the right balance between being prudent and putting on a decent event?'

'That's not the issue.'

'Of course it is.' She moved away from his torchlight, trying to avoid touching anything. It wasn't easy; there was stuff everywhere. 'We need to raise community awareness and give people a reason to visit the Starlight Playhouse. The way I see it, we either spend a lot of time and energy trying to publicise the playhouse over a long period, which may not result in an increase in users and risks losing the council funding...or we take a punt and throw everything at one big event.'

The ceiling creaked as the wind shook the rafters. Not a good development.

'It might not work, but at least then we'll know. The success of the showcase will give us a measure of what works and what doesn't in terms of fundraising.'

He shook his head. 'It's a risk.'

'Yeah, but the odds are stacked in our favour. Think about it. There are posters everywhere. The arts festival is being advertised on local radio, in the newspapers, even on the side of buses. Social media posts are already trending. Most of the work's being done for us. We'd be crazy not to take part. It makes good business sense.'

He rubbed his forehead. 'I'm not comfortable putting the playhouse at risk without consulting my mother. I tried

201

contacting her at the rehab centre to discuss it, but the manager refused to put my call through.' He sounded miserable.

Becca tried to imagine how she'd feel if it was her mum in rehab. Pretty terrible. But that's why they needed to do this. Carolyn wasn't able to turn things around herself, either physically or emotionally; they had to take action on her behalf. 'If Carolyn was here now, what do you think she'd say?'

'I have no idea. And that's the problem.' Frustrated, he stepped back, tripped over a travel case and disappeared. There was a thud, followed by a series of expletives. His torch bounced off something and it was suddenly very dark.

A beat passed. 'Tom, are you okay? Are you hurt?'

'I'm fine.' He didn't sound fine.

Where was he? She aimed her feeble light in his direction, but couldn't see him. She climbed over the travel cases, careful not to drop her phone. She found him lying on his back, wedged between two large trunks. 'What are you doing down there?'

He glared up at her. 'Funny.'

It was. Since the moment he'd arrived in Brighton, he'd been assertive, controlled and a pain in the arse. Her initial dislike might have softened, but that didn't mean seeing him in a compromising position wasn't hugely enjoyable. 'Are you trapped?'

He shielded his eyes from the glare of her phone. 'No need to sound so happy about it.'

She stifled a laugh. 'Just to clarify – you can't move or get up? And you need me to assist you. Is that right?'

He sighed. 'Why do I get the impression you're about to leave me here?'

'As if I'd do something so cruel. I have every intention of helping you.'

'Thank you.'

'As soon as you agree to the showcase.'

He stilled. 'You're blackmailing me?'

'God, yes.' She was enjoying watching him on the back foot for once.

He tried rolling onto his front and failed. He tried again, conceded defeat and swore...and swore again.

She watched him struggle, amused by his efforts. 'Anytime you need a hand, just say the word. I'm right here waiting.'

He surprised her by laughing. 'I'd forgotten how manipulative you could be.'

'I prefer to call it persuasive.'

'Either way, you had a habit of leading me astray.'

His comment stung. There'd been no accusation in his voice. He was teasing her, she knew that. But her mind had inevitably jumped back to the painful conclusion of their relationship.

She batted the sadness away, remembering the other version of Tom who used to meet her after school and walk her to dance class, wait outside for her to finish, and then walk her home afterwards.

'I don't recall you putting up much resistance.' She kept her tone light. Now wasn't the time or place to start rehashing

203

mistakes of the past. They had enough angst to deal with without fighting over events from twelve years earlier.

He pushed against the trunk pinning him to the floor. It didn't budge. 'Are you going to help me up?'

'Are you going to approve the showcase?'

He growled. 'Fine.'

'Fine?'

'I approve expenditure for the showcase.'

'Good. I also need you to stop giving Jodi a hard time. Give her a break, will you?'

He didn't immediately answer.

Becca adjusted the angle of the light. He was frowning. His hair was a mess and he was grinding his jaw. 'Come on, Tom. She's working her socks off. You have to see how much she's changed?'

He sighed. 'Okay, from now on I'll do my best to trust her.'

'Said with such sincerity.'

'Don't push it. I've agreed, haven't I? Now, will you please help me up?' He elbowed the side of the trunk. '*Ouch.*'

She wasn't done. 'One last request.'

He swore again. 'These are not requests. They're demands being agreed to under duress.'

'And being recorded.'

That shut him up. *Ha!* Not so clever now, was he.

'Not a smart move, Becca.'

'I think it's very smart.' She failed to hide the gloat in her voice. 'I'm not having you retract your consent at a later date.'

204

'I meant using your torchlight and video function at the same time. How much battery life do you have left?'

Oh. He had a point. She needed to hurry up. 'My last request is that we agree to stop battling over every decision and work together with Jodi to run the playhouse in your mother's absence. We might not always agree, but we need to stop butting heads. Whether you want to admit it or not, you need us.'

She could tell he was fighting the urge to tell her where to stick it. Tough. He didn't think twice about taking advantage of a situation, why should she?

She tried again. 'Agreed?'

'Agreed.'

Could he sound any sulkier?

'Thank you.' She was glad...relieved too. He was starting to wheeze and she hadn't wanted to leave him lying there any longer.

She tried moving one of the trunks, but it was too heavy. She shoved the other one, but that wouldn't shift either. A plan was needed.

'Careful with your knee,' he said.

Like she needed reminding.

'Make yourself useful and hold the torch,' she said, handing him her phone. She climbed over the trunk and moved the smaller cases out of the way. 'How did you know about my knee?'

He aimed the light in her direction. 'My mother told me. How did you injure it?'

She picked up a case. 'I tripped over a goat.'

His sudden laughter caught her off-guard. 'Is that a dance move or a euphemism?'

'Neither.' She shoved the cases onto a shelf. 'I was working at London Zoo. One of my tasks was to clean out the goats' enclosure. When a little blighter started peeing on my boot I jumped backwards, not realising another goat was behind me and I fell over him.'

'Sounds painful.'

'It was.' She'd made enough space to access the back of the trunks. 'I needed surgery to reattach my patellar tendon and spent eight weeks on crutches, followed by eight weeks of intensive therapy.' She sat down, shying away from the cobwebs catching in her ponytail. 'I've only recently started dancing again.'

'Why were you working at London Zoo?'

She tucked her feet under the shelving and pushed against the wall. 'Let's just say, my career never quite hit the dizzying heights I'd hoped for.'

'I'm sorry to hear that. But there's still time, you're only twenty-eight.'

She pushed hard, using her quads. 'Unfortunately not, it's game over. Professionally, anyway.' The trunk shifted a fraction.

'I thought recovery from tendon surgery was achievable these days?'

'It is, but I ruptured my Achilles a few years back, so I was already compromised.' She pushed again. The trunk shifted a bit further.

'Another goat?'

She laughed. 'Nope, dancing this time. I landed badly. I thought I'd been shot, it made such a bang.' She adjusted her position and pushed again. The trunk moved another few inches. 'It took me two years to recover and I only regained around eighty per cent of my ability. So when the second injury occurred eighteen months later, the surgeon warned me my career was probably over.' The trunk finally shifted.

'I'm sorry, Becca. I didn't realise.'

'Such is life. Some dreams we have to let go of.' She got up, brushing dirt and cobwebs from her clothes. It hurt a lot more than she was letting on. They'd agreed a fragile truce. She wasn't about to divulge all her weaknesses. He had enough power as it was. 'Anyway, enough about me. What's it like being a barrister?'

He squeezed himself out from between the trunks. 'It has its moments. It's not how I imagined it would be.' Even lit by the feeble torchlight, she could see he was filthy. His suit jacket was covered in dust and there was a tear in his trousers. He ran his hand through his hair, creating another flashback from their youth.

She pictured them sitting in his bedroom, legs entwined, holding hands and watching his mum's old portable TV. 'Do you remember we used to watch *Kavanagh QC*?' she said, resisting the urge to brush cobwebs from his jacket. Touching him wouldn't be a good idea. 'You wanted to be like John Thaw. The gruff barrister who always won his cases.'

Tom climbed over the trunks, using her shoulder to lean on. So much for not touching. 'Yeah, but that's only because he was never expected to defend an idiot who'd beaten his former business partner around the head with a child's scooter.'

His disgruntled expression made her laugh. 'Are you serious? That was your case today?'

'It was.' He shone the light against the wall. 'Now, where's the fuse board?'

'In the cupboard on the left-hand wall.' She squinted, trying to find it in the darkness. 'Eddie left me instructions.' She eased her way over to the wall. It was cold and sticky. Not the most pleasant of tasks. 'Was the man found guilty?'

'Yes.' Tom's hand brushed hers as they searched for the cupboard. 'Here it is.'

The cupboard housed an array of jumbled cables. 'There should be a master switch next to the fuse box.' She took the phone from him. 'You flick the switch and I'll hold the light. I don't want to get electrocuted.'

He gave her a loaded look. 'But you don't mind if I do?'

'It's your house.'

'Fair enough.'

Ignoring his almost-smile, she aimed the light in the cupboard. Her phone started to dim. 'How do you defend someone you know is guilty?'

He lifted the cables and looked underneath. 'It's not my

job to decide if someone's guilty or innocent. I only do what the client tells me to. And if they tell me they didn't mean to knock someone out with a plastic scooter and they were trying to disperse a swarm of attacking bees, then that's the defence I present to the jury. Even if it's a load of crap.'

'Over there.' She spotted the fuse box. 'The switch should be next to it.' She pointed to the lever. 'Innocent until proven guilty, eh?'

'Exactly. And if my client tells me they're not guilty, I have to take them at their word. Even if the evidence against them is strong and things will be far worse for them if the case goes to trial. What I think is irrelevant. It's up to others to decide about guilt or innocence.' He pulled the lever. There was a delay before faint light filtered through from the stairwell. 'Bingo.'

She turned away. She didn't want him to see the tears threatening to escape.

It was those 'others' who'd decided her guilt back in 2006. And what hurt the most…was that he'd believed them.

Chapter Seventeen

Friday 20th October

Tom wasn't having the best of days. He'd spent most of the morning enduring a wet and miserable four-hour drive to Lincoln to take part in a prison adjudication, where he'd had to undergo a full body search, including an x-ray and a springer spaniel sniffing around his crotch. He'd then been escorted across the miserable yard area in the pouring rain and through several locked gates before arriving at C wing, where he'd met his client who'd got into a fight with another prisoner in the canteen. Tom was required to defend him in front of a district judge. If found guilty, he'd receive an extra forty-five days in prison.

It wasn't the most exciting way to spend a day, and for very little financial reward. It didn't help that he was still preoccupied with the events of yesterday.

Izzy couldn't seem to grasp that she was no longer the legal owner of their apartment and was required by law to move out. When he'd arrived at the flat, he'd found her still asleep with no removal van booked and showing no signs of leaving.

She was smart enough to realise he was there to 'kick her out' and had resorted to trying to seduce him, inviting him to join her in bed. When that failed, she'd switched to crying, reminding him she had nowhere else to go.

He'd resisted caving in and continued packing up her things. This had resulted in her yelling abuse while he'd loaded her belongings into his car, and continuing to yell as he'd deposited her at a Travelodge. He'd tried to assuage his guilt by paying for a week's stay – which had cost him more than he'd earnt today in representation fees. Such was life.

His day had deteriorated further when he'd received a call from an unknown number. Assuming it was Izzy calling from the Travelodge, his resignation had been replaced by annoyance when his father's voice had come on the line. His mother had given Harvey his number. Thanks, Mum.

The conversation started out in its usual stilted fashion. His father reiterated his desire to be in his son's life, and Tom refused to forgive and forget. The subject had then switched to his mother and her stint in rehab.

Tom's annoyance had increased when his father had 'expressed concern' over Tom's involvement in the running of the playhouse and whether this 'distraction' would be detrimental to his son's career. Tom wasn't sure what had angered him most. His father's interference, or the man's willingness to see his ex-wife's business fail while she sought help for her addiction. His father's counter-argument had been to point out that Carolyn had appointed two deputies to run the playhouse in her absence and Tom's presence had never been requested or needed. Like his dad had ever cared about his mum! Flaming hypocrite.

Tom was just glad his father had no idea who the deputies were. Otherwise, all hell would break loose. He'd ended the call at that point. He'd been in danger of crashing his car and it was already damaged where he'd run into a recycling bin thanks to Becca chucking paint at him.

An image of Becca covered in paint briefly eased the tightness in his chest as he endured an equally miserable four-hour journey back to Brighton. He'd forgotten to pick up his inhaler this morning and the need for relief had been building all day. There used to be a time in his life when he would have been okay surviving for a day without drugs. Now it seemed he couldn't go twenty minutes without artificial stimulants.

Why he kept thinking about Becca, he had no idea. He supposed it was the realisation that her intentions regarding the playhouse came from a genuine desire to save the place. He'd been too hard on her.

But she'd inflicted her revenge, refusing to help him when he'd got stuck between two travel trunks on Wednesday night. It should have annoyed him. Instead, it had demonstrated her determination not to let his mother down. And that had endeared her to him – much as he hated to admit it. Over the past two weeks, he'd been reminded of the girl he'd fallen in love with. Becca Roberts was funny, energetic, clumsy and cute. Her endless playfulness was both an irritation and strangely infectious.

He'd agreed to the showcase, not only because it was a great idea, but he was also confident that along with Jodi, she could make it work. What he hadn't vocalised was his concern about his mother's ability to cope. If the playhouse became more successful with more hirers and users, would that put extra pressure on her? She'd be fragile when she left rehab and she'd need a stress-free environment, not additional responsibility.

But he hadn't felt ready to share his concerns with Becca. He might have moved past wanting to throttle her, but trusting her with his worries and insecurities wasn't something he was ready to risk. Being betrayed once was enough.

He pulled into the playhouse car park, relieved to be home. The tickling sensation in his chest was a warning sign. He planned to shower, drink beer and eat curry. But first, he needed his inhaler.

His plan to head upstairs and change out of his damp suit was scuppered when he heard raised voices coming from the office. Would his conscience allow him to ignore it? Probably not. Sighing, he marched across the foyer.

On reaching the office, his hand stilled on the handle. He could hear Vivienne shouting. He couldn't make out what she was saying, but she didn't sound happy. Taking a ragged breath, he opened the door and discovered Vivienne almost levitating over Jodi.

Under such an onslaught, Jodi might have appeared the underdog, but anyone who thought Jodi would be intimidated by the older woman's ferocity would soon learn otherwise. She had her hands on her hips, refusing to back down.

He cleared his throat. 'Is there a problem...?'

The sound of his voice momentarily broke the locking of horns. A beat followed before they advanced on him, both screaming words of accusation, both intent on relaying their version of events first.

He raised his hand, a feeble attempt to still them. When it didn't work, he took an involuntary step back. 'Will you both quit shouting?' They paused, not quite content to shut up, but enough so he could intervene. 'One at a time.' He looked at Vivienne. 'What's the problem?'

'*She* is the problem. I caught her stealing.'

'You did no such thing!' Jodi looked close to tears.

'Quiet. Both of you.' God, his chest hurt. 'Accusing someone of stealing is a serious matter.'

Vivienne recoiled. 'Are you accusing me of lying, Master Thomas?'

'I didn't say that—'

'But you immediately doubt my word.' Vivienne looked affronted. 'Of all the hurtful, insulting—'

'Just tell me what happened, Vivienne.' Christ, she could be dramatic.

'I walked into the office to find *that* woman...' Jodi was

subjected to one of Vivienne's glares '…with her hands in the safe.' She folded her arms, no doubt for dramatic effect. 'And now the money has disappeared. It doesn't take a genius to work out who took it.'

A rush of cold hit Tom in the chest. His breathing tightened even further. 'The money for the showcase?'

'All five thousand pounds. I came in here and there she was, her grubby little hands in the safe. She can't deny it. Jumped away like a scalded cat. Guilt written all over her thieving face. She knew she'd been caught—'

'Enough!' Tom turned to Jodi. He didn't think for a second she'd stolen the money. Why, he wasn't sure. She had a history of lying and theft. But Becca was right: Jodi had changed. She also wasn't stupid. He'd only withdrawn the money yesterday. Only a real idiot would take it so soon. 'I'm assuming there's an explanation?' She'd probably moved the money, like with the bank accounts. 'Where's the money?'

Her face radiated hurt. 'You think I took it?'

He felt himself frown. 'You mean, you didn't?'

'No, of course I bloody well didn't.'

'Then where is it?' Air seemed to be stuck in his chest. He was struggling to exhale.

'I don't know. When I came into the office and went to put the cheque book back in the safe, I realised the bank bag was missing. That's when Vivienne came in.'

Vivienne pointed a finger at Jodi. 'I caught you red-handed.'

'Then where's the money?' Jodi opened her arms. 'I haven't

left the office, so if I took it I'd have it, wouldn't I? Search me. Look in my bag. You won't find anything.'

'Who's to say you didn't take it earlier? Maybe you were covering your tracks. You've probably stashed it somewhere.' The black of Vivienne's floaty dress blurred Tom's vision. 'Shall I call the police, Master Thomas?'

Jodi looked stricken. 'Please don't do that.'

'You see? Guilty.' Vivienne was judge, jury and accuser all rolled into one. He was surprised she didn't fist-bump the air.

Jodi started to cry. 'I didn't take the money, I swear.'

Tom sagged against the door. He needed to lean on something.

'Then why shouldn't we call the police? Surely you want the culprit caught?' Vivienne's tone had switched to sarcastic. 'If you've nothing to hide, you needn't be worried.'

Tom knew exactly why Jodi didn't want the police involved. She had a criminal record. She'd been jailed for theft. They were hardly going to believe her word over Vivienne's.

Jodi shook her head. 'Please, Tom. I didn't take the money. I need you to believe me.'

And he needed his inhaler.

'Go home, the pair of you.' He turned to leave. 'I'll deal with this tomorrow.'

'But Master Thomas...?'

'Go home, Vivienne.'

He hadn't meant to snap, but walking had become difficult.

216

Hell, breathing had become difficult. His vision had blurred. His chest felt tighter with every step.

How he made it up the staircase, he didn't know. He gripped the banister, using all his strength to pull himself up. He was wheezing badly. His whole chest rattled. It was so loud it felt like it was coming from outside his body.

The faces of his ancestors on the walls seemed to be scolding him. Their stern expressions loomed down on him as he climbed the stairs. He barely made it to the top before the coughing began. It was official – he was having an asthma attack. Drugs awaited. Relief in the form of Ventolin. He just needed to get upstairs.

The galley corridor felt longer than usual. He staggered diagonally, pushing himself from one wall to another, unable to support his own body weight. He knocked over a chair, dislodging a painting on the wall. He could barely breathe. He was sweating. Shivering. Drowning.

He reached the stairwell for the east tower. One last push.

Every step slowed. Every step required more effort. Was he going to make it? He was near the top. The coughing became worse, rendering him unable to move. He was within a few feet of the table. His inhaler was just out of arm's reach.

Black spots appeared before his eyes. He slumped to the ground. Pain stabbed at his chest. The pressure building in his lungs pinned him to the floor.

He hadn't made it.

And then a cool hand touched his forehead. 'Tom...? Can you hear me?'

Was he hallucinating?

'Sit up,' the voice instructed. 'Use your inhaler.' Fingers helped him insert the inhaler into his mouth. 'Breathe,' the voice said. 'And again.' Another shot of Ventolin hit the back of his throat.

The pain gripping his chest eased.

'Relax,' the voice said. 'Lower your shoulders.' Hands rubbed his arms. Fingers kneaded the tight muscles along his shoulders, soothing and gentle.

Gradually the fog cleared. Light returned and the room drifted into focus.

Becca was in front of him on her knees. She checked her watch and then put his inhaler in his mouth. 'Again,' she said, pressing the button. 'Breathe in.' She was timing the gaps between puffs. How had she remembered that?

Trying to relax when you couldn't breathe wasn't easy. A lack of air induced panic. And panicking wasn't conducive to overcoming an attack. Tensing up exacerbated the difficulties of trying to draw in air or to exhale.

She checked her watch and gave him another puff of Ventolin. 'Slow deep breaths,' she said. 'That's it. You're doing really well.' Her smile was reassuring. 'Squeeze my hand if you can hear me?'

Her fingers closed around his and he gently squeezed them. She was crouched next to him, holding him steady. She smelt of strawberries. Her top was blue. Her lips were painted red.

As his focus returned, he realised he was in his bedroom,

slumped against the wall by the stairwell. He wondered how she felt about being up here? The room hadn't changed since she'd last been here. Stacks of vinyl records sat on the floor. A single bed was pushed against the wall under the slanted ceiling. A poster of The Clash still clung to the wall, curled at the edges, faded and torn.

She placed the inhaler in his mouth. 'And again.'

He sucked in another shot of Ventolin. His heart was racing, accelerated by the drug, but the pain in his chest was easing.

'Lean forward,' she said, easing him out of his suit jacket. She removed his tie and unbuttoned his shirt. She got up and walked across the room, pausing as if getting her bearings. Her hair was in a messy braid, the ends blue. Her tights were brightly patterned. She looked the same as she always had. Quirky, youthful, beautiful. She headed over to the chest of drawers and removed a hoodie. Bringing it over, she guided it over his arms and zipped it up. He hadn't realised he'd been shaking.

Another voice called up the stairs. 'Becca?'

He recognised Jodi's voice.

Becca went over to the stairwell.

'How's he doing?' he heard Jodi say.

'He's over the worst. Did you get hold of the doctor?'

'He's on his way. He said we should call for the paramedics if his inhaler doesn't work.'

'It seems to be easing things,' Becca said. 'But I'll keep an eye on it.'

'The doctor said a warm drink might help relax his airways.

I made tea. I'll wait downstairs and bring the doctor up when he arrives.'

'Thanks, Jodi... You okay?'

Tom didn't hear her reply. They'd both lowered their voices. He might not be able to hear what they were saying...but he could guess. Vivienne had accused Jodi of stealing. The money he'd withdrawn from the bank for the showcase had disappeared. It was a catastrophe.

Vivienne had wanted to call the police. But if the safe door had been left open, it could have been anyone. A chancer. A burglar who'd cased the joint. But if the door was closed, then it could only be one of four people. Him. His mother. Vivienne or Jodi. The only people with the combination. And that's why he hadn't reacted. He needed to get his head around the situation. Ask a few more questions before making any accusations. But first, he needed to breathe.

Becca reappeared holding a mug. She sat down next to him and handed him his inhaler. He administered it himself this time. Progress.

She rubbed his shoulder. 'You're still too tense. Drop your shoulders.'

He followed her instructions, amazed that she'd remembered how to handle an asthma attack. It'd happened a few times when they'd been together. Usually after a night dealing with his mother. She'd been the same then, caring and in control, even if she'd later admitted she'd been scared. Thank God she was here.

'Drink some tea,' she said, lifting the mug to his lips. 'The doctor's on his way.'

The warm liquid was soothing and welcome.

His chest felt like an elephant was standing on it, but his airways were loosening. He drank another few mouthfuls. 'Thank you,' he said, his voice croaky.

'It's Jodi you need to thank.' She lowered the mug. 'She's the one who came and got me and said you needed help.'

'That was good of her.'

'I think so.'

Especially as you'd just accused her of stealing.

She didn't say the words. She didn't have to.

The accusation hung in the air...right next to his guilt.

Chapter Eighteen

Sunday 22nd October

Jodi finished reconciling her aunty's accounts and shut down the computer. It had taken most of yesterday and a couple of hours this morning, but it was done now. She hadn't minded, she'd been glad of the distraction. Plus, it helped her aunty. The guest house finances were relatively straightforward compared to the Starlight Playhouse. But as to whether she'd be working at the playhouse anymore, she didn't know.

She got up from the desk and went over to the bay window. On a clear day, the view was like a picture postcard. Not today. The storm had subsided, but it was still grim outside. The sea looked foreboding, grey and dull. People were huddled under the sheltered seating on the promenade, their disposable ponchos flapping in the wind.

She was glad to be in the warm, wearing her slipper socks and fleece onesie. Hardly the height of fashion. She didn't care. She needed comfort today.

She hadn't heard from Tom since Friday's incident. In truth, she hadn't wanted to. He'd been in no fit state following his asthma attack, and she'd stayed away from the playhouse yesterday, figuring they both needed space. Maybe it was cowardly, but she couldn't face everyone. Part of her wanted to fight this latest accusation, stand up for herself and prove that she wasn't a thief. The other part of her wanted to crawl into bed and never face anyone again. Especially Leon. What must he think? Did he even know what had happened?

Only a couple of hours before Vivienne's accusation, she'd been floating on cloud nine having gone with Leon to the wholesalers to place an order for the showcase. They'd stopped off at The Lion & Lobster for lunch, and away from the playhouse the atmosphere between them had felt different. Like they could relax. They'd chatted about life in Brighton, his passion for writing songs, and her secret obsession with *Love Island*. He'd teased her, but had given himself away as a fan when he'd mentioned one of the contestant's names. Joking with him had been hugely enjoyable.

The conversation had moved on and they'd shared stories from their childhood. He'd admitted to hating school, which had allowed her to admit she'd struggled as a teenager too. She hadn't divulged much, certainly nothing about her criminal activity. But it was the first time she'd been semi-honest with a guy and she hadn't felt judged.

When she'd arrived back at the playhouse, she'd relived the conversations in her head. And then Vivienne had burst into the office and accused her of stealing and her good mood had shattered into a thousand pieces.

She climbed onto the padded window seat and tucked her feet under her, cuddling a cushion to her chest. Droplets of rain ran down the window, each one chasing the next.

She hadn't taken the money. But being innocent until proven guilty only applied if you didn't have a criminal record. Once you'd crossed that line, you were never above suspicion again. There was always a question mark hanging over you. If Tom decided to call the police, news of her conviction was bound to get out. She'd be questioned. Possibly arrested. Maybe even charged. And there was no way she was going back to prison.

Most people assumed prison was a dangerous place where gang violence reigned and hardened criminals controlled the system, like in *Orange is the New Black*. But for her, prison had been... How could she describe it? Humiliating. Degrading. Inhumane.

It was the small stuff she'd struggled with. Guards walking into her cell when she was on the toilet. Never being allowed to shower alone. Being supervised whilst drying her hair in case she held the dryer under the taps and electrocuted herself – as one inmate had done.

One time, a pair of scissors had disappeared from the craft room and the whole prison had to be shut down until the implement was found. As she was the last prisoner to leave the craft room that day, she was prime suspect. She'd been body-searched, questioned and disbelieved when she'd denied taking the scissors. A thorough search of her cell had followed with her few personal belongings being tossed to the floor.

The incident ended when the art teacher realised she'd miscounted and all the scissors were accounted for. There'd been no apology. No help to tidy her cell. As far as they were concerned, she was the only person who could have taken the scissors and therefore she was guilty by default.

And now it was happening again.

Her aunty backed into the study dragging the hoover. 'How are you getting on, love?'

'I've just finished.'

'Oh, bless you.' Her aunty stretched out her back. 'Give me a complex sewing pattern and I'm fine, but put me in front of a spreadsheet and I break out in hives.' Her smile was sunny...like her hair. 'Not looking any better, is it?' she said, noticing her niece's upward glance.

Jodi smiled. 'It's not that bad.'

'Fibber. But if my ridiculous hair makes you smile, it's a sacrifice I'm willing to make. How are you feeling today?'

She shrugged. 'I don't know. Flat, I guess. Ashamed.'

Her aunty frowned. 'What have you got to be ashamed about? You didn't take the money.'

'No one believes that.'

'I believe it.' Her aunty came over. 'You didn't take that money.'

'Vivienne thinks I did. Tom thinks so too.'

Whose side would Leon take? she wondered. There was nothing in *The Art of War* about dealing with injustice.

Her aunty tutted. 'Tom Elliot is too judgemental for his

own good. This isn't the first time he's jumped to the wrong conclusion.'

'Last time wasn't really his fault. He was put in a horrible situation.'

'Nonetheless, he should've allowed Becca the opportunity to explain, instead of letting that opinionated father of his influence him. And anyway, why are you defending him? He hasn't exactly been supportive of your efforts at the playhouse.'

Jodi hugged the cushion closer. 'I don't know. He looked conflicted on Friday, as if he didn't want to believe I'd taken the money.'

'Then he should've said as much, instead of letting that awful woman accuse you. I've a good mind to go up there and set them both straight.'

'Please don't. It'll only make things worse.'

'Fair enough,' her aunty said plumping up a cushion. 'But if things escalate, they'll have me to deal with. The woman with the yellow hair on the rampage.' She kissed Jodi's cheek, making her laugh.

Becca's head appeared around the door. 'Ah, here you are. I've just got off the phone with Tom.' She came into the room, looking stylish in her ripped jeans and leather jacket.

Quite a contrast to Jodi's snuggle-wear. 'How is he?'

'Better. He's been on bed rest and his breathing's much better. He asked me to thank you for what you did Friday night.'

'I should think so to.' Her aunty glanced from Becca's trendy outfit to her own baggy 'cleaning clothes' as she called them. Her expression indicated she felt as frumpy as Jodi did.

Becca dumped her leather bag on the floor. 'Leon's at the playhouse on his own today. I said I'd go in and help so Tom can rest up.'

The mention of Leon made Jodi cringe. Did he think she was guilty?

Her aunty shook out a duster. 'I don't know why you're putting yourself out for that man.'

Becca checked her phone. 'I'm not doing it for Tom, I'm doing it for Jodi and Carolyn. Me too. I need the win. My self-esteem can't take another failed career, even a temporary one.'

'Did Tom say anything about the money?' Although Jodi wasn't sure she wanted to know the answer.

'Not much. I told him you didn't take it. He doesn't think you did either.' Becca smiled encouragingly. 'So that's something.'

'Then why didn't he say that at the time?' Aunty Ruby said wiping the desk. 'Why did he let that dreadful woman accuse Jodi?'

Becca shrugged. 'He said he didn't want to make any snap judgements, or inflame the situation until he'd had a chance to investigate.'

'Shame he didn't take that attitude twelve years ago.'

Becca flinched.

Jodi felt a change of topic was needed. 'What about the

showcase? He wasn't keen before the theft. I can't imagine he'll allow it to go ahead now.'

Becca pulled out a flyer from her bag. 'I told him it was happening. No debate. The playhouse has already been added to the programme. See…?' She handed the flyer to Jodi. 'Tickets are selling fast and all the advertising is underway. If we pull out now it'll be a reputational disaster. The showcase has to go ahead.'

'But we have no money.' Why was she using the word 'we'? Jodi was no longer part of the team.

'We'll have to improvise. It's not ideal, but it's not impossible.'

Jodi studied the leaflet. 'What about the roof repairs?'

Becca looked ponderous. 'That's the sticking point. I'm not sure what our options are. I'll have a chat to Eddie about it. When's he arriving?'

'Sometime today.'

Okay, I'll talk to him later.' Becca went over to Aunty Ruby. 'Are you excited about having a new guest, Mummykins?'

Becca was subjected to a look. 'Ecstatic.'

'Sarcasm is the lowest form of wit, Mother dear.' Becca tickled her ribs. 'Isn't that what you used to tell us?'

'Yes, but it's do as I say, not as I do.' She tried to escape her daughter's tickling. 'Stop that.'

Becca stopped tormenting her mum. 'See you later.' She came over and hugged Jodi. 'Stay strong. We have your back, okay? Tom says he'll speak to you tomorrow.'

Jodi startled. 'He wants me in work?'

'Of course he does.' Becca picked up her bag. 'The showcase isn't happening without you.'

'What did you do, beat him into submission?'

Becca grinned. 'It was a joint decision. The truth will always out.'

That was what worried her.

When the front door slammed, her aunty turned to her. 'How's she coping seeing Tom again? She hasn't said much.'

Jodi shrugged. 'They fight. They disagree.'

Her aunty frowned. 'Why do I sense a *but* coming?'

'The energy between them is palpable. They're like magnets. Drawn to each other, even when they're fighting.' She wondered if Becca had noticed. 'I'm not sure how it'll end up, but there's unresolved chemistry that's for sure.'

'Just what every mother doesn't want to hear.' Aunty Ruby switched on the hoover.

Jodi let the noise of the vacuum wash over her.

It was strange watching Becca and Tom together after so long apart. The friction between them had definitely shifted, but the tension remained. Would they ever bury the hatchet and become friends again? It was a tall order.

And would she ever stop feeling responsible for their split? Unlikely.

Maude appeared in the study carrying a dead bird. At least, Jodi hoped it was dead.

Her aunty let out a cry of annoyance and flicked off the

hoover. 'Not on my clean floor!' Maude dropped the carcass by her feet, turned tail and sauntered out. 'That's right, leave me to clear it up.' She bent down and scooped it up with a plastic bag, just as the front doorbell chimed. 'If Dr Mortimer's forgotten his flaming key again, I'll wring his neck.'

Only it wasn't Dr Mortimer at the door. It was Eddie.

Judging by the look on her aunty's face, it might as well have been Charles Bronson standing there, looking like he'd just stepped off the set of *The Dirty Dozen*. Her scowl fell away and her jaw went slack.

Eddie leant against the doorframe, his roguish brown eyes twinkling. 'I hear you have a room available?'

Jodi hid behind the study door, intrigued by the sight of her dumbstruck aunty.

'You want to stay *here*?' Aunty Ruby stared at him. 'Are you sure?'

He laughed. 'Great sales pitch.'

Her aunty's blush clashed with her hair. 'I'm so sorry. Of course, please come in. Mind the step.' She stepped back into the hallway. 'Do you have any luggage?'

'In the car.' He held out his hand. 'Eddie Moriantez.'

Her aunty extended her hand and then realised she was still holding the dead bird. 'Oh, God!' Her blush was replaced by a look of pure horror.

Eddie turned his hand over, palm up. 'Let me dispose of that for you.'

'Oh...thank you.'

230

He tipped the bagged bird into his hands.

'It was my cat,' her aunty said, as he headed towards the door, clearly feeling an explanation was needed.

He glanced back. 'Well, I'd hoped it wasn't you.'

As he disappeared through the front door, her aunty started fanning her face. 'You could've warned me,' she said, running over to check herself in the hall mirror.

'Warned you about what?' Jodi came into the hallway.

'Why is it men improve with age, while woman simply... wilt,' she said, raking her hands through her yellow hair. 'Him upstairs has one sick sense of humour. I look like a complete fright. And I haven't even changed out of these awful jogging bottoms.' She pointed to the saggy knees. 'How embarrassing.'

Eddie returned minus the bird, now with a suitcase in tow.

Her aunty jumped away from the mirror.

Eddie pretended he hadn't noticed, and then spotted Jodi. 'Hey, there, kiddo.'

'Hi, Eddie. You found us okay, then?' If she wasn't mistaken, her aunty was being checked out. Jodi hadn't seen that coming.

Flustered, her aunty grabbed a key from a hook behind the counter. 'Can I take that for you?' She nodded to the suitcase by his feet.

He picked up the case. 'Thank you, I can manage.' He turned to Jodi and handed her a folded piece of paper. 'From Leon,' he said, squeezing her hand.

She unfolded the note, recognising Leon's looping

handwriting. *Chapter thirteen – Using Spies. All wars are, at their heart, information wars.*

Puzzled, she glanced up.

Eddie winked at her. She wondered if he knew what had happened on Friday. But then, maybe it was better not to mention it. She didn't want to embarrass the man.

She pocketed the note, resolving to revisit chapter thirteen as soon as possible.

Mrs Busby appeared from the breakfast room. She stopped when she saw them. Despite being eighty-something the woman was extremely astute. Not much got past her, which was a trifle awkward when you lived under the same roof. If her aunty ever did decide to partake in a reckless fling, it'd be in the local paper before the week was out.

'I see we have a new visitor, Mrs Roberts.' The delight on the old lady's face was flagrant. Jodi half expected her to rub her hands together in glee.

'We do, Mrs Busby. If you'll excuse me, I'm just showing the gentleman to his room.'

Mrs Busby didn't budge. 'Oh, my,' she said, beaming up at Eddie from her five-foot-nothing stance. 'You're a handsome devil.'

As far as Jodi could see, this was one of the few advantages of getting older. You could get away with saying anything.

Eddie held out his hand. 'Eddie Moriantez. Pleased to meet you.'

The old lady clasped hold with both hands. 'I'm Mrs Busby.

One of Mrs Roberts's long-term residents, along with Dr Mortimer. Have you met the doctor?'

'No, I haven't.'

'He's deaf, so speak up.' Mrs Busby twisted his left hand upwards for closer inspection. 'Not married?'

Eddie looked stunned by the direct line of questioning. 'Err...widowed.'

The old lady sighed. 'Oh, dear me. Mrs Roberts is a widow.' She lowered her voice, as though Aunty Ruby wasn't standing there. 'Heart attack. Twelve years ago. Very tragic.'

Eddie looked uncomfortable.

Aunty Ruby looked mortified.

'It's not right for a lady to be on her own. Don't you agree, Mr Moriarty?'

Eddie went from looking sympathetic to bursting out laughing.

Jodi doubted Mrs Busby had realised her slip. Eddie might have classic film-star looks, but the baddie professor in Sherlock Holmes? Hardly.

Oblivious, the old woman carried on. 'When did your good lady wife die?'

Eddie stopped laughing. 'A...a few years ago,' he said, trying to pull his hands away. His eyes shifted to Aunty Ruby, a plea for help.

Her aunty took the hint. 'Let's not keep Mr Moriantez hanging around, Mrs Busby. I'm sure he'd like to get settled in his room.'

233

Eddie managed to extract his hands. 'It was good to meet you, but you'll have to excuse me. I don't want to keep Mrs Roberts waiting.'

'Oh, call her Ruby, it's much more intimate. Don't you think?'

The noise her aunty made sounded slightly strangulated.

'You be sure to call on me if you need anything. I'm down the landing on the right. The Arc Deco Suite.'

Eddie raised his eyebrows.

Yep, he didn't need to point out it was odd. But no more so than Dr Mortimer choosing the Moulin Rouge Boudoir.

When Mrs Busby finally departed, her aunty turned to Eddie. 'I'm sorry about that. Mrs Busby can be a little... intrusive at times.'

Eddie grinned. 'Don't worry about it.'

For a moment, their eyes locked.

Jodi wondered if she should make a discreet exit.

But then her aunty seemed to check herself. 'Would you care to follow me?' She went over to the staircase.

Eddie followed, his eyes homing in on her backside.

Jodi followed too, trying not to laugh.

'Nice structure,' Eddie said, halfway up the stairs.

Her aunty spun around, nearly losing her balance. 'I beg your pardon?'

He looked surprised. 'The building...nice structure.'

'Oh, right.'

Jodi had to cover her mouth to stop herself laughing.

Her aunty led him down the hallway towards the Carpenter's Room. When she turned to show him the room, she discovered he wasn't behind her.

Eddie was looking in the room opposite. 'Is this the room?'

Her aunty laughed. 'The Floral Room? I'm not sure Laura Ashley bedspread and curtains would suit. Not unless you're gay.' And then realising what she'd said, she slapped her hand over her mouth. 'I'm so sorry. I don't know why I said that. It's none of my business if you're...you know...whatever.'

Eddie let her flounder for a few seconds. 'Not gay,' he said, joining her in the Carpenter's Room.

Her aunty looked relieved.

Eddie wheeled his suitcase into the room. 'What a fantastic room.'

The Carpenter's Room was painted dark grey with yellow fabric accents. All the furniture was bespoke, made by her uncle. The artwork on the walls and the wood-burner slotted into the alcove softened the edges. It was the perfect room for Eddie. Manly, yet sensitive. Just like him.

Rather alarmingly, her aunty's hair matched the colour of the cushions. They really needed to do something about that. Not that it seemed to bother Eddie. He was looking at her aunty like she was Julia Roberts.

'I'm so glad you like the room.' Aunty Ruby walked over to the door. 'I'll get you some towels. Perhaps after lunch I could trouble you to fill in a registration card. I need to keep the books in order.'

'No problem.' He sat on the bed and ran his hand over the grey duvet cover.

It was a few seconds before her aunty dragged her gaze away from the bed.

Jodi followed her into the hallway. 'Everything okay?'

'Absolutely peachy,' she said, opening the airing cupboard door. 'I think plain white towels might be best. I'm not sure I could cope with a six-foot Charles Bronson wandering about the place in floral terry towelling.'

Charles Bronson. Just as Jodi had thought.

Aunty Ruby was smitten.

For the first time since Friday night, Jodi felt a rush of happiness.

Chapter Nineteen

Saturday 28th October

Becca felt like a football coach standing on the sidelines yelling instructions at her players. Only she wasn't dealing with a bunch of muddy youths running around a pitch, she was trying to synchronise nine children into moving across the floor in unison to the song *Chandelier*. It wasn't so much an elegant and sophisticated ballet routine, more like prop-forwards entering a rugby scrum.

'Listen to the music,' she yelled, trying to hold her phone steady as she videoed them. 'You're out of time. Wait…wait… GO…jeté…pirouette…ronde…no, *ronde*, Ben!' The poor kid looked confused.

The showcase was in exactly four weeks. Had she been too optimistic in trying to get them to perform a routine? Based on this morning's debacle, hell yes.

On the positive side, her class size had increased. The latest pupils to join were a pair of cuties who had natural ability and already knew the basics. She'd waited for their mothers to criticise her lack of teaching ability, but so far they seemed quite happy with her methods – and this was their third week. Definite progress.

At least the dance studio was more presentable now. Unlike the art studio and grand ballroom, which had suffered due to the recent storms.

'You need to move quicker,' she yelled, pointing to where Ben should be standing. 'That's it, turn your feet out...good boy.' He was an adorable child, but he had the attention span of a goldfish. 'Big finish, everyone! Nice sweeping arms... relevé...plié...and slowly move into arabesque... Lovely. Well done.'

She gave them a thumbs-up as the music ended, even though most of them had fallen out of the final arabesque. Focusing on a polished ending was a challenge for another week.

'Gather round,' she called, beckoning them over. 'Great class, everyone. You should be really pleased with yourselves.' She was rewarded with smiling faces. 'I know the routine isn't perfect, but there's plenty of time to work on it.'

Who was she trying to fool, them or her? But the advice she'd received from Rosie had been spot on. Kids responded better to praise than constant criticism.

'You just need to practise at home. We've only got a few rehearsals left before the showcase. So I'm going to email your parents the video of the routine, and I want you to spend half an hour every day going over the steps. Can you do that for me?'

They all nodded. A couple of girls tugged at their too-tight hair-buns, eager to be released from the confines of ballet attire.

Phoebe raised her hand. 'What about costumes, Miss? Can we wear tutus?'

The other girls nodded excitedly, but Ben started crying, no doubt traumatised by the idea of wearing a tutu as well as getting the routine wrong.

'The costumes haven't been decided yet, Phoebe.' Becca went over and gave Ben a hug, trying not to fret over how she was going to finance a set of show costumes with no budget. 'I'll let you know in the next couple of weeks. Well done for today and see you all next Saturday.'

The end of class was always manic. Parents tried to locate lost items of clothing, children ran off before their parents were ready and mothers tried to coordinate diaries, play-dates, and lifts to next week's class.

Ben still had his arms around her waist. 'I can't do the steps...and I don't...don't want to wear a tu...tutu,' he said through tearful hiccups.

She hugged him close. 'I promise I won't make you wear a tutu. And you'll pick up the routine – you just need to practise. Don't give up now, you're almost there.'

His mother came over, looking tired and drawn. 'Everything okay?'

'Ben's a little worried about the routine, but I've assured him he just needs to practise. And I'm sure Phoebe will help, so there's nothing to worry about.'

Rosie ruffled his hair. 'Listen to what Becca's saying. Now go and get your things. I want a quick word with the teacher.' She waited until the other mothers had left and her children were out of earshot.

Oh, hell. Had Becca shouted too much during class? 'Is everything okay?'

'It's fine, it's just...' Rosie's hand shook as she held on to her walking stick. 'Will we have to pay for the costumes?'

Becca knew of several dance schools who charged for costumes, so it wouldn't be an outrageous request to ask the parents to pay. But she could see from the look on Rosie's face that money was an issue. Welcome to the club, she thought. They were trying to put on a showcase with a zilch budget. But she didn't want to burden the woman who'd supported her when she'd first started teaching. It didn't seem right. 'Don't worry, costumes will be supplied for the showcase. The kids just need to provide their own ballet shoes, which they all have.'

'Oh, that's good.' A relieved-looking Rosie gathered up her children's belongings and headed for the door, balancing on her stick. 'See you next week.'

Phoebe skipped over to the door. Ben trailed behind, dragging his bag on the floor.

Becca waved them off. Maybe she should simplify Ben's part in the routine? She'd give him a couple more weeks before deciding. She didn't want to embarrass the kid by singling him out.

When the studio had emptied, she changed out of her ballet shoes into her pink trainers and locked up. It had been a strange week, even more so than normal. Jodi hadn't been in work Monday or Tuesday complaining of an upset stomach, which was unusual. Jodi was never ill. She suspected her cousin's ailment was exacerbated by the stress of being accused of theft. And who could blame her? It was outrageous. When Jodi had returned to work, she'd stayed in the office working on ways to produce the showcase with no money, thus avoiding any non-essential contact with the other staff members.

Tom had been in court most of the week, although she suspected he was also lying low, and Petrit had been on annual leave, so it had been quiet. But things couldn't continue as they were. Decisions needed to be made. And she felt it was up to her to break the tension.

She went in search of Tom, knowing he'd arrived back from London early this morning. As she passed through reception, she spotted Eddie descending the grand staircase looking decidedly damp. 'Hey, Eddie. Have you seen Tom?'

'He's up in the roof,' he said, digging around in his pocket for a hanky. 'We've been trying to fix the leak. I'm heading out to buy more tarpaulin. How was ballet class?'

'Good, thanks. How are you finding the guest house?'

The mood at the guest house had changed since Eddie had moved in. It felt lighter, less like an old people's home and more like the holiday residence it was supposed to be. Even Mrs Busby had perked up, enjoying flirting with a 'handsome devil'.

Eddie grinned. 'Interesting. Your mum's a lovely woman.'

There hadn't been a man in her mum's life since her dad had died. Not to Becca's knowledge anyway. But maybe it was time for her mum to start dating again? And there was no one more decent or likeable than Eddie. Becca just needed to ensure her mum was receptive to the idea. 'She needs to get out more. Running the guest house is tiring work.'

He frowned. 'Anything I can help with?'

'There is actually. I've been trying to coax her along to the tea dances, but so far she's resisted. Now, if you were to come along, she might be persuaded to attend.'

He laughed. 'I'm a terrible dancer.'

'Good, that'll make her feel better.'

'I'm not sure how to take that. But I'll do my best.' He wiped his big hands on his hanky. 'Need anything from the DIY store?'

'Five grand to repair the roof and put on a showcase?'

His expression turned rueful. 'I think we all want that.'

'You don't think Jodi took the money do you, Eddie?'

He looked surprised. 'Not for a second.'

Good. 'Any idea who did?'

He shook his head. 'I'd have something to say to them if I did.'

He wasn't the only one. 'See you later.'

'See ya, kiddo.' He patted her shoulder, leaving her to climb the grand staircase in search of Tom.

As she passed by the portraits of Tom's disapproving

ancestors she poked her tongue out. It was childish, but they were a miserable bunch.

When she reached the top of the staircase, she stopped to get her bearings. The long galley corridor ran the length of the manor house. At each end was a set of concealed steps. Tom's bedroom was in the east tower, so she knew the layout, but she'd never ventured up to the west tower before. Access to the roof was via the attic at the top, so once again she found herself navigating a narrow staircase, fighting off cobwebs and spiders, trying to locate Tom.

She heard him before she saw him. He sounded like he was wrestling a crocodile, judging by the groans and grunts. As she climbed the makeshift ladder to the eaves, she saw him. He was dressed in a suit, minus the jacket and tie with the sleeves of his pale blue shirt rolled up.

She glanced away from his hairless forearms, focusing on the fact that he wasn't wrestling a large reptile, but fighting with a giant sheet of tarpaulin.

He stood up and smacked his head on a wooden beam. '*Shit!*'

Becca stepped over the floor joists to reach him. 'Watching you attempt DIY is like watching a toddler in traffic.'

He startled. '*Jesus!* Don't creep up on me like that.'

'I didn't. And if you weren't making such a racket you'd have heard me coming. What are you doing?'

'Baking a cake,' he said, rubbing the side of his head.

Sarcastic sod.

'I can see stars,' he said, blinking a few times.

'That'll be the hole in the roof.' She looked up at the daylight seeping between the slates. 'Need a hand?'

He looked at her ballet leotard and tights with white loose-knit jumper and pink trainers. 'Dressed like that?'

'Says the man wearing a suit.'

A smile twitched at his lips. 'I forgot to change.'

'Idiot.' She assessed the mess around her. 'What do you need?'

He nodded to the toolbox by her feet. 'Is there a hammer in there?'

She searched around and handed him the tool. 'Have you seen Jodi this morning?'

'Not yet. How is she?' He ducked under the beam and positioned the tarpaulin.

'Not too bad, considering she's been wrongly accused of theft.'

'Hold that, will you?' He reached up, his body almost touching hers as he leant over her. 'And I haven't accused her of anything.' His shirtsleeves were already soaked through. Why he hadn't thought to change first she didn't know.

She held the corner of the sheet in place, trying not to think about how close he was. She could smell his citrusy aftershave and a faint waft of fabric conditioner. The effect was alarming. 'But you didn't correct Vivienne when she accused her, did you?'

'I was having an asthma attack.'

'That was then. What's your excuse now?' When she turned, their eyes met, and for a moment they both stilled. She could feel the heat building and she had to resist the urge to lean in to him. What the hell was happening? She broke the tension by nodding to the hammer. 'Do you know what you're doing?'

Insulting his DIY skills did the trick. He glared at her. Good. It was safer that way. 'Of course I don't. You want to do it?'

'I'm helping, aren't I? And you haven't answered my question.'

'You haven't given me a chance.' His blue eyes penetrated the gloomy light. 'And I have been dealing with it. But I didn't want to jump in with both feet until I'd spoken to all the staff.'

'Meanwhile, Vivienne continues to slag off Jodi to anyone who'll listen, telling them she's a thief.'

He hit the nail. It buckled and fell out, disappearing between the rafters. 'I didn't realise she was doing that. I'll have a word with her.'

'Good, because according to you a person's innocent until proven guilty.'

He gave her a loaded look. 'I agree.'

'And no one has any proof that Jodi took the money.'

'I know.'

'And they won't find any proof, because she didn't do it.'

'I know.'

'And continuing to slander her is not on. In fact, isn't it a criminal offence?'

245

He waved the hammer at her. 'Are you listening to me? I said, I know.'

'Fine. Well, do something about it.'

He looked exasperated. He also looked hot, much as she disliked admitting it.

And then her brain caught up with her ears. 'You *know* she didn't take it?'

He rummaged in the toolbox for another nail. 'Not for certain, but like I said last weekend, I don't believe she took it. How to prove that, heaven only knows. The safe door was shut prior to Jodi discovering the money was missing. There were no signs of a forced entry, and Vivienne said the money was in the safe first thing that morning. The only other person who'd been in the office was Petrit, and he doesn't have the safe combination.' He selected another nail. 'Leon and Eddie weren't working, so that discounts them. I've talked to everyone who was there, searched the place and questioned Vivienne again about what she allegedly saw, but I've drawn a blank.' He stood up, managing to clip his head again. '*Shit!*'

She waited until he'd stopped rubbing. 'You haven't questioned me.'

It was a moment before he spoke. 'You're right, I haven't.'

'I'm surprised I wasn't the obvious suspect after Jodi.'

'Don't.' The look he gave her made it clear he didn't want to go there.

She didn't either, but how could she not? Her feelings were

246

as raw today as they had been twelve years earlier when he'd believed her guilty of a crime she hadn't committed.

In May 2006, Jodi was having a particularly bad time and her behaviour was heading towards self-destruction. Drugs had become a factor, so had alcohol. She'd begun taking money from her mum's purse. When it stopped being sufficient to fund her habit, Jodi had started stealing. Becca had tried to stop her, but her loyalties were torn, not knowing whether she should tell someone or keep quiet. She'd tried to reason with her cousin, but Jodi was already past the point of caring.

One Saturday afternoon while they were shopping in Boots, Becca realised Jodi was putting stuff into her bag without paying for it. She'd insisted Jodi put the stuff back, but Jodi had refused and ran from the store.

Becca had run after her and grabbed her cousin's bag with the intention of returning the stuff to the shop. Instead, the security guard caught her and her dragged back inside, by which time Jodi had scarpered. The police were called and Becca was placed in a holding cell until her parents arrived. She'd never been so scared in her entire life.

She hadn't let on that Jodi had taken the stuff. Consequently, she was given a police caution and received a humiliating telling-off by the duty sergeant. Her parents had been beside themselves, terrified that their normally well-behaved daughter was following in her cousin's wayward footsteps. She'd been grounded for two weeks and not allowed to see either Tom or Jodi for the duration. It had been torture.

It wasn't until Jodi was sent to prison a couple of years later that the truth emerged. But by then it was too late. Her dad had died, believing her to have committed the crime, and Tom had broken up with her. He'd assumed along with everyone else that she was guilty. And when his own father had banned him from seeing her or Jodi, claiming they were a 'bad influence', Tom had disappeared from her life.

When a sober and remorseful Jodi had been released from prison, the first thing she'd done was apologise to Becca. She'd even wanted to confess to the police, but Becca wouldn't let her. Jodi had been punished enough. She didn't want to see her cousin go back to prison, so they'd made their peace.

The same couldn't be said for her and Tom.

She shifted position, hiding her misery from the man who'd broken her heart. 'So where does that leave us? We have no money and no one accountable for the theft. How do we move forwards?' When she glanced at him, she realised he'd been watching her.

His expression was unreadable. It was a while before he spoke. 'I wish I knew. Any suggestions?'

She mustered up an enthusiastic tone. 'Well, cancelling the showcase isn't an option.'

He raised his eyebrows. 'I admire your determination, but how can we afford it?'

Her arms were beginning to ache. She shifted position. 'Jodi's already started on a plan. She's designed electronic tickets and switched all the advertising to social media outlets.

She's changed the exhibitors' contracts so they're responsible for insuring their work, and she's recruiting volunteers to help on the day. If we pull together, we can make this work.'

He looked sceptical. 'You really believe that?'

'Especially if we can temporarily fix the roof so we can use the ballroom and art studio.' She held his gaze. 'We can't let whoever took the money win, Tom.'

He nodded. 'I agree.'

'Good.' It was time to lighten the atmosphere. 'Now hurry up, my arms are killing me.'

He glared at her, looking scarily like his grumpy ancestors. 'Then move your fingers, before I squash them.'

She poked her tongue out, which made him laugh.

'Child.' He waited until she'd repositioned her hand before tapping the nail with the hammer. 'How many acts have we got booked for the showcase?'

'We have the tappers and the kids' ballet routine, and Jodi's showing around a landscape artist today who's interested in exhibiting. We've also had an email from another potential artist, and Leon's asked for a slot.'

'Leon?'

'Yes, he's a singer-songwriter.'

'I never knew that.' Tom tugged on the tarpaulin. 'Are you going to dance at the showcase?'

'I wasn't planning to.' She shook out her arms and handed him another nail. 'You need to fix the other side.'

'I'm aware of that.' He rolled his eyes, and flattened the

tarpaulin across the wooden slats. 'Why aren't you performing? Is it your knee?'

'Not really. It's been a while since I've danced properly.' She didn't want to admit it was her confidence and not her knee that had yet to recover.

He eased the nail into the splintered wood. 'I think you should consider it. No disrespect to Leon or the others, but you're by far the best advert we have for the playhouse.' The hammer slipped off the nail and hit his thumb. '*Shit!*'

She wasn't comfortable receiving compliments about her dancing. Not from him. It was too...intimate. 'You okay?'

He cradled his hand under his armpit. 'I'm fine.'

They might have formed a fragile truce, joining together to save the playhouse, but she wasn't ready to venture into more personal territory.

He tested out the tarpaulin. 'Right, that'll have to do. How long it'll last, I have no idea.' He dropped the hammer into the toolbox. 'Eddie's going to cover the flooring with tarpaulin, so if the roof does leak it shouldn't seep through to the rooms below. There's nothing more we can do.'

'Good. Right...well, if you don't need me anymore, I'll head down and see how Jodi's getting on with the landscape artist.' She was eager to escape and assimilate her thoughts. Spending too much time with Tom was confusing.

But as she reached the ladder, he called after her. 'Becca?' She glanced back, derailed by his sudden smile. 'Thanks for your help. I really appreciate it.'

250

The sight of his dimples made swallowing hard. 'No worries,' she said, reversing down the ladder and wishing she still thought of him as Tom-the-Tyrant, because dealing with his more likeable counterpart was a hell of a lot more challenging. And then guilt nudged her in the ribs. 'Oh...and thanks for believing in Jodi.'

He held her gaze. 'You're welcome.'

It was just a shame he hadn't believed in her.

That thought alone was enough to dull any fleeting attraction. He'd broken her heart once; she'd be a fool to go there a second time.

Leaving him tidying up, she headed down stairs, trying not to dwell on the past. But it was no good. Reminiscing over the events of twelve years ago had aggravated an old wound. The injustice she'd felt resurfaced. Maybe that's why she was fighting so hard to clear Jodi's name. She knew what it felt like to be wrongly accused.

As she neared the café, she could see Jodi talking to a woman in a kaftan. She guessed it was the landscape artist. Vivienne was standing by the kitchen door, her trademark sneer in place as her eyes followed Jodi. What did she think her cousin was going to do, run off with the plastic cutlery?

Leon was behind the bar refilling bottles of spirits, seemingly disinterested in what was going on around him. Her cousin had said she'd sensed a cooling off from her admirer over the past week. Something Becca hoped wasn't true. Surely Leon knew Jodi was innocent?

And then a man walked into the café. At first, Becca didn't recognise him, his once dark hair was silver and he wore black square-shaped glasses. But as he turned and caught sight of her cousin, his expression gave him away. Harvey Elliot.

'What on God's earth are you doing here?' he said, loud enough that all heads turned in his direction.

Jodi's confusion switched to shock when she realised who it was.

Becca ran over to rescue her cousin. 'Your son is upstairs, Mr Elliot. This way.' She needed to get him out of there.

But he wasn't budging. 'I said, what are you doing here?'

All eyes were on the floorshow.

Becca took Harvey's arm, trying to steer him out of the café. 'Jodi works here, Mr Elliot. As do I. Now, shall we go and find Tom?'

He shook her off. 'Let go of me.'

'Dad?' All heads turned. This time at the sound of Tom's voice.

Vivienne perked up, sensing trouble was looming.

Tom looked confused. 'What are you doing here?'

'Never mind what I'm doing here,' Harvey Elliot said, pointing at Becca and Jodi. 'I want to know why you have two people with criminal records working in your mother's playhouse?'

Jodi gasped.

Leon dropped a glass.

Vivienne looked like she'd won the lottery.

Chapter Twenty

...continued

It took a lot for Tom to lose his temper, but witnessing his father 'outing' Becca and Jodi in front of the playhouse staff sent him spiralling from infuriation into full-blown rage. Who the bloody hell did he think he was?

Without stopping to think, he grabbed his father by the elbow and dragged him from the café. 'Upstairs, now!' he bellowed, barely able to speak through his clenched teeth. An argument was about to happen and he didn't want an audience.

In his periphery, he saw the look of horror on Becca's and Jodi's faces, and the smug look on Vivienne's. Part of him wanted to stay and manage the aftermath of his dad's bombshell, but the bigger part of him needed to yell at his father.

As they ascended the grand staircase, he vaguely heard his father talking behind him. But he wasn't listening. He had no interest in anything his father had to say. He was too focused on breathing. His chest was tightening with every step. So much for rest and relaxation. Dealing with a damp roof, an unknown thief and a showcase they couldn't afford wasn't conducive to reducing his stress levels. And now he had to deal with his father.

By the time he reached the top, he was so breathless he had to use Uncle Henry's bust to lean on. Recovering slightly, he marched down the galley corridor to his mother's study, adrenaline and anger the only things spurring him on.

He pushed open the door and went inside, steeling himself. It was cold in the room, but he didn't light the fire. He didn't want his father getting too cosy.

His body was shaking, his chest rising and falling in short bursts. He took out his inhaler and administered a welcome burst of Ventolin. The pain in his chest eased a fraction. He noticed the state of his hands, dirty and bloody from hitting himself with the hammer. His suit trousers and waistcoat were smeared in cobwebs. Christ, he was a mess...unlike Harvey Elliot, who walked into the study looking pristine in his navy blazer and tailored trousers and wearing a totally unre-morseful expression.

Tom had to fight the urge to pick up the elephant-shaped paperweight on the desk and smash it over his head. 'What the hell were you thinking?'

His father looked mildly alarmed. 'I beg your pardon?'

'Downstairs just now. Telling everyone about Becca's and Jodi's past. Why did you do that?' He closed the door, in case Vivienne decided to eavesdrop.

'A more pertinent question would be: what are they doing working at the playhouse?'

Tom rubbed his chest. 'That's none of your concern.'

'Of course it's my concern. This is your mother's business. If you're making rash decisions that jeopardise the future of the playhouse, then it's my duty to intervene.'

Tom wondered if he'd heard correctly. 'Your duty? You have no right whatsoever to dictate what happens here. You gave up that right when you buggered off.' He marched over to the desk. The room suddenly seemed too small. Or maybe the furniture was too big. He couldn't decide which.

'Not this again.' His father sounded exasperated.

Tom spun around. 'How dare you walk in here and act like you're in charge. This is no longer your home.'

'But it's still your mother's. And if you're engaging the likes of that Roberts girl and Jodi Simmons to work here then your judgement is highly questionable.'

Tom banged his fist on the desk, making the framed photos wobble. His injured thumb began to throb. 'Firstly, I didn't hire Becca and Jodi, Mum did. And secondly, my judgement is none of your concern. I don't care if you agree with my decisions, but I do care about you walking in here and relaying private information about Becca and Jodi to the rest of the staff.'

'Your mother is an alcoholic. Her decision-making is impaired.' His father had switched to QC mode, sullying the credibility of the star witness.

Tom wasn't about to be outwitted. 'But mine isn't.'

'If you're trusting that pair to work here, then clearly it is.'

His father's voice was calm, measured, displaying his ability to be 'reasonable' despite provocation. 'Do you need me to remind you they both have criminal records?'

'And do you need me to remind you about the law of slander?'

That shut his father up. It was a small win, but one he would relish.

'Becca wasn't charged, she was given a police caution, and because she was under eighteen at the time there's no record of the offence on her DBS check. She's perfectly within her rights to sue you, and I for one would be happy to represent her.' God, his chest hurt. He glanced around hoping to find a bottle of water.

'You're being a little dramatic.' His father's patronising tone didn't waver. 'And the same cannot be said for Jodi Simmons. She has a record longer than my arm.'

'Now who's being dramatic?'

His father sat in the wingback chair. 'My point is, they cannot be trusted.'

To anyone else, there was nothing strange about a man taking a seat in a study. But nothing Harvey Elliot ever did was random. It was a tactic. A manoeuvre designed to unsettle the opposition. He was allowing his son the opportunity to present his 'opening argument'. No doubt, he hoped Tom would cave under the pressure and hang himself. Well, tough. That wasn't about to happen.

Tom picked up an almost empty can of lemonade and

drank the dregs. It was flat and disgusting. In the absence of water, it would have to do. 'You haven't seen them for twelve years. You have no idea what they're like now. But you don't care, do you? You've made your judgement and as we all know, the great Harvey Elliot is never wrong.'

His father crossed his legs. 'So there isn't five thousand pounds missing?'

Tom stilled. 'How did you know about that?'

'Vivienne was kind enough to enlighten me.'

'Oh, I bet she was.' Bloody woman.

'Do you think it's a coincidence that within weeks of those two showing up here money is taken from the safe?'

Tom needed to buy himself some time. He used the tissues on the desk to wipe his hands. The tick of the grandfather clock filled the silence.

Money had never gone missing before. So no, it wasn't a coincidence. But if Jodi didn't take the money then who did? He suspected it was a set-up to get rid of Jodi. But he had no evidence. And without proof, he didn't need his father to point out he had no case.

Binning the tissues, he faced his father, who looked annoyingly relaxed. He was reading the spines of the books filling the wall-to-wall bookcases.

'Whatever conclusions you've reached, you don't know the facts. I trust Becca and Jodi. They work bloody hard, and they're doing more to save the playhouse than anyone else. More significantly, Mum trusts them. She appointed them as

257

deputies in her absence and she's the only person who has the authority to reverse that decision. Not me, and certainly not you.'

His father tilted his head to one side. 'So who took the money?'

Good question. 'It's under investigation.'

'Are the police involved?' It was asked in such an innocent way that it was obvious he already knew the answer.

'Not yet. I didn't want a scandal to ruin the showcase event we have planned.'

'Ah, yes, the showcase.' His father brushed a piece of lint from his jacket lapel. 'I understand from Vivienne the missing five thousand pounds was to finance the event? Without the money, doesn't that rather foil your plans?'

Bloody Vivienne again.

Of course, it did. But he wasn't about to admit as much. Despite Becca and Jodi's best efforts, he was realistic enough to know an event that big needed financing. He'd been racking his brain trying to find a solution. He would have financed the show himself if the flat sale hadn't wiped him out. There hadn't been much equity in the property, and what little there was had been used up clearing the secured loan taken out to cover Izzy's debts. His income was currently lower than it had been, and he'd just forked out for Izzy's second week at the Travelodge to prevent her from becoming homeless. He was skint.

So he'd done the only thing he could think of. He'd

applied for a personal loan to finance the showcase and get the roof fixed. Maybe he was crazy, but he couldn't cope with the idea of letting his mother...or Becca...down. But with no security in the form of a property or fixed income, there was no guarantee his application would be successful.

His father's voice broke into his thoughts. 'After all this time, she still has a hold over you.'

Tom feigned ignorance. 'I don't know what you mean.'

'The Roberts girl. A schoolboy crush is one thing, but allowing her to distract you from your career and risk all you've worked for? Is she really worth it?' His father was a clever sod. The question was typical of a seasoned QC, loaded with a series of hidden insinuations that made it impossible for the defendant to answer a straight 'yes' or 'no'.

Tom's answer should be 'no'. They hadn't been involved for twelve years. They'd both moved on. And yet, he still felt a connection.

He hadn't ended the relationship because he'd fallen out of love with her. He'd been persuaded to walk away. He hadn't had the opportunity to talk to her about what had happened, or explain face-to-face why he was ending it, so there'd been no...closure. One day they were together, the next they weren't.

In her eyes, he'd betrayed her. He'd believed the worst and hadn't stood by her, hadn't resisted pressure from his father to break up with her. And she was right. But he'd been confused. He'd been unwilling to believe her capable of theft, but presented with the evidence, how could he think otherwise? And if Becca was heading for the same path as her cousin, then his father had been right: it could have affected his chances of becoming a barrister.

It was only months later that doubt had started to creep in. Becca had never been dishonest. She'd once insisted they return to a café when she'd realised they hadn't charged her for her second juice. It was difficult to believe her capable of shoplifting. So in that sense the answer was 'yes'. She did still have a hold over him.

'No one's distracting me from my career,' he said, staring down at the unopened copies of *Justice Weekly* lying on the desk. No doubt his father had spotted them too.

'That's not what Arthur Watson tells me.' His father tapped his fingers on the arm of the chair. 'Apparently, you've hardly been in chambers of late. Your trial rate has reduced to a fraction of what it was. If you're trying to commit career suicide, then you're going in the right direction.'

'Quit with the career advice, Dad. I'm not interested.'

'Well, you should be. Don't you want to make Silk?'

Tom rubbed his chest. 'Achieving Silk is your dream, not mine.'

'Surely it's what every barrister wants? And you have an advantage – someone willing to make it happen. Why would you reject that? For the sake of your pride?'

How could he explain that he'd become disillusioned with

the profession? He wasn't sure he wanted to be a barrister anymore, let alone a QC.

He'd been so chuffed to be called to the Bar and declared an 'utter barrister'. To be allowed to practise and call himself *learned* and wear a wig and gown. It had been so exciting. And now he was thinking of walking away. The reality of dealing with petty criminals, speeding motorists and those posing a nuisance to their community depressed the hell out of him. He'd wanted to make a difference. And he wasn't doing that.

'When it comes to career decisions, I'll decide what's best for me.' Tom leant against the desk, needing another puff of Ventolin, but unwilling to show any weakness in front of his father. 'I'm sorry if that disappoints you, but I stopped looking for your approval when you walked out on Mum.'

'So you're prepared to give up years of study to work at a rundown arts centre?'

'That's the bit you don't understand.'

'Then enlighten me.' His father opened his hands, a show of how reasonable he was being.

'This place means everything to Mum. She'd be devastated to see it close. Unlike you, I'm not about to let her down. So if that means taking time out to support her and keep things going while she seeks help for her addiction, then it's a sacrifice I'm willing to make.'

'Even if it damages your career?'

'Yes, Dad.'

There was no need to explain that he had no intention of ruining his career. His days as a defence barrister might be numbered, but he'd do something else law-related – he just wasn't sure what. His father would never understand, so there was no point discussing it.

'How is your mother?' His father uncrossed his legs.

Oh, so now he was showing an interest in his mother? 'No idea. She's not allowed visitors.'

'When will she be released?'

Jesus. 'She's not in prison.'

His father sighed. 'I meant, when is she coming home?'

'Not for another few weeks.' He pushed away from the desk. 'Now, unless there's something else, I think it's better if you left.'

His father stayed seated. 'I was hoping you'd join me for lunch?'

Was he for real? Tom rubbed his chest. 'Not going to happen.'

His father stood. 'I really do want to make amends.'

'Great. You can start by going downstairs and publicly apologising to Becca and Jodi for humiliating them earlier.'

His father didn't reply.

'Yep, just as I thought.' Tom walked over to the door and opened it. 'Have a safe trip back to London, Dad.' When his father reluctantly left, he shut the door behind him.

Tom lay down on the sofa and took two shots of Ventolin,

trying to slow his breathing. He focused on the swirl of the blue damask patterning on the curtain pelmet and listened to the grandfather clock. He wanted to check on Becca and Jodi, but arguing with his father had used up all his breath.

Chapter Twenty-One

Sunday 29th October

Jodi handed Aunty Ruby a wodge of cotton wool. 'You're dribbling,' she said, guiding her hand to where the dye was running down her cheek. 'Hold that, I'm nearly done.' She continued to paste on the dye, watching the colour darken and worrying whether her aunty had picked the right shade. She looked at the instructions again.

'Everything all right, love?'

'I think so.' Jodi turned the box over. 'What colour did you say this was?'

'Dark brown. Has it covered the yellow?'

Jodi looked at her aunty's hair. The mixture had been beige on application, but over the last ten minutes had rapidly darkened to a flat black. It didn't bode well. 'It's definitely covered the yellow,' she said, omitting to mention it'd also absorbed all the light in the room. Maybe it would wash out a lighter shade? She could only hope. She checked her watch. 'Another fifteen minutes.'

'Excellent. Cup of tea?' Her aunty climbed off the breakfast stool.

'Stay where you are, I'll do it. You'll drip dye all over the floor.' Checking the towel was firmly secured around her aunty's neck, Jodi went over to fill the kettle.

'And pop some bread in the toaster while you're at it. You haven't had any breakfast.'

'I'm not hungry.' Jodi's stomach was so knotted she could barely tolerate fluids, let alone food.

'You've got to eat, love. You need to keep up your strength.'

'What's the point?' Jodi unhooked two mugs from the stand, knowing she was being morose, but unable to shake it off. 'Nothing I do makes a difference. I don't know why I bother even trying.'

'You don't mean that.' Her aunty's consoling tone only made her feel worse.

'It was bad enough before Harvey Elliot showed up. Now it'll be impossible. Everyone knows about my criminal record. They'll never trust me.' She went over to the fridge, swallowing back the lump in her throat.

There was a brief pause before her aunty spoke. 'Have you considered this might be a good thing?'

She turned to her aunty. 'Are you kidding me? In what way?'

'Don't get me wrong, what's happened is awful and I could brain that bloody man for what he did. But the worst has

265

happened now. Everyone knows about your past. It's out in the open.'

'I don't see how that's a good thing.' It felt like the end of the world.

'Living with a secret is exhausting. You spend the whole time looking over your shoulder, waiting for someone to discover the truth. Well, they know now. Big deal. You've been punished, served your time and more than made amends. They no longer have a hold over you.'

'Nice theory, but reality doesn't work that way.' She blinked away tears. 'God only knows what Vivienne will do with this information. She's been itching to call the police all week. I'm amazed they haven't shown up here this morning to arrest me. And she's bound to tell Petrit.'

'Dealing with those two is going to be tricky, I grant you...' Her aunty shifted on the stool. 'If you don't stop stirring that tea, love, there'll be nothing left in the mugs.'

'Sorry.' Jodi fetched a cloth from the sink. 'I'm a little distracted.'

Her aunty fanned her face, trying to disperse the potent fumes radiating off the dye. 'What about the rest of the staff? How did they react?'

'Eddie didn't say much at the time, but he found me later and gave me a hug. He said his opinion hadn't changed and he knows I didn't take the money.'

'That was nice of him.'

266

'He's a nice man.' She mopped up the spill, noticing her aunty's pink-cheeked reaction to the mention of their latest houseguest.

'And what about the lad who gave you the book?'

Jodi stilled. 'Leon.'

'What was his response?'

Jodi averted her gaze, suddenly fascinated by the cherry patterning on the side of the mugs. 'I don't know, I ran out without looking at him.' She hadn't wanted to see the look of disgust on his face.

It wasn't like things between them hadn't already changed. Ever since the money had disappeared a week ago he'd been cool with her. Nothing major, no accusations, or visible hatred like Petrit and Vivienne, but there'd been no gifts, no hot drinks made to cheer her up and get her through the day. Whatever connection they might have experienced during their lunch out, it had evaporated the moment news of the theft broke. And she was sadder than she could have imagined. More fool her for believing a lovely, kind and decent bloke like Leon would be interested in a damaged, untrustworthy girl like her. Would she never learn?

'Give him time. I'm sure once he knows the facts, he'll come around.'

Jodi doubted it. She'd blown it with Leon. Once again, her past was affecting her future. She brought the mugs over to the table. 'Would you like a biscuit?'

'Not for me.' Aunty Ruby pushed the barrel towards her. 'But you have one. You need to eat something.'

Jodi sat at the kitchen table.

Her aunty unearthed a Penguin and unwrapped it. 'I know this is hard, and life feels cruel at times, but this is all part of moving forwards.' She handed Jodi the biscuit. 'This is your first proper job. You're being tested, just as everyone is when they start work. I know your situation's a little different, but workplace issues are commonplace. I had an awful time when I first started teaching. I had to deal with disgruntled parents, unruly children and a head teacher who didn't think I was up to the job.'

Jodi nibbled the biscuit. 'What did you do?'

'For the first month, I cried myself to sleep every night.' Her aunty tilted her head, causing the dye running down her forehead to change direction. 'During the second month I thought about quitting and trying something different, like working in a flower shop.'

Jodi reached across and dabbed the leakage with cotton wool. 'What stopped you?'

'The realisation that being a florist wasn't an easy job either. Early starts, long days, and cold weather? I hate being cold. I'd have made a terrible florist. My point is, whatever job you do, there's always an induction period to get through. A bumpy road before things get smoother. Your situation might be more extreme than most, but it's not unusual.'

'As Tom Jones would say.'

She laughed. 'Exactly. And he's a man worth paying attention to.'

Jodi nibbled her biscuit. 'So you're saying I should suck it up and not quit.'

'The truth is, wherever you go you're going to have to get over the same hurdle.'

God, what a depressing thought. But her aunty was right. She couldn't change her past. She was stuck with it. She discarded the Penguin, no longer hungry.

Aunty Ruby patted her hand. 'Like I said, the worst is over. It's out in the open now. Dig deep, keep your head down and work hard. Prove to everyone they're lucky to have you. Okay?'

She nodded. 'I'll try.'

'I know you will.' Her aunty sipped her tea. 'Lovely cuppa.'

Jodi checked her watch. 'Unfortunately, it's time to rinse off the dye.'

'Oh, well, it's probably a good thing. I'm getting high from the ammonia.'

Jodi followed her aunty upstairs, mulling over her advice. Maybe there was something to be said for not having to worry about her secret getting out anymore. She was dreading going into work tomorrow, even though Tom had assured her it would be business as usual. He'd phoned last night and apologised for his father's behaviour, assuring her he would personally deal with any attempts to undermine her authority. She'd just have to hope he stuck to his promise.

'How are things going with Eddie?' Jodi unhooked the showerhead in her aunty's en suite, glad to focus on something other than work troubles. 'Is having an extra houseguest making things harder or easier for you?'

'Both.' Her aunty leaned over the bathtub.

'I noticed he mended the hinge on the freezer door.' She rinsed off the dye, trying to ignore the stream of black circling the plughole. 'It must be nice having someone to help with that kind of stuff.'

'Oh, it is. If something needs fixing, he mends it. If the bins need putting out, he takes them out. If I've put a casserole dish into soak, he washes it up. Whatever needs doing, it's done before I have a chance to think about it, let alone do it. Last night he replaced the shower screen in Becca's bathroom.'

Jodi laughed. 'He's certainly very attentive. So what's the downside?' When her aunty didn't respond, she prompted her. 'Come on, share. What awful habit have you uncovered? Does he pick his teeth? Wear women's underwear?'

'Can you imagine!' Her aunty's laughter morphed into a coughing fit.

Jodi handed her a flannel. 'Am I drowning you?'

'I'm fine.' Her aunty wiped her face. 'I had a visual of Eddie wearing stockings and suspenders. It gave me quite a shock.'

It wasn't an image Jodi wanted to entertain. 'So what's his crime?'

'When he's around I get...flustered, and hot. I drop things and trip up the stairs. He always seems to catch me making

270

a...what is it you girls say? A complete tit out of myself... Is that the right phrase?'

Jodi laughed. 'Sounds to me like you have a crush.'

'More likely the menopause.'

She soaped up her aunty's hair. Even the shampoo turned grey as she lathered it through to the ends. Not a good sign. 'Why don't you tell him how you feel?'

'Goodness, no.'

'Stop shaking your head, you're spraying the tiles.' She rinsed her aunty's hair and covered it in a healthy dose of conditioner, hoping it might soften the intensity of the colour. 'Only a couple of weeks ago you were telling me you wanted some excitement in your life. You said running the guest house was hard work on your own. Well, now you have a hot bloke helping you out. The fact that he makes you feel all gooey is a bonus. Why wouldn't you want to embrace that?'

Her aunty had gone quiet.

'You know I'm right.' She massaged her aunty's hair. 'Eddie's old-school, a proper gent, so he's never going to make a move. If you want things to progress you're going to have to take a risk.'

'But what if he's not interested? I'll make a fool of myself and lose his DIY skills. I couldn't bear that.'

Jodi laughed. 'Trust me, the man's smitten. Nothing you could do will ruin that.' She rinsed off the conditioner. 'But if you're worried, start with something low-key. Ask him to

271

lunch, or say there's a film you want to see. Better still, come along to the next tea dance. He's promised to be there on Friday, and you know Becca would love it if you came, so what have you got to lose?'

'I would say my dignity, but I think I lost that years ago.'

Jodi reached for a clean towel. 'I promise you, if you ask Eddie out, he won't say no.' She rubbed her aunty's hair, hoping the cream towel wouldn't turn black. 'And if you were honest with yourself and stopped focusing on the negatives, you'd realise only a love-struck man would voluntarily take the bins out.'

Jodi stood back from the bathtub so her aunty could straighten and shake out her hair.

Oh, heaven, hell and damnation.

It was jet black. Worse still, the dye had stained her hairline. Her aunty looked like she'd lost a fight with an inkpot. 'Although, you might want to buy another hat first,' she said, turning her to face the mirror.

Aunty Ruby screamed.

Chapter Twenty-Two

Becca suspected her mum was hiding. Ever since the disaster with her hair, she'd taken to disappearing whenever Eddie appeared. Last night Becca had found her in the cleaning cupboard crouched behind the vacuum, waiting until Eddie had gone to bed before emerging. It would be funny, if it wasn't putting a spanner in Becca's efforts to matchmake. Both she and Jodi had agreed that her mum and Eddie would make a great couple. But that wasn't going to happen if her mum kept vanishing like Harry-bleeding-Potter.

Unable to find her mum inside the guest house, Becca went into the garden. The hanging baskets had wilted, but the shrubs were still going strong, protected from the coastal winds by the surrounding wall. In the height of summer, it was glorious out here. Not so much on a blustery November day.

A flash of polka dots revealed her mum's hiding place under the archway.

Becca headed over, careful to avoid Maude who was

273

creeping along the wall primed to pounce. 'What are you doing out here?'

'Like you don't know.' Her mum pulled a face, sounding like a petulant teenager. 'Has Eddie left yet?'

'He left ages ago. And your hair isn't that bad.'

Her mum pushed back the hood of her spotted rain mac. 'I look like the Wicked Witch of the East!'

She was right. The dead-black colour had faded. It was now moss-green. 'You're right, it's a disaster.'

Her mum looked disgruntled. 'What happened to lying to protect my feelings?'

'I'm not that good an actress.' She kissed her mum's cold cheek. 'I have a ballet class this afternoon so I can't do anything today, but on Monday we're going to book an appointment at the hairdresser's. No more home dye kits, okay?'

'I can't afford salon prices.'

'I'm paying for your hair, no arguments,' Becca said, trying to sound stern. 'You've spent the entire week avoiding everybody and you didn't come to the tea dance yesterday despite promising me you would, so action is needed.'

Her mum looked sullen. 'The ballet costumes won't make themselves.'

'I said I'd help with those.' Becca shivered, her teal jumper-dress and purple tights no match for the biting wind. 'I don't expect you to make them on your own.'

'It's easier if I do them myself. The sewing room isn't big enough for two, and three weeks isn't long to get them made.'

Like Becca didn't know. The showcase was rapidly approaching and there was loads still to be done. And no money. She was hugely grateful her mum had offered to make the ballet costumes, but she didn't want her to miss out on having a social life in the process.

Talking of which... 'Jodi and I have been discussing the future of the guest house.'

Her mum sighed. 'Not this again. I know you both mean well, but I'm fine. Bad hair, aside. It's just mid-life blues. Nothing for you girls to worry about.'

'But we do worry. We want to see you happy. Not running yourself into the ground.'

'Honestly, love—'

'Just hear me out. If you don't like our idea, we won't mention it again.'

Her mum's green hair fluttered in the breeze. 'Fine. What's your idea?'

Becca took a breath, preparing for her sales pitch. 'How would you feel about converting the guest house into four rental apartments? Two upstairs and two down. Jodi and I spoke to a local estate agent, who said the rental income from four apartments would be higher than you're currently getting renting out individual rooms, which is seasonal and not guaranteed income. Plus, you'll save heaps of dosh not having to cater for the guests. Think about it. No more running around after people, no more feeling tied to the business. You'd be able to travel and take holidays. And the best bit is you already

275

have tenants for two of the apartments. Jodi and I would share one, and Eddie's keen to rent the other.'

Her mum's lifted eyebrow was lost in a sea of mouldy green. 'You spoke to Eddie about this?'

'Not in any detail. But we wanted to sound out the idea to see if it had legs. So what do you think?' Becca desperately wanted her mum to be happy, and this might be a way of achieving that.

Her mum sighed. 'I appreciate you girls trying to help, and it sounds great, but it's not possible. Not while Mrs Busby and Dr Mortimer are still here.'

Becca had anticipated this. 'Mrs Busby and Dr M have been getting a good deal for a long time. They're crafty enough to look after themselves. And it's not like they'll be out on the streets tomorrow. You could always offer them one of the apartments. They could sign up for meals-on-wheels, or something.'

Her mum frowned. 'What about Daddy's dream? You hated the idea of selling up when I suggested it before.'

'I know, but this way we get to keep his dream alive.' She took her mum's hand. 'More importantly, we get to focus on Mummy's dream. Managing all this…' She gestured to the potting sheds next to the summerhouse. 'It's not what you want, is it? Be honest.'

Her mum shook her head. 'Not really.'

'It's time to do what's right for you.' She tucked her mum's green hair behind her ears, hoping it might soften the effect. It didn't. 'Will you think about it?'

Her mum nodded.

'Good. Now, I've got to go. I'm checking out a potential artist for the showcase, and I need to catch up with Tom later.' She ran over to the kitchen door.

'You're spending a lot of time with Tom Elliot,' her mum called after her. 'You be careful.'

The mention of Tom's name caused an involuntary flinch. Becca turned back. 'It's a business meeting, nothing more.'

'Sure about that?' Her mum tried to look serious – an impossibility with green hair. 'You're not falling for him again, are you? Remember what happened last time?'

How could she forget? 'That was twelve years ago. He was a boy then. He's a man now. He's...changed. Not that I'm interested, it's just, I don't think it would be fair not to acknowledge that.'

Her mum came over. 'Has he changed? He accused Jodi of stealing.'

'That was before. He knows Jodi didn't take the money. He's trying his best to protect her.' It felt odd defending Tom. She'd despised him for so long.

Her mum sighed. 'Fair enough. I just don't want to see you get hurt again. Be on your guard, okay?'

'I will.' Dropping her guard around Tom wasn't a mistake she was likely to make. 'Now come inside Elphaba...before a tornado strikes and a house lands on your head.'

Laughing, her mum followed her inside. 'Daft thing.'

Grabbing her worn leather biker jacket, Becca left the guest house, her mum's words ringing in her ears. She didn't need anyone reminding her of how Tom had treated her. She had the scars to prove it. But when people didn't give Jodi a second chance she was quick to complain. The same rules had to apply to Tom. And it wasn't like she was falling for him again. She just didn't hate him anymore.

The thought stayed with her as she headed towards the marina near Kemptown.

Becca stopped to check the map on her phone, trying to locate the artist's warehouse. She wanted to pop in and introduce herself in the hope he might be interested exhibiting at the showcase. But as she wandered through the streets checking directions, she was distracted by the sight of a guy standing outside the Black Dove pub.

He was leaning against the wall, wearing faded jeans, Timberland boots and a Harrington jacket. Coupled with his wavy blond hair and startling blue eyes, he looked like a male model. Only, he wasn't. Not unless he'd changed profession in the last twenty-four hours.

What was Tom doing outside a pub? He never used to drink. He'd said watching his mother had put him off. Still, it was no concern of hers. He could do what he liked.

She was about to walk off, when something stopped her. It was the expression on his face. He looked…lonely. Like he had the weight of the world on his shoulders. As painful as it had been to be 'outed' by his father last weekend, she imagined it couldn't have been fun for him either.

She hadn't seen him much this week. And when she had, he'd been either refereeing a disagreement between Jodi and Vivienne, or shut away in the office staring at his laptop. And now here he was, looking dejected and lost.

Her brain told her to leave him be and focus on dealing with her own issues.

Her heart had other ideas.

Sighing, she headed over. Visiting the abstract artist could wait.

'No suit?' she said. 'Have you ruined all your formalwear attempting DIY?'

He jolted at the sound of her voice. And then he grinned. 'This is me trying to relax.'

She avoided looking at his dimples. 'How's that working out for you?'

He shrugged. 'No idea.'

She zipped up her jacket. 'How did the meeting go with George yesterday? Did he sign up for the showcase?'

Tom scrolled through his phone. 'I have photos.'

She leant closer so she could see the screen. He smelt faintly of beer. He showed her three pictures of ice sculptures, only they weren't made of ice. The first one was a large irregular-shaped chandelier. The second was a set of twisted icicles, and the final one was...

'It's the soul,' he said, as if sensing her confusion.

She looked at him. 'The soul?'

'He was a bit peculiar.'

279

She frowned. 'Define peculiar.'

'Big holes in his earlobes, piercings in his neck and tattoos covering his face.' He glanced at her purple and turquoise boots. 'You'd have got on fine with him.'

Becca's hands went to her hips. 'I'd forgotten what a heathen you are.'

He flicked one of her bunches. 'Miss Blue Hair.'

She stepped away, one eyebrow raised. He was teasing her? 'How much have you had to drink?'

He held up three fingers. 'Two beers.'

She couldn't help laughing. 'How many pieces will George be exhibiting at the showcase? What size space does he need?'

Tom rubbed the back of his neck. 'When he started using words like *concept* I lost the will to live. I said you'd ring him Monday to finalise details.'

She rolled her eyes. 'Fine. It's probably safer that way. Do you need help getting back to the playhouse?'

'I'm not *that* drunk.' He shoved his hands in his pockets. 'But I need to eat. I'm hungry.' He hesitated. 'Fancy joining me? Not a date or anything. Just...eating.'

The sensible option would be to go home. A tipsy Tom was strangely endearing. But maybe time spent away from the pressures of the playhouse would help improve their fragile working relationship. 'Where do you want to go?'

'Chips on the pier?'

She laughed. 'How very touristy of you.'

He shrugged. 'The fresh air helps my breathing.'

She couldn't argue with that. 'The pier, it is.'

They headed for the marina and crossed the road to where the Palace Pier dominated the skyline. The flags on the turrets flapped manically as the wind blew across the huge illuminated construction. The iron legs beneath held firm against the battering of the lively sea. Seagulls circled above searching for discarded food.

They walked past the dodgems, the carousel, and the bright yellow helter-skelter, watching families enjoying a day out, unfazed by a lack of sunshine. The salty air mingled with the smell of hot doughnuts and sickly sweet candyfloss.

As they queued for food, she glanced at the stalls selling Brighton rock, Slush Puppies and ice cream. The acrid scent of vinegar hovered in the air, until the wind changed direction and it disappeared.

Tom opened his wallet. 'Marcus Forbes will be arriving at the playhouse on Wednesday to fix the roof.'

He spoke so fast she wondered if she'd heard him correctly. 'Marcus Forbes? But we have no money. We can't afford to pay him.'

'I wanted you to know in case I'm not back from court when he shows up.' Tom moved forward when the queue shifted.

She caught up with him. 'How will we pay him?'

'Let me worry about that.' He reached the front of the queue and put in his order, refusing her attempts to pay for her own chips. He handed her a napkin. 'Tomato sauce?'

'No, thanks. And stop changing the subject. You can't drop a bombshell like that and not expect me to ask questions. Does this have something to do with the council grant?'

He nodded. 'I received a letter this morning. They've refused my request for an extension. Unless they receive a detailed report by the end of the month, the grant will have to be repaid.'

'Oh, crap. And we don't have the money to repay the grant, do we?'

He shook his head. 'Nope.'

At some point since reluctantly accepting the dance teacher job, Becca had become emotionally attached to the playhouse. She'd gone from associating the place with sad memories, to realising how fantastic it was. The possibilities for a thriving community arts centre were endless. And now it was under threat. 'So how come we're getting the roof fixed?'

'I realised you were right. Unless we take action, the play-house will fall into receivership. We can't risk putting on a huge event and hoping it doesn't rain. If the showcase isn't a success, it's game over.'

She couldn't agree more. 'But that doesn't answer my question about how we're going to pay for the roof fix? Has Marcus agreed to an instalment schedule?'

'Something like that.' He collected their food and headed for a quiet shelter on the west side of the pier opposite Ivor's Tarot Reading cart. 'Have you had any more thoughts about dancing at the showcase?'

282

She sat next to him. 'So you get to ask questions, but I can't?'

He tucked into his chips. 'It would be a shame if you didn't dance.'

She gave up trying to talk about the roof. She'd try again when he was sober.

Instead, she considered his question. Ever since he'd put the notion in her head she'd been toying with the idea. She missed dancing. Teaching was more rewarding than she'd imagined, but it didn't replace the rush of performing. The longer she left it, the harder it would be to return. Her knee was feeling stronger and she'd been religiously doing her exercises every day, so maybe it was time to test herself.

'I'm considering it,' she said, not wanting to fully commit until she knew it was possible and she'd conquered the self-doubts filling her head.

He smiled. 'I'm glad.' There was a softness in his expression she hadn't seen for twelve years. The impact created a tightness in her chest...and she wasn't the one with asthma.

She popped a chip in her mouth, a welcome distraction from thinking about the man next to her.

'I saw Jodi's poster designs this week,' he said, licking ketchup from his fingers. 'Are you starting classes for people with disabilities?'

She dragged her gaze away from his mouth. 'It's an idea Jodi and I came up with to engage with hard-to-reach groups within the community. One of the ballet mums has multiple sclerosis. I did some research, and apparently, dance can alleviate all manner of physical symptoms. It's proven to help with mobility and mental health issues.'

She'd always known dance improved posture and breathing, but it was when Rosie had told her that since being diagnosed she felt invisible that Becca decided it would be worth exploring. She liked the idea of helping people take back control of their bodies and discover a new way of expressing themselves.

'Plus, it's another box ticked in terms of meeting the council grant requirements.'

Tom smiled. 'Sounds like a great idea. Let me know how I can support you.'

'Thanks. I will.'

Maybe she'd suggest meetings away from the playhouse more often. Out in the open, against a backdrop of the swirling sea and bracing wind, he was more pliable than normal. Less uptight...but then he was half-cut.

'We're also thinking about dementia-friendly screenings once the cinema is in better shape.' She'd got the idea from Dr Mortimer, who struggled to watch a film in one sitting these days. 'We figured if we created a relaxed environment and scheduled in regular breaks throughout the films it might prove popular with the older community.' She was surprised to find him watching her. 'What?'

'Mum would love that.' He looked doe-eyed and boyish. His blond curls danced around his face, softening the hard contours. He was slumped next to her, his hair unruly, his eyes glistening in the dull shelter lighting. This was a very different Tom to the man in a grey suit.

She swallowed awkwardly. 'Yes, well...hopefully the council will too.'

He was still watching her, the heat of his body keeping her warm.

She should move. She ate another chip instead. 'Do you want to play a game?'

He grinned. Not just any grin. Every feature on his perfect face joined together in an assault to produce the most wicked, mischievous smirk she'd ever seen.

She tried for a look of admonishment. 'Not that kind of game.'

His expression eased into laughter. 'I always used to beat you at the slots.'

'But I always won at Dancing Stage.'

'It was hardly a level playing field.'

They'd spent many a Saturday afternoon at the amusement arcades battling over the games. It was nice to be reminded of something fun. 'Do you remember playing guess the backstory?'

He laughed. 'I do, yeah.'

She turned to look at the queue for Ivor's Tarot Reading, momentarily bereft because she wasn't gazing at Tom's face anymore. A woman in her thirties was fiddling with her mobile looking unsettled. Careful not to be overheard, she leant closer so she could whisper in Tom's ear. 'Boyfriend issues.'

He snorted. 'Too easy.'

'You didn't let me finish... She met him on Tinder. He responded to her search for a romantic man who likes Chihuahuas and enjoys the earlier works of Phil Collins.'

His laughter caused a few heads to turn. 'Did she find him, the man of her dreams?'

'No. A bald man with a limp and an unhealthy interest in Leyton Orient contacted her.' She overrode his laughter. 'He might not have been ideal, but he was kind and attentive and turned out to be hopelessly romantic, buying her flowers, posh dinners and lavishing her with gifts—'

'Too good to be true.'

She sighed. 'Thank you for pre-empting my phenomenal climax.'

He turned sharply. 'You have phenomenal climaxes?'

It was her turn to laugh.

'Shush,' he said. 'Climax quietly, will you?'

She tried to ignore the flare of heat surging through her belly. 'Are you going to let me finish?'

'Of course, a gentleman always allows a lady to finish first.'

She tried to reason the shudder rolling through her was a result of her laughter and nothing else. But it was too late to stop her mind tumbling back twelve years.

In the first few months of them dating the subject of sex had never arisen. Yet it had still been an issue. Little looks between them, stopping kissing because things had got a bit

286

heated. An intensity to their cuddling, which left them both short of breath.

It finally happened the weekend of one of Fat Boy Slim's infamous beach parties. That afternoon spent in the confines of a shabby two-man tent, fumbling around and making a right hash of trying to lose their virginity, had altered their relationship in a way she could never have envisaged.

It hadn't been great the first time; in fact, it had been embarrassing and painful. She remembered crying afterwards, afraid he'd dump her because she'd been rubbish. But Tom had been so lovely. He'd stroked her hair and kissed her repeatedly, telling her how much he loved her. When she'd finally calmed down, he'd held her close, drawing patterns on her back with his finger and making her guess what he was writing. He'd wanted to know where she was most ticklish and made her give a score out of ten for every place he tried, until he found the spot that made her squeal so much she had to push him away.

They'd ended up laughing and messing about, rolling about the tent making the airbed wobble, until the inevitable happened. The second time was much less awkward; she hadn't felt quite so detached. She'd even managed to open her eyes at one point, mesmerised by the way Tom's face contorted as he collapsed on top of her.

Once the shyness and reserve was out of the way there was no holding back. His bedroom, outdoors at Preston Park, in the treehouse in the grounds of the playhouse. Whenever the opportunity arose, they did it. There was no pressure, no planning and no guilt. Things would start out as they always had, Tom would kiss her, touch her face, or do something as innocent as brushing the hair from her eyes and that would be it. They'd stop, look at each other, and then almost knock each other out as they came together.

She'd assumed – wrongly as it turned out – that sex would always be that special.

It never had been again.

The sound of Tom's voice brought her back to the present. He'd binned their empty chip bags and returned to the shelter. 'You were saying?'

'Oh, right...well, unfortunately the bloke turned out to be a conman. He talked her into borrowing money for him and disappeared, leaving her with a huge debt and nothing but Leyton Orient goalkeeping gloves.'

He laughed and settled in next to her.

'She's sent him several texts, but he's not replied, which is why she keeps staring at her phone.'

Tom glanced over at the woman. 'Maybe he'll have a change of heart, realise he loves her and return her money.'

'Or maybe she'll see sense and shop his sorry arse to the cops.' She didn't bother shushing him when he laughed.

'You're good at this game,' he said, leaning closer, his thigh resting against hers. 'Tell me another one. Do the man next to her.' She found herself drawn to Tom's partially opened

288

mouth. His eyes glistened, but they were tired. The effects of alcohol were waning, clearly.

'I'd rather do the guy sitting next to me.'

Tom groaned and closed his eyes. 'Now that's depressing.'

'You want to hear this, or not?'

He opened one eye. 'Go ahead, how bad could it be?'

She cleared her throat. 'Well, the guy next to me has it all—'

'No, he doesn't.'

'This is *my* story, remember?' When he mimed zipping his mouth shut, she continued. 'Thank you. As I was saying, the guy next to me has it all. He's...handsome, intelligent and hardworking. He's a criminal barrister, who helps his mother maintain the family's ancestral manor—'

'Sounds like an idiot.'

'But he does have his failings.'

'Naturally.'

'For a start he has a habit of interrupting.' Her glare made him smile. 'But his main problem is that his stress levels are through the roof and that has a detrimental impact on his breathing—' She placed a finger over his lips when he made to interrupt. Their eyes locked and for a moment, everything around them seemed to still. The noise of the arcades faded away. The blustery wind died down. The lights above dimmed. The feel of Tom's warm breath tickling her skin caused a hitch in her breathing. She removed her finger.

His face was so close, their noses were almost touching. 'And how would you suggest he lowers his stress levels?'

She swallowed. 'Well, for a start, he could wear jeans more often.'

He raised an eyebrow. 'Jeans?'

She nodded. 'He's much more relaxed when he wears jeans.'

Not to mention sexy.

And playful.

Oh, hell.

Chapter Twenty-Three

Friday 10th November

Jodi was exhausted. She'd spent the entire morning on the phone trying to secure sponsorship for the showcase without much success. Most of the companies didn't want to hand over hard cash, but some had offered their services to support the event. She supposed that was something. Income was still zilch, but at least she had extra manpower available.

She added the names to the list and ticked off the need to find additional bar staff and theatre ushers. It hadn't been a totally unproductive morning.

Needing to stretch her legs, she got up from her desk and picked up her notebook. She was about to leave the office when she backtracked and checked her desk drawer was locked.

Ever since the theft she'd been paranoid about covering her arse. Tom had changed the safe combination, which hadn't surprised her, but she wished he hadn't told her the new code. He said it would look more incriminating if he didn't give it to her. Like he didn't trust her and that would only invite more suspicion. She could see his point. But it didn't make dealing with the likes of Vivienne and Petrit any easier.

Checking no one was watching, she removed the key from its hiding place under the spider plant and dumped her rucksack in the drawer, along with her treasured copy of *The Art of War*. She'd taken to reading passages daily in the hope it would improve her warfare tactics for handling the terrible twosome. Locking the drawer, she replaced the key in its hiding place. Until the cloud of suspicion had lifted she wasn't taking any chances.

Closing the office door behind her, she turned and almost bumped into the Woman-in-Black. 'Crikey, Vivienne. You made me jump.'

Vivienne's eyes narrowed. 'Have I caught you doing something untoward, Miss Simmons?'

It would be so easy to react, but Jodi needed to pick her battles. Retaliating would only give her nemesis further ammunition. 'I've done nothing wrong, Vivienne.' She tried to move past, but the woman wasn't budging.

'But you do have a criminal record for theft?'

Jodi flinched. 'Keep your voice down.' A middle-aged couple had arrived for the tea dance and were making their way through the foyer. She didn't want them overhearing.

'I'm not saying anything that isn't true.'

'No, but this is a public area. It's not appropriate to talk openly about private matters relating to staff.' Remaining professional and delivering a consistent message was all Jodi could do to counteract Vivienne's allegations. 'If you'd like another copy of the policy relating to data protection, I'll happily supply you with one. If not, please refrain from mentioning this in the public areas again.'

'And let you get away with it? Why should I?' Vivienne raised her chin, her black hair showing flecks of grey. 'It's outrageous that you're allowed to continue working here. If I had my way, the police would be called and you'd be in prison. Locked up for committing *another* crime.'

How Jodi kept her temper she didn't know. Only an acute sense of injustice kept her from walking out. 'If you have a grievance, Vivienne, put it in writing. Becca and Tom will deal with it.'

'They won't do anything. You've got them fooled with your voodoo witchcraft. Not me.' Vivienne jabbed her chest. 'I know what *your* sort are like.'

'My sort?' The instant the words left her mouth, she regretted reacting. The conceited look on Vivienne's face was galling to witness. The woman knew she'd struck a nerve.

Jodi took the only sensible option and retreated from the battle. Vivienne wanted her to lose the plot and hang herself. No way was she giving her the satisfaction.

'I'll also send you a copy of *Discrimination in the Workplace*, Vivienne. It's clear you need a better understanding of the subject.' Jodi walked off, trying to cover the shake in her hands. Awful, horrible, ignorant woman.

'The only thing I need to understand is why you haven't

293

been fired,' Vivienne called after her. 'Or sent back to *prison*.'

Jodi's eyes burned from the effort of trying not to cry. She wouldn't succumb to Vivienne's bullying. Although how much more she could take, she didn't know.

It had been three weeks since the theft and two weeks since Harvey Elliot had dropped his bombshell. Tom had called everyone into the office the following week and apologised for his father's behaviour. But it hadn't stopped Vivienne's campaign to get rid of her. Tom had been at pains to point out that Becca didn't have a criminal record and his father's accusation had been unsubstantiated. Unfortunately, the same couldn't be said for her.

The shame had been almost unbearable. She'd stared at the floor the entire time, too humiliated to look anyone in the eye. Especially Leon.

Tom had said all the right things, talked about respect and privacy and the need to investigate before jumping to conclusions. But it hadn't stopped the daily abuse.

Aunty Ruby had told her she needed to ride out the storm, and she was trying, but it wasn't easy.

Jodi headed through the bar, but there was no sign of Leon. Not that he would have acknowledged her. Gone were the days when he'd make her a drink and leave her a little gift.

Shaking off the disappointment, she found Petrit in the kitchen, rolling out pastry.

Tom had offered to accompany her when she needed to talk to the surly chef and it was a tempting offer, but if Petrit knew he unnerved her, it would only encourage him. He had enough of a chip on his shoulder as it was.

With no supervision, Petrit had been allowed to come and go as he'd pleased, smoke wherever he wanted, and never be taken to task for his rudeness. According to Eddie, Carolyn hadn't been present enough to notice his behaviour, or if she had, she hadn't had the energy to deal with it. But they couldn't afford to keep turning a blind eye. The Starlight Playhouse was in serious financial trouble. Unless they pulled together and worked as a team, the place would close. And that would be a huge loss to the community.

Petrit looked up when she entered the kitchen. 'What you want, *thief*?' He'd taken to greeting her this way every time she spoke to him. No doubt he was hoping she'd eventually cave under the pressure and quit. But that wasn't going to happen.

'I've repeatedly asked you to use more respectful language, Petrit.'

'Why? You steal money.'

She held her ground. 'The matter is being investigated. Until we know the outcome, you need to stop making accusations.' She felt like a stuck record, repeating the same request every day, only for her authority to be continually flouted.

He grumbled something under his breath.

Ignoring him, she focused on work-related matters. 'The showcase is in two weeks. I've asked you several times to come up with catering requirements for the event. Have you done this?'

He banged the worktop with the rolling pin. 'You come in here, telling me what to do. Not your place!'

'It's a simple question. Yes, or no?'

'No!'

Her instinct was to back away, but she stayed firm. 'In that case, I'll contact Buddies Café and accept their kind offer to provide catering for the event. We would've preferred to use in-house facilities, but clearly that's not possible. I'll be noting your behaviour in your personnel file.'

He began shouting in Romanian – although the word 'thief' remained in English.

Jodi made a hasty escape in case he lost it completely and threw the rolling pin at her. She backtracked through the empty bar, wishing she still had Leon's support. What she wouldn't give to look over and see his reassuring smile. But she had to deal with this on her own now. And that saddened her more than she wanted to admit.

She'd almost reached reception when she heard Tom's voice. 'This is Jodi Simmons,' he said. 'One of the co-managers I was telling you about.'

She ground to a halt and turned to face them. Charging about the place was hardly professional.

'Elaine and Stewart are here to discuss exhibiting at the showcase,' he said, approaching.

Jodi mustered a welcoming smile. 'Hello.'

'Elaine makes pottery and Stewart is an abstract artist.' Tom turned to the couple. 'Jodi's organising the event. She's the one with the business expertise. We're very lucky to have her working at the Starlight Playhouse.'

Jodi shook their hands, hoping her palm wasn't clammy. 'Lovely to meet you both.'

Tom touched Jodi's elbow. 'Do you know where their work will be exhibited?'

'I've allocated the foyer for the paintings,' she said, gesturing to the space around them. 'And the art studio for the pottery. It's a bigger space, and the exhibits will be more protected from passing footfall.'

'As you can see, Jodi has everything organised.' Tom pointed behind the couple. 'If you'd like to come this way, I'll show you the art studio. The roof is currently being repaired, so I'll need to check it's safe to enter first.'

Tom glanced back and gave Jodi a thumbs-up. His smile was so genuine it almost made up for the horror of dealing with Petrit and Vivienne. Almost.

She watched him lead the couple towards the art studio.

Having calmed down from her run-in with Petrit, she made her way to the grand ballroom for the tea dance. She wasn't overly keen on ballroom dancing – she didn't know a waltz from a quickstep, but Becca needed her. Her cousin had supported her throughout the tough times, so it was time to repay the favour.

As she opened the ballroom door, Jodi was greeted by the dulcet tones of Frank Sinatra crooning softly in the background. He was periodically drowned out by bursts of drilling from above. The roof repair team were working directly over-head.

She half expected to see plaster falling from the ceiling, but there were no signs of damage.

The room was chilly, but light from the chandeliers bounced off the white and gold décor making the room glow. The large mirrors made the room seem bigger, creating multiple reflections around the room.

Becca was standing on a chair addressing those gathered for the tea dance. She was wearing an electric blue Fifties swing dress with red Mary Jane shoes. Her hair was pulled into a high ponytail, secured with a blue ribbon, the same shade as her hair. She looked both cute and sexy. A look Jodi had never managed to pull off.

'It's wonderful to see a few new faces,' Becca said, the petticoats beneath her skirt swishing as she moved. 'Thank you for attending the Starlight Playhouse weekly tea dance.' She clapped, encouraging everyone to join in.

Jodi felt self-conscious in her dull grey work suit and plain shirt. Especially as there were still faint tomato stains visible under the bright lighting. She wished she'd brought a change of outfit. Everyone else had made an effort.

'This afternoon we're going to focus on the social foxtrot,' her cousin said, radiating a confidence Jodi envied. 'This is a dance-hall classic and is particularly well suited to a crowded room. It's also easier to learn than the traditional ballroom foxtrot.'

Aunty Ruby stood close by, her green hair partially hidden under a black scarf. She was wearing a black dress with matching tights looking scarily like Vivienne. Thankfully, her aunty was nothing like the evil front-of-house manager. Her choice of clothing was probably an attempt to blend into the background. Jodi could empathise; it was a tactic she adopted herself.

Becca looked eagerly at the group. 'Before we start, I have some exciting news. On the twenty-fifth of this month, the Starlight Playhouse will be participating in the Brighton Arts Festival. We have numerous performances and exhibitions planned, but the event will conclude with a communal dance. It would be fantastic if you were able to join in.'

Mrs Busby raised her hand. She was wearing her best pale green pinafore dress. 'Are you asking us to perform?'

'Damned if I can remember what I had for breakfast this morning,' Dr Mortimer said, looking dapper in his military blazer, 'let alone learn a dance routine.'

A few people nodded, sharing his concerns.

'I'm not suggesting a choreographed routine,' Becca reassured them. 'It'll be a relaxed informal dance where people watching will be encouraged to join in and hopefully come along to the weekly tea dances.'

Eddie raised his hand, looking very smart in his dark jeans and checked shirt. 'I'm new to this. I don't know any of the steps.' Jodi suspected his motivation for 'dressing to impress' was her aunty.

'I don't know the steps, either,' Aunty Ruby said, voicing her agreement. 'It won't look very impressive if we don't know what we're doing.'

'The spectators will be encouraged to join in if they can see varying abilities,' Becca said, pausing when the banging above got too loud. 'We want to demonstrate that the tea dances cater for all abilities from beginners to seasoned pros.' She gestured to Mrs Busby, who beamed and patted the side of her new hairdo. 'Have a think about it and let me know. I'd really love for you all to take part.'

Jodi gauged the response. Her aunty and Eddie didn't look convinced, but the middle-aged couple she'd seen arriving earlier were chatting animatedly. As were two women dressed in Forties tea dresses and seamed stockings.

Becca clapped her hands, calling for a lull in the noise. 'Shall we get started? I'm sure you're eager to begin. If everyone could find a partner, we'll begin with a closed position. You need to face your partner square on.'

Becca climbed off the chair and turned up the music.

Jodi recognised the song. *It Had to be You.*

And then she spotted Leon. He was leaning against the grand piano looking relaxed and amused. He was wearing a fitted dark grey T-shirt and black jeans. He looked sexy and adorable. Her belly dipped at the sight of him.

When he looked over, she felt herself blush. He pushed away from the piano and walked towards her, his gait slow and sexy. Her pulse kicked up another notch. Was he about to ask her to dance? His reflection bounced off the mirrors lining the walls, creating multiple images. One Leon was enough to derail her composure. A roomful was overwhelming.

As he neared, butterflies filled her tummy, sparks of pleasure raced through her veins. Maybe he was still interested in her after all...

And then he stopped and invited Mrs Busby onto the dance floor.

Jodi tried not to let her disappointment show. A weight settled in her stomach, killing the butterflies dead. It was like the floor had disappeared from under her, dragging her from hope to the depths of despair.

To anyone watching, there'd been no slight. He hadn't been spiteful, like Vivienne. Or cruel, like Petrit. His reaction to seeing her had been polite, pleasant...and totally detached. And that's what hurt so much.

Dr M appeared. 'Would you do me the honour?' he said, tipping his non-existent hat.

She forced a smile. 'Of course, Dr Mortimer.'

'The man, or lead partner, starts on their left foot,' Becca instructed, shouting above the music and drilling. 'We're looking for a nice relaxed frame.'

Jodi tried to focus, but her mind was elsewhere. She'd known this would happen. Even when she'd first met Leon and he'd shown an interest in her, she'd known that once he found out about her past his attraction would fade. She hated being proved right.

Stupidly, for a brief moment she'd allowed herself to enjoy his attentions. Even hoped they might not be temporary. More fool her. And now it was over, and she was sadder than she could have imagined.

'We're going to step forwards for a slow count of two...and then backwards,' Becca yelled, 'followed by two quick steps to the side.'

Jodi flinched when someone jabbed her on the shoulder. She turned to find the Woman-in-Black looking grim.

'What is it, Vivienne?' She couldn't imagine the woman was there to foxtrot.

'There's a delivery.'

'Can't you deal with it? You can see I'm busy.'

'Yes, *dancing*. You should be working.'

Jodi felt aggrieved. She regularly worked extra hours, far more than she was paid for. 'I'm supporting Becca's efforts to increase visitors to the playhouse, Vivienne. I'd appreciate it if you dealt with the delivery yourself.'

'No.' And with that she turned and walked off, like a vampire bat returning to Dracula's coffin.

Apologising to Dr M, Jodi left the ballroom and headed for reception. She might not have been overly enthusiastic about learning to dance, but it was a damned sight better than dealing with the Woman-in-Black.

A guy with a clipboard was waiting in reception. He smiled when she approached. 'Afternoon, love. Where would you like these?' He gestured to a pile of boxes.

She wasn't expecting a delivery. 'Can I look at the paper-work?'

'Sure.' He handed her the clipboard.

The delivery was from London Theatrical Supplies. It was the curtains for the stage.

Puzzled, she looked up. 'I cancelled the order,' she said, wondering what had happened. 'Our funding situation changed and I emailed to cancel. There's obviously been a misunderstanding. I don't know how this happened. I'm so sorry but I need to reject the order. We don't have the funds to settle the account.'

'Nothing to pay,' he said, pointing to the 'paid in full' stamp on the document.

She looked at the paperwork again. 'How...I mean, who... I don't understand?' The contact name at the top said Mr T Elliot. Tom had placed the order?

'All I know is, I'm to deliver these boxes. Where would you like them?'

'Err...in the theatre, if that's okay. If you could wait a moment, I'll fetch the key.'

She headed towards the office, her head spinning. Tom had paid for the curtains? He must have taken on board her concerns about the stage looking too bare for the dance routines. She'd tried unsuccessfully to borrow curtains from a local theatre, and now they didn't have to. Just like the roof repairs, Tom had financed the work himself.

Lost in thought, she almost didn't see Petrit in the office.

He was crouched behind her workstation, sifting through the items on her desk. 'What are you doing?'

The sound of her voice startled him. He straightened, but far from looking 'sprung', he folded his arms. 'I need timesheet.'

'What happened to the one I gave you yesterday?' She didn't believe for a minute he was looking for a timesheet.

'I need replacement.'

She looked over at the safe, checking it was shut. He didn't have the combination, but his body language told her he was guilty of something. 'I'll print off another one.' She noticed the spider plant had moved. 'In future, please don't come in here and search through my desk.'

The next thing she knew his face was inches from hers. He'd moved so quickly she didn't have time to escape. 'You have something to hide?'

'Of course not. But that doesn't give you the right—'

'People who take money should be punished.' He reeked of sweat and cigarettes. She held her breath, partly because of the smell, mostly from the fear of what he'd do next.

He grunted and left the office.

She sagged against the wall, her heart racing, her hands shaking.

What had Petrit been looking for in the office?

Chapter Twenty-Four

Tuesday 14th November

Tom parked up behind the playhouse and switched off the engine. His head hurt, he was tired, and he was hungry. He should have stopped off to buy food, but the desire to get home had been stronger. Although how much longer the Starlight Playhouse would be his home was anybody's guess. The way things were going the place would be closed in a matter of months. It was a depressing thought. Although not quite as depressing as today's trial.

He climbed out of the car and walked over to the side door, letting himself into the darkened playhouse.

His client today had been acquitted of domestic violence charges, which didn't sit well with his conscience. There'd been no doubt as to the man's guilt, or the strength of the evidence against him, but his wife was too frightened to testify against him.

Tom was fed up with representing lowlifes. But if nothing else, today's trial had confirmed his decision to switch career paths. It was time for a change.

As he neared reception, he realised a light was on. He became aware of a faint banging sound. At first he couldn't work out where the noise was coming from, but as he rounded the bend he was halted by the sight of Becca sitting on the floor hitting the radiator pipe. 'At last!' she said, stopping. 'I thought I was going to be stuck here all night.'

'The trial ran late,' he said, going over. 'What do you need?'

She looked sheepish. 'I may have glued myself to the floor.'

Whatever he'd been expecting her to say, it wasn't that. 'How the hell did you do that?'

She gave him a look of admonishment. 'Well, clearly I sat on some glue.'

He raised his eyebrows. 'That's where you're stuck?'

She nodded.

He burst out laughing. He couldn't help it. It was the perfect antidote to a crap day.

'Oh, yes, it's hilarious.' Her disgruntled expression only added to his enjoyment.

'How long have you been like this?'

'Long enough to have set.' Her blue-blonde hair was piled on top of her head. Loose tendrils framed her face and she had a smudge of red ink on her cheek. She looked adorable.

'Why didn't you call someone for help?'

She gave him a loaded look. 'Because my phone's in the office, smartarse, or else I would've done.'

He crouched down next to her. 'Let me get this straight. You're currently stuck and need my assistance?' He scratched

306

his chin. 'Goodness, this is familiar. A lesser person might use this situation to their advantage and blackmail the other person into doing what they want.'

The look on her face was priceless. 'I never blackmailed you.'

'Coerced, then.'

She folded her arms. 'Fine. You win. What it is you want?'

So many things came to mind – including rubbing the smudge of ink from her cheek. 'Nothing. I just wanted to see you squirm.' Grinning, he stood up. 'Okay, stay where you are. I need appliances.'

'I'm hardly likely to go anywhere, am I?' she called after him.

He went in search of Eddie's toolbag, chuckling to himself. She'd glued herself to the floor? Life was certainly never dull with Becca Roberts around.

He returned to reception with Eddie's toolbag, noticing the large display adorning the far wall. *One night only! The Starlight Playhouse presents a showcase extravaganza! Book now! Tickets selling fast!* Each exhibitor had their own poster with accompanying photos. The whole display was surrounded by gold bunting and varying-sized cut-out stars.

'Nice work,' he said, setting the bag down next to her. 'Eye-catching.'

'Thanks. I wanted to make an impact.'

'Although, you didn't have to include yourself in the display.'

She glared at him, but he could see she was fighting back a smile. 'Funny guy.'

Sparring with Becca was definitely a tonic. 'Where's the glue you used?'

She handed him the box.

He read the instructions. 'You used Araldite? This is heavy-duty glue, Becca.'

'I know, but Pritt-Stick wouldn't hold the bigger stars. They were too heavy. I found this stuff in the cleaning cupboard. I made a bit of a mess mixing the tubes together. The instructions said to hold it in place for fifteen minutes, so I did. But that's when I realised I was stuck and I didn't have my phone.'

He crouched down next to her. 'Has the glue seeped through to your skin?'

'I'm not sure.' She yelped when she tried to lift her leg away from the wooden floorboards. That answered that question.

'Can you wiggle out of your jeans?'

He was subjected to another glare. 'They're skinny cut.'

'Humour me.'

She sighed. 'Fine.'

Watching her ease down the zip of her jeans and attempt to wiggle out of them was hugely distracting. Not to mention hypnotic. He found himself mesmerised by a flash of red silk, before she whacked him on the arm and said, 'Stop gawping.'

It quickly became apparent that there was no way she could get herself out of the jeans. She was well and truly stuck. She looked up at him with a pair of dejected blue eyes. 'Any other suggestions?'

He had a sudden urge to touch her, but resisted. He unearthed a pair of scissors from the toolbag instead. 'Yes, but you might not like it.'

Her eyes grew wide. 'You're kidding me?'

'It's that, or I call the fire service?'

'Oh, God.' She covered her eyes. 'How has my life descended to this? Do not draw blood.'

'I'll do my best.' He shrugged off his suit jacket and rolled up his shirtsleeves. He felt like a surgeon about to go into theatre. 'Okay,' he said, stepping over her. 'We need to do this in two stages. Stage one is to cut off your jeans.' He slid the scissors under the foot of her jeans and began to cut, slowly and deliberately up her leg. When his hand slid up her thigh, she let out a tiny gasp. He stopped cutting. 'Painful?'

'Nope, it's okay.' She sounded slightly breathless. 'Carry on.'

Slowly undressing a woman as gorgeous as she was should be erotic as hell. Unfortunately, when the woman in question was glued to the floor, it put a real damper on the proceedings. 'Can you lie down?'

She blinked. 'Excuse me?'

He grinned. 'I need you on your back.'

'You're enjoying this, aren't you?'

He tried to look bashful. 'Why would you think that?'

She started laughing. Shaking her head, she lay down. 'You're not filming this, are you?'

'Of course not. Only a sick person would film someone in

309

a compromising situation.' He tried to focus on the job in hand, and not on the rise and fall of her chest. 'Stop wiggling.'

'Sorry.' Her jeans were now cut open and her leg was on display.

For a moment, he didn't move. He couldn't. Lust had rooted him to the spot.

She raised herself onto her elbows. 'Finished?'

'Not quite.' Again, he didn't move.

'I meant cutting, not gawping.'

'I'm not gawping, I'm appreciating,' he said, removing a wallpaper scraper from Eddie's bag.

Her eyes grew wide. 'What are you doing now?'

'I need to get the cloth away from the floor.'

As gently as he could, he used the scraper to prise her away from the floorboards.

Grappling with a woman's bare thigh wasn't exactly conducive to maintaining a platonic friendship. Add in the faint scent of strawberries, the lure of her glossy lips and he was wishing he *had* called the fire service. But then, he wouldn't be happy about a load of firefighters gawping at her, so maybe it was better he did it.

When he was done, he took her hands and pulled her to her feet. One leg was still encased in fabric, the other was sporting a patch attached to her thigh. The rest of the garment flopped about like a mudflap, revealing the full length of her leg and her underwear.

'Nice pants.'

'Oh, put a sock in it.' She shoved him playfully, making him laugh.

'You're on your own for this bit.' He handed her a bottle of white spirit. 'Soak the material. See if you can ease it away. Shout if you need me.'

'Oh, now you choose to be a gentleman.' With her sass returning, she marched behind the reception desk, hiding her lower half from view.

'I've had an idea about the showcase,' she said, her face a picture of concentration as she tried to remove the patch of material. 'I think we should invite the council along.'

He nearly dropped the scraper. 'Are you serious?'

She glanced up. 'Think about it. It's better than a stuffy report. We can demonstrate how we're meeting the conditions of the grant. It'll have a much bigger impact than writing to them. We can show them our vision and persuade them to believe in us.'

He raised an eyebrow. 'Us?'

She shrugged. 'I'm as invested as you are.'

'Because of Jodi?'

'Partly, yes.' She returned to removing the material. 'I'd be lying if I said I didn't want my cousin to succeed and gain a permanent job out of this. But I need to do this for me too. For the last seven years, I've been part of a tightknit community. Dancing is about evoking passion, connecting with people and providing escapism. People need that in their lives. Whether it's my tappers looking for friendship, or my ballet kids dreaming of being the next Darcey Bussell. The Starlight Playhouse provides an opportunity for the whole community to leave behind their ordinary lives and enter a world of the extraordinary.' She winced as she tried to remove the material. 'And I need that optimism in my life as much as the next person. I think you do too.'

Did he? 'Not really.'

'Oh, come on. You love playing the hero.' She continued battling with the stuck material. 'It's what drives you. Underneath that conservative exterior is a man who secretly enjoys taking risks and being adventurous. Isn't that why you became a barrister, so you could save the day?'

He honestly didn't know anymore. But maybe that's why he found defending criminals so unsatisfying. He was on the wrong side of the equation.

After much puffing and panting, she admitted defeat. 'It's no good. There's no way I'm getting this material away from my thigh. You're going to have to help me.' She appeared from behind the desk. 'Where do you want me?'

Tom had several answers. None of which were appropriate. 'Lie down again.'

She dutifully obeyed. This time on her front, so he could gain access to the back of her thigh.

He knelt behind her. Slowly and carefully he dabbed at the material, trying to ease it away from her skin, which was cool and soft...unlike a certain part of his anatomy, which was getting increasingly warm and definitely not soft. *Jesus!*

He jumped up. 'You know what, I think it's better if someone else does this.'

'Someone else?' She rolled onto her back.

'Yeah, like Jodi, or your mum. Someone...female.' Someone who wouldn't fantasise about removing her knickers. 'I'll drive you home,' he said, grabbing his jacket and handing it to her. 'Wrap this around you.'

Puzzled, she took it. 'Thanks.'

'My pleasure.'

When he got back, he was going to take a very long cold shower.

Chapter Twenty-Five

Saturday 18th November

It was only after Becca had walked into her dad's old study and seen the look on her mum's face that she'd realised her mistake. She should have waited until after the meeting before changing into her Harley Quinn costume.

Oh, well. Too late now.

Reacting to the shocked expression on her mum's face, Mrs Busby turned to see what the problem was. When she saw Becca's skimpy outfit, complete with tiny leather shorts, ripped fishnets and bare midriff below her top emblazoned with the slogan *Daddy's Lil Monster*, she tutted. 'Such an exhibitionist.'

Becca gave a sheepish grin.

In contrast, Dr M smiled. 'Goodness me,' he said, loosening his collar. 'That's not something you see every day.'

'I should hope not.' Mrs Busby elbowed Dr M when he continued to stare.

'I'm going to a fancy-dress party,' Becca said, sitting on the window seat.

Her mum gave her a disapproving glare, which held more

weight now she was minus the green hair. They'd gone to the hairdresser's earlier. Becca's freshly bleached hair had been dip-dyed with a purple ombré effect, and her mum's hair had been cut into a short pixie style and dyed a deep red. Despite her mum's apprehension that at fifty-two she was too old to have her hair done at a place called *Punktured,* she'd emerged feeling buoyant and looking ten years younger.

Any remaining doubt had dissolved when they'd arrived home and Eddie had performed a comedy double-take. 'Nice hair,' he'd said, his expression that of a bewitched man.

Her mum had shrugged off the compliment. 'Yes, well…it needed a trim,' she'd said, disappearing into the kitchen, blushing profusely.

Back to the present, and Mrs Busby and Dr Mortimer were eager to know why they'd been summoned. They were sitting on the leather two-seater, perturbed that their Saturday evening telly schedule had been interrupted.

Mrs Busby tapped her watch. 'You asked to see us, Mrs Roberts?'

'I did, yes. Thank you for coming.' Her mum got up from the wingchair and perched on the corner of the desk, clearly aiming for casual and relaxed.

Mrs Busby folded her hands in her lap. 'I was saying to the doctor earlier, perhaps Mrs Roberts has some news for us. The sound of wedding bells perhaps?'

Becca's laugh resulted in a glare from her mum.

'No wedding bells, Mrs Busby.' Her mum sounded slightly strangulated.

'What a shame. Especially as you and Mr Moriarty are so *intimate* now.'

Her mum flushed a deep red. 'I have some news that affects the guest house,' she said, avoiding eye contact with her grinning daughter. 'I'm...converting the building into four apartments.'

Mrs Busby and Dr Mortimer didn't react. No yelling. No surprise.

Clearly wondering if they'd heard, her mum raised her voice. 'I said, I'm converting the building into apartments. It will no longer be a guest house.'

Still no response.

Becca signalled for her mum to continue.

'Even if we had a full complement of guests, I'd still struggle to make ends meet. And the upkeep is getting too much for me. So, you see...' she gave them an apologetic smile '...that's why I've made this decision. I'm so sorry.'

Mrs Busby turned to the doctor. 'I told you something was afoot.'

Dr Mortimer screwed up his face. 'Speak up, woman. Damned if I can hear what's going on.' He cupped his ear. 'What did she say?'

'She said she's giving up the guest house,' Mrs Busby shouted.

'Ha!' The doctor slapped his thigh. 'That's ten pounds you owe me.'

Mrs Busby harrumphed. 'A lucky guess.'

Becca and her mum exchanged a glance.

'I think it's about time we told her, don't you?' Mrs Busby patted the doctor's knee. 'My dear, Ruby. The doctor and I have wanted to move out for years.'

Her mum's expression was priceless. 'You have?'

'We only stayed because we knew you couldn't keep going without us.'

Her mum shook her head. 'What are you saying?'

'We're saying you can stop worrying. The doctor and I will be gone before New Year. There's a nice little cottage in Hove we've had our eye on for some time.'

Her mum gasped. 'You mean...' She pointed between them. 'You two...?'

'Why, of course. Surely you aren't that blind.' Mrs Busby hauled herself to her feet. 'Come along, William. Time to start packing.'

'Goodness, Mrs Busby. I didn't mean for you to leave immediately. There's plenty of time.'

'Don't get your knickers in a twist. The doctor and I have booked a holiday.' Mrs Busby beamed at Dr Mortimer. 'We went to the travel agent's late yesterday. A last-minute deal. We fly to Palma a week tomorrow to pick up the boat.'

Her mum's mouth dropped open. 'B...boat?'

Mrs Busby nodded. 'We're going on a cruise.'

An odd mixture of admiration and envy flooded her mum's face.

'Can you imagine it, Mrs Roberts? Sailing around the Greek islands, eating gourmet food in Italy, shaking maracas in Spain? What an adventure.'

Her mum forced a smile. 'An adventure indeed, Mrs Busby. I'm delighted for you both. I'm sure you'll have a wonderful time.'

They left the room. There was a few seconds' delay before her mum screamed.

Becca rushed over. 'Before you have a complete meltdown let's focus on the positives.'

'Positives? All this time I've been running around after them, cooking, cleaning, making beds, and the whole time they were staying because they felt *sorry* for me?'

'It's upsetting, I know. But it could've been worse.'

'How?'

Becca tried not to laugh at her mum's disgruntled expression. 'You expected them to be devastated by the news and they weren't. You were panicking about where they'd live and the guilt you'd feel at making them homeless. Now you can stop worrying. They're going to be fine. Best of all...' she took her mum's hands '...there's nothing stopping you from booking a holiday now.'

'Like the pair of them you mean?' She stamped her foot. 'A *cruise*?'

Becca darted over to the bookshelf and removed the travel brochure Jodi had told her about. 'It's galling, I know. Why don't you open a bottle of wine, curl up on the sofa, and pick out a holiday for yourself?' When her mum looked sceptical, she added, 'Come on, Mum. You deserve this.'

Her mum took the brochure. 'I'm in shock.'

'Me too. But that'll wear off, and then you'll see this is a better outcome than we could've hoped for.' She kissed her mum's cheek, leaving a smudge of lipstick. 'Mrs Busby and Dr Mortimer? Blimey. Who knew?'

'Well, not me, that's for certain.' Her mum fanned her face with the brochure.

The grandfather clock struck nine p.m. 'Right, I've got to go. The bus is due at ten past. Don't wait up... Love you.'

Leaving her stunned mum to recover, Becca headed into the hallway. She didn't see Maude leap out from behind the reception counter until a loud screech was followed by pain shooting up her leg.

Her yelp alerted Eddie, who appeared looking concerned. 'You okay?'

Becca rubbed her leg. 'I'm fine. Just as well these tights were already ripped, or I wouldn't be happy.' She glared at the cat, who in typical Maude fashion sneered.

Eddie picked up Maude. 'How did it go breaking the news? Does your mother need consoling?'

'It went surprisingly well. Although...' A plan was starting to formulate. 'How would you feel about a holiday, Eddie?'

He raised an eyebrow.

'Mum's always wanted to travel, but she hasn't been able to. Now things are changing we're hoping she can be persuaded to book something. Travelling alone isn't much fun...but if she had someone tagging along?'

He grinned. 'Leave it with me.'

'You're a star, Mr Moriarty.'

He laughed.

She went to hug him, but Maude hissed. 'Mum's in the study looking at a travel brochure. Strike while the iron's hot.' She unhooked her leather jacket from the coat stand. 'I'm off out. Night, Eddie... And thank you.'

He winked at her. 'My pleasure.'

'And thanks for the bloody leg, Maude!' Poking her tongue out at the cat, she left the guest house and skipped down the steps to catch the bus.

Her leg was still sore from being glued to the floor on Tuesday. It had taken several attempts to prise the material away, and she'd been left with an unattractive red patch, which she'd had to cover up with make-up for tonight. The memory of Tom's long fingers trailing up her bare thigh ignited another flare of heat within her, and she had to shake the image away. It was getting increasingly hard not to think about him.

Luckily, the bus pulled up just as she reached the stop. She hopped aboard, searching in her jacket pockets for tissues to wipe her leg.

Ignoring odd looks from those aboard the bus, she found a seat and settled in for the short journey to Preston Park.

Nick from her tap class had phoned yesterday in a panic. The venue for his wife's thirtieth birthday party had cancelled last minute and he wanted to use the playhouse instead. It was the perfect venue for a big function, so they'd spent the day decorating the grand ballroom, ensuring the party would be amazing and Cassie would have a great night. The theme was Heroes and Villains. Hence her Harley Quinn outfit.

Jodi had taken charge getting the party started, but she was working at the restaurant tonight, so it was up to Becca to oversee the latter part of the evening.

As Becca exited the bus and walked up the long driveway to the Starlight Playhouse, she was once again blown away by the view. The building looked impressive against the dark skyline. Fairy lights outside made it look inviting. Cars filled the driveway, an unusual sight. Although not as unusual as the sight of Dracula pulling up in a Land Rover.

Smiling, she headed inside.

The foyer was full, a gaggle of bodies dressed in bizarre and elaborate costumes. There were several comic book characters. Make-up, false limbs, S&M accessories, fake blood – you name it, it had been incorporated. It was a shame Vivienne wasn't here. The Woman-in-Black would have fitted in perfectly.

Becca shrugged off her leather jacket and tucked it behind reception.

Guy Fawkes appeared in front of her. Even under his vendetta-style hat and false moustache she could see it was Nick. 'You look great! Where's Cassie?'

'Dancing in the ballroom. Thanks so much for coming to our rescue.' He trod on his cape and dropped his stick of fake dynamite. At least, Becca hoped it was fake.

She picked it up for him. 'No problem. Glad to help. And besides, you're helping me by taking part in the showcase next week. Are you looking forward to it?'

He grimaced. 'Not really.' He was honest, if nothing else. 'Actually, that's not true. I'm just a bit nervous. We both are.'

'Nerves are a good thing. It means you care. You'll be fine. The rehearsal on Wednesday went really well.' She was such a liar. The tappers had yet to make it through the routine without messing up. And with the council now attending the showcase, there was even more pressure to succeed. However, pointing this out wouldn't be helpful.

'I hope you're right.' He gave her a sheepish grin. 'Can I get you a drink?'

'I'll help myself. You enjoy the party.' She left him battling with his cape and made her way through the throng of people, enjoying encounters with Harry Potter and a Death Eater before making it to the bar.

A huge witches' cauldron sat on a table. Beetlejuice was ladling up potent-looking punch for the guests. It was a second before she realised it was Leon under the stripy suit and blackened eyes.

He handed her a glass. 'Hunch Punch?'

She could smell something fruity. 'What's in it?'

'Peach vodka, pineapple juice and Sprite.'

'Sounds suitably inebriating. Give me a large one.' She took a sip. 'God, that's good.'

He grinned. 'Is Jodi coming tonight?'

Becca raised an eyebrow. He'd stopped asking about her cousin after the theft. 'She's working at *Pho-King Good* tonight.'

He cupped his ear, assuming he'd misheard. 'Come again?'

'The Thai restaurant.'

He looked surprised. 'I didn't know she had a second job.'

Becca gave him a reprimanding look. 'There's a lot you don't know about my cousin. Despite what some people might think Jodi's very hardworking. She's honest, loyal and nowhere near as tough as she looks. Anyone who thinks otherwise is sorely misguided.'

Something flickered across his face. It was hard to decipher what under the make-up. 'Enjoy the party,' he said topping up her drink and moving on to the next partygoer.

Leon was a conundrum. He'd never sided with Vivienne or Petrit when they were being shitty to her cousin, but he didn't jump to Jodi's defence either. Not since the theft. He was the Switzerland of the playhouse, staying out of any arguments.

But there were moments when he'd glance at Jodi, a sad expression on his face. Becca wished he'd believe in her. Still, if he couldn't see what an amazing person she was then he didn't deserve her.

She backtracked through the bar, past where the food was laid out, sidestepping the Grim Reaper fondling Cinderella. Not surreal at all.

She spotted the door to the art room was ajar and went to close it. They didn't want people venturing inside. But as she pulled the door to, she heard a low thumping sound from inside. Before she could reason her actions, she opened the door, unprepared for the sight of an Egyptian Mummy 'doing' Wonder Woman up against the shelving.

Becca's brain tried to compute what she was seeing. The couple didn't appear to notice the intrusion, or if they did, they were too absorbed to care. Wonder Woman had her eyes closed, her head dropped back against a stack of paintbrushes, as she panted, 'Naughty...naughty...Mummy.'

When the Mummy groaned and hoisted Wonder Woman up, revealing more than Becca needed to see – even without the lights on – she stepped back and closed the door.

Guests shouldn't be in the art room, and certainly not getting down and dirty. But no way was she about to attempt 'coitus interruptus'. She'd pop back later when they'd 'finished' and lock the door.

Downing her drink, she stopped off for a refill, before heading into the ballroom.

The familiar sound of Beyoncé's 'Crazy in Love' greeted her as she entered the room. It was lovely to see the ballroom full. Bunting decorated the walls, along with fairy lights and large posters showing Cassie at various stages in her life.

The birthday girl was on the dance floor. Watching Mary Poppins 'twerking' was almost as surreal as seeing the Mummy and Wonder Woman 'at it'. Maybe not quite. Becca hoped the image would rapidly fade from her brain.

Cruella de Vil waved at her from the side of the room. Judging by the mannerisms and lack of height, she guessed it was Miriam. She headed over.

Mi-Sun was next to her, dressed as Batman. 'I hope this isn't what you're wearing for the showcase,' Becca said, trying not to laugh at the sight of Mi-Sun with her underpants over her tights. 'Maybe I shouldn't have let Wanda take charge of the costumes.'

Miriam grunted. 'The less said about that the better.' She pushed her half-black half-white wig from her eyes. 'She's talking about white bodysuits. Can you imagine me in Lycra?' She gestured to her rotund middle. 'Think again, I told her. People aren't paying good money to see my wobbly bits on display.'

Mi-Sun lifted her mask. 'Wanda doesn't have any body hang-ups like we do.'

'Tell me about it. You should see the costume she's wearing tonight.' Miriam tutted. 'Wonder Woman, would you believe?'

Becca spurted punch everywhere and started coughing, soaking her top.

Miriam smacked her on the back. 'The woman looks a right spectacle. Skirt up to her armpits.'

Yep, that just about described what Becca had seen too. 'Excuse me, I need to clean up.' Brushing her top, she left the ballroom, her head spinning from the realisation that Wonder

Woman was Wanda. She'd never be able to look the woman in the eye again.

Becca made a detour for the office when she remembered Jodi had wet wipes on her desk. It was only when she reached the door she realised it would be locked. Except, it wasn't. Cautiously, she popped her head around the door.

Tom was sitting at his desk typing on his laptop.

'You're working when there's a party out here?'

His eyes grew wide when she walked into the room.

'What?' She looked down. 'Oh, right. I spilled punch down myself.' Technically, she'd spat punch down herself. She figured he didn't need to know that.

His gaze travelled the length of her body. 'I hadn't noticed.'

'No? My leg then? Maude attacked me.'

'Not that either.' His head tilted to one side, a strange look on his face. 'Who's Maude?'

'My mum's evil cat.'

'Right.' He swallowed. 'Nice...outfit.'

'Thanks. Why are you working?' When he didn't respond, she clicked her fingers, snapping him out of his trance. 'Tom.'

He blinked. 'What?'

She studied his flushed cheeks. 'Is your breathing okay?'

'It's been better,' he said, ruefully.

She frowned. 'I thought your asthma was getting better?'

'It is.' He rubbed the back of his neck. 'Do you have to stand like that?'

'Like what?' Her hands were on her hips, her weight resting on one foot. 'I often stand like this.'

'Yeah, but normally wearing more clothes.' His eyes were dark and hot, and sent something liquid running down her spine.

Her outfit was a little skimpy. Still, it was quite reserved compared to some of the things she'd worn dancing. But then he was Mr Conservative, favouring a suit for all occasions. Although not tonight...and that wasn't helping her efforts not to jump him.

She went over to Jodi's desk and removed a handful of wet wipes. 'Jeans again? You're listening to my advice then?' She lifted her top and began wiping. 'Is it working? Are you feeling more relaxed?'

'Not right at this moment,' he said, shaking his head. 'Did you want something?'

'I came in here for these.' She indicated the wet wipes. 'You didn't answer my question. Why are you working?'

'I thought I should stay close by in case anything happened. How's the party?'

She deliberated whether to tell him about Wonder Woman and the Mummy. Probably not. It was his family home, after all. 'It's great. Nick and Cassie are ecstatic. The place is buzzing.' She wiped her sticky hands and binned the wipes. 'It's a good dry run for next week. The display in reception is attracting a lot of interest.'

Mentioning the display acted as a trigger. She could tell

from his expression that his mind had tumbled back to Tuesday night. The atmosphere between them since had been charged, like an electrical current was crackling around them. It was happening again now.

She cleared her throat. 'Anyway, I'm hoping people will come back for the showcase.'

'Let's hope.'

She sauntered over to him. 'The stage curtains look great, by the way.'

'Good.'

'And the roof is fixed now.'

'I know.'

She leant on the desk. Two glasses of punch had lowered her inhibitions. 'Are you going to tell me how we paid for the work?'

His eyes dipped to her bellybutton ring. 'Nope.'

'Are you going to explain how we suddenly have printed flyers, a stocked bar and new spotlights in the theatre?'

His mouth twitched. 'Nope.'

'Fine.' She turned and sat on his desk.

He started typing. After a minute, he sighed and sat back in his chair. 'Are you going to sit there all night?'

'Depends.'

'On?'

She smiled. 'On how resistant you are to joining the party.'

'I'm not invited.'

'You can be my plus-one.'

328

He gestured to his T-shirt and jeans. 'I'm not in costume.'

'Costumes aren't compulsory.'

'I should be working.'

'No, you should be relaxing.' She gave him a look. 'Remember?'

He sighed. 'You're not going to go away, are you?'

'Hell, no.' She swung her legs around and hopped off the desk. 'Dancing is an excellent relaxer.'

'I'm not dancing.'

She leant over his shoulder and closed his laptop. 'No point fighting.' Her face was inches from his. A warning voice in her head told her she was playing a dangerous game. But the alcohol in her bloodstream fuelled her desire to have some fun. It had been ages since she'd enjoyed herself. She wanted to dance.

More significantly, she wanted to strip away Tom's protective layers and see whether the eighteen-year-old she'd once adored still lurked somewhere deep inside.

There was a long drawn-out moment where they both looked at each other. Her skin began to prickle with heat, but she refused to look away.

Eventually, he let out an exasperated laugh and rubbed his eyes. 'Christ.'

She took that as victory and sashayed over to the door.

He got up from the desk and came over to her. 'You should come with a government health warning.'

'I'll take that as a compliment.'

329

He followed her out, locking the door behind him.

She slid her hand into his and led him through the mass of people and into the grand ballroom. The dance floor was packed. The sprung wooden flooring moved beneath them as people jumped about to 'Love Shack'. He was tentative at first, unwilling to join in. He shook his head in an amused fashion as she began dancing.

Her 'nightclub' dancing, as she called it, was no better than anyone else's. It wasn't choreographed, or structured. It was gyrating, shaking arms and legs, and letting the music dictate the moment.

He loosened up a fraction during 'I Gotta Feeling', moving his feet from side to side. She laced her fingers into his, trying to get him to relax. He laughed at her efforts. When 'Dancing Queen' came on she slid her arms around his neck. In six-inch heels, she was almost eye level, able to enjoy the pained expression in his eyes. His shoulders were like blocks of concrete, rigid with tension.

'Relax your shoulders,' she shouted above the music.

He rolled his head, trying to loosen up. He only managed it when the music took a slower turn. Ed Sheeran starting singing 'Perfect'. Tom let out a long breath, his shoulders lowering with the motion.

She set the pace, moving with the rhythm, guiding the pair of them around in a circle, their bodies relaxing into each other.

It was like being transported back to 2006. No longer

fighting one another, but in total unison. His arms slid around her, pulling her closer. She rested her head on his shoulder and let the music fill her senses, enjoying his warmth, his smell. The vice around her heart began to slacken for the first time in what felt like forever.

'What do you miss about being a teenager?' she asked.

He rested his chin on her head. 'I can't answer that without incriminating myself.'

She sighed. 'I miss snogging.'

His burst of laughter made her head bobble against his chest.

'We used to kiss for hours.'

He looked down at her. 'I remember.'

'You can't do that as an adult.'

He smiled. 'You can't?'

'When we used to kiss it never used to lead on to anything else...' She paused. 'Well, not in the beginning, anyway.' It was safer not to think about where it'd led after that. 'I used to love kissing you. You made me feel...I don't know, like I could just enjoy it without my behaviour being...questionable. You could never snog someone like that now and just stop when you'd had enough. You have to be so guarded, in case things move quicker than you're ready for them to. I miss that. I think adults skim through the best bits, too eager to get laid.'

He laughed again. 'You think kissing is the best bit?'

She paused. 'It's not just the kissing; it's what goes with it.

That lovely feeling when you can't wait to see someone and the nervous excitement when you do. Feeling giddy when they touch you and wanting more, but not getting it, and then by the time you do...wow.' She sighed. 'Grown-ups miss out on that, don't you think?'

He didn't say anything.

'You don't agree?'

'No, it's just...'

'What?'

She looked up at him, but his expression was unreadable. 'That feeling never wore off, Becca. Even after we'd...'

The room seemed to stop spinning.

Chapter Twenty-Six

...later that night

The grand ballroom looked a sorry sight. Gone were the flashing disco lights and thumping music. It was now littered with discarded bottles and glasses, and remnants of food smearing the floor. At least it was empty. The drunken partygoers dressed in bizarre costumes had departed, returned to their homes where sore heads and hangovers awaited. It was gone midnight before the party had started to wind down. Tom had intended to clear up, but decided it could wait until the morning when the cleaners would arrive.

For now, he needed to ensure there were no stragglers left in the building and lock up. His bed awaited.

Thoughts of his bed led to thinking about Becca and the image of her dressed as Harley Quinn. Christ, she was hot. She'd always been beautiful. Now she was mind-blowing. As a teenager, she'd been cute with big blue eyes and long blonde hair. Aside from the appeal of her dancer's physique, she'd always worn a smile, her persona animated and playful. And even though their relationship had developed into intimacy over time, it had been based around love and affection. Most of all fun.

Seeing Becca again after so long had ripped open a wound that had never healed. And that made him angry. He hadn't wanted to revisit his past. He didn't want a reminder of how things had once been. It was torture. Gut-twisting. But over the last couple of weeks something had changed. And he was still coming to terms with the shift in their relationship.

It was impossible to stay angry with someone so…adorable. Whatever illegalities she may have been guilty of at sixteen it hadn't affected the woman she'd become. She defended Jodi with a passion that was admirable, and her desperation to save the playhouse showed the depth of her kindness and desire to help people.

But there was one big difference between the teenage version of Becca and the adult version. And that was sex appeal.

He backtracked through the foyer towards reception.

Liking her again was one thing. Wanting to carry her upstairs and remove her fishnets with his teeth was quite another. He wasn't sure when things had changed. His attraction had been growing steadily over the last few weeks. Chipping away at the barriers he'd built to protect himself from getting hurt again. But at some point during the last week he'd gone from wishing he'd never laid eyes on her to dreading never seeing her again. And that scared the shit out of him.

334

But he could no longer deny what he felt. When they'd danced together all remaining resistance had melted away. The feel of her in his arms, the smell of her skin, the sound of her voice and laughter. It was like he could finally breathe. What that meant for the future, he had no idea.

He noticed the door to the art studio was open and the light was on. He hoped he wasn't about to discover a drunken partygoer passed out on the floor. It was bad enough Captain America had fallen asleep in the bar and needed lifting into a taxi. Tom's back was still complaining.

There were no partygoers in the art studio. Only Becca. She was balancing on a table, trying to reach the tall sash window. Her arms were raised above her head, lifting her skimpy top and revealing a tattoo of a twirling dancer on her lower back. The muscles in her legs flexed as she reached up, making her shorts ride up. He could see a faint red patch on her thigh where she'd glued herself to the floor. Lust rooted him to the spot.

Only the precariousness of her unstable position prevented him from continuing to admire the view. 'Need a hand?'

She jolted at the sound of his voice, kicking over the chair she'd used to climb up. She flailed about, trying to regain her balance.

He darted over and grabbed her by the legs. But far from playing the 'hero', as she'd accused him of doing on Tuesday, all he managed to do was topple her off the table. He caught her, but as he stepped backwards, he collided with the upturned chair and lost his footing. There was an almighty crash as they landed on the table, which promptly collapsed.

She let out a painful yelp.

He banged his elbow on something, but he was more concerned about her. She was clutching her knee. 'Shit! Are you okay?'

Her face was screwed up. 'I'm not sure.'

'I'm so sorry,' he said, mortified at having injured her. Supposing she never danced again and it was all his fault. 'What can I do? Do you need ice?'

'Just give me a minute,' she said, rubbing her knee. 'The pain might subside.' She bent her leg, wincing when she straightened it.

'I can't believe I dropped you.'

She managed a self-deprecating smile. 'It's not the first time I've been dropped. I've had my share of inept male dance partners. It's no big deal.'

He felt himself frown. 'It's a big deal to me.'

She surprised him by laughing. 'Lighten up. It's only a knock, I'll live.'

He frowned. 'You're bleeding.'

She glanced at her leg. 'That was Mad Maude, remember? And you're bleeding too. My bracelet must've caught you.' She trailed a finger down the side of his cheek. 'Sorry.'

His breath hitched. But that could just be the sting in his face. 'It's fine.'

Her eyes stayed locked on his. 'Are you hurt anywhere else?'

He shook his head. 'You?'

'Nothing major. Can you help me stand up?'

He got to his feet and pulled her up. 'Can you put any weight down?'

She tested her leg. 'Yep, all good.' The pained expression on her face didn't match her words.

He slid his arm around her. 'Liar.'

She laughed. 'Stop worrying, will you? I just need to walk it off.'

'Lean on me, then. Take it easy.' He took her weight as she hobbled around the room. 'Why were you standing on the desk?'

'I was closing the window.'

'Why was it open? No one was supposed to be in here.'

She laughed. 'That's the thing about parties, people get carried away.'

'And randomly open windows?'

She looked at him. 'I'm guessing they opened the window because things got a little steamy in here.' She raised an eyebrow, waiting for him to catch on.

It took a moment. 'You're kidding? In here? Tonight?'

She laughed, her purple bunches swaying with the motion. 'Afraid so.'

'It wasn't Superman, was it? I saw him getting frisky with Maleficent in the bar.' And then he changed his mind. 'Actually, I don't want to know.'

She leant against him. The scent of her perfume made him feel light-headed.

337

'How's your knee?'

'Not too bad. Hopefully, there's no permanent damage.' She stopped walking. 'I might need to sit down for a bit.' When he picked her up in his arms, she laughed. 'What are you doing?'

'Redeeming myself.' He adjusted her position and carried her out of the room. He'd been wanting to do this for weeks. 'You'll never make it up the staircase with a bad knee.'

'We're going upstairs?' She had a playful look on her face.

He stilled. 'Unless you'd prefer me to call you a taxi?'

'I'd prefer it if you called me Becca.'

His laughter made carrying her across the foyer more challenging. He could feel the warmth of her body pressed against him, the texture of her skin soft through the rips in her tights. Her arms were snaked around his neck. The brush of her hair against his face made him shiver. He wanted to kiss her. He wanted to do more than that. But she was injured and he needed to negotiate the stairs.

He stepped over the rope cordoning off the private quarters. He felt quite manly as he lifted her over. Tarzan, eat your heart out. But then his trail leg snagged on the rope and he toppled forwards. With his foot ensnared he couldn't stay upright, and his balance had gone south. They fell to the floor together and this time he landed on top of her.

She smothered a yelp.

This was not the way to impress a woman. He pushed himself onto his elbows. 'Becca...? Are you okay?'

When she laughed, his insides melted. 'I'm fine, Casanova.'

A tiny voice in his head told him he should move. He was lying on top of her, arms either side of her head, knees either side of hers, trying not to squash her. He was also panting heavily.

It wasn't the worst position he'd ever found himself in. Despite being sprawled on the floor, it didn't stop the intensity of the moment registering with a certain part of his anatomy. The feel of her chest rising and falling beneath his only added to the tension. He was close enough to touch her, to whisper in her ear. It was the ideal moment to tell her how he felt...but come to think of it, how *did* he feel?

He risked a glance down and found her staring up at him. 'Shall I move?' he whispered.

She shook her head.

The next thing he knew they were kissing.

Her lips were warm and willing. She responded with such passion it knocked him sideways. Any thoughts of self-control went flying out the window. He'd been dying to do this ever since the moment he'd set eyes on her again. He moved against her mouth, drawing her in, making her moan. He wasn't sure it'd been anything like this as a teenager. She was clinging hold of him like she never intended to let go.

When she wrapped her legs around him, he nearly lost his mind.

He could taste her, smell her; everything he'd forgotten came flooding back, reminding him why he'd been so crazy for her. Why he'd fallen in love with her in the first place. But that wasn't going to happen again. This was just snogging.

The hell, it was.

Her hands were laced into his hair, gripping hold, her body pressing against him, urging him on...and he really didn't need any encouragement.

'Tom...?'

'Oh, God, Becca.' He wanted her so much.

'Tom?' Her voice was sharper this time.

He kissed her neck, his tongue trailing over her soft skin. 'What is it...? What do you want me to do?'

'*Tom!*' This time a command.

He jerked back, his brain drugged with lust and desire. It took a few seconds to compute it wasn't Becca calling his name, but... *Shit!*

He dragged himself upright, as though branded by a cattle prod. Becca yelped when his knee hit her thigh. 'Sorry...sorry.'

It was too much to hope it was an apparition. A bad dream, or his brain playing dirty tricks. Standing in front of him, hands on hips, staring down at him, was his sodding ex-girlfriend. 'Izzy?'

'Hello, darling.' Her forlorn expression switched to calculating when she spotted Becca. 'I didn't mean to interrupt. I'm Tom's girlfriend.'

'*Ex*-girlfriend,' he said, feeling as poleaxed as Becca looked. He offered Becca his hand and carefully pulled her to her feet. 'Are you okay?'

'I'm fine.' He kept hold of her. He didn't want her running off.

Izzy gave Becca the once-over. 'What an unusual outfit. Are you some sort of hired entertainer?'

Becca's cheeks flushed.

'Let me get you upstairs,' he said to Becca, ignoring Izzy. 'You need to ice your knee.'

Izzy feigned concern. 'Oh dear, are you hurt?' She swished her long hair over one shoulder. 'Must be all that rolling around on the floor.'

Tom shot her a look. 'Pack it in, Izzy.'

'Have I said something wrong?' She attempted a butter-wouldn't-melt look.

Becca shook her head. 'I think it's best if I go home.'

The weight of disappointment settled in his chest. 'There's no need. Izzy's not staying.'

Izzy faked a concerned smile. 'The taxi's still outside if you need to go somewhere. I didn't have enough cash to pay the driver so I asked him to wait.' She removed her camel-coloured coat and placed it on the suitcase by her feet. A not-so-subtle hint that she intended to stay. 'Be a love and settle up for me, darling.'

Becca's eyes drifted to the suitcase. 'I'll leave you to finish locking up.'

Every fibre in Tom's body wanted to hold on to her. There was so much he wanted to say. But the moment had gone. Ruined by his ex. 'I'll see you out.'

She held him at arm's length. 'No need.'

He dug out his wallet. 'Let me give you some money.'

'Twenty-five quid, plus tip.' Izzy smoothed down the front of her fitted black dress. 'It's double fare after midnight.'

He handed Becca fifty quid. The money he was supposed to be giving the cleaner in the morning. 'Text me when you get home. I need to know you're okay.'

She gave him an incredulous look. 'Go and deal with your girlfriend.'

'*Ex*-girl—'

'Whatever.' She sighed. 'I'm tired. I'm going home to bed.'

Izzy gave her a little wave. 'That's probably for the best.'

Tom focused on Becca. 'Let me help you out to the taxi.'

'I can manage.' She hobbled away.

'Nice meeting you,' Izzy called after her.

Tom waited a beat before storming over. 'Quit with the sarcasm. Why are you here, Izzy?'

She touched his chest. 'Aren't you pleased to see me?'

'No.'

She baulked at his answer, but he knew her well enough to realise it was an act. He watched her face morph from shock, to hurt, to upset. How had he been so blind to her manipulations for so long?

'Let's go upstairs and talk,' she said, sliding her arm through his, no doubt hoping Becca would see before she disappeared.

He unhooked his arm. 'I'm not in the mood for your games. Why are you here?'

She looked around. 'What a great place. It's a shame you've never brought me here before. I like it. Can I have the full guided tour?'

'No. Answer the question.'

'You're bleeding?' She touched his cheek. 'Let me tend to that for you.'

He stepped away. 'Why are you here, Izzy?'

'Why don't you fix us a drink and then we can chat.'

'Answer the bloody question!'

The smile fell from her lips. 'Fine. I need a place to stay until Harry gets back from New York.'

Who the hell was Harry? Maybe he was the guy who'd turned up at the flat with her? Tom no longer cared. He just wanted her gone. 'Why didn't you stay at the Travelodge?'

'I didn't like it there. I was lonely.' She sounded sulky.

'Can't you stay with your parents?'

'Daddy's stopped my allowance. He says I need to get a job.' She made it sound like this was the most ridiculous suggestion ever. 'It's just a couple of days. Surely you can put me up for two days? You owe me that much.'

He ran his hands through his hair. 'You're unreal.'

'Oh, come on. It's not a huge ask. Two days...three max.' She batted her eyelashes.

'Izzy, you're not staying here.'

Her bottom lip wobbled. 'I have nowhere else to go.'

'That's not my problem. And you had somewhere to stay. A place I was paying for.' A fact that irked more now he knew she was seeing another bloke. Why wasn't *he* paying for Izzy's accommodation?

Tears ran down her face. 'It's because you have another woman, isn't it? You've no idea how much it hurts to see you with someone else. I still love you.' She moved towards him. 'I want us to be together. I always have.'

He wasn't falling for that old chestnut. 'No, you don't, Izzy. You just don't want anyone else to have me.'

'That's not true.'

'Yes, it is. You want me on hand to bail you out, to pick you up when your life spirals out of control. That's not love. It's need.'

Her hands went to her hips. 'So, I need you. What's wrong with that?'

He had a flashback of Becca standing in the office adopting the same stance in her Harley Quinn outfit. A sense of yearning engulfed him. He wanted her so much.

In fact, he'd never wanted a woman more.

But Becca's 'hero' accusation had struck a nerve. He'd thought of little else all week. He'd realised she'd been right. But his need to 'rescue' people didn't come from a sense of bravery or heroism. It stemmed from guilt. He felt guilty for breaking Becca's heart twelve years ago. Guilty that he hadn't been able to save his mother from alcoholism. And guilty for pursuing his own career while his mother struggled to run the playhouse.

If he'd been able to rescue Izzy, then it might have eased

the torment of letting everyone else down. Izzy was constantly yo-yoing between drugs, alcohol and partying. She hadn't wanted him when her life was good, but relied on him when she crashed and burned. And he'd tolerated it because he felt guilty.

It was time to rectify that mistake.

He faced his ex-girlfriend. 'Our relationship is over, Izzy. You can't keep relying on me. It isn't healthy. Or fair. On me, or you. You keep saying it's one last time, but it never is. I thought things would change when we split up, but they haven't. You need to do as your father suggests and sort your life out, and without me there to keep bailing you out. We need to make a clean break so we can both move on with our lives.'

Her expression hardened. 'So you're going to throw me out on the streets?' She shoved him in the chest. 'Callous bastard.'

He wouldn't do that, it was gone one a.m. 'You can stay for tonight.'

Her anger disappeared, replaced by a seductive smirk. 'Thanks, baby. I knew you wouldn't let me down.'

He stepped away when she tried to touch him. 'But in the morning, I'll drive you back to London.' He picked up her suitcase. 'And then I never want to see you again.'

Doubt crept into her smile when she saw his resolute expression. 'You...you don't mean that.'

He held her questioning gaze. 'Yes, Izzy. This time, I do.'

Chapter Twenty-Seven

Thursday 23rd November

Becca winced when feedback from the headset penetrated her ear. She removed her earpiece, waiting until the noise ceased. Eddie was in the lighting booth, showing the students from the Brighton Music Institution how to plot the effects board. It was slow progress. But as they were providing their expertise free of charge she wasn't about to complain.

She took the opportunity of a lull in proceedings to go over to her mum, who was seated in the stalls making a few last-minute alterations to Phoebe's costume.

'I think Eddie's got his work cut out with the students,' she said, plonking herself down on one of the theatre's fold-up seats.

Her mum focused on threading a needle. 'I'm sure he'll manage. He's a very resourceful man.' Her cheeks had coloured, which thankfully no longer clashed with her hair.

Becca laughed. 'Resourceful?'

Her mum glanced up. 'Less than a day after mentioning I needed to find a surveyor to provide quotes for the guest

346

house renovations, one turned up.' She dug the needle into the chiffon. 'He's already checked out what planning permission I'd need, and spoken to the water company about moving sewerage pipes.'

'Don't you want his help?'

'It's not that. I'm grateful. Really I am, but it's all moving a little too fast.'

Becca glanced into the wings, checking her ballet kids were behaving themselves. 'So ask him to slow down. Say you need time to adjust to the changes.'

'It's not me I'm worried about.'

Becca turned to her mum, puzzled by her concerned expression. 'You're not worried about me, are you? I'm the one who suggested it, remember?'

'I know, but you've always been so adamant about holding on to Daddy's dream. This change is going to be hard for us all. And you've looked so dejected this last week. I wondered if you were regretting the suggestion?'

It was true that the guest house renovations had opened an old wound. The idea of seeing her dad's handiwork being knocked down was gut-wrenching, but it wasn't the sole cause of her sombre mood.

Her mum took her hand. 'The relationship you had with your dad won't be affected by any changes we make. You know that, right?'

Becca shrugged. 'I guess. It still makes me sad that he died believing I'd broken the law. I hated disappointing him.'

347

Her mum looked shocked. 'Oh, sweetheart. Your dad knew you hadn't taken that stuff.'

Becca frowned. 'He did?'

'Well, not straight away. But once the dust settled, he realised you were covering for Jodi. You were far too honest to steal anything.'

Time seemed to slow. 'But...why didn't he tell me?'

'He could see you were troubled by something. We both could. He figured you'd tell us the truth when you were ready.'

But she'd never got the chance. He'd died before she could confess.

Her mum took her hand. 'I'm sorry, love.'

'But when Jodi left prison and confessed all, why didn't you admit you already knew?'

'Goodness, I'm not sure. It was a long time ago. I was probably too focused on supporting Jodi's efforts to turn her life around. I feel terrible now. I'm sorry, love.'

Becca was too relieved to be angry. 'It's okay. At least I know now.'

Her mum shoved her sewing to one side. 'Your dad was really proud of you, and don't ever think otherwise.' She was pulled into a tight hug. 'Come here.'

Tears threatened. Her dad knew she was innocent? It was too much to get her head around. She pulled away and wiped her eyes. If she let go now, she'd collapse completely. 'As for the renovations, don't hold back on my account, okay? I'm fine with it. Really.' She glanced up at Eddie in the lighting booth. 'And it would be a shame not to utilise the services of someone so *resourceful*.'

Her mum gave a sheepish smile. 'He's asked me to go on a cruise with him. Can you believe that?'

'I hope you said yes.'

Her mum looked shocked. 'I hardly know the man.'

'So get to know him. Ask him on a date.'

'That's what your cousin said.' Her mum picked up her sewing. 'I haven't dated anyone since your father.'

'Then it's about time you got back out there. You deserve to be happy, Mum. And Eddie's a catch.'

Her mum resumed sewing. 'I'll think about it.'

'Good. Because we all need to move on.' And wasn't that the truth.

She kissed her mum's cheek, flinching when her headset crackled. A tentative voice announced a one-minute cue for the ballet routine. With her mind still whirling over the news that her dad had known the truth about the theft, she stood up and gave the nervous student a thumbs-up. Turning to the stage, she clapped her hands. 'Okay, kids. Places, please.' She had to shout to be heard.

With a bit of prompting from the stage crew, the kids ran onstage. They looked cute in their costumes, silver leotards with pale pink chiffon tutus. Ben had been given silver shorts to wear, much to his relief. Her mum had done a sterling job.

'You're opening the showcase, remember,' she called from the stalls. 'You'll need to be in your starting positions behind the curtains before the music starts.' They ignored her. 'Are you listening to me?'

Amongst excited chatter a few of the kids nodded. Most weren't paying attention.

Consequently, when the music started panic ensued.

What should have been a beautiful and heartfelt ballet routine turned into a cattle charge as the kids thundered across the stage trying to pick up where they should be. It didn't help that one of the kids was missing with a tummy upset and Phoebe's substitute skirt kept tripping her up.

It might be funny if they didn't have a paid audience watching in forty-eight hours' time – or the council visiting to pass their judgement.

'You're behind the music,' she shouted, trying to be heard over Sia's 'Chandelier'. 'You need to move quicker!'

The second half of the routine improved. The kids grew in confidence, moving almost in harmony. The end arabesque went reasonably well, although the spacing was wrong. She'd have to work on that.

When they finished, she clapped loudly. 'Well done!'

They rushed to the edge of the stage, eager to hear her thoughts.

'Brilliant job. You did really well. We have to finish now as the tech team need to plot the next number. We'll go over the spacing again on Saturday morning, but it's looking good.' She gave them an encouraging smile. 'Please be here by ten a.m. at the latest for the dress run. And don't forget your costumes,' she yelled as they ran offstage, already losing focus.

'God help us,' she said, returning to her mum.

'It wasn't that bad. The costumes looked nice.'

'Thanks to you.' Becca dragged her sweatshirt over her head and stripped down to her costume. 'And now it's my turn.' Her knee wasn't up to a full-throttle run-through of her routine, but she planned to mark out the number so the tech team could plot the lighting and gauge the timing of her performance.

'Are you worried your knee won't hold up?' Her mum spotted the heavy strapping on her leg, a contrast to her floaty lilac stretch-dress with jagged hem.

She hadn't mentioned re-injuring it on Saturday. 'It doesn't feel great, if I'm honest.'

'Is something else bothering you?'

Becca frowned. 'Why do you ask?'

'I've seen you dance through injury before – you're normally so stoic. What's different this time?'

A lump formed in Becca's throat. Trust her mum to see through her bluster. 'I'm worried I've lost my spark. I've never doubted myself before, but now the thought of going onstage terrifies me. What if the council retracts their funding because of me? I'll never forgive myself.'

'Oh, sweetheart. Sit down a moment.' Becca obeyed, landing with a heavy thud on the seat. 'Now listen to me. You're still grieving for the loss of your career. Of course, it's going to be painful. And yes, it's natural to have doubts. But you're never going to know whether you can still do it unless you try. The spark comes from in here...' she placed her hand over Becca's heart '...and that can't be eradicated by injury. And as for the council, one performance isn't going to be the difference between them sticking with the playhouse, or pulling the plug.'

Her mum was right, as usual. 'I'm being a wuss.'

'You're certainly being too hard on yourself. Now, get on that stage. You don't have to push it. There's no audience, so it doesn't matter if it's not perfect. See how you get on, okay?'

Becca nodded and made her way onto the stage. She took up her starting position in the centre and waited for her cue. The view from the stage was familiar. Footlights glared casting the empty seating into shadows. The glitter-ball above spun slowly creating twinkling lights. In her periphery, she could see movement in the wings as the backstage crew silently worked away.

Eventually, the lights dimmed and Ed Sheeran began to sing 'Perfect'.

She'd switched song choice after last Saturday night. Since dancing with Tom her emotions had been in turmoil. A confusing mixture of embarrassment, desire and heartache.

Maybe that's why she'd chosen this song. She didn't have to dig deep to produce the emotion required to convey the intent behind the moves. It was there, scratching under the surface, waiting to drive her across the stage and elevate her jumps.

When the spotlight hit her, she began to move. Her knee felt stiff and heavy...like her heart. Her rationale had been clouded by Hunch Punch, lust, and a longing to re-create the past. Physically, she wanted Tom with an urgency that clawed at her insides. Emotionally, she'd known it would end in calamity.

He had a girlfriend. Current, or ex. It didn't matter. He was entangled with someone else. She'd been a fool to believe they could turn back the clock and pick up where they'd left off.

Sadness killed any vibrancy in her dancing – injured knee aside. Her moves felt laboured and awkward. The ache in her knee was almost welcome. It gave her something tangible to hold on to. Punishment for letting herself fall for Tom Elliot... again.

The music ended.

The lights lifted and she glanced around the empty stage.

Her mum jumped up and started clapping. 'That was beautiful,' she shouted from the stalls. It wasn't, but Becca was grateful nonetheless.

She headed offstage to change. Her limp was getting more pronounced. If she wanted to dance on Saturday she needed rest and ice. With so much organising to do that might prove impossible.

Her mum rushed over and hugged her. 'You see? I knew you could do it.'

Eddie climbed down from the lighting booth. 'Well done, love. That looked great.'

'Thanks, Eddie.'

His praise evoked a smile from her mum, who blushed and glanced away.

Eddie remained oblivious. 'I think we're done for tonight,' he said, focusing on her mum. 'It's looking good. Do either of you ladies need a lift home?'

Her mum fussed with her sewing bag. 'I have my car here. But thanks for the offer.'

Becca was struck by an idea. 'Actually, if you don't mind going home with Eddie, Mum, could I borrow your car? I'm not quite done yet, and my knee's a bit sore to walk home.' Becca made a point of rubbing it, ignoring her mum's suspicious glare. Well, she wasn't lying. Her knee *was* sore. She turned to Eddie. 'If that's okay with you?'

'No problem, at all,' he said, ever the gentleman. 'Can I take your bag for you, Ruby?'

Her mum handed over her bulky bag and dug out her car keys. Becca was subjected to a look that said she knew what her daughter was up to. 'I'll see you at home later.'

Becca didn't mind being in her mum's bad books.

Just as she'd needed a push to start dancing again, her mum needed a push to start enjoying herself again.

Becca watched them walk off, Eddie chatting away, her mum trying not to stare at him.

Smiling, she removed her knee-brace, before changing into her comfy sweats. Her tappers' technical run wasn't until tomorrow night, so she was done for the evening. But having fibbed, she couldn't go home yet, so she headed for the café. A hot drink might ease the ache in her chest. A bag of ice might do the same for her knee.

She hadn't seen Tom since the party. She'd managed to avoid him all week, ignoring his text messages asking whether she was okay. No, she was not okay. Jodi had assured her that Izzy was no longer staying at the playhouse, but Becca wasn't taking any chances. The last thing she wanted was another chance encounter with the woman who'd caught her fooling around with Tom and insinuated she was a hooker.

Talk about humiliating.

She was so preoccupied with her thoughts, she didn't see the lone figure sitting in the café. Not until she heard Harvey Elliot's distinctive voice.

'You're still here, then?' he said, causing her to turn sharply.

What the hell was he doing here?

He was sitting at one of the tables reading a broadsheet. 'My son didn't take my advice and terminate your employment then.' He licked his thumb and turned the page. 'Your cousin too.'

Becca wasn't in the mood for one of Harvey Elliot's character assassinations. She'd had enough of those twelve years ago. 'If you're looking for Tom, he's not here.' She went to hobble away, but wasn't quick enough.

'Will you join me?' he said, closing his paper.

'I'm busy.' She needed ice for her knee.

He gestured to the chair opposite. 'This won't take long.'

Much as she didn't want to engage, she figured it might stop him bad-mouthing her to Tom. She sat down. 'What do you want?'

It was a while before he spoke. He adjusted his glasses. Crossed and uncrossed his legs, as if considering how best to word whatever it was he wanted to say. It didn't take a genius to work out what was coming.

Finally, he cleared his throat. 'The Wentworth family have a long heritage dating back several centuries,' he said, looking at her intensely. 'Were you aware that Tom's grandfather was the Earl of Horsley?'

She raised an eyebrow. Did he think she was dim? The playhouse was littered with historic portraits and family busts. Anyone visiting would quickly become aware of the family's blue blood.

Sensing her irritation, he continued. 'As such, Tom has obligations to ensure the future and reputation of that title is preserved. As his father, I have a responsibility to protect him from situations I feel might not be in his best interests.'

She didn't like where this conversation was headed. 'And your point is?'

'I have reason to believe you and my son have renewed your...liaison.'

She felt her cheeks burn. 'I don't know where you heard that.'

'Why else would you still be here?'

She drew back stung. 'Excuse me?'

He held her gaze. 'What you do in your private life is none of my business. But the well-being of my son is very much my concern. His career is at stake. Not to mention the future reputation of this family, which could be jeopardised by an... unfortunate association.'

Had they been transported to a Jane Austen novel?

She rubbed her knee, eager to occupy her hands so she didn't thump Harvey Elliot. 'I resent the implication that I'm here for any other reason than to progress my *own* career and save the playhouse from closure.'

He shook his head. 'Whether we like it or not the world is a judgemental place. As the grandson of an earl there are certain expectations in terms of who it would be appropriate for Tom to form a relationship with.'

Her knee began to throb. She knew what he was implying. Her less than pristine past coupled with her cousin's criminal record might tarnish the family's good name.

'As I've already told you, we're not involved.' She straightened her leg, trying to ease the stiffness. 'And besides, Tom appears to already have a girlfriend.'

His eyes narrowed. 'Let's not be naive, Miss Roberts. It wouldn't be the first time a man has enjoyed the company of more than one woman.'

That did it. She stood up. Insulting her was one thing, but attacking Tom's character was out of order. 'You don't have a very high opinion of your son, do you, Mr Elliot?'

'I simply meant that—'

'I know what you meant.' She balled her fists, trying to keep her hands under control. 'And it seems that I have more respect for your son than you do.'

His face coloured.

'Anyone with half a brain can see your son is honourable and decent, with morals and integrity. He's kind...funny... generous...and spends so much time taking care of the play-house, his clients, his mother, that he's ill with it. The guy can barely breathe for Christ's sake. He puts everyone else's needs ahead of his own. He works long hours, never gets a break, and what thanks does he get?' She pointed at him. 'His own father bad-mouthing him.'

'I never—'

'And you know what?' She took a step closer, anger clouding her brain. 'I don't care if you dislike me, or think I'm not good enough for your son. But before you start making accusations about my behaviour, maybe you should look at your own actions.'

'Meaning?'

'It wasn't me who left their teenage son to deal with his alcoholic mother.' She shushed him when he went to inter-rupt. 'You should be grateful and proud of the way Tom dealt with those difficult years. And if you're not...well...that says more about you than it does about him.'

She was on a roll.

'And furthermore, Tom doesn't need *protecting* from me. If you knew your son at all, you'd know that he's honest and law-abiding, and even aged eighteen he would never have allowed himself to be led astray. Not by me, and not by Jodi.' Her whole body was shaking. She leant on the table. 'You want to know the reason I'm still here?'

He drew back when she jabbed her finger at him.

'Because unlike you, I don't quit when things get tough!'

He flinched.

'So if there's nothing else...' she gestured to the exit '...I suggest you leave. The showcase is in two days and we have a lot to do.'

Harvey Elliot just stared at her.

She stared back. No way was she backing down.

Eventually he stood up, folded his newspaper and pocketed his wallet. He paused on his way out. 'I underestimated you, Miss Roberts.'

She held his gaze. 'Yeah, well...don't do it again.'

The shake in her legs made her feel unstable. She couldn't believe what she'd just done. But she'd probably never see him again, so what did it matter.

Twelve years ago, she should have stuck up for herself and she didn't. It might be long overdue, but this went some way to repairing the damage caused by her lack of courage aged sixteen. It wouldn't help resolve things with Tom, but it sure as hell made her feel better about herself.

Chapter Twenty-Eight

Friday 24th November

Becca's insides were hurting from trying not to laugh. Or was it cry? It was hard to tell. Her tappers were wearing their costumes for the showcase. White trousers and waistcoats for the women, white trousers and jacket for Nick. They had on white trilby hats with a black trim and matching neckerchief. In theory, they should have looked smart and stylish. Unfortunately, Miriam's bust was too big for the waistcoat. Cassie's trousers were two inches too short. Mi-Sun's trousers were too long and Nick's were too wide. Only Wanda's costume fitted perfectly. Funny that.

With only twenty-four hours until curtain up there wasn't much Becca could do – other than hope her mum was up for a spot of late-night sewing.

They were in the theatre running through the routine. Far from adding the finishing touches to a polished routine, her tappers looked like petrified wildebeest being chased by lions.

'Don't change direction!' she bellowed, struggling to be

heard over One Republic's 'Counting Stars'. 'You should've split into two lines by now!'

Mi-Sun turned and got caught in the glitter curtain, knocking her hat off. When she bent down to pick it up she bumped into Nick, who lost his footing and bumped into Cassie. They were like dancing dominoes.

'Pick it up, guys! Spread out, you're too close together.' They moved apart. 'That's it... That's far enough... Stop... *STOP!*'

Too late. Miriam disappeared off the side of the stage.

Everyone rushed over to check she was okay.

A beat later, Miriam's face appeared, minus her hat. She climbed onto the stage, banging heads with Wanda who'd tried to help. They bounced apart, both rubbing their foreheads.

Becca rubbed her own forehead...for an entirely different reason. 'Cut the music,' she yelled, miming a slicing movement across her throat.

The student running the sound cues killed the music.

Removing her headset, Becca moved through the auditorium and onto the stage, trying not to panic. Her tappers were suffering from a severe case of pre-show jitters.

'It's a disaster,' Wanda said, still rubbing her head.

'We're not ready.' Cassie looked close to tears. 'We're a laughing stock.'

Nick and Mi-Sun nodded in agreement.

'It's not a disaster,' Becca assured them. 'It's live theatre. These things happen.'

'I fell off the stage!' Miriam pointed to the dirty smudge on her white trousers.

'So act like you meant to do it.' Becca knew they were past the point of responding to critique. All she could do was try and boost their confidence and hope a pep talk calmed their nerves. 'It's like when you're walking down the street and you trip up the kerb. Ten minutes later, you'll have forgotten all about it.'

'It's hardly the same thing.' Miriam sounded morose.

Cassie fiddled with the waistband of her too-short trousers. 'We keep messing up.'

'We don't want to let you down,' Nick said. 'We know you've got a lot riding on tomorrow.'

Becca's heart pinched. Oh, bless them.

'We've been practising at Miriam's house,' Mi-Sun said. 'We wanted you to be proud of us.'

Becca hadn't realised they'd been putting in extra rehearsals. She had to fight back tears. They weren't natural dancers, and yet they'd supported her transition from failed dancer to inexperienced teacher with good humour. She owed them big time. They hadn't dumped her when she'd messed up. And she wasn't about to do the same to them.

'I'm so proud of you,' she said, meaning it. 'You're doing something new and pushing yourselves out of your comfort zones. Two months ago, some of you had never danced before. Now look at you! Performing a complex routine at a showcase. It's amazing.'

Miriam brushed dirt from her backside. 'But it's not perfect.'

Becca looked at their five worried faces. 'I'll let you into a secret. There's no such thing as a perfect performance. There'll always be something you're not happy with. During my career I made mistakes. I fell over, hit scenery and bumped into other dancers. I've never met a dancer who hasn't made a mistake. At the time, it seems like a great tragedy, but you soon learn that it doesn't matter. The key is to get up, carry on, and finish the show.'

'I'm so nervous,' Cassie said, wringing her hands together. 'I'm physically shaking...look.' She held out her vibrating hand.

'Me too.' Nick's hand was equally wobbly.

'Nerves are healthy,' Becca said, warming to her subject. 'Everyone gets nervous. Once you're onstage the nerves will switch to adrenaline. And you're not doing this alone. You're part of a team and that sense of togetherness will keep you focused.'

They looked doubtful.

'I'd be worried if you weren't nervous. Being nervous means you care about getting it right. Over time you'll learn how to deal with nerves. Some people jump up and down, or have a bit of fun and make jokes. Others meditate in a quiet corner. Whatever works for you.

'Feeling nervous prior to a performance will never go away. But being nervous and lacking confidence are two entirely different things. You're doubting yourselves and questioning whether you can do this. I promise you, you can.' As Becca was suffering from the exact same condition, she wondered if it was time to listen to her own advice.

She moved around the group, trying to reassure them. 'You all know the routine. I've seen you do it. You've rehearsed and prepared. You're ready to perform. Don't let being nervous undermine your confidence. You *can* do this. And you will be wonderful. Okay?'

They gave half-hearted nods.

Becca's hands went to her hips. 'Well, that wasn't very convincing. Let's try again. Can we do this?'

They nodded with a little more conviction. 'Yes.'

'Good.' She gave them all a hug. It was out of her hands now. All she could do was pray the routine wasn't a complete disaster...and that no one else fell off the stage. 'See you all tomorrow,' she said, waving them off. 'Ten a.m. sharp for a dress run, okay?'

Chatting away, they packed up, still nervous about performing, but determined to try their best.

When the theatre had cleared, she locked up and went in search of Jodi. Along with Eddie and Leon, the three of them had been working flat out all week to ensure everything was ready for tomorrow.

Becca had been secretly relieved Tom's time had been taken up juggling court hearings and organising the showcase. It meant she hadn't had to talk to him about what had happened last Saturday.

As for her cousin, she wanted to check Jodi was okay and wasn't being abused by the terrible twosome, whose commitment to the showcase was non-existent.

She found her cousin in reception wearing jeans and a T-shirt, a sweatshirt tied around her middle. Her hands were filthy.

Becca frowned. 'Everything okay?'

Jodi shook her head. 'Not really. One of the men's loos is blocked and Elaine's flight has been delayed. It's touch and go whether she'll be back in time for the showcase. The pottery exhibition is one of our main attractions.'

Becca's heart sank. 'Isn't there anyone else who could oversee the exhibition?'

Jodi shook her head. 'She says not, but she's going to update me when she knows more.'

'Well, let's hope she makes it back in time. What about the loo? Do we need to call a plumber?'

'Eddie's gone to find a plunger. But if we can't clear it ourselves, we might have to.' Jodi's expression indicated unblocking a loo wasn't high on her list of enjoyable pastimes.

They'd be hard pushed to get a plumber out this late. Not to mention the additional expense.

Jodi rested her hands on her knees. 'This better be worth it.'

Becca rubbed her back. 'Of course, it will be. The council are going to be blown away by the showcase. Carolyn will return to find the playhouse thriving, and you're going to finally receive the credit you deserve.'

Becca was subjected to an incredulous look.

'Okay, so it's wishful thinking, but a girl can hope.'

Jodi straightened. 'I appreciate the pep talk, but I'm not naive enough to believe I have a future here. My contract ends soon. And even if we manage to win over the council, the situation with Vivienne and Petrit is unbearable. They want me gone.'

Becca frowned. 'We can't let them succeed. When Carolyn returns, Tom will tell her what they've been up to and she'll take action.'

Jodi didn't look convinced. 'Carolyn will be far too focused on her recovery to bother with petty staff issues. And she shouldn't have to.' She stretched out her back. 'I've loved working here, despite the terrible twosome, and getting to hang out with you has been a dream. I've even managed to win over Tom, but it's not enough.'

The mention of Tom caused a surge within Becca.

Jodi shrugged. 'The best I can hope for is a successful showcase. The council letting Carolyn keep the grant and a decent reference. Maybe now I've got some office experience, another employer will be willing to take me on.'

Becca hugged her cousin. 'God, I hope so.'

Leon appeared, breaking the moment. His dark eyes darted between the hugging cousins. 'Sorry for interrupting. We've finished cordoning off the car park.'

366

Jodi tucked a loose strand of hair into her ponytail. 'Thanks for letting me know.'

He took in her dishevelled state. 'Anything else you need doing before I head off?'

Jodi shook her head. 'We're good, thanks.'

He hesitated before walking off. 'See you tomorrow then.'

He'd almost reached the door, when Jodi called after him. 'Leon?' She went over. 'Thanks for everything you've done this week. We couldn't have done it without you.'

There was a long drawn-out moment where neither one moved. Becca was tempted to make a discreet exit, but the moment was broken when Leon said, 'No worries. Anything for Carolyn,' and walked out the door.

Jodi's shoulders slumped.

Becca went over and hugged her.

'Well, that told me,' her cousin said, with a self-deprecating laugh. 'He hates me.'

'No, he doesn't. And don't be quick to assume the worst. Leon cares more than he's letting on.'

Jodi broke the hug. 'He cares about the playhouse, sure. Carolyn too. Every day he continues to be sweet and kind and funny...just not with me. Not that I can blame him. Decent blokes like Leon didn't want trouble. And they certainly don't want a woman with a criminal past.'

'You need to stop thinking like that. There's so much more to you than that.'

'Leon doesn't seem to think so.'

'Then more fool him.' Becca turned Jodi to face her. 'Mum and I were talking last night about how we both need to move on with our lives.'

'That's what I'm trying to do.'

'I know, but you also keep justifying people who treat you badly. Like somehow you deserve it. Well, you don't. Mum needs to find the courage to start living again. I need to build a life after dance, and you need to forgive yourself for messing up when you were a kid. You're a good person, Jodi. The best I know.' She kissed her cousin's cheek. 'It's time for us to let go of the past. Okay?'

Jodi nodded. 'I'll try.'

'Good.'

Eddie appeared in reception armed with a plunger. 'Look what I found.' He stopped when he saw tears running down Jodi's face. 'What happened?'

Becca gave her cousin a squeeze. 'She's tired. It's been a long week.'

Eddie came over. 'Why don't you head home, love.'

'There's too much to do—'

'I'll sort out the blocked loo,' he said cutting Jodi off. 'And there's nothing we can do about the Elaine situation until we know about her flight. She'll either be here, or she won't. It's out of our hands. Go home and get some sleep. Things always look better in the morning.'

Jodi half-smiled. 'Am I allowed to wash my hands first?'

Eddie smiled. 'Of course.'

Becca could've kissed Eddie. 'While you're washing up, I'm going to fetch some ice from the kitchen. Then we can head home together. Okay?'

Jodi nodded and headed off to the ladies'.

'Thanks for that, Eddie. She wouldn't listen to me.'

'No problem,' he said, heading off to fix the loo. 'See you back at the guest house later.'

Becca went into the kitchen. When she'd run through her routine again tonight, she'd been able to push a little harder, which was a good sign. Her movement had felt a lot freer. The bad news was that her knee was now stinging like crazy.

She wrapped some ice in a tea towel and backtracked into the café, where she sat down to wait for Jodi, balancing the ice pack on her knee.

A door slammed somewhere in the distance.

She heard Tom's voice before she saw him. 'Here you are,' he said. 'You've been avoiding me.'

She supposed their paths had to cross at some point.

He sat next to her, looking relaxed and happy. He obviously hadn't bumped into his father last night. No way would he be in such a good mood if he had. He probably didn't even know Harvey had been here. She wasn't about to enlighten him.

'Good news,' he said. 'I have the programmes for the show-case.' He handed her one, his fingers brushing against hers. 'Don't they look great?'

She ignored the flutter in her belly his touch created. She

369

needed to stay strong. If she had doubts about getting too close to him before last night, her row with Harvey had cemented her decision. She refused to be treated as an embarrassment.

She studied the front of the programme. The image depicted the Starlight Playhouse at twilight. The building was bathed in moonlight and surrounded by stars. It was beautiful. Under the main heading was the caption '*Starring professional dancer Becca Roberts*'.

She handed the programme back to him.

'Don't you want to look inside?' He flicked through the pages showing her the colourful contents and exhibitor adverts.

She had to admit the programme looked good. Where had he got the money to pay for them?

He spotted the ice pack on her leg. 'How's your knee? Will you be able to dance tomorrow?'

She glared at him. 'Is that all you're worried about? Whether I'll be able to dance?'

He frowned. 'I'm not following.'

She took a breath. 'The last time I saw you Tom, you had your arms around your girlfriend.'

'*Ex*-girlfriend,' he said, his smile long gone. 'And I didn't have my arms around her, she had them around me.'

'Same thing.'

'No, it's not.' He dragged his chair closer. 'She turned up here uninvited. I had no idea she was coming.'

Becca held his gaze. 'So she didn't stay the night?'

He paused.

Just as she'd thought. And to think, last night she'd defended his behaviour to his father. 'You know what, it's none of my business.'

'Don't say that. It is your business, but there's nothing going on with Izzy.' His expression was pleading. 'I promise you.'

'It didn't look that way.'

'That's because...' he paused, closing his eyes briefly '... she's struggling to adjust. But I swear on my life it's over between us.'

She shrugged. 'It doesn't matter. Carolyn will be home from rehab soon and you can return to London. We'll never have to see each other again.'

He looked stung. 'That's not what I want.'

'It's for the best—'

'No, it's not.' He touched her arm. 'I'm not going back to London. That's why I've been so busy this week – I've been looking at premises.'

She shrugged away from his touch.

'I'm going to set up a practice in Brighton and switch to family law.'

If he was expecting a fanfare, he'd be disappointed.

He searched her face. 'I thought you'd be pleased.'

'Why? It's nothing to do with me.' She rubbed her chest. She had a pain to rival the throb in her knee.

'Are you kidding me? What about last Saturday night?'

She shrugged. 'What about it? We got a little carried away. It happens. It was a kiss, nothing more. Not a reason to relocate.'

'Why are you being like this? We reconnected, you know we did. Don't try and deny it.' His confusion was palpable. 'So this is what...cold feet? Jealousy that my ex showed up? What? Because I don't understand.'

He never would, and that was the problem. She couldn't deny falling for him again. It would be pointless even trying, but that wasn't the issue. They were skirting around the elephant in the room.

She turned to him. 'Look at it from my perspective. A beautiful woman shows up here at one a.m. in the morning and calls you *darling*. She reacts badly when she discovers us fooling around on the floor and makes it obvious she wants me gone. And then she stays the night.'

He closed his eyes. 'I know how it looks. And you're right.' He opened his eyes. 'All the evidence points to us still being an item. But you have to believe me, we broke up ages ago. I'm not with Izzy anymore.'

She swallowed past the lump in her throat. 'I believe you.'

'You do? Then what's the problem?'

It was time to address the elephant. 'Twelve years ago, you didn't do the same for me.'

He tilted his head to one side. 'I'm not following.'

'When presented with hearsay and gossip, you believed me capable of theft. You assumed the worst. You didn't give me

372

the chance to explain. You allowed your father to shame me and my family. No email, no text, no phone call. Nothing. You just walked away.' A fact that hurt more now she knew even her dad hadn't believed her guilty.

His cheeks coloured. 'But you'd confessed to the crime. You were caught red-handed, arrested and cautioned. What was there to explain?'

Sadness filled her heart. 'And that is why we will never be together again.'

Jodi appeared from the loos. Her expression turned wary when she realised what they were discussing. 'Ready to go?'

Becca struggled to her feet. 'Definitely.'

And with that, she hobbled away, leaving Tom shaking his head in bewilderment.

Chapter Twenty-Nine

Saturday 25th November

Jodi checked her watch. Time was running away from her. In less than an hour's time the doors of the Starlight Playhouse would open to the public.

Hordes of people had already descended on Brighton for the arts festival. The town was buzzing, filled with street entertainers, classical recitals and open-house tours. The event had kicked off with a silent disco, led by DJ Guru wearing an orange spandex catsuit, who'd caused numerous traffic delays as he'd guided fifty or so dancers through the streets of Brighton.

At least the weather was good. It was a mild day. Local radio was following the events, ensuring people knew what was happening. The festival promised to be a massive success. The only problem was the Starlight Playhouse wasn't ready for business.

Jodi skimmed the list of items still unticked on her schedule. The pottery exhibition had been the main cause of the delays. Elaine's late arrival had caused havoc, requiring a team of six to carry her 'From Clay to Creation' display into the art studio. Still, it was done now. Jodi could tick it off.

Buddies Café were currently setting up a makeshift kitchen in the café, much to Petrit's annoyance. Too bad. He'd turned down the opportunity to organise something himself. Feeling disgruntled because a rival chef was 'on his turf' was his problem.

The volunteers had arrived to work behind the bar and support Vivienne with front-of-house duties. Not that Vivienne was happy. But then the Woman-in-Black was never happy.

As if sensing she was the subject of Jodi's thoughts, the woman appeared. She was dressed in her usual bespoke head-to-toe black, and made a point of looking peeved when the people setting up the circus exhibit got in her way. 'A group of homeless individuals are in reception claiming they're here to help with the showcase.'

'That's right. They're from the night shelter. I did warn you to expect them.'

'You didn't tell me they were *actually* homeless.' Vivienne had obviously led a very sheltered life.

'Does it matter? We're grateful for the help.'

'I don't see how engaging the services of the great unwashed will be of much use.' Vivienne's inner snob was never far from the surface.

'As a thank you, I've offered the volunteers use of our shower facilities and a hot meal before the playhouse opens to the public.' Jodi checked her watch. 'Which is in forty-five minutes, so we'd better get a move on.'

Vivienne didn't budge. 'I can't imagine madam would approve.'

'On the contrary, I think Carolyn would love the idea. Either way, Tom's in agreement and so is Becca. You'll find a box of T-shirts in the office for the volunteers.'

'We're purchasing clothing for them too?' Vivienne tutted. 'Really, considering the lack of funding—'

'I'm not discussing funding with you today, Vivienne. I'm too busy.' Jodi cut the woman off before they got into another bust-up regarding the missing money. 'We're running behind schedule. Please take the volunteers to the changing rooms next to the dance studio and advise them of their duties.'

Vivienne recoiled as though Jodi had suggested she personally strip them down and lick them clean. 'I will do no such thing.'

'And when you're done please change into your uniform for the day. Did you bring something red to wear?'

'I did not.' Vivienne's nostrils flared.

'In that case, please select one of the printed T-shirts.'

A look of horror sharpened Vivienne's features. 'I've never worn a *T-shirt* in my life.'

'Then it'll be a new experience for you. Everyone else has adhered to the dress code.' Jodi gestured to the people working around them.

Aunty Ruby was wearing a red tunic over black trousers.

Eddie was wearing one of the red printed *Starlight* T-shirts they'd had designed for the showcase, as was Leon. Everyone had been asked to wear a combination of black and red, and they'd all adhered...except for Petrit, who'd refused to remove his chef whites. As Jodi suspected he wouldn't be hanging around for the showcase, it was a battle she was willing to concede.

Vivienne stared at Jodi's new black Primark suit with red shirt, complete with 'Showcase co-ordinator' name badge. 'Madam will be hearing about this.'

'I do hope so.' Jodi turned her back on the Woman-in-Black...who should be the Woman-in-Black-and-Red if she wasn't so bloody stubborn. 'Excuse me, I need to get on.'

Ignoring Vivienne's mutterings, Jodi checked her list. Becca was in the dance studio running the dance numbers. Tick. The volunteers had arrived to help Leon with the bar. Tick. The music students weren't due until after lunch, so she didn't need to worry about them yet.

She glanced over to where Eddie was briefing his team of Sussex Sea Cadets on their duties for the day. Even they'd managed to incorporate elements of red into their uniforms by adding an armband.

That just left the debacle in the café. Far from looking like a circus, it was currently a safety hazard. Tom was overseeing the exhibits, but he was struggling to juggle the needs of 'creative types' who wanted their displays to be 'organic' and not 'formulaic'. George was being indecisive about where he wanted his ice sculptures, and the abstract artist felt his 'vision' for his presentation clashed with the 'energy in the room'. Tom's patience had been tested further when he'd realised the circus exhibit included a flying trapeze.

At that point, Jodi had decided to step in and help.

She called Eddie over. 'We need another pair of hands to hoist the trapeze.'

The two men lifting the contraption weren't tugging on the pulleys in unison. Consequently, the outstretched mannequin kept swinging around and whacking people on the head.

'It might help if we had a third person underneath.' Jodi repositioned the stepladders. 'I'd go up myself, but my skirt's too tight.' She would have brought a change of clothes, if she'd realised so much physical labour would be required.

'No problem.' Eddie climbed the ladder, placing his big hands on the mannequin's sequin-clad bottom. When Aunty Ruby glanced over he smiled, which distracted her from easing the second mannequin into a pair of large clown trousers and she bumped heads with the dummy, making Eddie laugh.

Since making the decision to turn the guest house into apartments, it was like a weight had been lifted from her aunty's shoulders. She'd taken to smiling for no reason, singing along to the radio and wearing lip gloss. Jodi suspected Eddie's attentions were a factor in her improved spirits. And why not? Her aunty deserved to be adored.

A commotion drew her attention. Why was Petrit shouting at the Buddies Café chef?

She marched over and pulled Petrit to one side. Didn't he realise these people were doing the playhouse a huge favour? 'What's the problem?'

His sneer made her take a step back. 'He want microwave.'

'So? Let him use the microwave.'

He grunted. 'If he want microwave, he should bring microwave.'

'Well, clearly he hasn't. So let him use the one here.'

'No.' His spittle landed on her face.

Jodi wiped her cheek. 'It's not your property, Petrit. It belongs to the playhouse. Now let him use the microwave.'

'No.'

Several pairs of eyes watched the exchange. She wanted to retreat, but that would be disastrous. She had to hold her ground. This was a key battle.

The cavalry came in the shape of Leon emerging from the kitchen carrying the microwave. 'Here you go, mate,' he said, handing it over to the Buddies Café chef. 'Anything else you need just ask.'

Relief swamped her. She wanted to run after Leon and thank him, but he'd already returned to the bar. He might not like her anymore, but he liked tyrannical chefs even less.

Petrit grunted and returned to the kitchen, barging through the swing doors.

Jodi returned to the mayhem. The trapeze artist was hoisted halfway up dangling from the ceiling. Eddie was at full stretch. They needed a longer ladder.

He'd realised this too and climbed down, heading off in search of one. The mannequin was left swaying at head height. Worst-case scenario, they'd have to exclude any visitors taller than six foot.

Jodi checked her watch. Thirty minutes left. Time was running out. 'We need to start clearing away these boxes,' she called, opening the door to the storage room.

Vivienne appeared. 'Why is the office door locked?'

'Because I locked it.'

'Were you worried one of your homeless friends might *steal* something?' Vivienne wasn't sheltered Jodi decided, she was downright ignorant.

'That's a very judgemental remark, Vivienne.'

The Woman-in-Black held out her hand. 'I need the bar float from the safe.'

Jodi handed over the keys. 'Bring them back when you're done, please.'

Vivienne snatched the keys and marched into the kitchen. She emerged a few moments later with Petrit. The pair headed in the direction of the office. What were they up to?

Jodi wondered whether she should have found a new hiding place for her drawer key. There was nothing in there other than her rucksack and *The Art of War*, but she couldn't be too careful where Vivienne and Petrit were concerned. After all, someone had nicked five grand. And it wasn't her.

She checked her watch. Twenty minutes left.

Aunty Ruby had almost finished dressing the clown

mannequin. The boxes were being moved. That just left the trapeze to sort out.

There was nothing she could do until Eddie returned with the longer ladder, so she focused on the spotlight, which was currently pointing downwards like an interrogation lamp.

She dragged the stepladders over and was about to climb up, hoping her skirt wouldn't split, when Leon appeared.

'Need a hand?' he said, holding the ladder steady.

She fought the urge to look at him. 'I'm fine, thanks.'

'Is there much left to do?' No one watching would guess he'd once fed her chocolates and left her gifts. It was business only now. Still, it was favourable to being ignored.

'I don't think so. We're going down to the wire, but hopefully we'll be ready.'

'The place looks good. Carolyn would be proud.'

Jodi swallowed awkwardly. 'I hope so.'

Leon wasn't a factor in her leaving, but he was definitely a reason not to stay. Spending each day knowing the man you'd fallen for didn't respect or trust you was torturous. It was almost worse than dealing with Petrit and Vivienne.

Eddie appeared. 'Jodi, love. You're needed in the office... The police are here.'

'The police?' Her brain mentally ran through her checklist. She was sure she'd obtained the correct licenses. She'd made a point of checking with the council. 'What do they want?'

Eddie looked uncomfortable. 'They're here to question you.'

'Question me? What about?'

Eddie glanced at Leon. 'The missing money. Vivienne reported the theft.'

Time seemed to slow – something she would have appreciated an hour ago. Not so much now. She blinked, hoping to snap out of her shock. It didn't work. Neither would her throat, which had constricted.

Eddie touched her arm.

Wordlessly, she walked towards the office, aware of Leon and Eddie beside her. White noise filled her head, blocking out the sound of them talking. Someone's hand touched the small of her back, she didn't know who.

The office was more crowded than it had been on the day Carolyn had called an emergency staff meeting and announced she was booked into rehab.

Tom stood by the main desk looking angrier than she'd ever seen him.

To his right, Petrit had his arms folded, his dark unibrow twitching.

Vivienne was positioned between the two desks in front of the safe.

Eddie and Leon followed Jodi into the room.

In the middle stood two police officers.

The female officer spoke. 'Are you Jodi Simmons?'

Jodi nodded.

'I'm Sergeant Matthews. This is my colleague Constable Withies. We're responding to an allegation of theft.' She checked her notebook. 'The sum of five thousand pounds, which Ms King alleges you took from the safe.'

This was all Jodi's nightmares colliding. Her past catching up with her. Being humiliated in front of people she cared about. Never escaping the label of thief.

Tom glared daggers at Vivienne. 'Ms King had no right to contact you.'

Vivienne raised her chin. 'I couldn't stand back and let madam be defrauded. Miss Simmons is the only one who could've taken the money.'

Sergeant Matthews addressed Tom. 'Is that true?'

Tom rubbed his chest. 'At the time of the theft four people had the combination for the safe. My mother—'

'Who was away,' Vivienne interjected.

Sergeant Matthews noted something down. 'Go on.'

'My mother. Myself. Vivienne King and Ms Simmons.'

Jodi didn't need a solicitor to know this looked bad. She was the obvious suspect. She was new to the playhouse and she had a criminal record. Means and motive.

'I'd hardly call the police if *I* took the money,' Vivienne said, looking self-righteous. 'And everyone knows how much Master Thomas dotes on his mother, so by default it has to be Miss Simmons.'

Jodi agreed. Except she was innocent.

Sergeant Matthews addressed her. 'Ms Simmons, on the twentieth of October this year did you steal five thousand pounds from the safe at the Starlight Playhouse?'

Jodi could barely make her head move. 'No, I didn't.'

Vivienne smoothed down the front of her dress. 'Who else could've taken it?'

Sergeant Matthews glanced at her colleague. 'Who's the legal owner of this place?'

Tom chipped in before Vivienne could. 'My mother, Carolyn Elliot-Wentworth.'

'Is she here?'

He shook his head. 'She's due back next week.'

Sergeant Matthews closed her notebook. 'I think it's best we wait for the legal owner to return. If she wishes to report the theft, we'll consider investigating. Until then—'

'That's it?' Vivienne looked outraged. 'But I've reported a theft. I've told you who took the money. Why aren't you arresting her?'

Jodi's insides clenched into a painful knot. She wanted to confront Vivienne, to yell that she was innocent, but her mouth wouldn't work.

The officer continued. 'It wasn't your money that was taken, Ms King. The owner may not wish to press charges.'

'Of course she will! She's been robbed.'

Sergeant Matthews shrugged. 'Sorry. Nothing more we can do.'

'What if I told you I know where she's stashed it?' Vivienne pointed to the desk. 'In there. Locked away. Why else do you think she hides the key? If you don't believe me, look for yourself. You'll see I'm telling the truth.'

384

All eyes turned to look where Vivienne was pointing. Jodi felt Leon brush against her as he backed out of the office. He'd seen enough. No doubt his opinion of her had just lowered even further.

Sergeant Matthews turned to Jodi. 'Do you have the key?'

Jodi knew they'd find the money inside. It was a set-up. It had to be. She looked at Petrit. His smile was that of a lottery winner.

Tom stepped forwards. 'I'm sorry, but this doesn't make sense. If Jodi took the money, why would she be daft enough to leave it on the premises?'

Sergeant Matthews tapped her notebook. 'He has a point.'

Jodi was grateful for Tom defending her. Would he continue to after the police found the money? She doubted it.

Vivienne and Petrit shared a look. 'I didn't say anything before, because Master Thomas hasn't been well. I didn't want to add to his stress levels. Madam asked me to keep an eye on him.'

Tom shook his head. 'That's bollocks, Vivienne.'

'And the reason Ms Simmons hasn't absconded with the money is...well...she hasn't had the opportunity. I've been keeping an eye on her. She was probably waiting until the heat was off before making her getaway.'

Jodi wanted to refute Vivienne's ludicrous explanation. After all, she'd been on her own on several occasions, but her mouth still wouldn't work.

Tom rubbed his chest. 'Jesus, Vivienne. You've been reading too many detective novels.'

Sergeant Matthews pocketed her notebook. 'Like I said earlier, I think we'll wait until the owner returns—'

'Did you know she was jailed for theft?'

Jodi wasn't shocked; she'd been expecting it.

Tom rounded on Vivienne. 'That was years ago, Vivienne. And it's not relevant.'

Vivienne gasped. 'You don't think a known criminal working at a place where money goes missing is suspicious?' Vivienne redirected her attention to the police. 'All I'm asking is that you search her drawer. If I'm wrong so be it. But if I'm right...?' She left the question hanging.

Sergeant Matthews exchanged a look with Constable Withies.

She turned to Jodi. 'May I have the key, please?'

There was nothing Jodi could do. Making a fuss would only look more incriminating.

With a heavy heart, she went over to her desk and was about to retrieve the key, when the door burst opened and Becca rushed in. 'You have to get outside now...a gang of heavies are wrecking your ride.'

Jodi's hand stilled on the spider plant.

Sergeant Matthews frowned. 'I beg your pardon?'

Becca's expression turned sheepish. 'Err...I said, you need to get outside now...a group of heavies are wrecking your ride?'

Sergeant Matthews barged past her. 'Withies, come with me.'

Becca rushed over to Tom and whispered something in his ear.

He turned to the group. 'Until the police return, I think everyone should leave so there's no question of anything untoward going on. Vivienne? Petrit?' He ushered everyone out of the office, including Jodi.

What the hell was going on?

The song 'Fame' blared out from an amp in reception.

Jodi followed everyone outside...where she discovered the tappers dancing around the police car. They were waving their hands in time to the music and singing about how they were going to 'live forever' and 'learn how to fly'.

The redheaded American woman climbed onto a low wall and attempted a star-jump, which nearly saw her tumbling off.

'Get down!' Sergeant Matthews shouted, before turning to her colleague, who was trying not to laugh. 'Don't just stand there, do something!'

Two of the tappers managed to get in the poor copper's way when he tried to reach the woman on the wall. The routine only ended when the woman lost her balance and fell into the arms of the policeman, who staggered to the ground under her weight.

Sergeant Matthews switched off the music. 'Unless you want to be charged with damaging police property, get away from that vehicle *now*!'

The crowd queuing at the barrier started clapping, whistling and laughing. Mostly at the redheaded woman, who was making a meal of getting off the young policeman.

'Back inside!' Sergeant Matthews yelled.

Like naughty children, they filed inside and returned to the office.

'I don't know what's going on, but unless you want me to slap you with a charge for wasting police time, open the drawer and let's get this mess sorted.'

Jodi had no idea what was going on, but she knew her time was up.

Resigned to her fate, she went over to her desk and lifted the spider plant. As she handed the key to Constable Withies, all eyes were on him as he eased open the drawer and removed two items. Her rucksack and *The Art of War* book.

Jodi was surprised when she realised Leon had returned to the office. He was standing by the door. When he saw what book it was, a flicker of something passed across his handsome features, but it was only fleeting. She wished he'd stayed away. This was torturous enough without him there to witness her humiliation.

'Any trace of the money?' Sergeant Matthews asked.

'Nothing, Sergeant.' He continued to rummage inside the rucksack, removing several items, none of which resembled a wodge of cash. 'The money isn't here.'

Jodi startled. It wasn't?

Vivienne looked annoyed. 'It must be there. Look again.'

'Try the safe,' Leon said, casually leaning against the door-frame.

Vivienne swung around to glare at him. 'Why would the

money be in the safe? *She* stole it.' She pointed at Jodi, who was still staring at the empty drawer in disbelief.

Leon shrugged. 'Who knows? A misunderstanding? An accounting error?'

Tom went over to the safe. 'Would you believe it?' he said, removing the money bag.

Sergeant Matthews frowned. 'Is that the missing money?'

Tom studied the package. 'Looks like it. It's the same bank bag.'

'Are you now saying there hasn't been a theft? The money was in the safe all along?'

Tom shrugged. 'It would appear so. Apologies for wasting your time.'

Jodi didn't know whether to laugh or cry. The money hadn't been in the safe this morning. She knew that for a fact, so who'd put it there?

With an exasperated sigh, Sergeant Matthews beckoned her colleague. 'Next time you think a crime has been committed check first before calling the police.' She opened the door. 'And if I discover any damage to my car, expect a bill.'

Tom waited until they'd left before addressing the group. 'What the hell is going on?'

Becca stepped forward. 'Vivienne and Petrit had the money all along. They planted the five grand in Jodi's drawer and then called the cops.'

Jodi's legs went from under her. Eddie caught her and lowered her onto a chair.

Vivienne looked outraged. 'We did no such thing.'

Tom dumped the money bag on the desk. 'No? Then what's your explanation?'

'She...must have moved it. She knew she was about to be caught and panicked.'

'How did Jodi move it?' Becca squared up to Vivienne. 'She was outside with the rest of us.'

'It was you, then. You're protecting her. Thieves in it together.'

Leon stepped forward. '*I* moved the money from Jodi's drawer to the safe.'

That shut Vivienne up.

Jodi gasped. 'You...you? Why?'

Vivienne jumped in. 'Because he's protecting his own. Your sort always stick together.'

Leon turned to her. 'You're right, Vivienne. *Our* sort always do, so that nasty individuals like you don't get away with ruining an innocent person's life. You and Petrit put that money in Jodi's drawer. I saw you do it.'

Tom's expression hardened. 'Is that true?'

Vivienne looked flustered. 'Of course not, Master Thomas. You mustn't listen to him. They're in it together.'

Jodi's mind had gone into a spin.

Leon dug out his phone. 'I have video footage,' he said, playing the recording. It was taken through a narrow gap in the doorway and showed Vivienne and Petrit stuffing the money bag into Jodi's rucksack and placing it in her drawer. 'You set her up.'

Petrit grunted. 'Her, not me.'

Vivienne glared at her disloyal accomplice, before turning to Tom. 'It's not what you think, Master Thomas.'

'Spare me.' Tom looked beyond angry. His blue eyes bore into Vivienne. 'I trusted you. My mother trusted you. And this is how you repay us? By stealing from the playhouse?'

'I was doing it for you...for your mother. I never intended to keep the money. I only took it to make you see reason. The woman can't be trusted. She's wicked.'

'The only wicked person in this room is you.' He turned to Petrit. 'And you.'

Jodi barely noticed the office door opening.

Tom was on a rant. 'Jodi has worked her socks off trying to manage the playhouse. She's had to endure the pair of you abusing her, discriminating against her, and making her life hell. And through it all she's remained professional and dedicated, showing more loyalty towards my mother than the pair of you put together. And unless you want me to have you both charged with perverting the course of justice, you'll both leave the playhouse now and never set foot in here again.'

'Tom?' The sound of Carolyn's voice startled everyone.

All heads turned to see the playhouse owner standing in the doorway.

Behind her, stood the four men from the council.

Oh, hell.

Chapter Thirty

...continued

There was a collective intake of breath, and for a long drawn-out moment, no one moved or spoke. All eyes were on Carolyn. Tom was the first to recover.

'Mum? What are you doing here? I wasn't expecting you until next week.'

'Clearly.' Carolyn stood by the door, her arms folded. 'Would someone like to tell me what's going on?'

Eddie came to his rescue and bundled Vivienne towards the door, ignoring her cries of protest. 'You see to your mum. We'll deal with these two.'

Petrit didn't wait to be escorted off the premises. He stormed out, followed by Leon, who no doubt wanted to check he actually left.

Becca addressed the men from the council – who were looking decidedly perplexed. 'Gentleman, welcome to the Starlight Playhouse. If you'd like to come with us, we'd be delighted to give you a guided tour.' She dragged Jodi from her chair. 'Isn't that right, Jodi?'

'What?' Poor Jodi still looked shell-shocked. 'Oh, right... yes, of course.' She forced a smile. 'This way, gentleman. Shall we begin with the pottery exhibition?'

Bless her. Tom could see she was shaking, but she did her best to cover it. He owed her an apology. He might not have believed she'd taken the money, but he hadn't prevented Vivienne and Petrit making her working life hell. He'd been a coward. Unwilling to rock the boat. And that was something he needed to make amends for.

Becca and Jodi ushered the councillors out the door. 'I think you'll be pleased with our progress,' Jodi said. 'We have several local groups supporting the event, and perhaps later we can detail our plans for diversifying the services offered at the playhouse.' She glanced back.

Tom mouthed a 'thank you.' Once again, Becca and Jodi were saving the day.

That just left him and his mum.

'Are you going to tell me what's going on?' she said, clearly unhappy about returning to discover two long-standing staff members being unceremoniously sacked. Who could blame her?

Tom closed the door. The playhouse was filling up with visitors. They didn't need an audience. 'It's a long story. In short, Vivienne was disgruntled because you gave Jodi the business manager job instead of her. Together with Petrit, they framed Jodi by stealing five grand of the grant money and tried to get her fired. When that didn't work, they reported her to the cops.'

His mother's expression was priceless. 'They did *what*?'

'Don't worry, Leon realised what they were doing and foiled their plan. The money has been returned. I had no option but to fire them.'

She rubbed her temple. 'Vivienne's always been so loyal.'

Tom leant against the door. 'In her warped way I think she was trying to prove her loyalty. But she was so blinded by misconceived injustice she failed to recognise that everything Jodi did was about protecting the playhouse.'

His mother raised an eyebrow. 'Someone's changed their tune.'

He shrugged. 'I was wrong. I admit it.'

'And what about Becca?'

'The same. She's talented, resourceful, creative and bloody stubborn.'

His mother laughed.

It'd been a while since he'd heard her laugh. Not without booze being a factor. 'They make a formidable team. While you were away the council threatened to withdraw our grant funding if we didn't do more to improve community engagement. Becca and Jodi weren't about to let that happen. They came up with the idea of a showcase to promote the place.'

'Well, let's hope it works,' she said, heading over to the desk. 'Especially as I've decided to offer them permanent co-management of the place.'

He startled. 'You have?'

She turned to look at him. 'It's time I took a back seat. I'd like to stay involved but hand over the day-to-day running to someone else. It'll allow me the space I need to maintain a sober lifestyle. And let's face it, this place has been on the decline for years, which I blocked out by drinking. With any luck, they can turn things around.' She picked up one of the showcase flyers. 'If today's anything to go by, they're halfway there. I've never seen the car park so busy.'

'They've done a great job. Becca has some amazing ideas, like dementia-friendly cinema screenings and dance classes for people with disabilities.'

She smiled. 'I knew they were the right people to leave in charge.'

'And you were proved right.' He shrugged. 'So how was rehab?'

She slumped against the desk. 'Painful, but necessary. Detox was the hardest part, but then I always knew it would be. That and letting go of my denial.' Her smile was self-deprecating. 'Dealing with the shame and guilt of being an alcoholic was pretty torrid. Not to mention exhausting. But I found the counselling sessions useful, and the cognitive behavioural therapy.' She fiddled with her necklace, as if needing to occupy her fingers.

He waited for her to continue. He didn't want to interrogate her, as she'd once accused him of doing.

'I learnt a few coping techniques to help me remain sober, which I'll need to practise every day.'

He watched her expression. 'How do you feel about that?'

'Resigned,' she said, with a shrug. 'It's a bit like being an athlete. If you don't exercise every day, you won't stay fit. I think that was my mistake before. I'd get sober and assume the hard work had been done. I'm learning that my recovery is still in its fledgling stage.'

'Will the centre continue to support you?'

She nodded. 'They recommend I attend regular AA meetings and family support sessions for at least twelve months. Right now, I don't want to drink, but I'm not naive enough to think that'll last. If I can get past the first ninety days, then my chances of maintaining abstinence will improve. In the meantime, I need to recognise the early warning signs of a relapse and embrace the things that will enable me to live a sober lifestyle.'

He'd never heard her talk about her addiction this way before. It felt like a breakthrough. 'I'm so proud of you, Mum. And just so you know, you won't have to go through it alone. I'm staying in Brighton.'

'You don't need to do that.'

'I want to.'

She came over. 'You need to stop trying to protect me. I know it won't be easy, but I have to live my own life and make my own mistakes. You're not responsible for me. If I fail, it's down to me, no one else.'

'I can't stand back and do nothing.'

'But if I keep relying on you to save me, I'll never learn to stand on my own two feet. It's time for me to be the parent in this relationship.' She stroked his hair. 'You need to find your own path in life, not be dragged down mine, waiting for me to stumble. I love you too much to allow that.' She curled a lock of his hair around her finger.

He wanted to believe her. But abandoning her completely wasn't an option. 'There's another reason staying in Brighton appeals.'

'And what's that, my love?'

'I've decided to move into family law, specialising in domestic violence cases. I think I'd be better suited to prosecuting perpetrators than defending them.' It was a new direction for him. One that excited him.

She tilted her head. 'You don't need to be in Brighton to do that.'

'True...but there's another reason I want to stay.'

She smiled. 'Becca Roberts?'

'That obvious, huh?'

'Mother's intuition.' She studied his face. 'So staying in Brighton is also about reconnecting with Becca?'

He mulled over how much to admit. 'That's what I want... but I messed up. We went from butting heads, to forming a truce, to having fun...but then she backed off, saying we could never be together. She hasn't forgiven me for walking away twelve years ago. I don't blame her. I behaved like a jerk.'

'Then apologise.'

'I've tried. She's not interested.'

'If that were true, then why did she tear strips off your father for bad-mouthing you?'

He wondered if he'd heard correctly. 'She did what? When?'

'I don't know the exact details, but your father was quite taken aback. By all accounts she gave him a right telling-off. I think it changed his opinion of her. And of you, for that matter. Does that sound like the behaviour of a woman disinterested?'

'I don't know.' *Did it?* 'Hang on, when did you speak to Dad?'

'He picked me up from rehab this morning.'

Tom tried not to feel hurt that she hadn't asked him to collect her.

'If you want Becca, then you'll have to fight for her.' She cupped his cheek. 'But first, will you please go and find your father and talk to the wretched man.'

'You mean, he's still here?'

'He didn't want to leave without seeing you.'

Tom shook his head, dislodging her hand. 'I'm not ready to forgive him.'

She gave him a stern look. 'And you think Becca's stubborn? You know, the anger you feel towards your father isn't wholly justified.'

Was she delusional? 'He left you.'

'And with good reason. I made his life hell. He was right to leave.'

'How can you say that?' When she'd needed his dad the

most, he'd walked out. Left her to battle her addiction alone.

She sighed. 'Because it's the truth. You need to stop being so harsh on your father and punishing him. He isn't perfect, but then who is? Certainly not me. I wasn't there for you when you were growing up, and your poor father had to care for the pair of us. It was unforgivable of me.' Tears pooled in her eyes. 'I've messed up time and time again, but you've always forgiven me, haven't you?'

'That's different. You have an illness.'

'It doesn't excuse my behaviour. Haven't you just been telling me how distressing it is that Becca won't forgive you? Even though you're sorry, she won't move past it?'

'That's different.' At least, he was pretty sure it was.

'No, it's not. It's the same thing. Your dad wants to make amends. To both of us. And I need to do the same. But that won't be possible if you two are still at loggerheads. Do it for me, if not for yourself. I need my family. Even your dad.' She hugged him. 'Please, Tom. Let him be a part of your life.'

He hugged her back. She no longer smelt of booze. He didn't know why, but that tiny fact made him well up. 'Fine. I'll do it for you.'

'Good, boy.' She released him and ruffled his hair, like she'd done when he was a kid. 'And when you've made up with your father go and find Becca. You'd be a fool to lose that girl a second time.'

Like he needed telling.

*

399

Considering how the day had begun, Tom had expected the showcase to be a full-blown disaster. But anyone visiting the playhouse now would be oblivious to the earlier dramas. All the exhibitions had been well received, and the café area was heaving, filled with families being entertained by Benny-the-Buffoon. The sound of laughter echoed through the playhouse, accompanied by sudden bursts of trumpet when Benny blew into his instrument.

Following Vivienne's departure, Becca had taken over her front-of-house duties. She looked happy and energised, chatting with visitors and demonstrating sensitivity when dealing with the volunteers from the night shelter. Tonight's finale event had sold out, which was brilliant news. A testament to her hard work and determination to improve the fortunes of the playhouse.

He'd been a fool for not believing in her sooner.

But despite his mother's optimism, he still felt like he'd blown any chance of being with her again.

Jodi appeared in the foyer regaling the councillors with facts about the showcase and their plans to develop the arts centre. He didn't need to intervene, she had them eating out of the palm of her hand. No one would guess that only a few hours earlier she'd been tearful and close to being carted off in a police car.

He conducted a sweep of the premises. Eddie had a handle on security, and Leon was managing the packed bar with ease. Satisfied the event was running smoothly, he went over to his father, who was studying the photo exhibition with the other patrons.

'Enjoying the showcase?' he said, pulling up a chair. See? He could do conciliatory.

His father looked startled, but then smiled. 'It's good to see the place thriving.'

Tom looked around at the masses of people crammed into the bar, laughing and joking. 'It's just as well I didn't get rid of Becca and Jodi as you suggested.'

His father flinched. 'I guess I asked for that.'

And then some.

But he'd promised his mother he'd make the effort. 'How's your health?'

'Not too bad. I'm sticking with soft drinks.' He nodded to his glass of juice on the table. 'What about you? Your skin's less sallow than last time I saw you.'

Tom had noticed that too. He'd barely used his inhaler this week. 'It's improving.'

Something else he had to thank Becca for. Encouraging him to relax and have fun had been a much-needed tonic. And maybe now the Izzy situation was sorted his breathing would continue to improve.

His father shifted in his chair. 'Can I get you a drink?'

'I'm fine, thanks.' A pause followed. Thankfully, the bar noise masked their awkward silence.

His dad cleared his throat. 'You weren't the only one who found it difficult, you know.'

401

Tom frowned. 'Found what difficult?'

'Dealing with your mother.'

And there it was. He supposed if they stood any chance of reconciling then it was a conversation that had to happen. 'Go on.'

His father paused, looking uncharacteristically unsure of himself. 'I found it...difficult trying to juggle working with raising a family and contributing to the upkeep of a four-hundred-year-old manor house. And so I buried myself in work. That way I didn't have to deal with what was happening at home. In truth, I stayed away because I didn't know how to handle it.'

Tom felt his chest tighten. And his breathing had been so good of late. 'So you left a teenage kid to deal with his alcoholic mother?'

His father sighed. 'You seemed to cope better than I did. You don't know what it's like to get a phone call telling you your wife is wandering down the middle of the road falling into cars and swearing at the police. It's—'

'What, Dad? Humiliating?'

'Yes.'

'Too damned right!' When a few heads turned, Tom lowered his voice. 'And who do you think went and got her when you weren't there?'

'I didn't know what to do.'

'And neither did I.' Tom rubbed his face. How many times had he come home from school to find his mum slumped in one of the wingchairs, her clothes creased, her hair a mess? 'You don't walk away from someone you love just because life isn't always easy.'

'You make it sound so clear cut. It wasn't. And I never walked away from you. That was your doing not mine.'

Tom baulked. 'So you're blameless?'

His father crossed and uncrossed his legs. 'That's not what I'm saying. I just think that maybe…' He cleared his throat. 'In hindsight…perhaps I handled you wrong.'

Tom raised an eyebrow. Unless he was mistaken, it sounded like his dad was about to admit he'd made a mistake. Impossible.

'I didn't know what to do, especially when you argued back. I didn't want to be seen backing down.' His father pushed his glasses up his nose. 'You were so like your mother. Stubborn. You still are. I could never handle her either.'

'You hated that.'

'Yes, I did.' He leant forwards, encroaching on Tom's space. 'I loved your mother. It tore me apart to watch her ruining herself with drink. I didn't know what to do.' He rubbed his forehead. 'And yes, I hated that.'

Tom had never seen his father vulnerable before. Gone was the invincible Silk. In his place, was a fragile middle-aged man with a heart condition. 'So where do we go from here?'

His father must have sensed a chink of hope. 'Is there a chance we could leave the past behind and move on? You're an adult now. You have a successful career. You're no longer a rebellious teenager trying to prove a point. And I've changed too. I've reduced my hours, which means I'll have time to help you. I know you don't want to achieve Silk, but maybe I could help in another way. Your mother tells me you're planning to relocate to Brighton? Will you let me fund premises for you? Or help source an associate partner? I'll do whatever it takes.'

Tom looked away. 'Thanks, but I've told you, I don't need your help.'

'You mean, you don't want it?'

He shrugged. 'I'm stubborn, remember?'

It was a beat before they looked at each other and laughed.

Tom rubbed his forehead. 'Christ, you're not going to give up, are you?'

His father shook his head. 'Never.'

Tom watched a couple study one of the photo exhibits. They were holding hands, exchanging adoring looks. It evoked a deep sense of longing within him. 'I hear you had a run-in with Becca?'

His father nodded. 'She told me a few home truths.'

'I'm sure you deserved it. You were a bastard to her twelve years ago.' But then, so was Tom. He was projecting his guilt onto his father.

'I know, and I'm sorry. But I was scared for you. I didn't want to see your potential wasted.'

Tom folded his arms. 'It's not me you need to apologise to.'

'And I will, I promise.' His father looked at him. 'But that'll be hard for me to do if I'm not in your life. If you'd forgive

404

me, then it'd make it easier for me to make amends, to both of you.'

Tom laughed. 'Ever the negotiator.'

His father held out his hand, a hopeful look on his face. 'Is that a yes?'

Tom made him sweat a bit longer before conceding. 'Fine. You're forgiven.'

Harvey Elliot pulled Tom into a hug. 'I'm sorry, son.'

Tom swallowed past the lump in his throat. 'Me too.'

He'd done as his mother had asked and buried the hatchet with his father.

Now all he had to do was work out how to do the same with Becca.

Chapter Thirty-One

...later that evening

Jodi was standing in the wings watching the finale. She hadn't wanted to be out front with the crowds. Her feet hurt from wearing court shoes all day and she was exhausted from trying to put on a brave face with the councillors. She was content to hide in the shadows and remain invisible. She hadn't eaten since breakfast and her throat was dry and scratchy. She craved a warm drink. Maybe once the show was over. For now, she had no desire to move.

The children finished their ballet routine and received a tumultuous round of applause. They'd looked endearingly cute in their pink tutus, floating around the stage like tiny rose petals. They hadn't put a foot wrong – not that she could tell. Becca might think otherwise, but she doubted it. Her cousin was standing on the opposite side of the stage, her hands clasped together willing the kids to do well. As they ran offstage, Becca hugged and praised them, before sending them back onstage for a second bow.

Tom appeared next to Jodi in the wings. 'It's going well,

isn't it? All that hard work has paid off. You should be proud.'

She shrugged. 'I guess.'

The house lights dimmed. Murmured voices filtered through from the auditorium.

'Just as well no one listened to me.' Tom stepped back to allow the tappers past. 'I never thought we'd pull it off.'

Five bodies dressed in white shuffled across the dark stage and took up their positions in front of the glitter curtain. 'It hasn't exactly been without its issues.'

He glanced at her. 'None of which was your fault.'

'Are you serious?' She lowered her voice. 'Without me things would've run a lot smoother. Vivienne and Petrit would still be employed and Carolyn wouldn't have returned from rehab to find the police leaving. Today could've been a disaster.'

'But it wasn't.'

They were interrupted by the start of the tap routine. The lights lifted. The music began and five tappers turned one-by-one to face the audience and lifted their hats.

Tom leant closer so he could whisper in her ear. 'Vivienne and Petrit were fired because of their own stupidity. You're the glue that's kept everyone together. You've worked endless hours, overcome obstacles and never given up. You had to endure Vivienne and Petrit giving you abuse and me being a tosser. Most people would've quit weeks ago.'

One of the tappers stumbled, but quickly recovered.

Jodi sighed. 'It's not like I was inundated with other job offers.'

A few audience members clapped along to the music.

'Doesn't make it any less impressive. This place was on the decline. You and Becca halted that. I'm really grateful. Mum is too. Not to mention winning over the council.'

She glanced at him. 'You don't have to say that.'

'Yes, I do. I owe you an apology, Jodi.'

Onstage, the tappers responded to the enthusiastic audience, their nervous smiles turning into beaming grins.

Tom leant closer. 'When you first started working here, I was judgemental and narrow-minded. My mother saw that you'd changed, but I didn't. I was a jerk.'

One of the tappers lost her hat. When she bent down to pick it up the male tapper tripped over her foot. Becca gestured from the wings, urging them to keep going.

Jodi adored her cousin. Aunty Ruby too. They'd stuck by her, no matter what. Never judged her, always forgiven her and encouraged her to be a better person, which made what she had to do next a little easier.

She waited for the tap number to reach its crescendo. 'I appreciate the apology, but there's something you should know about what happened twelve years ago.'

'It doesn't matter,' he said, one eye on the tappers. 'Whatever it is, it's in the past. It's no longer relevant.'

'I wish that were true, but it's the reason there's still friction between you and Becca.'

Tom stilled.

The tap number ended and the place erupted with applause

and whistles. Five happy tappers soaked up the response, bowing and waving as they exited the stage. When the clapping continued, they ran back on and took another bow. It was a while before the audience settled and the lights faded to black, ready for the next number.

Jodi watched her cousin walk onto the darkened stage and take up her starting position. Even motionless she looked elegant, animated and breathtakingly beautiful.

Jodi wasn't the only one who thought so. Tom's gaze was fixated on her cousin.

'Becca never stole from Boots,' Jodi said in a hushed voice. 'It was me.'

The music began and the sound of Ed Sheeran filled the auditorium.

Tom dragged his eyes away from Becca, his expression a mixture of confusion and disbelief. 'What?'

It was time to confess. There was no turning back. 'She ran after me, hoping to persuade me to return to the shop. When I refused, she tried to take the stuff back herself, but the security guard caught her.'

He blinked a few times, as if processing what he was hearing. A beat later, his focus returned to watching Becca. Jodi was glad. It was easier without him scrutinising her.

Becca's routine started slowly, her movements fluid and balletic. If her knee was hurting no one would guess. She looked strong, confident and assured.

'To this day, I don't understand why Becca didn't give me

409

up,' Jodi whispered. 'Even when the police arrested and cautioned her she kept quiet. Her parents grounded her. Your dad banned you from seeing her. But she still protected me.'

Even in the dim lighting she could see Tom had paled.

As the music built so did the energy in Becca's moves. Her purple dress hugged her slim body as she twirled, the chiffon trailing behind her like angel wings.

Tears pooled in Jodi's eyes. 'The worst thing was, I didn't care. I was so hooked on drugs and booze I let her take the fall. It was only years later when I left prison and got clean that I realised the enormity of what she'd done. By then it was too late. I wanted to confess, but she wouldn't let me. She said there was no point. You were long gone.'

Tom didn't say a word. His focus was on Becca, watching the emotion in her pour out through every movement. From the tips of her fingers, to the point of her toes, she oozed class, elegance and passion. The audience were mesmerised. Stunned into silence.

A series of complicated moves saw her seamlessly combine twists, turns and leaps, before landing one-footed and spinning on the spot. It looked effortless. Jodi knew it wasn't. As the music faded, Becca's body softened, her limbs retracting as she uncurled from the spin and slowly sank to the floor.

A few seconds of complete silence preceded the place erupting with whistling and shouts for an encore. The audience were on their feet.

'Maybe now you understand why you don't owe me

anything. Certainly not an apology.' Jodi picked up the bouquet of roses by her feet. 'It's me who's in the wrong. And you have no idea how sorry I am.' She handed Tom the flowers. 'Will you do the honours?'

Without a word, Tom joined Becca onstage and handed her the bouquet.

Her cousin clearly hadn't expected flowers. She covered her shock with a shy smile, thanking Tom, before resuming curt-seying to the crowd.

Tom returned to the wings. 'No wonder she hates me.'

Jodi caught his arm. 'She doesn't hate you. Christ, are you kidding me? But she'd never have told you the truth. She'd see it as a betrayal to me, which is crazy. She owes me nothing.' She nodded to where Becca was leaving the stage. 'There's still a connection between you two, but there's also a barrier. I figured the only way of enabling you both to move past it was if I came clean.'

The house lights dipped to black. The audience continued to murmur, discussing the routine they'd just witnessed.

Tom sighed. 'I appreciate you telling me. It can't have been easy.'

Jodi shrugged. 'It's not like I had a future here.'

The thought of walking away from the playhouse filled her with sorrow. But she'd made her bed. She had no one to blame but herself.

'I wish things were different. But I'll always be grateful for this opportunity. Thanks for sticking up for me, Tom. You made life hard for yourself by choosing to believe in me. It means a lot.'

Onstage, Leon appeared with his guitar and placed his amp on the floor. Jodi's heart ached at the sight of him. He looked nervous. Handsome too, wearing his red *Starlight* T-shirt. She couldn't believe it when Becca had told her it was Leon who'd orchestrated the plan to distract the police so he could move the money and foil Vivienne's plan. But then, he was a good man. Too good for her.

Jodi wiped her wet eyes. 'I'll spare you the awkwardness of asking me to leave. Once I've helped clear up tomorrow, I'll be gone.'

Tom rubbed the back of his neck. 'That's not going to work.'

'I'll make sure everything's in order,' she assured him. 'I won't leave you in the lurch, I promise.'

Pre-recorded music covered Leon tuning his guitar.

Tom shook his head. 'That's not what I meant. Mum wants you and Becca to take over management of the Starlight Playhouse.'

Jodi couldn't have been more surprised if he'd said Petrit had signed up for the weekly tea dances. 'I'm sorry...she's what?'

He shrugged. 'It's time she took a back seat. The stress of running this place won't help her recovery. She trusts you and Becca. She knows you'll take care of the place and give it a fighting chance of success.'

It was hard to separate the multitude of emotions coursing through her. Elation, hope, excitement – all wiped out by crushing disappointment when she realised she couldn't accept the offer. 'I'd love to accept, really I would. It's a dream opportunity. But how can I after what I've just told you?'

He frowned. 'It doesn't change anything, Jodi. Am I pissed off? Hell, yes. I walked away from the only woman I've ever loved believing her to be capable of something she didn't do. But that was my mistake, not yours. You may have messed up, but so did I. I should've believed in her, and I didn't.'

Was she hearing him correctly? It suddenly occurred to her that she had a golden opportunity to repair her cousin's broken heart. 'For what it's worth, I don't think it's too late for you and Becca. Everyone deserves a second chance, right? You're forgiving me. My cousin needs to forgive you. I'll be sure to remind her of that.'

He smiled. 'Good. I need all the help I can get. But you won't be able to do that if you quit. So, will you please accept the job?'

'It's more than I deserve.'

He nudged her. 'It's the least you deserve. You're not the same person you were twelve years ago. What you did then has no bearing on who you are today. Anyone can see that. Will you stay?'

She could hardly believe it. 'If you're sure?'

'Positive. And besides, my mother would kill me if I let you quit.' He kissed her cheek. 'Enjoy the rest of the finale. I have some grovelling to do.'

'Good luck,' she called after him.

It was down to Becca now. Hopefully her cousin would see sense and forgive him. She deserved a happy ending. And Tom deserved a second chance.

Onstage a spotlight lifted on Leon. He cleared his throat and tapped the mic. 'Hello, Wembley!' The audience laughed.

He looked nervous. She'd never seen Leon wrong-footed before. He was always so confident. It only made her want him more.

'This is a song by Bob Dylan,' he said, glancing over. 'It's called 'Masters of War'. It's for my warrior princess.'

Her breath hitched when he smiled at her.

For the next fifteen minutes, she indulged in her own private concert. Tucked away in the shadows of the darkened wings she watched Leon perform. Nerves got the better of him to start with and he hit a few wrong notes, but he gradually relaxed as the audience warmed to his playing.

She'd never heard the song before, but it instantly became her new favourite. He followed the song with two he'd written himself, which she loved, and two further covers. His voice was warm and enticing, and by the time he'd finished she was his biggest fan. She clapped and cheered from the wings, along with the audience.

He exited the stage and disappeared. She hadn't expected anything less. It didn't stop disappointment welling up inside her.

The finale was over. Only the tea dance remained. She waited until the audience had filed out of the theatre and the backstage crew had cleared the stage before gearing herself up for the next challenge. But before she could move, Leon appeared next to her in the wings.

'I'm guessing you haven't drunk anything all day?' he said, handing her a steaming mug of coffee. 'Sorry I rushed off. Nerves had played havoc with my bladder.'

Is that why he hadn't come over? 'I enjoyed your performance.'

'Thanks. It went okay. A bit shaky.' He leant against the wall. 'The cappuccino has extra sugar, by the way. I figured you'd need the energy.'

She was touched by his kindness, but emotion still constricted her throat.

As if sensing this, he nodded to the mug. 'Drink up. It'll help.'

She took a sip. She hadn't realised how shaky she was until her tremors started to subside. She'd been running on neat adrenaline all day.

He smiled. 'See? Not so hard.'

It was like the Leon of old had returned. Gone was the cool reserve, replaced by chattiness and smiles. Not that she was complaining.

He waited until she'd drunk most of her coffee, before he said, 'Can we talk about today?'

She paused. 'I guess so.' Not that she wanted to relive the

415

events of earlier. The humiliation was still raw. But that was her problem, not his. 'I haven't had a chance to thank you. I'd be facing charges if you hadn't proved I didn't take the money. It was lucky you caught Vivienne and Petrit on film.'

He frowned. 'Luck had nothing to do with it. I suspected they were behind it. I just couldn't prove it. That's why I backed off. I figured I stood a better chance of catching them off-guard if they thought I'd lost interest in you. It worked. They went from stopping talking when I was around to being indiscreet. It enabled me to overhear conversations. I knew they were up to something. I just needed proof.'

It took her mind a moment to compute what he was saying. 'I don't understand. You knew it wasn't me? But what about when you found out about my past? You must've suspected me then?'

He shook his head. 'It made no difference. I knew you hadn't done it. It was obvious you'd had a rough time. When we went to the pub that time, and you told me about your childhood, I could tell from your body language there was more to the story. The way you shied away from a compliment as though you didn't deserve it. The way you allowed Petrit and Vivienne to abuse you, like their punishment was justi-fied. I knew something had happened to make you that way. I just didn't know what.'

'I had no idea it was that obvious.'

'Maybe I was looking closer than anyone else.'

She felt herself blush.

'Only someone trying to turn their life around would've worked so hard or put up with so much crap. And confronting Carolyn over her drinking? That was really brave. I think that might've been when I fell in love with you.'

Jodi jolted so quickly she almost dropped the mug. 'Wh... what?'

He scrutinised her. 'Is it so hard to believe?'

'But...you backed off, you stopped...you know?'

'Flirting?' He smiled. 'I told you, I only did that to throw Vivienne and Petrit off the scent.' He took the mug from her and squeezed her hand. 'I just told you I'm falling in love with you, and you look close to tears. That's not great for my confidence.'

She hadn't answered because she was still too fixated on the feel of his warm hand holding hers. 'Even though you know I went to prison?'

'Jodi, I don't care what happened in your past. I'm only interested in being a part of your future.'

She almost had to pick her jaw up off the floor. 'You are?'

His expression turned rueful. 'You're killing me here. Can you please put me out of my misery? Do you like me?'

Like him? Christ! 'I do.'

He closed his eyes. 'You had me worried there.'

'Sorry, I'm still trying to get my head around everything. I thought you'd stumbled across Vivienne's and Petrit's plan by accident. I had no idea you'd been working undercover.'

He laughed. 'James Bond eat your heart out.'

It was her turn to laugh.

His fingers laced into hers. 'You were innocent. It was up to me to prove that.'

'It wasn't, but thank you anyway. I can't tell you how grateful I am. How can I ever repay you?'

He considered that. 'A dance would be good?'

She smiled. 'I hear they're holding a tea dance here tonight.'

He slid his arm around her. 'What are the odds?'

And as they headed for the ballroom, Jodi felt the tightness inside her melt away. She'd ridden the storm and emerged the other side. She'd been offered her dream job. She'd made amends for her past. And she'd found a man who knew the worst about her, but still wanted to be with her.

For the first time in her life, she felt like she could finally move on.

Chapter Thirty-Two

...later that night

As the showcase started to wind down, the playhouse seemed to sigh with relief. Most of the exhibitors had packed up; so had Buddies Café and the bar. All that remained were a few people in the ballroom enjoying a last waltz before the tea dance concluded.

Needing to rest her knee, Becca found a quiet alcove and sat down. She allowed her mind to drift back over the events of the evening. The kids' ballet routine had been faultless, much to her surprise. They'd exceeded her expectations. The mayhem and distractions that hampered weekly classes had been replaced by nine focused mini prima ballerinas rising to the occasion.

The tappers had been great too. Not perfect, but entertaining. The audience had loved their routine. From the mismatched costumes to the bumping into each other onstage. The audience had laughed along, assuming it was a send-up. Several people had commented on the excellence of the tappers' comic timing. There was no need to tell them it hadn't been intentional. The important thing was the tappers had got through the routine and they'd enjoyed themselves.

The evening had been a turning point for her too. Her knee had ached throughout the routine, but it hadn't felt weak. If anything, the pain had given her strength. From now on, dancing would be purely for pleasure. Like it had been when she was young. No more exhausting shows, demoralising auditions, or late nights in nameless cities. She wanted to lay down some roots and build a home in Brighton.

It was the first time since her career had ended that she'd felt excited about her future. Watching her students had filled her with an acute sense of satisfaction. She'd felt like a proud parent standing in the wings witnessing them overcome their insecurities. Teaching had challenged her. She'd had to develop new skills and overcome adversity, but the rewards were tenfold. Even before Carolyn had tracked her down and offered her co-management of the playhouse, she'd decided that whatever happened next, her future involved teaching.

She watched the dancers circle the ballroom. It'd been lovely to see so many people waltzing around the room. With the fairy lights twinkling and bouncing off the gold décor, the space had glowed.

Live music still hugged the air, the quartet of musicians from the Brighton Music Institution as reluctant to pack up as the players on *Titanic*. They were a talented bunch, even if they looked like the Marx Brothers in their ill-fitting charity shop tailcoats. It didn't detract from the beauty of their playing.

A burst of laughter drew her attention to the dance floor. Mrs Busby and Dr Mortimer were enjoying a last dalliance before heading off on their cruise tomorrow. Aunty Ruby was dancing with Eddie, and Carolyn was dancing with her ex-husband. Watching Tom's parents was a lesson in forgiveness. Carolyn's illness had driven her husband away, and yet he still wanted to help her. In turn, she'd forgiven him for leaving her. Seeing them smiling and dancing showed that no matter what mistakes had occurred, bridges could be rebuilt.

Of course, the best part of the evening had been watching Jodi dancing with Leon. She'd had to stop herself running over and hugging them both. She couldn't imagine they would have appreciated the intrusion. Instead, she'd watched from afar as they'd exchanged shy smiles and moved tentatively to the music, shifting from work colleagues to a couple on the brink of romance. Shyness had given way to playfulness, and all awkwardness was soon gone.

Her cousin was currently sitting across the ballroom with Leon. When she got up and left the room, Becca went after her. She'd been waiting for an opportunity to talk to Jodi all evening.

She caught up with her by the ice sculptures. 'Who'd have thought we'd end up running the Starlight Playhouse together?'

Her cousin turned at the sound of Becca's voice. 'I know, right? It's the stuff of dreams.'

They both squealed and rushed towards each other, dancing around like idiots. Becca felt a surge of joy. It'd been so long since she'd felt motivated by what lay ahead, and the best bit was, she was getting to do it with her cousin.

She hugged Jodi. 'Nobody deserves this more than you. After everything you've been through, you've stuck at it and won through. I couldn't be happier for you.'

Jodi hugged her back. 'And you have a new dream too. Carolyn loves your ideas for making the playhouse more inclusive.'

Becca beamed. 'We make quite a team, if I do say so myself.' It was lovely to see her cousin so happy. 'How do you think the showcase went?'

'Brilliant. We've had loads of positive feedback. Elaine's interested in hiring the art studio to run weekly pottery classes, and we've given out loads of flyers. Oh, and a few people have asked about adult ballet classes too.'

'I'll add it to the list.' Becca was relishing the endless possi-bilities for expanding the playhouse. Assuming it stayed open. 'How did the council react?'

Jodi grinned. 'We won't hear officially until next week, but they're happy with the progress we've made since their last visit. The grant is safe.'

'Yes!' Becca punched the air. 'Thank God, for that.' She hooked her arm through Jodi's. 'And what about you and a certain bar manager? How are things going with him?'

Jodi blushed. 'It's early days, but so far so good. We had a long talk and cleared the air. I'm still trying to get my head around the fact that he saved my arse today.'

Becca grinned. 'You should've seen his face when he rushed into the theatre saying he needed help, and my tappers came up with the idea to re-enact the *Fame* number.'

Jodi laughed. 'I was too traumatised to find it funny at the time, but that poor copper's face. I really hope someone videoed it.'

'Me too.'

The sound of approaching voices distracted them. Eddie and her mum were heading their way. 'You left your wallet on the table,' her mum said, handing it to Eddie.

Eddie chuckled. 'What would I do without you, Ruby?'

Her mum stopped walking. 'Now you come to mention it, that's a very good question.'

Becca dragged Jodi behind the icicle statue. 'I think things are about to get interesting,' she whispered to a confused-looking Jodi.

When her mum spoke again she sounded hesitant. 'I was wondering if...you'd like to have lunch sometime?'

Eddie tilted his head to one side. 'I make it a point to have lunch all the time, Ruby, not just sometime.'

Her mum looked flustered. 'What I meant was, would you like to have lunch with *me* sometime...as in a...a date.'

Jodi gasped.

Becca nudged her in the ribs. 'Shush.'

A brief silence ensued. Eddie said, 'A date?'

Even hidden behind the ice sculpture, Becca saw her mum roll her eyes. 'Yes, Eddie, a date. As in two people sharing time together. I'm asking if you'd like to start dating.'

It was Becca's turn to smother a laugh.

Eddie looked amused. 'I thought we already were.'

Her mum's expression was priceless. 'What on earth made you think that?'

He seemed to consider this. 'Well, we're going on a cruise together, aren't we? And we see each other every day, we have breakfast together, and watch TV.'

'You call that dating?' Her mum's voice had shot up several notches.

Eddie frowned. 'Don't you?'

Jodi leant in and whispered, 'He's winding her up.'

Becca grinned. 'I know.'

'No, Eddie, I do not. That's called friendship...companion-ship. It's not *romantic*.'

'Oh, right.' Eddie scratched his chin. 'And you think lunch would change that?'

Her mum growled. 'Men!'

She went to walk off, but Eddie caught her arm. 'Why are you so mad, Ruby?'

She swung around. 'I'm mad, because you think we're dating, and we are most definitely not dating. I mean, it's not as if you've even kissed me.'

Eddie stepped towards her mum. 'You want me to kiss you?'

'Yes, Eddie, I want you to—'

424

Jodi gasped.

Becca was a little shocked herself. Eddie had some moves on him.

She turned to her cousin. 'I think Mum and Eddie just started dating.'

Jodi mimed fanning her face. 'I think so too. Are you okay with that?'

'I won't lie, it feels a little odd. I'm not used to seeing her with anyone other than my dad. But I want her to be happy, and Eddie's a great guy. I'm pleased for her.'

Jodi hugged her. 'How much longer do you think we're going to have to stay hidden?'

Becca's phone beeped. *Blast!*

Her mum jumped away from Eddie. 'Is someone there?'

They'd been sprung.

Becca emerged from behind the sculpture, dragging her cousin with her. 'Only us,' she said, sheepishly. 'Jodi and I were just admiring this exhibit. It's a fascinating piece. Almost sensual in its design. Don't you think, Jodi?'

Jodi nodded. 'Very sensual. One might even say...intimate. Like two snowflakes *kissing* in the snow.'

Their collective giggling was met with a steely glare. 'You're not too old to be grounded, you know.' Her mum tried to cover her blush with fake outrage.

Eddie put his arm around her. 'Look on the bright side, Ruby. You don't have to break the news to them now that Mummy's dating.'

She sloshed him. 'And you can pack it in, too. Don't think I don't know you were winding me up.'

Leon appeared from the ballroom. 'There you are,' he said, coming over. 'I was wondering where you'd got to. Everything okay?' His arm went around Jodi's shoulders.

Becca looked between her mum and Eddie. And then her cousin and Leon.

'Everything's perfect,' she said. She couldn't be more pleased that they were all moving forwards with their lives. The pinch in her chest was a result of too much dancing, nothing more.

And then her phone beeped again. Two messages from Tom.

I'm in the treehouse. x

Don't forget your torch. x

She blinked at her phone. What on earth was Tom doing in the treehouse? She glanced up. 'Are you guys okay to lock up? There's someone I need to see.'

Her mum raised an eyebrow. 'Is this someone six foot with blond hair?'

Becca nodded. There was no point denying it. 'Are you okay with that?'

Her mum sighed. 'I suppose it was inevitable.'

Jodi pointed to the exit. 'What are you waiting for? Go.'

Becca ran for the door, just as the grandfather clock in reception struck twelve. Bloody hell, she felt like Cinderella!

The moment she stepped outside the playhouse, a shower of glitter filled the night sky with a loud bang. The fireworks on the Palace Pier had started. A fitting end to the festival.

As she ran across the courtyard and down the steps leading to the grounds, another explosion lit up the sky. This one was blue and gold. Lights flickered then dispersed, fading into blackness. They seemed closer, as if somehow Becca could reach out and touch them.

As the lights from the playhouse faded, she switched on her torch function. The ground surrounding the treehouse was boggy and impossible to wade through. Trying not to end up face down in the mud when it was daylight was a challenge. In the pitch dark, it was virtually impossible.

She used the series of wooden pathways with rope handles to aid her. They'd been built on top of the muddy ground to make the treehouse more accessible, but they were unstable and precarious.

Another explosion filled the sky. Sprays of silver and purple glittered above.

A faint light appeared in the distance. Tom was standing on the treehouse balcony holding a lantern. She couldn't imagine he'd summoned her here to discuss business. At least, she hoped not. Still, she wouldn't get her hopes up.

'You could have chosen a better meeting place,' she yelled, trying to centre her balance. 'Climbing into the attic would've been preferable.'

'Mind your footing,' he yelled. 'There are some slats missing.'

'Oh, great. Like this isn't difficult enough.' Thank heavens she had good core stability. 'I hope you're going to rescue me if I fall in? I'm wearing a new dress.'

'The red one with the frilly top and low neckline?'

She grabbed a rope handle. 'That's the one. If I'd known I'd be climbing trees tonight, I'd have changed outfits.'

'I'm glad you didn't.'

Another firework exploded above.

'How are you getting on?'

'Piece of cake,' she said, and then her feet parted company. Her body flailed as she tried to hold on to the rope handles. She narrowly avoided landing in the mud. 'Are you laughing?'

'Of course not.'

Liar.

Another firework crackled and fizzed.

'My mother tells me you've accepted the offer of co-managing the playhouse?'

Her excitement had yet to wear off. 'I still can't believe it.'

'She loved your ideas for expanding the place.' He waited until she'd stepped onto the last section. 'I know she says she doesn't want the stress of running the place, but it would be great if she could still be involved. You know what they say about idle hands.'

'I'm way ahead of you. How do you think she'd feel about teaching art to people leaving rehab?'

A few seconds passed before he spoke. 'I think she'd love it. That's a great idea.'

'Good.' She looked up at the balcony. Tom was leaning over the edge holding the lantern. 'Do I get a sonnet?'

He laughed. 'No, but you do get a lantern. I've left it by the stairwell.'

She pushed open the door. It had been twelve years since she'd been inside the treehouse. Nothing much had changed. The rattan table and chairs remained downstairs, along with a small generator providing electricity for the fridge. There were no lights, only lanterns. Heat came in the form of a log-burner, which was lit. She was grateful. The weather was mild, but it was November nonetheless.

She picked up the lantern and climbed the stairs. 'The tea dance went well,' she said, her skirt brushing against the sides of the narrow staircase. 'It was a shame you missed it.'

'I hear my parents danced together.'

'They did. It was lovely.' She angled the lantern so she could see Tom waiting at the top. His blond hair was messy and he wore a hoodie over his red *Starlight* T-shirt. 'How do you feel about them becoming friends again?'

'Weird. I thought Mum was only doing it to force me into forgiving him. But I realise she's genuinely okay with what he did. I guess if she's willing to forgive him, I should too. If only for her sake.'

The stairs creaked beneath her.

Tom offered her his hand. 'Thanks for having a go at him, by the way. Whatever you said, it worked. He wants to help me set up my law practice in Brighton.'

She took his hand and let him guide her up the last two steps. 'I'm pleased for you.'

Arguing with Harvey hadn't been fun, but if it resulted in Tom's father supporting him, then it had been worth it. She wasn't a fan of Harvey Elliot, but she knew it would be better for Tom if they could put their differences aside.

She reached the top. 'I'm not sure which was more surreal, seeing your parents dancing together, or my mum smooching with Eddie.'

Tom looked shocked. 'They smooched?'

'Intimately.' She let go of his hand and looked around. The layout upstairs hadn't changed either. It was compact with barely enough room for a double bed. Glass doors led onto a balcony, providing the perfect view of the fireworks. The treehouse was basic, but it was a far cry from camping alfresco.

Two bottles of wine were sitting on the floor next to two glasses and a portable stereo. A thick blanket covered the air bed, which was inflated.

She looked at Tom. 'Expecting company?'

He looked embarrassed.

She moved past him and picked up a bottle of wine. 'Still, now I'm here it seems a shame to waste a perfectly good bottle of wine.' She read the label. 'I say perfectly good.' She turned to look at him. 'It's non-alcoholic. Are you abstaining to help Carolyn?'

He unzipped his hoodie. 'Not really. She'll have to get used to being around booze. But if we're going to run a programme for people leaving rehab then we'll need a decent selection of soft drinks too.'

'Fair enough.' She unscrewed the cap. 'Maybe we could serve both?' She poured two glasses. 'And you never know, it might be delicious.' She handed him a glass. 'Here's to a successful showcase, and winning over the council.'

'I'll drink to that.' He clinked glasses with her. 'Cheers.'

They simultaneously took a sip, grimaced, and then laughed.

'Or maybe not,' she said, putting her glass down.

Outside, the fireworks continued.

She walked onto the balcony. 'It's such a great view from up here.'

He joined her. 'When the sky lights up you can see the Palace Pier.'

She strained to see where he was pointing. 'You're right, you can.' She let the moment linger, unwilling to break their relaxed humour too soon. The air was chilly, but she didn't mind. She was content to breathe in the scent of burning wood below and Tom next to her. He always smelled so good. 'I think it's about time you told me how you financed the showcase.'

He took a sip of wine, frowned and placed the glass on the floor. 'I took out a loan.'

She'd thought as much. 'That was risky. You could've lost the lot.'

He turned to her. 'I knew how much it meant to you.' His expression was earnest. 'And the future of the playhouse means a lot to me too. I realised it was riskier not to try something.

431

You and Jodi were right when you said we couldn't keep going as we were.'

'Using your own money was still a big gamble.'

He shrugged. 'It paid off.'

There was no denying Tom Elliot was a good man.

She broke eye contact and resumed watching the fireworks. It was easier to think without the impact of his intense gaze.

'I'm sorry I believed you capable of theft all those years ago.'

She turned sharply. 'What made you bring that up?'

He shoved his hands in his jeans pockets. 'A conversation I had with Jodi tonight. She told me you didn't steal anything. It was her.'

And there it was. Out in the open. 'Why would she tell you that?'

He shrugged. 'You'll have to ask her. But she said she didn't want there to be a barrier between us anymore.' He removed his hands from his pockets. 'I'm sorry I believed you were guilty.'

His words stung, but could she really blame him for thinking she was guilty? She'd never denied it. On the contrary, she'd allowed everyone to believe she was guilty. Even her parents. Tom hadn't behaved any differently to anyone else. And yet she'd expected more from him. Was that unfair?

'We all make mistakes,' she said, stepping away from him.

'But you were right,' he said, closing the gap between them. 'I should've trusted my gut and believed in you. I shouldn't have accepted what my dad said. I should've had the decency

432

to talk to you face-to-face.' He continued moving towards her. 'And most importantly, I shouldn't have walked away. I acted appallingly. I'm truly sorry.'

She'd backed into the glass door behind, cutting off any means of escape. 'Maybe I didn't do Jodi any favours by taking the blame,' she admitted. 'Maybe she would've changed her ways earlier if she'd been charged instead of me? At the time, I thought it was the right thing to do. Now?' She shrugged. 'Who knows?'

His body was almost touching hers, one hand resting on the door behind. 'You were protecting your cousin. I get that.'

His face was breathtakingly close. She could see the beginnings of blond stubble forming on his jawline. 'But I lost you in the process.'

Silence descended, broken only by the crackle of another firework. Neither of them moved. Only air separated them. She could see the torment in his eyes. The way his hair lifted in the breeze. His eyes travelled over her face, her shoulders, her chest, absorbing every curve, every blemish. He reached out and stroked her arm. 'You're cold.'

She was, but that wasn't the cause of her shaking. Her clumsiness might be under control, but he still had the ability to derail her. She ducked under his arm and went inside.

He followed, closing the doors behind him.

He crouched down and pressed play on the stereo. Ed Sheeran began singing 'Perfect'.

'Fitting,' he said, standing and offering her his hand. 'I loved watching you dance tonight. I'd forgotten how mesmerising you are.'

She took his hand, allowing him to pull her close.

'It reminded me of watching you all those years ago,' he said, sliding one arm around her waist. 'I was captivated. I still am.' He looked deep into her eyes. 'You've always brought out the best in me, Becca. You stand up to me and challenge me. You never let me settle.'

As she looked at his earnest expression, she realised she'd been so hurt by his betrayal that she'd forgotten what an honourable and decent man he was. Even at eighteen, he'd shown extraordinary kindness and tolerance when dealing with Carolyn, and resilience and stoicism when on the receiving end of Harvey's rants. Maybe it was time to forgive him?

His gaze hadn't let up. 'I love you, Becca Roberts. I think I always have.'

Her breath hitched. It had felt like forever since she'd heard those words. She wanted to savour the way they sounded: soft, sincere and heartfelt.

His blue eyes searched hers, laced with uncertainty, as though everything rested on what happened next. 'I'm staying in Brighton so I can lead the life I want. I'm tired of keeping people at arm's length, afraid of letting them close. I was so angry when Dad left, but I behaved no better. I walked away when things got tough, just like he did. But I've learnt my lesson. I'll never give up again. I want us to be together. I want the chance to make amends.'

434

She held his gaze. 'Just to clarify...you want us to forget everything that's happened in the past and pick up where we left off twelve years ago?'

His eyes briefly closed. 'I'm asking a lot, I know. Maybe it's wishful thinking, but—'

'I love you.' The words tumbled out before she had the opportunity to assimilate her thoughts. But her shock was short-lived. She'd spoken the truth. She loved him. She'd never loved anyone else. It was time to stop pretending otherwise.

He looked stunned. 'You love me?'

She reached up on tiptoes to kiss him. The feel of his warm lips against hers filled her with a rush of joy. She ran over to the airbed and jumped on it, making it bounce. 'Come on, then?'

'Just like that? No arguments? No making me beg?'

She gave him a playful smile. 'Well, if you're having second thoughts—'

'I'm not.' He ran over and landed next to her, sending her flying into the air. The sight of his dimples creasing his cheeks made her feel like she was home at last.

They collapsed in a fit of giggles, which turned to heated cuddling, which morphed into frantic fumbling, resulting in them rolling around the bed like two sex-starved teenagers, knocking heads and sending the lantern flying.

The years melted away. They'd gone full circle. Ending up back where they'd started twelve years earlier. Lying on the squeaky mattress in his dad's treehouse...and snogging.

Love doesn't always bloom the way you expect...

'Warm, witty and wonderful'
Rosanna Ley

The
Forget-Me-Not
Flower
Shop

Tracy
Corbett

Love Tracy Corbett? Then why not read her first novel.

The Saunders sisters need a bit of Cornish magic this summer...

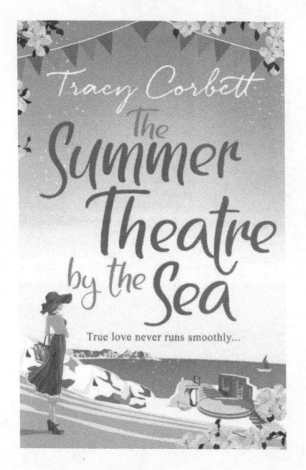

Escape to the Cornish coast with Tracy Corbett.